The Goddess of Greengrass

By An∞n

Dedicated to uncounted victims of the Grenfell Tower fire, Royal Borough of Kensington & Chelsea, West London, 14 June 2017

"To die, to sleep - to sleep, perchance to dream - ay, there's the rub, for in this sleep of death what dreams may come" - Hamlet

Greengrass

Jadd holds Ilaha, wrapped in a soaking wet blanket, across his lap in the bathtub.

Heat.

Noise.

People screaming.

Screaming beyond the walls and above the ceiling. Below the floor. Like spectres, shrieking. Eternal pain in their screams. Emotional, physical, spiritual.

Outside, beyond the windows, beyond the walls, more noise. Horns. Sirens. Voices. Wind. A rushing wind, up, up, pulling at them both, at the hot thick air inside the flat, at everything.

Jadd holds Ilaha close. This makes her warm, too warm, but makes her feel safe.

Ilaha is immaculate and innocent.

Unaware how unsafe she is. She is very unsafe. In mortal danger.

Jadd holds her.

"You will be safe, child," he promises softly into Ilaha's ear.

Darker. Blackness now. Hotter. Louder. Synaesthesia, touchingtastinghearingsmellingseeing blending into one. Feel a color. Taste a touch. Hear a flavor. Smell a sound. See a scent.

Ilaha is melting. She is becoming sick. She can hardly breathe.

"Stay here, blessed granddaughter. Do not move. I will return quickly," Jadd commands.

He lets Ilaha go and stands up.

Ilaha remains lying in the bathtub. She straightens and tightens her legs, hugs herself into her wet blanket, and tries to block everything out.

Jadd comes back. During the instant the door is open the air in the loo rushes away into the flat, sucked violently toward the infinite volume of fiery heat and noise and suffering beyond the door.

Jadd kneels next to the tub.

"My darling child, you must stand now," he tells her.

Ilaha stands up.

"You can drop the blanket, child, you will not need it," Jadd instructs her.

Ilaha lets the soaking wet blanket fall away.

Even after dropping the blanket, Ilaha does not cool at all. Her white sweats are soaked, her white hoodie, hood up, is soaked. The room is too hot; the soak is too thick, for anything to ever cool.

"Ilaha, do you remember the stories I told you about the prophet Muhammad?" he asks.

Jadd is kneeling, facing her eyes to eyes, wiping grime from her bare feet.

"Yes Jadd, I remember them all," Ilaha nods to affirm.

Jadd smiles.

"Good girl. Do you remember the story about the night Muhammad flew?" he asks her.

She nods. "Yes Jadd."

He reaches out and hands Ilaha a stuffed animal, a white horse with wings. She takes it from him.

"Hold Buraq, child, to your heart. Hold Buraq tight," Jadd tells her.

Jadd stands up and steps into the tub with Ilaha.

He wraps his hand in the wet blanket Ilaha has shed and punches through the opaque window pane. He cleans away as much glass as he can to create a full opening.

Through the opening, to the west, Jadd sees a waning moon, bright, and a planet.

Jupiter?

He is sure it is Jupiter, he feels connected to Jupiter. Solstice in about a week, the sky is not as dark as it may be, but the moon is bright and Jadd is sure he sees Jupiter.

Jadd turns to pick up Ilaha, lifts her in his still very strong old arms, and sits her down on the ledge of the window frame, facing him. She feels hot air rising over her back, just hot enough to be uncomfortable.

Ilaha realises she is partly outside now, way above the ground. Dozens of stories up.

The flat is six floors down from the top floor of Greengrass Tower.

Ilaha starts to feel breathless and scared.

"Jadd I am scared, please bring me in," she pleads.

He holds her there, firmly.

"Ilaha my dearest child, do you remember those stories, about Muhammad?" he asks her, again. "He was brave, Ilaha, like you. You are brave. You are strong, precious one. And you can fly."

Ilaha stares at him, not disbelieving, not afraid, not quite understanding. Her Jadd has always been a source of safety, strength, power.

Her Jadd would never tell her an untruth.

"I can fly, Jadd?" she asks.

"Yes, Ilaha, you can fly. You are going to fly now, Ilaha, like Muhammad did," he tells her.

"I have always dreamed the biggest dreams for you," Jadd tells her, crying, heaving. "They will all come true, and so many more, my love. Fear not. God is infinite."

He kisses her, tears streaming down his face, onto hers, into her mouth.

Salty.

She clutches at Buraq.

Jadd shoves Ilaha with all his might from the burning flat, through the opening to the west he has created for her.

He pushes her towards the moon, upon which man has walked. To the west, to a future of infinite possibility.

Ilaha feels herself fall away from the window, and from her Jadd. She clutches Buraq and whooshes into a weightless and magnificent, miraculous night flight.

Inside the flat Jadd collapses into the tub. He has expired. He has nothing left, at all.

He can taste a Madeleine.

Jadd mentally indexes his life, smiling and laughing and crying, missing so much, so much already gone, so much never to be seen. He prays for Ilaha, and dreams the biggest dreams for her. A lifetime of lives imagined and real and future and past and here and now stream through his brain, all at once, unconnected to time.

Jadd sees all. Clarity. Truth.

Revelation.

God is infinite.

He suffers tranquility.

Dreaming.

Jadd sees the door to the loo burning through. The heat is too much to bear.

He resurrects himself and climbs up and through the window frame, his feet dangling way above the ground, hanging on, prepared to face infinity, but unwilling to let go of possibility.

Dreaming.

Hotter now. Louder. No air. Deafening. Time has long since stopped. No sense at all of how much time, or of time itself, at all, in any sense, even as a sense. Pain now, fear now, bliss now, but he won't scream.

Unbearable. Flashpoint. Insufferable.

Dreaming.

Surrender.

"Allāhu 'akbar!"

Falling.

Bright white. Nothing else. No sound, no feeling, no smell. Just pure whiteness, comprehensive, infinite whiteness. Jadd enshrouded in the whitest of whiteness, bigger than senses, bigger than geometry, bigger than humanity.

Falling.

The whiteness breaks. Jadd hovers, face down, well above the ground, floating weightless. Breathless. Below him is a vast field of beautiful green, under a bright sunny blue sky, with sharp white lines laid out upon the perfect green.

The green is grass. The lines are chalk.

4

Falling.

In the field below Jadd sees a form, modestly clothed in pure perfect white, only a blissful smiling face, bare feet and bare hands displayed.

A girl, a young woman, lying there, flat on her back, arms clutching at a tennis racket. On the black strings there is a silhouette of a white horse with wings.

She appears not unlike a version of the crucifixion.

Brown skin, white pants, white top, white headpiece. Clutching Buraq.

Ilaha.

The Biggest Dream

Avatar

Lily Lacey, one-time British pop star, not a one hit wonder, more of a hit after hit hits wonder, idles away on Twitter. She tweets a lot. Millions of followers, despite going on ten years since her last album. Not the biggest following on social media, of course, but all right, still.

Social media is essential for Lily Lacey Primrose Tudor, real person, to become Lily Lacey, celebrity.

Young Lily builds a following online. A big one. She is a cyber Pied Piper of sorts who attracts millions to her cinéma vérité stream of consciousness blog.

She documents her emergence as a musical genius, as a pop Siren, as a diva, not fully understanding what she is really doing.

Real people or celebrities?

This is what her older half-brother asks whenever he happens across Lily gossiping with her mates. Before she debuts her first album. Before she is real people *and* celebrity.

Back when her snark is just funny and harmless, because she is just a real person. It is offered for a live audience of a few friends, also real people. Always at the very least for an audience of one, herself.

Definitely real, herself.

Eventually her avatar goes online for a virtual audience of millions of cyber mates, potentially not even sentient, because Morpheus has shown us the Matrix isn't real.

Real people or celebrities?

The rules of etiquette for real people and celebrities are not the same.

Example. A single mum, struggling, receiving public aid, lives in a council tower. Terrible heat wave. She opens a window hoping to cool her stifling flat. There are no screens or window guards. Disrepair. Budget cuts. Zoning violation overlooked.

Mum suffers a momentary lapse of attention to answer the phone. A debt collector. Her toddler climbs up onto the windowsill and falls to his or her death.

Not funny. You cannot make jokes.

Example. A rock star is living in a posh high rise penthouse. The windows have been opened by the maid for cleaning. Very expensive, custom, fashionable windows. Sills very low to the floor. Very, very unsafe for children. There are no unsightly window guards, of course. Zoning exception for posh flats.

The rocker's statuesque nanny, a member of the Swedish bikini team, ignores his toddler to exfoliate her utterly buttery perfect skin. The unattended toddler runs at an open window and falls to his or her death.

The rocker writes a hit song about it. Issues a press release announcing to the whole world that he has gotten sober to honor the dead child. Discusses his grief endlessly on TV, radio, and in print to promote his hit song.

Even cries on cue for the camera.

Funny. You can make jokes.

Real people, people who toil and boil and bubble and trouble per hour, they get what they get, and probably need all of it. Marxist alienation is not obvious or relevant to real people.

I assemble widgets. What do I care if I assemble widgets or blidgets or fidgets? A paycheck is a paycheck.

Real people perform a task, leave work, go to the pub for pints, and they are real people among other real people. They leave work at work. At the local, one is not what one does for work.

Real people exist as real people.

For celebrities economic alienation is different. Celebrities are their own merchandise. They embody the whole class struggle. They do not sell their labour, they labour to sell their very self. They never leave work. And the work never leaves them.

Celebrities are not real people.

Celebrities are concepts. Fictional characters. Their gravity warps the social fabric of the etiquette universe.

This is why they are referred to as "stars."

They don't work at all, really, because they *are* a product.

They cannot just up and go back to being real people at their convenience.

It wouldn't be fair, TBH.

Cincisprezece Ritualuri

As a child Lily is always in the company and God forbid care of one or another level of celebrity. She grows up adjacent to it, surrounded by it, familiar with it.

Lily's father, a minor celebrity, is always out and about. Hardly one to stay at home to properly care for Lily. He wants to party, so he just brings her along. Dump little Lily in a room with a telly and a Toblerone and she will be fine for hours.

Her mum, much more grounded, a professional woman, formally educated, is always attached to varying levels of celebrity artist performer types after divorce from Lily's dad. There is something about Lily's mum that artistic types seek out. She possesses qualities they often do not.

Put simply, she is an adult.

School does not work for Lily. It is hopeless. She gets terrible grades and acts out. Expelled more than once. Way too cool, for school, the future Lily Lacey.

So she quits. Young. Fifteen.

Her mum says get a job or go back to school. You won't loaf about in my home all day doing nothing.

So Lily runs away to Romania.

She discovers that in Romania there is a village, Satul Pian, where all of the girls learn piano. It is a rite of passage, at age fifteen. They call it "Cincisprezece Ritualuri." In the eight weeks prior to summer solstice, all the girls go through intense training on grand pianos in a great hall in the village square.

10

On solstice they play a fantastic concert outdoors on the grand pianos, which are given to each of them. Generations of women who have completed Cincisprezece Ritualuri attend the event.

It is beautiful, and magical, and for Lily impossible to believe that it is real.

Satul Pian is a dying village with a wonderful tradition that is not expected to last. The prior two years there have been no girls aged fifteen to complete the rite. There are few young girls left in the village. Families are leaving for cities to find better lives. Nobody is moving to Satul Pian, excepting an occasional old folk returning home to expire.

The village is considering allowing outsiders to participate in Cincisprezece Ritualuri for the first time in more than four hundred years, but has not decided on that yet.

Lily prints up a dossier and is on a train the next day.

Two days after leaving home she is in Satul Pian begging and pleading her way into the Cincisprezece Ritualuri. Eight weeks later she plays a grand concert under candlelight and a fading solstice sun. She plays a survey of the finest piano pieces, from Mozart and Beethoven to Ravel and Rachmaninoff.

Perfectly.

She returns home sure of herself. Sure of her future. On her path.

With a beautiful grand piano.

Eternally grateful to the people of Satul Pian.

Lily commits herself to making music.

She immerses herself into a self-directed PhD program in pop culture. It all goes in, pop through the ages, filtered through her senses, and comes out as brilliant lyrics and masterful compositions.

Thanks to her parents she has access to the creators of pop culture, some of them, some of it. She is curious and always asking asking asking. Because she is precocious, they indulge her.

Lily can measure herself against them, so she knows she is good. Really good. Talented. From young, she just knows. Now she becomes convinced by evidence.

Monkey see, funky do, I am good, just as good as you.

Lily Tudor is lucky to soak in the people behind the celebrity curtain, and perhaps make better sense of her Wizard of Oz than Dorothy ever could.

Poor dumb Dorothy stuck trying to figure out how to get home on the Yellow Brick Road. Dragging along Tin Men and Cowardly Lions and Scarecrows. Drudging off toward some Emerald City.

Believing in the Wizard.

Sucker.

Lily Lacey never has to worry about any of that, because as it turns out her home isn't a place at all, like a farm in Kansas. She needs no Yellow Brick Road to follow. Her home is a milieu, not very far from Abbey Road. She knows the Wizard from young.

He isn't in Emerald City.

He vomits on her dad's sofa one night.

Just like Dorothy, after exposing the man behind the curtain, covered in his own vomit, Lily has an epiphany.

She clicks her heels, and after forty days in the desert where music is revealed from on high, she comes down from the mountain cave with a complete catalogue.

She just needs to write it down.

Within days it is recorded.

Within weeks it is on BBC Radio One.

Within a month she has a groundbreaking record deal.

Within a year she is being handed all of the most prestigious awards in pop music.

And now she is famous. A celebrity.

No longer real people.

Sirens

Lily is all alone, at home, compulsively tweeting @ a few million followers that may actually be zero real people.

She has no zeal to know what's right or what's real. Social media taught her how to feel and real life has lost its appeal.

She will never know for sure fake from real, because that is not possible. Life does not offer a red pill you can take to see the truth. It offers an unexplained ink blot. You see whatever you choose to see.

Lily is older. She is old, almost. Certainly no longer young. Not twenty two.

Not an ingénue.

Teens to twenties and now well through thirty in a blur. Irony, of course, because she sings about it. About an emerging spinster with a look in her eye wondering how and why.

The song charts at number one.

Lily Lacey's life is hardly over, of course. She is simply on hiatus. Indefinite hiatus. Not quite back to being Lily Lacey Primrose Tudor, but no longer Lily Lacey, really.

The full circle may simply be impossible, in fact. Celebrity may just be a one way street of uncertain length, which leads right into a Daily Telegraph obit, if you get lucky.

Lily is sitting there tweeting away when she hears sirens.

They sing to her.

Very loud, deafening as they rush past her beautiful home. She stands up from the sofa, still holding her phone, and goes to the front door to see what is about.

To the east Lily sees a giant geyser of fire filling the sky.

Greengrass Tower is ablaze, apparently engulfed from ground to roof.

She can hear Greengrass crackling when it gets quiet between the screaming vehicles that rush past. Can she? Is that possible, from here? To hear the fire? From blocks away?

Nosey. A buttinsky. She must go see what is happening.

It is hot outside. Very hot. Lily puts her bare feet into some sheepskin boots that are in the entryway. They feel nice going on, inside an air conditioned home, so she goes through the door and takes off to the east into the hot night.

Lily doesn't get far before it becomes clear this fire is a disaster. Ambulances rush by, and the filth drive past with sirens blaring. There are not as many fire trucks as might be expected, however. Lily is making her way toward the burning tower, phone in hand, still looking at Twitter.

She should avoid Greengrass altogether, but she can't help herself in being drawn to it. Rather than just stay home, Lily heads east straight at the fire in the sky.

As she gets closer to Greengrass everything gets louder, and hotter, and more crowded. The entire building is burning, with giant hot flames spewing toward the night sky like crude oil spewing from a blowout. Lily can swear she feels the heat of the building, but this is not possible, given how far she is from the tower.

Regardless, she feels it.

Not sure, exactly, what she is doing, Lily turns to her phone and tweets.

Tweet: *#Greengrasstower on fire. Going there now. Anyone in neighborhood should go as well.*

Tweet: *Bring …*

Toiletries
Sanitary products
Phone chargers
Toys
Clothes
Water!!
Towels

Tweet: *If u are dbl parked on Clarion Row, move your f#%$ing car!!!*

She snaps the car's plates and tweets the picture.

Tweet: *re pic: #londonfilth, roboticket pls!*

Lily reaches Asphodel Meadows, an open field near the Greengrass Tower. She is very close now, and the fire in the sky has come down to earth and gone vertical. From here she must look straight up to see the flames rising into the heavens.

Untold numbers of Greengrass residents are making their way from the burning tower and organically collecting themselves here, on Asphodel Meadows. Dozens, perhaps hundreds. Anonymous, invisible, there will never be a proper accounting of them all. They will simply pass into oblivion from here.

For now they seek an open space. Grass to sit upon. Cooler air to breathe. A reprieve from their hell. They speak different languages, chattering in so many tongues.

Neighborhood people are filtering into Asphodel Meadows from the surrounding area as well, carrying blankets and such, anything they can grab in a rush that makes sense to help.

An old lady ambles behind a trolley announcing she has tea.

Lily keeps tweeting, snippets of what she is seeing, but now she is confronted by a hipster dragging a waggon full of water.

"You, there, drag this waggon. Over there. To that tent they are putting up," the hipster commands.

Lily never utters a word. She puts her phone in her pocket, takes the waggon handle and watches the hipster rush away. Probably scurrying off to fetch even more material for the rapidly escalating aid effort. The water load is heavy, and the waggon wheels are less than ideal for the grass, but she is strong enough and she manages.

Lily makes it to the tent, being assembled in the fire shadow of the burning tower. The crew is official, sent by the State.

"I have water," she announces.

Nobody turns, nobody notices. They utter babble. They don't care. They are too focused on putting up the tent where Greengrass refugees will be housed to care about her, or even the Greengrass refugees who will be housed.

They want to build, upward, higher, bigger, and grander, to the heavens, an irrational obsession. Lily looks for someone who looks like maybe they are, well, in charge, but there are only those who babble.

A bookish looking dweeb of a man approaches the State crew, dressed in red, wielding clipboards. Lily hears him explain that refugees must register to vote prior to being admitted into the care system. He keeps saying "we" want more voters. The State crew no longer babbles. What they say is very clear. With enthusiasm they each take a clipboard to register refugees to vote.

Lily leaves the water and drifts away from the scrum. It is a bit overwhelming, really, the whole scene.

Lily sees a little child, standing alone in just a nappy, crying, and she breaks down. Freezes. Lily can hardly breathe. She steps catatonic toward the child, but that instant the child is scooped up by dad and rushed away to somewhere … else.

Lily needs air now. Space. To go somewhere … else.

She turns away from Asphodel Meadows and heads north, away from the fire, away from the tragedy, toward the bright moon, and Pluto, visible in the sky.

Orphan

Lily finds her way into an empty lot quite far from Greengrass Tower. The pavement is in ruin. Tall grasses grow everywhere through wide cracks. There is a single car, abandoned, without tyres, amidst the tall grasses.

Lily is tall, and from a distance she sees something moving on the roof of the car. She passes through the tall grass to get closer. It is a child.

Lily moves a bit faster. She gets close enough to hear a voice. Leaning up against the passenger door, Lily sees a girl in white sweats and a white hoodie, hood up, clutching a stuffed animal.

A white horse with wings.

The girl is saying something over and over.

"Ilaha can fly."

The words register in Lily's brain, and an odd thought occurs to her.

I believe you.

Lily feels a rush, a panic, and understands she must get this child off the collapsed roof of the car. She reaches out and takes the girl into her arms.

The girl is very warm, hot and soaked. Her clothes are drenched. She is not small. Lily can't really tell her age, but luckily she is small enough that Lily can pick her up and carry her.

"Ilaha can fly."

Lily holds the girl, head resting on her shoulder, legs wrapped around her waist. She starts off for the nearest emergency, quite a walk with a child to be carried. Pretty close to the point of exhaustion, after taking multiple breaks to sit, more than one of which for a fag, Lily and the girl reach the emergency department.

"Ilaha can fly."

The girl has not stopped saying it. Lily assumes that she is talking about herself, that her name is Ilaha.

Lily stays with the child for hours waiting for care, holding her. When she checks her in, hours prior, she puts herself down as caretaker, for procedure. Not knowing the child's name, and being required to provide first and last, she lists her as "Ilaha Tudor" to appease the person taking the form.

Lily and Ilaha wait, and wait, and wait. Finally they are seen. The doctor checks Ilaha over, determines that she is not meaningfully injured, treats a few small scrapes and cuts, and is ready to discharge her when Lily reiterates that she has no idea who the child is, or where she belongs.

"She must have family? They will look for her," Lily pleads, "Isn't there some system for caring for her and making sure she gets where she belongs?"

The doctor looks at her, cuts right through her nonsense, and reprimands her.

"You are Lily Lacey, right?" Lily confirms she is.

"You are rich, right?" Yes, she concedes.

"You have a posh flat here, in Babel?" A house, but yeah, I live here, she admits.

"You know how many people live in Greengrass? You were there, at the fire? The single best thing that could ever happen, at this point, for that girl, is for you to just take her home. When the time comes, they will find her," the doctor tells Lily.

Lily sees this is obvious and feels a bit dumb.

"Just keep an eye on her. If she starts getting dizzy or nauseous or worse in any way, get in your car and drive to an emergency far away from here. Because you can. Because you are rich, and a celebrity, and can get her seen quickly somewhere else," the doctor instructs.

The doctor abruptly signs off on Ilaha's release, hands a slip of paper to Lily, and leaves to help someone in real need.

"And give her a lot of water," the doctor says over a shoulder.

Lily takes Ilaha home and spends the night with her, giving her sips of cool water, never leaving her side.

@LilyLacey is Labour

The day after the Greengrass fire the First Class publishes a full-page tabloid cover of an exhausted Lily Lacey holding a sleeping Ilaha Tudor in her lap. A pieta of sorts, that someone tweets from emergency, over a headline.

"The Goddess of Greengrass."

The buggers find out the little girl in Lily's lap is listed as 'Ilaha' on the emergency admission form and google it posthaste. They learn that Ilaha is an Arabic name that means 'goddess.' Below the big headline is a lead in, "Lily and Ily - Posh Helps Skint in Babel."

They put it all together. Speak off the record with the person who admits Ilaha. The doctor. Others in the waiting area. The one who tweets the pieta pic.

Lily Lacey, former pop star, drags a child who survives Greengrass into emergency the night of the fire then takes her home.

The First Class hasn't run a Lily Lacey story in years, so this narrative has big potential for them. There is a time when she helps them sell a lot of papers.

For free, of course.

Papers pimp celebs out for free, not a fee.

Two way street.

They make you famous, keep you famous, and you let them sell papers in exchange. You get "fame" and are left to the alchemy of spinning it into whatever gold you may. They sell ads and copies of the paper and make real money from the fake news.

When Lily is relevant, when she is young and a pop star charting hit songs, the First Class runs a story or more a day about her for months at a time. Fake news, for sure, but classic junk food journotainment.

Example. They print up razzi snaps of Lily in sweats with no makeup eating fro-yo from a cone, then make up a legally safe allegation that she is assuaging a broken heart with sweets. See the new cellulite on that celluloid, BTW? LMFAO.

Example. They print a picture of Lily apparently stumbling drunk out of a club, and with no risk of losing a libel judgment hint clearly at a future in rehab, she won't go, no no no, or vaguely suggest the morgue, as if they are hoping for both, in a drawn out sequence they can cover. OMG.

There are some items they run that can be called actual borderline 'news,' but rarely anything more than fully vetted celebrity gossip.

The Royal Borough of Babel community, where Lily lives, where Greengrass Tower is located, is very wealthy. Community members converge onto the scene at Greengrass right away after the fire. In Britain the State provides services, but even in Britain the community level zeal to help cannot be suppressed by Big Government.

Lily goes to help, taking Ilaha along, hoping to find her people. Without contriving to do so, at all, Lily and Ilaha become a symbol of the kind Britain, the caring Britain, and the Labour Britain that believes in ideals of not so soft socialism.

The whole thing starts to snowball, and with reluctance Lily and Ilaha are pulled into a very public role Lily did not mean to seek. They really go to help. Honest. To maybe find Ilaha's people. Seriously. Only good intentions send them back to the site in the days after the fire.

The problem of it is when the spotlight goes on, Lily's instincts kick in and she performs. Resurrected, like a phoenix, she ascends. With tact and grace she elevates the tragedy beyond itself into a much larger political salience.

This is not about shabby public housing. It runs deeper. It is about Brexit, isolationism, about state services, open immigration, and about being citizens of the world. We need the world; we are obliged to cooperate with the world. We must help each other as a policy.

Lily, a natural, but a bit rusty, quickly recovers her knack for playing a crowd and plays the Greengrass oeuvre like a virtuoso. Lily is Labour, Lily is engaged, and Lily articulates her position. Simple, genuine, passionate. Naive.

Compelling.

Lily helps to create an irresistible groundswell for Labour.

Prior to the fire there are stakes, machinations already underway that are now threatened by derailment. Brexit passes, a shock to many, even to those on Lombard Street who are very well paid to never be shocked.

The Tory Prime Minister resigns, having vocally opposed Brexit and badly missing the mark.

Looking to strike while the Brexit iron is hot, the Tories call for a snap election to consolidate a bigger majority in Parliament. This fails, in the wake of Greengrass, with some credit due to Lily. All of a sudden what appears to be a clear path to a more deeply conservative Britain is grown over by a liberal political jungle.

Lily steps into the light while sentiment is swirling. She has her moments, she does.

On telly she challenges official Greengrass mortality estimates. *Why won't they give us a realistic number?* She demands immigration amnesty on behalf of all Greengrass refugees. *Have they not suffered enough, only to be deported now?* She leads a cry for immediate renovation of all existing public housing to meet the highest fire safety standards. *Shall we immolate more innocents for want of sprinklers and alarms?*

Things may otherwise subside but Lily moves forward, a socially crusading Joan of Arc. In a stepwise fashion she goes from being in the moment, doing whatever she can to help Greengrass refugees on the ground, to leading a bit of a political crusade.

Her efforts help topple the Tories, who are put aside by a no confidence vote. In an open election Britain decides on a Labour-led coalition government aspiring for the grandest of collective ideals. A Brexit revote is drummed up and Brexit is reversed.

Lily finds herself with political capital, suddenly, that she does not set out to accumulate but will not squander.

As the dust settles and feeling improves, public sentiment favors relocation and restoration for Greengrass refugees. They are promised immigration amnesty. The Greengrass property is conditionally declared a public housing site in perpetuity. Preliminary plans for a new tower pass, and emergency renovations in the remaining state buildings that have fallen into dangerous shambles are tentatively approved.

Lily Lacey, former pop star, becomes a rapidly rising political player, and appears on her way into an office.

Adoption

Lily cares for Ilaha from when she finds her, but she is not an ideal candidate to adopt her. Single, divorced, political, celebrity, sex and drugs and rock n' roll and all.

The problem for Children and Families is that Lily takes Ilaha *Tudor* home from the emergency as instructed, with a signed NHS release form, and then the following day she contacts her legal counsel and tells them the situation.

Counsel advises that it will be better for Ilaha to stay with Lily than to go into the hands of Children and Families. Counsel asks if Lily will file for temporary custody.

Lily tells them yes, definitely. *I will care for her.* Lily is already irreparably inseparable from Ilaha.

Temporary custody is granted. An oversight by the court, perhaps, but pragmatic. Lily is officially Ilaha's legal guardian when the placement process begins. By the day, taking Ilaha away from Lily is becoming, well, more complicated. Especially if she presses to maintain guardianship.

Despite every effort to identify next of kin for Ilaha, none can be found. It is simply impossible. DNA matching is a dead end. Nobody comes forward to identify her. There is no way to match her to any public record. In terms of her official existence, Ilaha is a case of Immaculate Conception.

She must be documented, though, so they can arrange her adoption. Children and Families quickly establish all of the necessary records.

They fabricate a birth certificate despite no small trouble deciding on her age.

27

Ilaha has all of her baby teeth, which generally start falling out about age six or seven, but she reads like a Year 6, a grade level for ten and eleven year olds. They decide she is eight, a bit arbitrary, deferring toward dental science and accepting that she may be precocious.

Settling on a birth date is also an issue. They initially establish fourteen June as her birthday. The date of the Greengrass fire. This makes sense, until it is pointed out that every year Ilaha will be reminded of the tragedy on her birthday. Seeing no harm in moving the date a bit, they settle on twenty one June instead. Solstice. The longest day of the year, a great day for a birthday.

Britain maintains convoluted citizenship laws. To keep things simple and unambiguous it is decided Ilaha Tudor was born on 21 June 2009 to married British citizen parents, Adam and Eve Doe.

She is therefore a natural born British citizen.

Having given up on finding kin, Children and Families makes Ilaha's adoption a top priority. She cannot stay with Lily indefinitely. Having her in the hands of Children and Families simply will not do, either.

No Dickensian State orphanage for the Goddess of Greengrass.

The committee assigned to place Ilaha for adoption comes up with a list of candidates as a starting point. Her DNA sample makes it clear she is of Arab descent and assumed a Muslim. Under the notion that placing Ilaha with "her own kind" is the best idea, a long list of prominent British Arab Muslims is compiled.

This effort falls flat, as candidate after candidate expresses reluctance to legally adopt Ilaha. Perplexed by this, an assistant to a committee member decides to google "adoption under Islam" and discovers that it is a bit complicated.

Under Islam it is considered a duty and a blessing to care for an orphan. Candidates are very eager to care for Ilaha in accordance with Islam …

… But they will not adopt.

It is forbidden.

The candidates on the list are modern and western, but they are devout, and they will not directly violate Islam by adopting.

For legal and political reasons this situation will not do. Ilaha's case must be a western adoption. Permanent placement. Equal status. Surname change.

The Crown will not place Ilaha as a form of houseguest.

While this process is carrying on, Lily is gaining political traction. She is already well known to Britain's public for her status as a one time pop star, but her previous rabble rousing efforts at more intellectual public discourse are generally dismissed.

Things change, and Lily's prominence at street level after the Greengrass disaster leads to a series of public appearances. She sits shoulder to shoulder with the intellectual leadership class on telly. She goes from the tabloids to the broadsheets, frequently appears on BBC News, impresses with an editorial published in the Financial Times, and experiences an image makeover.

It is understood that Lily is well on her way to being groomed for office, if that path is desirable …

… So the placement committee is told to start seeing Lily as a prime candidate to permanently adopt Ilaha.

Outside forces intervene into the process and pressure the committee to send out a feeler to Lily.

She is moving too far, too fast, into areas of public discourse that are best left neglected. A multi-partisan shadow government that really runs things acts to neutralise the possible threats she may create. *Let's give her Ilaha;* they plot, under the expectation that she will not pursue a career of public influence, *for the good of the girl,* of course.

Mama Lily enthusiastically agrees to adopt Ilaha.

In a very public way, in front of the media and neighbors at her home, it is announced that London Town's own Lily Lacey will legally adopt Ilaha, the Goddess of Greengrass.

Mama Lily speaks and insists she has no political aspirations. She wishes to focus on being Ilaha's mum.

Soon after Mama Lily adopts Ilaha, liberal fervor triggered by the Greengrass disaster dissipates. The public moves on. Nothing changes, really. The political ecosystem reverts to a copacetic stasis.

Seventy one officially dead and mourned in St. Paul's and now move on, shall we, to bigger matters, like maximizing the Greengrass site for full GDP creating public benefit.

Yesterday's disaster just a mild kerfuffle.

The knee-jerk political promises are forgotten. Refugees are never relocated. Citizenship is never granted. Maintenance is never done. Greengrass Tower is razed and replaced with a posh multi use property managed by a private equity firm.

History speaks, interrupts, really, and concludes that Greengrass is dormant.

Elysium

From the very first days with Mama Lily, as a little girl, Ilaha watches tennis on the telly. If anyone ever changes the channel she screams until they change it back.

No Teletubbies. No Paddington. No 3rd & Bird.

Only tennis.

Ilaha's first life decision, made very soon after she comes home with Mama Lily, is to get to Wimbledon. To that magic place she sees on telly. Her consciousness quickly begins to revolve around Wimbledon. It is her holy season, really, the most important moment of her year.

Years go by and Ilaha remains committed to tennis. Her devotion only strengthens as she grows.

Ilaha drags Mama Lily to the courts in the park every day. Upwards of five times a day. Year round. Weather aside. Rain or shine. She insists on hitting on Christmas day! Ilaha has a passion, devotion, and Mama Lily will not discourage it.

The public tennis courts become Ilaha's personal place of worship. She never waits. As if by a miracle, as soon as she shows up, someone on a court defers, ending their play to allow her on.

Hello Ilaha. So nice to see you. Are you hitting well?

Ilaha gushes and spills out the details of her training.

"I am working on backhands today," she explains.

Minutes later Mama Lily is out on the court tossing balls from a hopper to Ilaha's backhand. Manicured fingers, posh outfit and in fabulous shoes, bejeweled and made up, the former rocker tosses tennis balls to her adopted daughter.

Respectful crowds gather and watch.

Ilaha is aware of them, but never uncomfortable. They are always there. She does not recall a single trip to the courts when there is nobody watching her. It is the most normal and natural thing, as normal and natural as waking into her dreams at night, taking them over as if playing a video game, clutching at Buraq, and feeling herself fly.

Ilaha wails at every ball with maximum passion. She is slight but powerful, and purposeful, and fierce. Mama Lily tosses the balls and instinctively cowers; hoping Ilaha will not misdirect and blast right at her.

When Mama Lily gets hit by a ball it hurts, and she is not one for racket sports to begin with. She tosses the balls from a sense of love, and from an understanding that a healthy childhood obsession should be encouraged. But she dislikes tennis.

Tory game.

One day at the courts among the spectators is a razzi. This razzi is adept at not making what he is doing obvious, but to Mama Lily it is as clear as day. And very much unappreciated. Feared, really. This was coming, a very unpleasant business.

Ilaha hits out the last of the balls Mama Lily has to toss. She walks around the net to the hopper and jaunts off to gather up her strokes. The deal is that Ilaha must gather. Mama Lily helps carry gear and tosses balls, but does not

33

gather. Gathering is her chance to take a break, usually in the form of a fag.

"We are gonna go now, Ilaha. I want to get home," Mama Lily calls to the girl.

She wants to flee the razzi. Ilaha, feeling shorted, pouts a bit but resigns herself to leaving.

On the way home Mama Lily gently leads Ilaha into a conversation about the future.

"Ilaha, dear, have you noticed that most of the other kids have a mum and a dad at home?" Mama Lily quizzes her.

Ilaha confirms that yes, she knows that. Dads work mums mum.

"I am a single mum," Mama Lily goes on. "And have you noticed I do not work?

Ilaha nods affirmation.

"How is it you think I am able to stay home, Ilaha, with no husband?" Mama Lily asks her.

"Do you have a husband who is away?" Ilaha asks.

"No, Ilaha, I do not," Mama Lily tells her. "I had a husband but we divorced. He isn't away. We are no longer married. Do you know what divorce is?"

Ilaha tells her that she does, because many of her classmates at school have divorced parents. Two Christmases, she says. They like it.

"I am able to be a mama for you because I made a lot of money once," Mama Lily explains. "I still have a lot of it left and I do not have to work."

"Do you notice how everybody in the neighborhood knows us? How they all say 'hello' to you and they all know your name?" Mama Lily continues.

Ilaha thinks nothing of this. They always have. She cannot remember a time when they did not.

"And they all know me? They all know who I am and greet me by name even if they are strangers, and sometimes ask me to sign pieces of paper for them?" Mama Lily asks.

Ilaha laughs.

"Autographs, yes," Ilaha says.

Mama Lily smiles.

They reach home and enter through the rear gate into the garden.

Gethsemane.

The socialite gardener Norah Lindsay designed and named it. She previously owned Mama Lily's home. The garden was used as her sketch pad for the remodel of the National Trust gardens at Blickling Hall.

Mama Lily and Ilaha stop and sit on the stone bench under the olive tree.

"Ilaha, you are becoming a target for the press. I used to be quite famous, and the press stalked me very aggressively. You are perhaps more famous than me, at this point," Mama Lily explains. "You survived a great fire at the old

Greengrass Tower and you are a political symbol for many people. You are a sort of hero, and there are a lot of people who love you."

Ilaha giggles.

"You have always been treated well by strangers but things will become different, very soon, I fear," Mama Lily goes on, "I need to make sure you understand that there will have to be changes. We must move out to the country, Ilaha. London is not a good place for us now."

Mama Lily knows it is the only choice. The razzies do not move slowly, and once one of the tabloids prints just that perfect picture of Ilaha hitting at tennis, or eating an ice cream cone, or getting in a spat at school recess, it will be no more freedom to roam. No more going to the courts five times a day. No more dining al fresco. No more trips to Tesco. No more tea time out of home, or movie nights on the public lawn, or anything.

The community shelters Ilaha now, but when the walls come down it will be Bedlam long enough that the poor girl may become damaged. There will be at least one cycle of tabloid nonsense for her to deal with. Her mates will punish her for it, as kids are wont to do, and she will probably end up blaming it all on Mama Lily.

Not unfairly.

Lily Lacey threw down with the tabloids, and any expectations Mama Lily harbors for being simply left alone are unrealistic.

Mama Lily holds Ilaha's hand and looks her right in the eyes.

"Ilaha, we are going to move," she tells her. "To our country house. Elysium. The City is no longer a good place for us to be. So come September when school is back in, you will start off new."

Ilaha resists, as kids will do.

"But my friends, Mama Lily. My teachers. My courts. The garden here. I love it. I do not want to go!" she complains.

Mama Lily is firm.

"Ilaha, we are moving to Elysium," she reiterates. "It is wonderful and beautiful and I actually prefer it, honest. You can have pets. Rabbits or chickens, dogs or cats, and grow veg and go about without me being with you every minute. It will be brilliant."

Ilaha understands, but still has a great fear.

"What about courts? I must have courts. Are there courts?" she demands.

Mama Lily can't say. She has not looked for courts and suspects that maybe there are none.

"Ilaha, we have means and property. If there aren't courts, we will build you a court," she promises.

Her own court!!!! Ilaha's heart swells and she stands bolt upright.

"Let's pack!" she squeals.

As rapid as that, she wants to move.

They pack the Range Rover and move straight to Mama Lily's country home, Elysium, the next week. It is summer, a good time to move.

From the first days a daily routine is established.

They wake when they wake, nibble on a light meal, dress, and make their way into town. They shop for the day's bigger meals, browse the newsstand and bookstore, cross paths with neighbors and friends, and perhaps stop in for tea or chocolate at the coffee bar.

It is idyllic and perfect.

Very quickly after moving into Elysium Ilaha's tennis court is completed. It is decided she will play on a hard court, as maintenance is less and she plays hard courts in the City. Once her court is built, the daily routine includes getting home and letting Ilaha hit balls for hours and hours, tossed from a ball machine that never cowers, never makes a terrible toss, and never gets tired.

Mama Lily watches her from the kitchen window, with a glass of wine, smoking. She marvels at the girl's tireless resolve. Hitting ball after ball, every swing passionate and purposeful.

Sun dropping, darkness filling the sky, Ilaha hits and hits and hits, hardly able to see the ball.

"That girl will wear out that machine before it wears her out," Mama Lily thinks to herself.

Club Dagobah

One rainy Saturday Mama Lily takes Ilaha over to the village tennis club.

Club Dagobah is pretty posh, really, but working class affordable. There are indoor courts, including clay courts, and outside there are beautifully arranged courts that are lighted at night. Eight of them surrounding a beautiful central garden with a large patio.

There is also a practice court with a ball machine.

Mama Lily fills out a form, pays for membership, and Ilaha bolts off to the practice court to use the ball machine. Mama Lily waits for her in the lobby, tweeting away and passing time. After about an hour she goes to the practice court and summons Ilaha.

"Come on, Ilaha. Time to go," Mama Lily calls.

On the way home Ilaha pleads for lights for her court, but Mama Lily tells her no, that will not be happening.

"Honestly, small woman, if I had even bothered to find out if there was a club, we never would have built the court we have," she complains. "I was just afraid I'd have to drag the gear so far I'd break me butt. At night you can go to the club."

Mama Lily makes it clear that is that. No lights.

Ilaha goes to Club Dagobah …

… At night, in the morning, during the day. She is there all the time. She is there so much she comes to know everyone at the club very quickly, young and old, punter to pro. And they all know her. Ilaha Tudor. Not the Goddess of Greengrass, just Ilaha, the girl who is always at the club.

Ilaha has passion, and she has an appetite for playing. She also has a rare and special talent. Ilaha has a sort of forceful compulsion that very few players have. If you watch her hit balls, with a trained, discerning eye, you can see it like a bright light turned on. You can see it in her eyes, and hear it in the sound her ball makes.

Ilaha achieves levels of action, pace and spin, that few players ever achieve. She has no way to know. It comes to her naturally, so it seems mundane. She has never actually played a match. Just hit balls. Tossed by Mama Lily, launched by a machine. She enjoys no basis for comparison.

One day when Ilaha is hitting on the practice court a capable man walks close enough to hear it …

… That sound.

He has heard it before, a real rarity. This is a clarion call. Unmistakable. He walks toward the sound, around the tarp that surrounds the practice court.

He sees a small girl wailing away at ball after ball. Every ball hit dead perfect on the sweet spot of the string bed. Every ball boring through the air, pulsating over the net like a missile and then turning down hard into the court, careening high and hard into the tarp behind the baseline on the other side.

Over and over and over.

It is a marvel. The man does not look at the girl producing these shots; he simply focuses on the ball. This is a small child but her ball is moving like a professional player's ball.

40

The girl keeps hitting, focused only on the next ball. The man walks down the sideline along the fence to the net, to observe clearance. About a meter. Ball after ball lands hard near the baseline. Misses into the net are very rare. Misses long are good misses. This girl really has something.

The man saunters back toward the baseline where the girl is hitting. The machine runs out of balls and Ilaha comes his way to get the hopper so she can gather up the balls and go at it again.

"You really like to hit balls, yeah?" he asks.

"Is there anything better?" Ilaha smiles wide.

A professional gets there by hitting a lot of balls, and they probably enjoy hitting every one of them. In fact, for some serious players, the joy of hitting balls can get in the way of actually playing the game.

"Are you a member at this club?" the man asks her.

Ilaha explains that she is new to the village and has only recently joined. She is excited about being able to play at a club.

She always hits with her mum, Ilaha goes on, but now she has a court at home and a machine she can use whenever she wants.

"You have your own court and machine?" the man asks.

Yes, she confirms. She uses it all the time at home but she likes coming to the club.

The man excuses himself and leaves Ilaha to go back to hitting.

Later in the day Mama Lily comes into the lobby of Club Dagobah. Ilaha is supposed to be outside, waiting to be picked up, but has lost track of time and is still on the practice court hitting balls.

Mama Lily approaches the man who can hear that sound. He is at the front desk.

"I left my girl here to use the practice court and she is probably still out there. Can I go back there and fetch her?" Mama Lily asks him.

"Sure," the man replies. "I'll go with you, in fact. I'd like to talk to you. I saw her hitting. She is really something."

The man comes around the desk and leads Mama Lily back toward the practice court.

"New to the village?" he asks.

Mama Lily explains that no, in fact she bought a farmhouse, Elysium, some years ago. She lived in the village for a while, but moved back to London. She has been living there until recently.

They reach the practice court and Mama Lily gently castigates Ilaha.

"Ilaha," she yells, making sure the girl hears her. She points at her wrist, even though there is no watch, and follows up. "I said five o'clock, Ilaha, gather up and let's go."

Ilaha still has balls left in the machine and Mama Lily knows she will hit them out before gathering up, but at least if she stands there the girl won't start a new round.

"You say she is good?" Mama Lily confirms with the man.

It never occurs to her where Ilaha ranks in the pecking order of tennis. Ilaha never actually plays, she only hits balls. Loads and loads and loads of balls. So many balls.

"I am sorry to be forward, but I think I recognise you. Are you Lily Lacey, the musician?" the man asks. Mama Lily confirms that yes, indeed, she is Lily Lacey, the musician. "And are you here, in the village, permanent, or just for a break from London?" he follows up.

Mama Lily tells him it is permanent, for Ilaha to start school.

"You know who she is, Ilaha?" Mama Lily asks the man.

He does not. Mama Lily puts her hand on the man's arm.

"Ilaha is 'The Goddess of Greengrass,'" she explains. "I found her outside Greengrass Tower the night of the fire. Took her in, and she never left. They could find no next of kin and I was allowed to adopt. Muslims don't adopt. Funny thing."

"The papers built her up into this big political symbol and she got a bit famous," Mama Lily goes on. "I started seeing razzies in the neighborhood in London when we would be about and she is getting old enough to get harassed. We moved here to protect her. I am hoping she will fit in as a regular girl and the razzies will leave us alone."

"Well, she may not be such a regular girl," the man asserts, "She seems possessed by hitting tennis balls and to be frank, she is awfully good. Special, really, how she hits. I've only seen a few hit it like her, and they were some great champions."

Ilaha hits out all of the balls and starts gathering. She exits the court and approaches Mama Lily and the man. He introduces himself, realizing he has yet to do so.

"I am Harmon, by the way. I run the place. Anything you need, I can get." Ilaha reaches out to shake his hand and Mama Lily strokes her head. Harmon makes a suggestion for them both, "Ilaha, you should think about playing some matches. We have people you can play with. It can be arranged."

Ilaha beams. She never plays matches.

"I want to. Right now? Is there anyone to play now?" she begs.

Not now, she is told by Mama Lily. It's late, I am tired and we are going home.

On the way out of the club, Harmon tells Mama Lily that Ilaha needs training.

"She hits, she has fire, she has rare talents," Harmon asserts, "But she should learn how to prepare and play matches. Bring her around and let me help her develop. She can go far."

"Harmon, is it? We will do that," Mama Lily thanks him. "Can't keep her off a court, and as long as I don't have to lug gear or chase around, bully for her."

bennosuke (弁之助)

Ilaha is too strong a player for the girls her age, but she is socially graceful and plays at the appropriate level for whoever is over the net. They mostly just hit balls, back and forth, not playing out points or games.

There would be no point in points or games.

Never, ever a bully, Ilaha smoothly drops into a beautiful, slowed down, buttery version of another fiercer self when she hits with peers. She hits right into the other side's strike zone, dampens her severe action, and guides them around the court into favorable situations. It is just a more formal version of exercise, after all, so why be mean?

This is why she never lacks for eager hitting partners. She makes them feel great about their game. She brings out their best by no accident, seeing it and feeding it.

Harmon decides to test Ilaha's limits. She is too comfortable being gentle and kind. It is time to let her brutal side out.

Harmon arranges a friendly match against an older boy, a lefty. A good player, a tough player, a fierce competitor, but also a bit of a rager. Fiery. Good, not great, more hustle than talent, who wins mostly by sheer will, often against better players.

"Connor, this is Ilaha," Harmon introduces them. "Ilaha, Connor."

They shake hands, and then Ilaha and Connor warm up a bit, hitting balls back and forth, taking serves, feeding each other volleys and lobs.

Something is a bit off during warm up. The practice court girl who makes that sound is not making that sound. Her ball is a bit dull, dead, not the lively monster Harmon has seen.

Ilaha wins the spin for serve and elects to receive. Not the typical choice, but so be it. Connor takes position to serve, calls out, "These are good," and starts the match.

His first serve is to the sideline, pulling Ilaha wide off the court. She returns wide across court, pulling Connor wide to his backhand, where he chooses the riskier shot down the line.

Ilaha anticipates this, runs it down, and slices a backhand high and deep to reset the point. They go back and forth down the middle of the court until Ilaha drops a shot short just so and Connor tries to do too much with it and hits it wide.

0-15.

The game carries on into deuce, with Ilaha placing shots very, very well and Connor willingly using an apparent power advantage to push her back. Ilaha seems to always have a response. They trade advantage a number of times until Connor has serve, down advantage, into the ad court.

Connor serves wide to the ad sideline all game, forcing Ilaha to hit backhand returns, but on first serve he goes down the T. He serves hard, places well, but Ilaha looks for that serve. She steps into the court, center inside the baseline, and blasts an off forehand through Connor's ad court.

That sound. Harmon is lurking about near the court, not watching, listening. He hears that sound. He knows who created that sound.

46

Game, Ilaha.

A bit surprised, Connor drops the balls and they change sides.

Ilaha sets to serve, announces, "These are good," and hits her first.

Some players can serve. Really serve. The great champions have fierce service games that simply overwhelm their opponent.

Sampras. Federer. Steffi. Serena ...

... Ilaha.

Her first serve whistles down the T, hitting the line, and bores hard into the tarp behind the court. Connor hardly moves. If he moves it is wasted effort. He is not getting to that serve.

Harmon hears it, but cannot believe he hears it. He makes his way to the court to watch.

Ilaha is a monster. She makes efficient use of her whole body, starting with a deep knee bend and culminating in a full-fledged vertical launch into a powerful explosive strike. Her ball drills through the air, with enormous pace and overwhelming action, with remarkable precision into impossible spots.

Over, and over, and over.

The match ends at 8-1. They were to play one superset, first to eight win by two. Connor manages to hold serve only once, in his final service game.

The boy is very upset.

He plays hard, he always plays hard, and he plays to win. He does everything he can, and he simply cannot answer what Ilaha throws at him. Connor plays a lot of matches, plays a lot of tournaments, and never encounters what this little girl forces upon him.

The whole thing is pointless, really. If they play a thousand times, Ilaha will win a thousand times.

Connor simply isn't good enough.

He is so upset because he realises it, right then, and right there.

Connor and Ilaha shake hands, exchange post-match pleasantries, and Connor leaves.

Harmon is awestruck.

"Ilaha, where did you learn to serve like that?," Harmon interrogates her. "Have you had lessons? Tell me the truth."

"I haven't had lessons, I swear," Ilaha insists. "I watch a lot of tennis on telly, and I just do what I see them do on telly."

"You know how well you can serve?," Harmon asks.

Ilaha confirms that yes, she knows.

"I practice serves, a lot, at night, when I lose the sunlight," Ilaha confesses. "I can practice service in the dark, because I don't need to see the ball. I can just toss it to where I will hit it."

"How can you tell if they are going in," Harmon asks her, a bit skeptical.

"From how it feels when I hit them," she responds. "They go in, trust me, I know they are going in."

Masamune (正宗)

Harmon leads Ilaha to the club lobby. They enter the pro shop, and Harmon takes Ilaha's racket.

He holds it up. He can tell it is not a player frame. The grip is so thin in his enormous hand. He reads the markings on the handle. Four inch grip. He measures the racket. Twenty five inches.

It's light. About ten ounces, he estimates. Harmon puts the racket on a scale, to weigh it. Nine and nine tenths ounces. Very light, really. Heavy, perhaps, for a child Ilaha's age and size, but very light nonetheless. Too light.

Harmon tests her string tension. Under fifty pounds. Too loose. To control the ball with strings that loose, Ilaha must hold back, withhold power by making a lower speed swing.

No good.

"You are done with this racket, Ilaha," Harmon tells her. "We are getting you into player equipment. Who is your favorite player?"

Ilaha knows them all. She admires them all. She loves them all, in different ways. But one is the best, the very best of all, the player she wants to become.

"Federer," she tells him.

Harmon stops. He looks at her, unblinking. He smiles, very much impressed.

"Federer, huh?" he confirms with her.

"Yes, Federer," Ilaha insists.

"He is the best. I want to be that good," she declares.

"What about Serena Williams? She is incredible," Harmon suggests.

"Nope," Ilaha insists. "Serena is awesome, sure, but she could never beat Federer."

"You want to beat Federer, huh?" Harmon asks her.

He is not mocking her, not treating her as a naive and silly child. He is taking her at her word, treating her as a peer, respecting her aspirations.

"Well, not right away, but someday, yeah, that is who I am shooting for," she tells him.

"Ilaha," Harmon tells her, looking her right in the eye, "If you are serious about that, you need new gear. I'll order you a new racket."

"Can I have my racket back?" she asks.

Ilaha wants to hit.

"No," Harmon tells her. "It is too small. You are done with that one. If you want to hit, use this."

He goes into his office and comes back with a wooden racket. Black. Donnay. It is a Bjorn Borg Donnay made by Jose Thiry. Borg used it at the French Open.

"Wood?" she asks, not quite understanding.

"Yep," Harmon tells her, "It's tiny, and heavy. Great training tool. Hit with this for a few days. Promise me you will only use this racket."

Ilaha promises she will, grabs the racket, and runs off to the practice court to hit.

Hagakure Kikigaki (葉隠聞書)

Ilaha arrives at Club Dagobah carrying the wooden Donnay racket she has been using. Hitting with it is hard, because the string bed is so small, but she figures it out over the few days of using it. It's really not so bad. Requires a much longer swing to create good action. Once you get the knack, it's great.

She anxiously calls on Harmon in his office to see if her new racket is in. Again. She has peppered him over the new racket repeatedly since he took away her gear. She is very eager to go back to modern gear.

Harmon holds up the new racket and displays it for her.

She drops the Donnay on the floor and reaches over his desk to grab the new racket. Harmon draws it back, not letting it go.

"It is a Wilson RF ninety seven frame," Harmon tells Ilaha. "Used at Wimbledon, in matches, by Federer. This racket has hit aces, and winners, and won matches, Ilaha."

She beams. Her joy is maximum. She can hardly believe it is hers.

"Before you run off and start wailing away at balls," Harmon lectures Ilaha, "You need to hear a few warnings. First, you must make it a point to hit from the feet up and out. Do not get handsy with this racket, Ilaha, you will injure your elbow. It is very heavy and very stiff. Requires a full body swing."

Harmon reaches into the drawer of his desk and pulls out a tailor's tape measure. He gets up and goes around the desk to where Ilaha is standing.

Harmon motions for Ilaha to pick the Donnay up from the floor. She does and they swap rackets. Ilaha holds her new racket feeling its weight and size.

"Extend your arm and raise the racket to shoulder height," Harmon instructs her. While Ilaha strains to support the racket, Harmon takes measurements at her wrist, elbow, and shoulder. The figures are jotted into a pocket calendar.

"Ilaha, a couple more things," Harmon resumes his warnings. "Do not hit for more than an hour today. And focus on solid contact. Hit the ball on the strings, on the sweet spot of the string bed. Do not keep framing balls. Focus."

Ilaha is dying to go hit, and practically bolts from his office.

Harmon comes along after about half an hour to check up on her. He is not hearing that sound, and he does not see the same girl who always hits everything pure.

Ilaha is struggling with her new gear. This is to be expected. Harmon leans against the fence that surrounds the practice court and addresses her.

"Not so easy to hit with, huh?," he observes.

She stops hitting and grunts her agreement.

"Right!," she laments, "It's like hitting with a paddle. Not soft, at all. Feels terrible."

Harmon walks onto the court and reaches out for the racket. Ilaha hands it to him.

"This racket doesn't do the work, Ilaha," Harmon explains, handling it deftly, with great ease, and visible comfort. "You do the work. The frame is very stiff, and I strung it very tight. Compared to what you were hitting, yeah, it is basically a paddle."

Ilaha is displeased. Hitting with her old racket feels so much better, and produces much better shots. Why must she switch over to this awful thing?

"You will have to adjust, Ilaha, but it will be worth it," Harmon promises. "The paddle quality you observed puts you in control. The less work the racket does, the more control you have over it. You can learn techniques to get back lost power and action. Once you do, the precision that this kind of gear creates will be very valuable."

Ilaha wants to hit more balls, but Harmon tells her to call it a day and leads her back to his office. He pulls out the tape measure.

"Okay let's measure again," he tells Ilaha.

She extends her arm and raises the racket to shoulder height. Harmon measures at the wrist, elbow, and shoulder.

"Three per cent swelling," he says, after jotting down the new figures. "Fine. Right in line, no concerns about injury. How do you feel? Arm okay?"

Ilaha confirms that her arm feels fine. A bit sore, but okay. She could hit.

"No more hitting," Harmon declares. "Two days. Come back in two days. Until then, no hitting."

Ilaha is a bit upset by this. She loves to hit. She has never taken two whole days off from it.

"We need to make sure you are really okay, Ilaha," Harmon explains. "You don't have rackets at home, do you?"

Ilaha considers lying to him, but decides against that. She tells Harmon she has a bunch of rackets at home.

"Okay," Harmon says, picking up his phone and handing it to Ilaha. "Call mum and tell her to bring all of your gear. It is being retired. You are getting new gear. When you get back from your break, you will have new weapons."

Ilaha calls Mama Lily, tells her to come pick her up, and to bring all of her rackets. She is taking a couple days off from hitting to make sure her arm is okay after hitting with her new racket.

Mama Lily is ecstatic. She rushes around Elysium gathering Ilaha's rackets, dumps them into her car, and speeds to Club Dagobah.

"That is all of her gear?" Harmon asks when Mama Lily comes into his office with an armful of rackets.

Ilaha nods to confirm. That's all of it.

Harmon stacks the gear on his sofa and takes a book off a shelf behind his desk.

"You read, right?" Harmon asks Ilaha.

"She is a little professor," Mama Lily interjects, with pride. "A real bookworm. She reads all day. Hitting tennis balls or reading. All she does."

"Great," Harmon says, smiling at them both.

He opens the book and makes an inscription on the inside cover.

Harmon hands the book to Ilaha.

"This is a special book. It was given to me by someone special, and now I am giving it to you. Wear it out. Read it, and really think about it," Harmon implores Ilaha. "It will make what you are setting out to do a lot more believable."

Ilaha and Mama Lily leave Harmon's office and exit Club Dagobah. In the car Ilaha looks over the book Harmon gives her.

It is a vintage copy of *Hagakure*, hardbound with a beautiful design on the dust cover. Ilaha holds it, handles it, and leafs through the thick, heavy pages. She clings to it, possessing it.

On the inside cover are two inscriptions.

"See it through - Gramps," appears to have been inscribed long ago. In pencil. It is fading but still legible.

"G∞D - Harmon E," below it. Perfect script, unwavering, no drags, no spacing errors, spills or drops.

Written with the skill of a trained calligrapher.

Hira

The two days without tennis are a whirlwind.

On the first day Mama Lily and Ilaha binge Netflix, gorge take away, and walk the countryside. They happen across a carnival and play games of chance, eat cotton candy, and ride creaky rides. It is wonderful. They talk and bond as never before.

Day two, 10 June, Mama Lily takes Ilaha to the Chislehurst Caves. They tour the caves with a group, and then wander about on their own.

"Mama Lily, I have dreams that I think are memories," Ilaha says, unprompted.

Mama Lily goes cold, then braces.

The moment is here.

She feels like her first time on stage at Glastonbury. You imagine and visualise, prepare and train. You know in your brain you can do it, that you can thrive. Then it is real, and for a moment you freeze. You feel as if you will vomit. Soil yourself. You must sync with the universe. Then you do, and you arrive.

Time to really be a mum.

"In my dream it is always the same," Ilaha starts, "It is very hot, and very dark, and so loud. I am so hot, like I am melting. And soaked. I am wrapped in a wet blanket and an old man, my grandfather, is squeezing me. It gets hotter and darker and louder and he leaves me, then he comes back. He picks me up and hands me Buraq, and then he shoves me through a window and I am falling. Then I fly."

Buraq, the horse with wings, her stuffed animal. She always knows where it is and every night, all night, she clutches Buraq to her heart as if she will die if she lets go.

"Is it scary, this dream?" Mama Lily asks her.

"No," Ilaha answers, "It isn't. I sort of wake up and step into the dream. The falling stops feeling like falling and starts feeling like I am flying. I fly through the cool air as much as I want. I am in complete control. It feels wonderful, especially after all the heat and noise and darkness. Free to fly. Then I land, softly, really, given how fast I am flying. I usually wake and find myself in bed hugging Buraq."

"The old man is alive, in my dream," Ilaha goes on. "I am sure he is my grandfather. I remember his hug, and he tells me I can fly. That he loves me. That he dreams the biggest dreams for me." Ilaha starts to well up. "He tells me all of the dreams will come true, and more. He says, 'God is infinite.' He tells me to hold Buraq and I feel his strong arms holding me tight way above the ground before I fly."

She cries and reaches to hug Mama Lily.

"Does he have a name, your grandfather?" Mama Lily probes, stroking Ilaha's hair.

"Jadd. I call him Jadd. When I talk to him, I call him Jadd. When I think about him inside my dream, his name is 'Jadd,'" Ilaha wails. Mama Lily asks about other relatives or people in the dream. "There isn't anybody. They are all gone and I never see them, or hear their names or anything. Just Jadd."

"Ilaha," Mama Lily mumbles, squeezes Ilaha, and cries. "That may be a dream or that may be a memory. All I know is this, I bless the day I found you. You were on top of an

59

abandoned car quite far from Greengrass, and you were saying, 'Ilaha can fly.' I believed you then and I believe it now. As far as I am concerned the only way you could have gotten there was to fly."

"Mama Lily!" Ilaha blurts out, laughing through her tears. "I can't fly! How would I fly? I am just a girl."

"No, Ilaha," Mama Lily insists, giggling along. "You are certainly not just a girl! You are my girl. You are 'The Goddess of Greengrass.' Listen. Listen to the caves. They are telling you that you can fly! You did fly, and that is why I am able to be your mum!"

Mama Lily and Ilaha continue wandering in the caves, the mood joyful. Mama Lily loves Ilaha, but she feels a duty to reunite her with her kin.

"Ilaha," Mama Lily asks, "Do you think maybe you can remember more if we go see a psychiatrist or something? They can maybe hypnotise you and find out who your kin are."

Ilaha stops, stands up tall, and faces Mama Lily.

"You are the only kin I know," Ilaha asserts. "I suspect all my kin are dead. I have googled and heard things. I know what happened. About Greengrass burning up and how I was thrown from a window. That is enough."

Mama Lily is curious about what else Ilaha knows. About herself, about Mama Lily before she is Ilaha's mum.

"So you google, yeah?" Mama Lily asks Ilaha. "You've snooped around online and found out about yourself a bit?"

Mama Lily is a prominent citizen of the World Wide Web, from far enough back that it is actually known as the World

Wide Web. She is a bit nervous about what Ilaha may have seen.

"Sure," Ilaha confirms, "I've seen myself on the cover of the First Class. 'Goddess of Greengrass.' It's really weird. When I first saw it, it made my dream easier to understand."

"Have ya ever googled me, Ilaha?" Mama Lily asks cautiously.

God forbid! Ilaha is one 'Lily Lacey' search away from a wealth of, well, results.

Ilaha laughs out loud.

"Of course!!! There are pictures of you and stories about you all over. You're Lily Lacey!" she declares.

The Fundamental Theorem of Tennis

Ilaha comes back from her time in the desert raring to hit. She rushes into the club and chases down Harmon.

"I wanna hit," Ilaha declares.

Harmon goes into his office and grabs her racket. He hands it to her and tells her to extend her arm and raise the racket to shoulder height. He wants to measure. Wrist, elbow, shoulder. He records the figures.

"No elbow pain. No soreness. You feel fine?" Harmon grills her.

Ilaha affirms yes, she is fine.

"Really?" Harmon presses. "You are not covering because you want to hit so bad?"

"Nope. Truth. I feel fine," she tells him.

Ilaha runs off to the practice court. She fires up the ball machine and starts wailing away, ball after ball, two line drill, forehand, backhand, forehand, backhand.

Harmon follows along and he hears it, again, over and over.

That sound.

It is denser now, heavier, and grander than it is with her undersized junior racket.

Ilaha feels it.

Power.

She feels like King Arthur must feel the moment he wields the Sword in the Stone.

Thor has a magic hammer.

Superman dons a suit with a cape.

Batman is literally just a rich guy who pays for gadgets.

Wonder Woman.

Wonder Woman descends from Gods and possesses magical powers, but even Wonder Woman has accoutrements. Lasso of Truth. Indestructible bracelets. Boomerang tiara. A sword and a shield.

Ilaha Tudor, the Goddess of Greengrass, wields a tennis racket.

Ilaha hits out the hopper and gathers the balls. Harmon addresses her from off court.

"Ilaha, how does it feel? Sounds great, looks like you have picked up a bit more pace," he observes.

Ilaha approaches him. She intends to drill him with questions.

"I feel a bit loose," she grouses, "The ball feels a bit out of control. I can't tell where it is going to go. It feels a bit wild."

Harmon takes in what she has to say. The heavier, bigger racket demands subtle changes. Explaining is no small matter. And explaining the nuance of adjusting for better ground strokes misses the bigger opportunity.

Harmon delivers a dissertation.

"Every ball you hit possesses three traits," Harmon begins, "Spot, speed, and spin. One of these will be the predominant characteristic for every shot. The thing that makes a winner a winner."

Ilaha nods that she follows. Harmon believes her, so he continues.

"Spot, speed, and spin interact. You can hit a shot to the right spot, but if you hit it too soft or with too little action, your opponent will play it back." Ilaha confirms understanding, so Harmon goes on. "Now, imagine infinity. Do you know what infinity is?"

"It's unlimited," Ilaha answers. "It is when something is so big it never stops."

Impressed, Harmon confirms her notion of infinity.

"Great. So imagine that you can hit to almost any spot you want, any time you want, with an easy shot. There should be some spots where you can hit that shot for a winner, right?" Ilaha agrees. "Now, imagine that you can hit a little bit harder. How many spots can you hit the harder shot now that create a winner?"

"More!" Ilaha shouts.

"Okay," Harmon continues, "Now imagine you can hit as fast as possible, so fast nobody can even see the ball, but you can still hit the court. How many spots can you hit to for a winner?"

Ilaha starts jumping up and down.

"All of them, all of them!" she exclaims.

Ilaha understands the notion. Start changing things, incrementally, and outcomes change.

"Ilaha," Harmon asks now, "What if you hit with more spin, how many spots on the court can you hit to now?"

More. More more more.

Harmon talks Ilaha through the calculus of incremental change, and Ilaha is right there with the right answers.

Hit from a given spot, at a given speed, with given action, at an opponent in a given spot. Picture how many spots you can hit to for a winner. Now hit a bit harder. How many more spots create winners? Now hit with more spin. How many more spots?

"Do you understand the visuals of this?" Harmon asks. Ilaha looks a bit unsure. "Look at the court as a big graph, color coded, where bright green is the places where a shot you plan to hit creates a winner, where bright yellow is the places where your shot comes back over the net but you can play it, and bright red is where you create a loser."

Ilaha walks out onto the court and stares over the net. She thinks about what Harmon explains and she sees it. Right before her eyes. Inside her brain.

Ilaha sees herself playing a shot from a given spot, sees her opponent in a given spot, and sees the color coded graph of where a hard flat forehand becomes a winner. Or a hard diving heavy topspin forehand that clears the net low. Backhand. Slice. Topspin. Lob.

She imagines it all. It becomes second nature for her.

"Ilaha, this is really, really important," Harmon implores her. He pauses to be sure she is paying full attention. "You must always visualise how the shots you plan to hit will color the graph. More important, you must learn how to select the shots that create graphs with a lot of bright green to hit at. If the graph is mostly bright red, pick another shot."

Ilaha sees it now. She forever sees the tennis court as a video game, of sorts, a color coded graph that displays how a shot is supposed to work out. Pick shots that create a lot of green. Do not pick shots that create a lot of red.

Her vision updates in response to the ball, to where she is on the court, to where her opponent is and how they hit and move. All she needs to do is perfect her vision.

It is not perfect, yet, but it will be.

The Manhattan Project

Harmon does not want Ilaha to play the junior tournament circuit. He does not want her involved with Big Tennis. Harmon does not believe playing alleged peers will help her at all.

Ilaha agrees with Harmon.

She prefers to train, mostly on her own with help from Harmon, and to play spectacular friendlies against people at Club Dagobah.

She revels in playing the middle aged men, who she toys with and pounds into dust with her sheer power. Against bigger stronger players she insists on making a brawl of it with kick serves and coming to net. She never plays a match without an audience.

Once word gets out Ilaha is playing, people show up to watch.

Ilaha plays like a man, but she looks every bit a beautiful, striking woman.

Olive skinned, her complexion is smooth and clear. Her jet black hair spills from her skull like a blowout from an oil rig, gushing with great force from every slight opening in her scalp. She has never allowed it to be cut. It is tied up in a giant bun when she plays.

When Ilaha's hair falls, it reaches her waist and stays behind her ears and between her shoulders.

Her eyes are striking. Piercing, bright, focused eyes. Always alert, always transmitting thought. Hazel. Hard to pin down, really, the color of her eyes. As if in flux, flowing seamlessly within bluegreenbrowngrayorange part of each all of none.

Ilaha is serious and consumed. Intellectual. She approaches training like an engineer. Like a research scientist. With a sense of industrial urgency.

She is working to solve a very big problem.

At first she films her practice sessions, goes home, watches the video, and charts dots where her shots land. She always has a thick stack of blank paper diagrams of a tennis court.

This is fine, but unsatisfactory.

She needs to know more than just where the shots land. How hard are they hit? How much and what kind of action do they have? Is a shot a winner, something that comes back playable, or a loser?

Ilaha improves her analytical system. She enlists a local stationary store to locate or create a triangle shaped stamp for her.

With the triangle stamp, Ilaha is able to add layers of information to her two dimensional graphs.

She watches the video of her practice sessions four times.

The first time through she stamps a triangle where every shot was hit and where it lands. The base of the triangle is always parallel to her baseline.

Then she watches the video again, and on each landing triangle she marks a dot to indicate the mix of spot, speed, and spin that defines the character of the shot.

A dot on the apex of the triangle means spot was the primary attribute of the shot. A dot on the lower left corner is for speed. Lower right, spin.

A dot away from a corner means the shot is not dominated by one or another characteristic. It is defined by a blend of attributes.

All of the shots are watched again for a third and finally a fourth time. The third time each triangle is numbered one through N to identify the shot pairs, and then the fourth time each pair is color-coded. Green means the shot is a winner. Red means the point is lost. Yellow means the ball comes back playable.

Ilaha wants to produce green triangles.

The amazing thing about Ilaha is that emotionally speaking she is indifferent to how she makes the triangles green. She has no preference, at all, for spot, or speed, or spin. Whatever works best is what she wants. She seeks the easiest shot she can hit that creates a green triangle.

Ilaha abhors giving away free points with errors of any kind. Decision, execution. Mistakes are anathema. Indecisive an unacceptable condition.

Much of her analysis is based on judgment, of course, but Ilaha has very good judgment. She does a lot of research. Ilaha spends hour upon hour with a stopwatch charting how far and how fast the top pros can go to run down a ball.

Based on this research, she color-codes her triangles. She knows what shots create what result based on her research. Her opponent starts at the ball machine. Ilaha hits a shot. Her opponent can or cannot run it down and send it back from where it goes.

Facts. Science.

Ilaha focuses her research on the men, the top men. The men who are best at getting to every ball, the fastest most athletic and smartest men.

Rafael Nadal is the best at this. Ilaha is a crazed fan girl. She always, always, always visualises playing Nadal, on grass, where his strengths are perhaps dampened, but hardly weak. Ilaha understands that the game is a race, ball versus man. If she can hit balls Nadal can't get to, nobody else can get to them either.

Ilaha's charting system works well, but producing the charts is painfully time-consuming. Her obsessive nature quickly leads her to analytics version two.

Ilaha dives into computer programming and figures out a way to hack her laptop to capture the same shot data automatically using the built-in camera. After many weeks of testing she determines the program is in fact taking good readings. For a few weeks she derives shot speeds from the video by hand, adding a new layer of data to analyze, but quickly automates that as well.

Version two is really impressive, but not nearly as good as the highest end systems being used in professional tennis.

Ilaha will not settle on inferior. She googles the PerfOculus system that is used to capture shot data during professional tennis tournaments. It is perfect, but very, very expensive. She discovers a lower priced alternative.

BallMap.

Ilaha clicks through a web page into a court locator. The nearest BallMap court is two hours drive. Ilaha convinces Mama Lily to drive her and she demos the system.

She is sold. She peppers the pro at the club with questions about BallMap and gets all the information she needs.

Club Dagobah is getting a BallMap system. Ilaha will make it happen. It is decided.

On the ride home, Ilaha pitches Mama Lily.

"Mama Lily," Ilaha asserts, "I need ten thousand pounds."

Mama Lily, caught a bit off guard, laughs.

"Why do you need so much money?" Mama Lily counters, giggling.

"I want to buy a computer system to install at the club to track all of my shots," Ilaha explains. "I have looked into it. The perfect system, PerfOculus, costs nearly a hundred grand, but that is for places like Centre Court at Wimbledon. We don't need that," she concedes.

"Welllll, as long as we don't need that," mocks Mama Lily.

"There is another system," Ilaha continues her pitch. "It is called 'BallMap.' I think it can be had for ten thousand. How can I get that much?"

Mama Lily realises Ilaha is serious about this. This is not a lark. Ilaha really wants this. She will find a way. She is that kind of girl.

"I will not just pay for it, Ilaha," Mama Lily asserts, "It's maudlin, the whole idea of that. My parents didn't just buy me eight-o-eight drums and studio gear every time I asked."

"I am not saying to just buy it for me," Ilaha defends herself. "But I want this, so how do I get ten thousand pounds? What can I do?"

Mama Lily admires her commitment.

"I'll tell you what, it's been forever since I performed, so here's a deal," Lily proposes, "You know everyone in the village like a pal. Arrange a charity event and I'll perform to help raise the money."

Ilaha smiles wide.

"I can produce a Lily Lacey show in the village to raise the fifteen grand to buy the BallMap for the club?" she confirms.

"Yep," Lily tells her, feeling like a giant waking from a slumber.

Lily Lacey, Lazarus

The next day Ilaha tracks down Harmon at the club and explains that she wants to raise money to buy a BallMap system for Club Dagobah. He is familiar with it and immediately agrees it is a great idea.

"So you are settling on BallMap, huh? Why not shoot for PerfOculus, Ilaha?" Harmon is joking, of course, but Ilaha does not brush the idea off.

"I looked into PerfOculus, but it may be impossible to raise that much money. BallMap is more realistic. Fifteen grand US." Ilaha has thought through every angle. "I am not even sure having Mama Lily headline at Glasto would raise enough money for PerfOculus!!!"

Ilaha does a lot of work, goes through all of the proper channels, and obtains a permit for a show on the village common.

The concert is to be held in a fortnight. It is not promoted widely, and not promoted online.

Flyers are pinned up around town and passed out at local youth sports events. Posters are displayed where they can be, in store windows and on public kiosks, cork boards inside local pubs.

The artwork is really cool, actually. It depicts a zombie Lily Lacey ascending steps from an open grave and walking toward a piano. The date, time, and location of the show are on the headstone. The sheet music on the piano is a visual riddle hinting at her set list.

It depicts a large round stone with Mick Jagger's big red lips and set of leering eyes rolling toward Bo Derek wearing a top hat over her cornrows, in a gold one-piece bathing suit.

The whole thing has a Mexican Día de Muertos visual quality.

In the days preceding the show the posters keep disappearing. Ilaha is bothered by this, but she is quick to replace them. She wants the show to be a success, so she does the work. It happens multiple times. She does not complain, she just puts up new posters.

Lily Lacey catches the performance bug, as aging pop stars are wont to do. She plans to play her Cincisprezece piano. It is in storage in London, but she wants it for Elysium. She sends movers to bring it to her so she can practice.

Lily Lacey works on her set list. She prepares with zeal. All day every day for the two weeks prior to the concert. She has not played a show in years, but like riding a bike it all comes back quickly.

Masterful.

Lily Lacey is going to kill, she knows it.

The Cincisprezece arrives at the village common the evening of the concert. Harmon is organizing the event on the ground. He instructs the delivery crew to place the piano on the gazebo nestled in the crux of the common.

Harmon sits at the piano, admiring it, gently fingering but not playing the keys. From a distance Lily sees him at her piano and makes her way to the gazebo.

Harmon never turns but he knows Lily is there.

"It is a Cincisprezece, right?" he asks her.

A bit surprised that he knows, Lily confirms that it is.

"Can I play it?" he asks.

Even more surprised, she tells him sure, go ahead.

Harmon sets himself with great affect and then launches into "Chopsticks," prompting Lily to slap him on the shoulder. Harmon smiles at her and promises to be serious.

He sets himself again, in perfect posture, enormous hands and bulging forearms splayed elegantly over the keys. He looks like a master pianist.

He is.

He strikes the keys.

Perfectly.

Lily does not recognise what he is playing. Not yet. It is teetering on an edge in her mind. She hears it and it sounds like she knows it, but she cannot name it yet.

Harmon continues. Brilliant, Lily thinks. She is aghast at his play. She hears and sees how difficult what he is playing really is. Harmon plays, perfectly, and Lily searches to recognise.

He nears the end of the first movement, and Lily gasps.

"Gaspard!," she blurts out loud, over applause from a small crowd that has gathered to listen.

Harmon plays the Ravel perfectly, right before her eyes. A piece written to be difficult, to test and challenge the virtuoso players.

He finishes the first movement, gets up from the piano, and bows to applause.

"It is a real treasure," Harmon says of the Cincisprezece. "Just beautiful. A perfect thing. You are very lucky to have it."

Lily is silent.

Harmon leaves her with her piano.

A bit shaken, Lily Lacey organises her set sheets and prepares herself to play.

An enormous crowd has gathered. Upwards of ten thousand. Crowded trains from London empty into the village all afternoon with people from the City coming to see Lily Lacey.

Some of them bring posters to be autographed, the missing ones, which are purchased in online auctions.

The concert is a public event. Lily Lacey is Labour, and the notion of a public concert carrying an admission price is flatly rejected. Ilaha enlists friends to walk the crowd collecting donations. People pay according to their means, and enjoy according to their appetite.

Simple.

It is a beautiful summer evening and the gazebo is a great spot to play. A DJ friend from Lily Lacey's pop star days has over engineered the sound system so the acoustics are great.

Lily Lacey taps a few piano keys to set herself, does a quick sound check, and then it is show time.

"Hey there!" Lily Lacey calls out. "What a turnout. All we did was put up posters and pass out flyers around town and look at you!!!"

The crowd cheers, cutting her off. Lily is genuinely surprised about the turnout, and the cheering. Shocked, really. But flattered.

They like her, right now, they really like her.

"I'd like to invite anyone and everyone who would like, please record this show," she announces. "Go ahead and set up wherever you like. Video, audio, whatever you want. Just keep in mind when you donate. All right, let's play. We will start out with a bit of fun."

Lily Lacey strikes up the first notes of a very popular hit, "LDN," by her namesake Lily Allen. Faithful to the original, but adapted for piano. Scrubbed of explicit lyrics and blue images.

The hometown crowd recognises it after just a few notes. A great and utterly surprised cheer goes up, and Lily Lacey is forced to loop the intro until the cheering dies down.

Lily Lacey has never played a cover. She is famously militant about that. Only her own music, her own lyrics and her own instrumentals.

Lily Lacey was once asked why she never plays covers, and why none of her songs ever include "featured" artists. Why she never employs co-writers, or has studio players on her tracks. Why she refuses to work with anyone else.

Why don't you collaborate? Everyone collaborates.

"Covers are for soda pop," she famously retorts, "And features are for creatures. I play for me. Can't play for me collaborating with ye."

In the crowd there is more than one no longer young lady wearing a vintage reproduction Lily Lacey concert shirt they just bought. It is iconic, actually, for ladies from LDN of a certain age.

Black T shirt, v neck, with a generic red movie theater soda pop cup that says "Soda Pop," plastic lid on top, straw sticking out, below her quote, "Covers are for soda pop."

Finally she plays, with a giggle and a smile to a great ovation. They love her "LDN," and they love her, Lily Lacey, one time celebrity, and perhaps even Lily Tudor, real person, just a little bit.

Now onto the real work.

Lily Lacey will play the Rolling Stone Top Ten Songs of All Time. Unaccompanied, adapted for piano solo, with vocals.

Number ten, Ray Charles. *What'd I say.* Her piano is perfect, her vocals an appropriate adaptation. No creepy appropriation, just Lily Lacey style genuine in the spirit of the original.

Number nine, Nirvana. *Smells Like Teen Spirit.* Not an easy adaptation for piano, but she makes it work.

Number eight, The Beatles. *Hey Jude.* Number seven, Chuck Berry. *Johnny. B. Goode.* Number six, The Beach Boys. *Good Vibrations.*

Lily Lacey skips number five. She will play it as her finale.

Number four, Marvin Gaye. *What's Going On.* Tough vocal. She nails it. Number three, John Lennon. *Imagine.* She practically whispers the lyrics, breathy, throaty, and it silences all. Number two, The Rolling Stones. *(I Can't Get No) Satisfaction.* High energy, engaged crowd. Lily Lacey plays bigger than the venue. Great crescendo piece. Number one, Dylan. *Like A Rolling Stone.* No overdone vocal affectations or cheap imitating, just a full rich authentic voice with nuanced lyrical emphasis.

Finale.

Number five, Aretha Franklin.

Respect.

It is Otis Redding's song. He wrote it, and he released it first. Nineteen sixty five. His version is a great, great song.

Not great enough.

Nineteen sixty seven. Aretha Franklin drinks Redding's milkshake. Right there, in plain view, for the whole world. She stakes a claim and forever after it's hers.

A de facto feminist fight song.

Lily Lacey does it more than justice. She does her best work adapting this particular song for piano solo with vocals. It has meaning for her. The crowd is loud while she plays, but she stays above them, pulling at them until they can no longer hold on and then escaping gravity to sock it to them.

Her piano is virtuoso, and when her rendition comes to an end the crowd rises and surges into wild applause. It is really a moment. They see a genius play deeply, powerfully, masterfully the best work of other geniuses, upon their shoulders, and it has an impact.

You could say it is just music, it is just a show, but Ilaha watches it. She absorbs it. Every sound. Every word.

Harmon marches her out to an acoustically perfect location right at the beginning of the show.

"Watch," he commands, clearing a spot for her, "And listen. You are about to see greatness. Absorb it. There is greatness in you. Watch your mum let hers out. You are gonna do the same thing someday soon."

Ilaha does. She is moved. More than just impressed, or excited or proud.

It is spiritual.

Ecstasy.

Ilaha stands upright frozen throughout the show. She loses her senses, but her heart expands to practically break free of her chest. It grows many more than three sizes that day, from already boundlessly big. She swims in infinity, she goes blind, and she experiences the sublime.

As it ends, as Lily Lacey closes out *Respect,* while she socks it to 'em, Ilaha comes back to the here and now all at once.

Changed.

People who record the show post it online straight away, and by the time Ilaha rushes to her Mama Lily and hugs her, shouting, "That was the greatest thing I have ever seen!" the concert is downloaded tens of thousands of times.

The show is a complete success.

Donations total over twenty grand, pounds. In addition, poster and T-shirt sales add in another twenty grand, pounds.

Harmon hears Ilaha grousing about the missing posters as they go missing. He goes online and finds auctions selling them for upwards of a hundred pounds. He figures that the concert may end up bigger than is understood, so he bets on a big turnout and buys a supply of posters and tees to offer. It all sells out rapidly.

Harmon donates all of the sales, including what he spent.

Ilaha is going to get her BallMap.

And Lily Lacey will finally get to work on her magnum opus.

The Science of Hitting

Ilaha is at the club all … the … time … once BallMap is installed.

Harmon gives her a set of keys to Club Dagobah.

With access to higher quality data she is able to really ramp ahead into a cutting edge game. A game like no one has ever seen.

Harmon spends hours telling her about wooden rackets, about humidity and gut strings. He tells her about aluminum, about graphite, about composite fibre. It is very much in depth, nuanced and scientific.

It is a graduate course in the science of hitting.

Harmon does a lot of explaining, forcing Ilaha to understand how equipment affects how you play the game. How all of the elements of Grand Slam tennis interact, driven by the tool in the hand of the player.

Harmon loves to talk Ilaha through "time machine" thought experiments.

If you put Federer in a time machine and send him back to play Borg, he can probably hold up very well. Agassi, great as he is, not so much. Djokovic, Murray, eh. Tough call there. Great, tough athletes both, but never touched wood. Nadal does fine at any point in time, including the future, but suffers a bit going backwards. Equipment. Backwards in time is a more vertical game. Now, if you put Billie Jean King in a time machine and move her forward to today, she has big trouble. Too small. She would not hold up against Serena or Venus. Players like that, too big and strong.

Ilaha loves listening to Harmon.

She sits there, for as long as he will talk, absorbing everything he tells her.

Borg, the iceman who dominates until he becomes bored. Harmon's sentimental favorite player. Ennui defeats Borg more than any opponent. At eighteen Borg wins a Grand Slam. Nineteen seventy four. By nineteen eighty one he wins eleven, dominating both sides of the Channel year after year.

Then poof, he quits.

In eighty one Borg loses to McEnroe in the US Open final. After the match he literally just walks away, skipping the trophy ceremony.

Borg is a racket nut. The great champions are. Borg's Donnay rackets are made for him and only him, all by Jose Thiry. Borg's rackets are strung so tight that they require extra wood to support the frame against the tension of the strings.

In one case, Borg's racket simply explodes after he hits a ball, from a combination of the force of his stroke and the tension of his strings. It is all perfect, that collision, with shards and bits of racket flying into the startled crowd.

Borg is a savant regarding his gear. A load of rackets is shipped to New York, and Borg knows they are off. Too heavy. Three grams too heavy. He is sure. They weigh the rackets. Four hundred eighteen grams.

Three grams too heavy.

Jose, sure his work is perfect, realises the rackets picked up water weight from humidity in shipping.

"Put them on the radiator," he instructs.

83

There are fifty of them.

The Ritz arranges with thrilled guests to allow Borg access to twenty five rooms. They turn up the heat and the rackets sit on the radiator.

They dry out and go down to exactly the right weight, four hundred fifteen grams.

Harmon explains how string tension works.

"Ilaha, you will hear much nonsense about how a ball behaves during the collision with the strings," he warns her. "Ignore it. For every ball, there is an optimal tension where as little energy is absorbed by the strings as possible, while as little energy is absorbed by squishing of the ball as possible. At this tension, and with this ball, you deliver maximum energy to your ball," he explains. She is unblinking. Rapt. "At maximum energy, your ball moves as well as it can."

"Mustn't I spin the ball?" she asks.

"No," Harmon tells her, "The ball spins itself, and spin is created in an instant. Spin is a tradeoff. Energy is energy. It can be spent spinning or moving forward, but never both."

"Don't think about spin," he preaches, "Think about trajectory."

"Idle spin is pointless," he asserts. "The ball is flying through a medium, the air. It curves because Newton says it will curve. It bounces off the air, and it is pulled down by gravity. It isn't spin that moves the ball; it is momentum versus air resistance. Plain and simple. And a ball that is not spinning at all bounces off the air the most."

"You cannot defy Newton's third law, Ilaha," Harmon insists. "And you cannot resist gravity. Spinning balls get pulled down mostly by gravity and only appear to be spinning down."

Ilaha is open to this thinking, but unsure.

Harmon, certain, takes her onto the court to prove it.

"BallMap is perfect for this," he says. "Watch me."

Harmon grabs a racket and two balls. He sets himself at the baseline and prepares to serve.

Ilaha has never seen him serve, and is feeling a rush now.

Harmon, normally a bit slouched and mundane in posture, comes alive. He sets, goes into his service motion, and tosses.

Knees bent, pushing on the earth with bare feet, lifting off the ground with great force, he hits a laser beam kick serve right down the T. The sound the ball makes when it is hit shocks Ilaha.

She has never heard such a sound.

Harmon motions Ilaha over to the BallMap terminal.

"Okay, look at this serve," he tells her. "You saw it move and how it broke down into the court."

They look at a three dimensional image of the flight of the ball, noting speed and spin at every point on its journey.

"Study the graph," Harmon tells Ilaha. "The shot covers about sixty one or sixty two feet, from racket to ground. This is because of the bend. Look at the spin rate. Four thousand one hundred eighty nine revolutions per minute. 'RPM.' Remember that acronym. That's pretty high for a man's serve. Now I'll hit again. Watch, close."

Harmon sets to serve again. This time he tosses a bit higher, squats a bit deeper, and really explodes violently but gracefully into his serve.

The ball literally whistles down the T to the same spot, explodes into and up from the court, and blasts into the tarp behind the baseline. Where the ball hits, the tarp is stretched.

The ball leaves a mark.

Harmon goes back to the BallMap monitor.

"Look," Harmon implores Ilaha, "I hit both balls from the same spot, no?"

Ilaha looks at the two graphs, overlaid onto the screen. Sure enough, both shots are hit within inches of each other on the toss. And both land within inches of the same spot on the court.

Harmon clicks away at BallMap and sets both graphs to have the same landing point.

"Look at the second shot. How much spin, Ilaha?" Harmon gestures toward the reading on screen.

She wonders if there is an error. Sixty RPM.

"Now look at the path," he traces them both with separated fingers. "My second ball cleared the net higher, Ilaha, and broke harder into the court. That second serve is not coming back. Nobody does anything with it."

Ilaha is aghast.

Harmon is not done.

"The second serve does not waste energy on spinning," he explains. "Look at the speed. The first is a hard serve. Leaves the racket at a hundred twenty five miles per hour, lands at ninety. Kicks nicely, hard and high. But the second. Look at it!!! Leaves at one forty five lands at one ten. Bam!!! And the kick, look at the path."

Ilaha sees that the second serve is always above the first, as if nestled into the first like a slice of deli meat into a sub roll, only more severe. It stays higher, clears the net higher, breaks harder to the same landing spot, then kicks even higher.

Ilaha stares. She sees lines and annotations and data, but it does not register. Her mind is frozen. She is numb.

All this time and she has never seen Harmon hit a ball. Now she watches the man blast two serves from cold, no warm up, that any Grand Slam champion would envy.

Who is he?

Harmon makes his point. Ilaha witnesses proof. And truth.

"Don't think about spin," Harmon sums up. "It is a MacGuffin. Focus on trajectory, and hitting the ball solidly. They all sink because of gravity. The more energy you put into the ball, the harder it breaks. The harder it pushes against the air. Just focus on maximum energy and launching at the right angle."

Ilaha comes back to earth, and Harmon finishes up that day's sermon.

"Ted Williams was like Borg, in a way," he tells Ilaha. "Savants, both. I studied baseball before tennis. I read Williams' book over and over, tattered the pages, wore it out. Nobody ever knew more about hitting things than Williams. He wrote all about it. It is all there, in print, his best explanation."

Harmon pauses and smiles, remembering. He meets Williams once, briefly. As a small boy. Harmon reads his book and must ask him something.

He hunts Williams down and asks him a single question.

Williams is astounded.

He tells Harmon a secret. One that Harmon agrees to never pass on.

"People say all sorts of foolish things about why Williams was such a great hitter," Harmon observes. "He could see better, had twenty-ten vision. Could read the print on the ball while it was coming at him. Could count the rotations of the ball, could calculate the curvature of the ball in his head," Harmon chuckles, "It is all nonsense. Williams himself insisted he could do none of it. But ignore him, right? They all know better than him what he knows."

Harmon goes on and on. Williams. Hogan. Tom Seaver. Newton. Borg again. Sampras. Federer.

Harmon realises he has departed from the moment, has run amok, and stops.

"Enough for today. It cannot be understood at once," Harmon breathes deeply, displaying a hint of exhaustion. "Here is the key concept, Ilaha. You need to produce maximum energy and hit it at the right trajectory.

"How do I do that?" Ilaha asks.

Harmon laughs out loud, grateful to have her as a compadre.

"You hit a lot of balls and just figure it out," he concludes. "The next ball can always be the one that makes it all clear."

Mushroom Cloud

A few days later Harmon calls Ilaha over to his office when she enters Club Dagobah. He hands her a racket. A Wilson ProStaff six point o with a tan leather grip.

One of Pete Sampras's rackets.

It was used in a U.S. Open final. He won.

Knowing this thrills Ilaha to no end.

It is heavy, and small. It feels like an axe. Ilaha's hand hardly gets all the way around the grip. The racket feels so, so different from hers. How in the world will she hit on that tiny string bed?

"Give this a try today. It's a gem, actually. One of Pete's. From the St. Vincent factory," Harmon beams, "Hard to get. Not cheap if you buy one. This one's for you. It is strung with gut at the moment, but you will break that soon enough and we will put in some poly. Strung tight. Pete's tension, seventy five pounds."

The metrics of the specs did not carry meaning for Ilaha. Seventy five pounds? How many pounds is her racket?

"It is so small, Harmon," she complains.

Only eighty five inches square. A sort of evolutionary relic. Made with modern materials, but at throwback scale.

Sampras, a power player, a serve and volley player, plays with a wooden racket as a child. In a Rolling Stone interview he credits playing wood until age fourteen with making him great. No accident. Harmon knows all of this, and is now passing it on.

"Ilaha, the ball contacts the strings within a very small area. It is effectively a single spot," Harmon declares, "All you need is that spot. So go out there and find that spot, and hit the ball on that spot."

Ilaha stands with the racket, older than her, by many, many years, looking unenthused.

"Come on Ilaha, feet, squat, push, open, drag, and pop. Feet up and out, no hands," he reminds her. "Simple."

Her practice session is difficult. At first her ball has less action. It flies and sails. She has trouble hitting the court, but over time she finds a groove.

Balls are frequently mishit, partially on the frame, but even mishit balls are shaped and worked. Hitting balls with this racket feels terrible until you catch one just right, and then you feel perfect solid nothingness.

The best feeling she ever feels.

After a bit Harmon whistles at Ilaha.

"So how is it going?" he asks her.

Ilaha tells him she got past spraying balls quickly.

She is fascinated by how the racket plays.

"It doesn't twist very much," she observes.

Harmon explains that the racket is narrower, so the edges are closer to the lengthwise axis of rotation.

"Imagine trying to push open a really narrow door. No leverage. The narrowness makes it harder for the ball to rotate the racket. Great for volleying." Once again, Harmon gives Ilaha the words and everything becomes clear as day.

"It is so heavy!!! Is it because of the lead tape here, on the frame?" she asks.

Ilaha demands sleek, clean, factory look gear, not messy and visibly customised. This racket is not aesthetically pleasing.

"Well, yes and no," Harmon explains. "For a fact it is heavier than your gear. Fourteen ounces, you play closer to eleven ounces. Heavy. Too many players want lighter, bigger. It's stupid."

"So yes it's heavy," Harmon goes on, "But what matters is how the weight is arranged. That's called 'swing weight.' A racket weighted toward the head feels heavier than a racket of the same weight that is weighted toward the handle."

"That racket you have," he points, "Is very head heavy. It is really an axe. Perhaps not match practical, but a great training tool."

Harmon reaches for the racket.

"I want to hit. Turn on the machine." Ilaha feels a rush. She has only seen Harmon hit two serves, and now he is going to hit ground strokes.

Harmon sets himself mid-court just inside the baseline and casually stands ready to hit. Ilaha turns on the machine and runs a topspin two line drill. Forehand, backhand, forehand, backhand.

The first ball flies to Harmon's forehand side.

He turns, micro adjusts his feet to play the ball into his strike zone, squats into his stroke, and in an invisible whoosh does exactly what Ilaha is always told to do.

Feet, push, twist, drag, and pop!

He misses the shot slightly, toward the frame, but it still bores through the air, well over the net, and breaks hard into the ad corner. When it hits the tarp behind the court it sounds out an amazing thud.

She rushes to the BallMap terminal.

Harmon is hitting a forehand very much like what Nadal hits. Not quite so much spin, but a lot of it. From his backhand he creates a nearly identical shot. Very hard and flat off the racket, but breaking hard after clearing the net high to crash down into the court.

After a bit he starts hitting slice backhands. The difference from his topspin backhand is startling. Not really in terms of spin, but in terms of flight and pace.

Harmon can see that the machine is running down to last balls, and on the very last ball, a forehand, he really, really uncorks a missile. Ilaha can hardly believe her eyes when the shot comes up on the BallMap. One hundred and forty miles per hour!!! It hits the court, too!

"How in the world can you hit a groundstroke as hard as a serve?" Ilaha demands to know.

Harmon looks at her as if she is not well.

"Ilaha, I can transfer much more of my body weight into a groundstroke than a serve. Of course a player can hit a harder groundstroke than a serve, if done right," Harmon states flatly.

Ilaha thinks about it. Not one to just accept, she thinks a bit.

"But that's not right," Ilaha argues. "The moving ball loses energy in the collision. You need to use up power to reverse the ball. A serve is sitting still, so all of the energy can go into moving the ball forward."

Impressed, Harmon talks her through the specious part of her argument.

"Clever, Ilaha," Harmon compliments her, "But a service toss possesses less energy when it is hit. All it really has is potential energy from its height off the ground, right?" Ilaha thinks it over and agrees. "So even though a moving ball has to be turned back, and it loses energy in the collision, there is more energy to work with. Losing energy does not mean zero energy, right?"

"Coefficient of restitution," Harmon says, very deliberately enunciated. "The ratio of how fast a body rebounds from a collision. You want it to be above one. Ball goes back faster than ball comes in."

She sees her error. Power creates its own power. Energy compounds into more energy. It shows on her face, in her eyes.

Harmon sees her see it.

"Ilaha, you just touched infinity," Harmon implores her. "You are privy to an insight. You should feel a bit numb. All of this, everything we are doing, it is about compounding energy. Feet knees hips shoulders elbow wrist strings. That is all about multiplying instead of adding."

"Lesser minds add, Ilaha," Harmon declares. "We are thinking people. We compound. Think about everything you do in terms of how it feeds itself toward mushrooming energy."

Harmon hands her the racket and walks off the court, leaving Ilaha to ponder and hit balls.

It's there. Her insight. Her intuition. Ilaha does exactly what Harmon tells her. She focuses on finding the beneficial feedback process.

Thereafter, when Ilaha is given pace to use, she feasts. She learns to find the energy, and borrow it, and use it to generate much, much more of it from itself.

Mind Walks on Thursday

Harmon visits with the man every Thursday. He catches the first train from the village into London, and then switches trains to exit London for Cambridge University, where the man lives. They meet at a coffee shop near campus.

The man is very old now, but sharp. He is not an official member of the Cambridge faculty, but he is held in high esteem by the academics at the school. He is living out his old age playing the role of intellectual raconteur.

The man occupies a University provided flat, spending his days translating and editing a modern version of the Quran for the world renowned Grand Mufti Ibrahim Ainfasal.

Dr. Assad Rasheed, PhD, Harmon's father-in-law.

Assad is born elite in his home country. His family is royalty, owners of property and occupants of positions of power across politics, religion, law, and the military. Assad can be a general, or judge, or anything else he desires.

He chooses medicine. Science. Academic study. When civil war breaks out he chooses the battlefield, working on the ground under fire to save fallen soldiers. He is an innovative healer. He is practical and open minded, not dogmatic.

Example. Assad does not have access to modern pharmaceuticals to treat infections during the war, so he searches for alternatives.

Maggots.

He learns that properly cultivated and applied, maggots very effectively treat infections. Countless men in Assad's homeland walk today, or labour with both arms in a trade, because Assad saves a limb with an innovative maggot therapy he develops.

Assad is analytic. Closed end thinking is his great strength. He looks over any problem and breaks it down, uncovering the limits and potentials of it. From repairing a taxi transmission to controlling blood pressure during surgery, Assad always cuts through the noise and grasps a great solution. Or he determines correctly that there is no solution.

Either way, problem solved once and for all.

Assad sees bravery in Harmon. Harmon, smart, remarkably smart, is not moved by ideas. Intellectually adept and perfectly capable, but unmoved. A bit of a troglodyte, really.

Harmon is a warrior.

Harmon is about the heart, but not the feelings of the heart, the righteousness of the heart. Assad holds Harmon in awe, because in any situation of conflict Harmon moves quickly and fearlessly, taking the right side and defeating anything or anyone that threatens it.

Harmon is cold, of course, and remorseless, as a result. He will not bully, but he will destroy.

Harmon teaches Assad that the calculus of right and wrong is always simple, and always based on observing who is on what side.

The bad guys are on the wrong side …

… And the wrong side is the losing side.

When Harmon arrives at the coffee shop, every Thursday, they embrace, deeply, upright, for more than a moment.

"Assad, father, how are you doing this week? Tell me what fascinating mysteries of nature you are toiling over." This is how Harmon addresses Assad.

It is the procedure. A ritual, of sorts. Assad states the matter on his mind for Harmon. Stating it helps him clarify it. Harmon listens, ponders, digests, and responds with his own insights.

This week Assad is pondering mortality. A subject with which he is all too familiar and worse experienced. He proposes a notion to Harmon.

"To what lengths are the living obliged to accommodate the dead, Harmon?" Assad asks.

Harmon has never thought it through but has already thought it through. This is how his mind works. He speeds through his intuition on the matter very rapidly.

"It is not an absolute. It is situational, and personal," Harmon responds.

"I have been reading about this, but what I have come up with is a bit vague and soft," Assad complains, "There's law, of course, regarding mostly the execution of wills and estates. There are religious customs, many largely overlapping, but little that I could find about the philosophy of obligations. Must we remember? Must we honor with ceremony? And for how long? And for whom?"

"Have you considered the alternative case, what obligation the dead have to the living?" Harmon counters.

Assad has not.

"Do the dead have any obligation to simply go, to let the living be?" Assad responds, thinking aloud.

"I am familiar with a notion in African culture that says the dead actually remain alive until nobody remembers them," Harmon offers, "If you follow through on that, the living have a moral imperative to sustain memory in the same spirit that they are expected to sustain life itself. Taken to the extreme this would mean that nobody should die, that the living should keep them in mind ad infinitum."

"Like the so called Matrix, Harmon?" Assad jokes.

They chuckle. A modern day evil demon made possible by the perverse dream that bits and bytes stored on machines can replace carbon based people.

Philosophy full circle.

It goes on like this for an hour or two, every week, over a few coffees and maybe some snacks, until the coffee shop gets more crowded and the time comes for a real meal.

"Let's go to the faculty for lunch today, Harmon," Assad suggests, "I'd like to find Doctor Raglan."

In the dining hall Assad is greeted by one after another of his acquaintances, each of whom serves him a notion or quip that he volleys back or allows to pass.

Assad barely eats, and unenthusiastically.

Harmon eats an apple, including the core and the stem. He always eats the whole thing. Some theory about building immunity to cyanide.

A very tall woman approaches Harmon with a great smile.

"Agent Mulder!" she practically shouts, laughing greatly.

"I want to believe, Esther," Harmon replies. He stands and hugs her. He likes her. They share a fanaticism for The X-Files and an appreciation for the beauty of Black-Scholes. A pair of conspiracy buffs and math geeks.

Harmon states the kernel of an idea that wins Dr. Esther Ferris a Swedish Bank Prize, the economics equivalent of a Nobel Prize. Her paper, *Algorithmic Finance and Systemic Black Swan Exposures,* does not credit Harmon as a co-author but it should. At his insistence it does not. Just seeing what is done with the idea is a thrill for him.

He desires no credit.

"What are we discussing today, fellows?" she inquires.

Dr. Ferris has joined them many times, and she always enjoys hearing anything there is to hear about these Thursday mind walks.

"The obligations that the living may or may not have to the dead," Assad relays, "But we have moved on. I want to find Doctor Raglan."

Dr. Ferris has just seen Doctor Raglan, out on the quad, flying kites. Hurry, Doctor is probably still there, she tells them.

"The truth is out there, Agent Mulder," she says to Harmon with a laugh as he leaves with Assad.

Assad and Harmon go outside to the quad and find Doctor Raglan flying numerous kites of various sizes, but all of them kites. Doctor has anchored them to wooden spikes.

"Assad, Assad, Assad. What do you see here, old man?" Doctor Raglan asks.

"I see a mind of the highest science trying to recapture lost youth," Assad replies with a laugh.

"Indeed, Assad," Doctor Raglan concedes. "I pine for the days when the simpler things were like magic and the magic was left to the imagination."

Doctor is a great, great mind. On par with the greatest of great minds. Minds that are so far ahead of their time that no contemporary biographer can document them properly.

Doctor has multiple male siblings, all of whom become great successes. Statesmen, conductors, magnates, artists. Every one of them a supreme achiever. Truly the best and the brightest.

To a man they all stand in awe of Doctor, who is different in every way. Intimacy of family has made them privy to exactly how powerful Doctor's genius is.

In the eighties, when Rubik's cubes are a thing, all of the Raglan boys rush to get their hands on them. The Rubik's cube is one of those pop culture IQ tests of a very discrete nature. You solve it the first few times you use it, because you have that kind of smarts, or you pore over it and work at solving it, because you persevere.

Most people just set it aside, unsolved.

Doctor Raglan's siblings all manage to solve it pretty quickly.

Doctor Raglan never plays with it. Doctor never even handles the cube, as far as anyone can recall.

When Doctor's brothers are playing with the cube, battling to be the first to solve it and then orchestrating competitions to solve it as fast as possible, Doctor is often nearby with pencil and paper.

During one of the competitions, blindfold solve racing, Doctor shouts out with a loud laugh. Doctor picks up a pile of papers, a proof, and breaks into the race.

"I solved it. Brilliant, really," Doctor eurekas at them. "It takes no more than twenty moves to solve, from any starting state. When you guys do these competitions, you must be sure you are all using a cube in the same N-order starting state or you are not running the same race!"

They don't understand, and they don't even really want to know, so they just brush Doctor off and keep cubing.

Eventually fighting starts, of course, as one brother posts an absurdly low time to solve and is accused of cheating. *How can I cheat, we randomly draw cubes!!!!* Something just isn't right about his time, way under ten seconds, so a kerfuffle.

Doctor is drawn to the ruckus.

"I explained this already, guys," Doctor asserts a bit frustrated.

Doctor arranges the remaining unsolved cubes.

"Cubes occupy twenty, only twenty, classes of unsolved starting state. Each class defined by the maximum number of moves necessary to solve. This," Doctor says, picking up the cube at the far left, "Is a twelve move cube. Watch."

Doctor begins to manipulate the cube.

None of the brothers has ever seen Doctor so much as pick up a cube. Apoplectic, they see it smoothly solved out in exactly twelve moves.

"And here is an eight move cube," Doctor asserts.

The brothers do not believe that, but they watch in amazement as Doctor solves another cube in seconds, with just eight moves.

Years later, many years later, all of them long ago having forgotten the Rubik's cube, Doctor watches nieces and nephews playing with cubes at a family gathering.

"Isn't it funny how such a thing comes back to capture the minds of another generation?" one of Doctor's brothers asks, sidling up. "They don't even realise that we played with the cube when we were their age."

The brother cuts into the crowd of kids.

"Hey guys, did you know Doctor is a wiz at solving the cube?" he tells them. They scoff, as kids will do. "No, I am serious," the brother goes on, "Doctor can solve it faster than any of you, I swear."

They want to see, so someone tosses Doctor a scrambled cube. Doctor looks at it, a certain feeling memory rushing back, and goes to work on solving it.

"This is a sixteen move cube," Doctor tells the kids, "So I can solve it in sixteen moves, but I don't go fast. I always preferred minimum move cubing to speed, since I am a bit clumsy."

Doctor is speaking while making moves, and sure enough after just a minute or two the cube is solved in exactly sixteen moves.

One of the nieces, the biggest cube enthusiast among them, practically shouts at Doctor.

"How can you tell how many moves the cube takes?" she pleads. She actually competes at solving cubes, so for her this secret is a potential bounty.

"The solve classes possess distinct marks that you can see," Doctor explains, "And once you know how to make the counts you can count the number of moves. No cube requires more than twenty moves."

The niece is amazed. It is only very recently that the people who work on such ideas are able to prove that "God's number," as it is known in cubing, is in fact twenty.

Proving it requires a lot of computer processing power. It is done by brute force. It takes thirty five CPU *years* to prove, finding solutions for every one of the 43,252,003,274,489,856,000 positions the Rubik's cube can occupy.

"How did you know that? That it only takes twenty moves? They just proved that," the niece protests.

Doctor is not terribly excited about the matter.

"Well, 'they' did not. I know because I proved it years ago when your uncles went through a Rubik's cube phase. They played with the cube as a toy, and I solved it once and for all as a mathematical fact," Doctor states flatly, but with a wry humor. "Now they all make boatloads of money and occupy positions of great power and enjoy phenomenal success, and

I am just a lowly professor who has yet to find the mathematical white whale!"

With age Doctor Raglan's sentiments go backwards, back to the simple, beautiful problems that draw one into a life of mathematics. Doctor always enjoys finding a deep understanding in clean, elegant, and powerful truisms. The fun is putting them into physical form for the aesthetics of it.

Thus the kites.

"Do you know why they are called 'kites'?" Doctor asks Assad and Harmon. They do not. "'Kite' is the Euclidean geometry term for a quadrilateral with two pairs of adjacent sides of equal length. Sort of like a diamond, where a diamond is a special case with all four lengths equal." Doctor continues to tinker with the kite array. "The term has been bastardised, where 'kite' means anything attached to a string that flies in the wind. Shame, really, so much is lost in making the term so generic."

Doctor keeps tinkering, and manages to arrange the kites into a formation in the sky that has an obvious structure. A mystery, but clearly structured.

"Doctor, I have some questions for you," Assad tells Doctor Raglan, who continues to tinker with the kites.

"Me first, Assad," Doctor counters, finishing up with the kite array. "Harmon, Beatles or Beach Boys?"

"Beach Boys," Harmon declares immediately.

Harmon looks up at the kites, earnestly ruminating over them.

"Exactly, Beach Boys," Doctor Raglan pats Harmon on the back.

Assad and Doctor drift a few yards away from Harmon, speaking quietly enough that Harmon does not hear what they are discussing. He doesn't care, actually, at all. He is studying the kites, above in the air, trying to make sense of their structure.

Harmon studies the kite array, running through concepts trying to recognise what they mean. Not language, not a translation of words into space. Not a mechanical analog. The kites do not represent some other physical process. Not from the soft sciences or philosophy. Makes no sense to try that. Not a visual interpretation. Harmon has a keen eye for visual pattern. This is not an interpretation of some visually meaningful thing.

He looks, and looks, and thinks, and thinks. His database of ideas nearly used up, he finally hits on it! Harmon smiles up at the kites, satisfied in his insight.

He knows.

Assad and Doctor Raglan end their conversation. Assad calls to Harmon, summoning him to their next stop.

"Doctor, join us for pints?" Assad invites.

Doctor declines.

Doctor Raglan turns back to the kites. They are wavering above against a blue sky in a manner that only a mind like Doctor Raglan's sees as orderly. Precise, in fact. Musical.

This is Doctor's aim.

Doctor will never explain to anyone how the geometry of kites has been converted into a visual expression of specific musical notes, whatever the wind. Doctor sits on the grass, dons headphones, and lays back looking up at the magical musical kite array.

Doctor Raglan, perhaps the finest mind, has installed a most beautiful temporary art installation in the quad at Cambridge. It is based on a powerful insight into the geometry of the real world that rivals anything science has uncovered. It exists now on the very ground that Newton himself once walked.

Doctor Raglan is conducting nature to play a recognizable symphony bar by bar and nobody notices.

The most beautiful song ever written, according to some.

It is there, obscured by trivial commotion, and for any and all to see and only Doctor Raglan sees it. In seeing it Doctor hears it, and in hearing it Doctor feels it.

This is the loneliest and most exciting thing, the thing Doctor lives for, anonymous, in solitude. To understand and thus feel. To connect with truth, and touch infinity.

Assad and Harmon start off toward the pub, but Harmon lags behind. Assad notices Harmon is not at his side and turns. He sees Harmon kick Doctor Raglan's foot.

Doctor removes the headphones. Harmon points up at the kites, and then he says something to Doctor Raglan, who leaps up and hugs Harmon in a great desperate grasp.

Harmon catches up to Assad, who is dying to know what Harmon said.

"God Only Knows," he tells Assad.

Kingdom of the Blind

Ilaha works very hard to develop a perfect service motion.

All of the subtle moves that are the difference between service being a slight advantage and service being an overwhelming advantage become natural for her. She trains herself to do the right things automatically, not as a product of effort.

She grows big and strong into an overwhelming service game.

Headed into Year 11 Ilaha stands through six feet tall.

She is powerful.

Broad shoulders, muscular thighs, solid core. Very, very strong.

Graceful.

Lithe.

Feminine.

"Ilaha, it is time to play tournaments," Harmon tells her.

He doesn't push, but he makes it clear that she has gone as far as she can with BallMap and friendlies at Club Dagobah.

"I'd love to, I think," she tells him, without pausing from hitting.

Harmon can see with one eye just how good she is.

Better than any of the women in the Grand Slams.

Ilaha is already the best female player in the world.

By a wide margin.

Fact.

Science.

Harmon knows.

Harmon has seen the ball. All that matters is the ball. Ilaha can do things to the ball very, very few can do. None of the women. Only a handful of the men. Harmon has been on court across the net from Ilaha, has seen her ball fly at him, and he is intimately aware of how good that ball is.

Harmon can rank her ball as a matter of science.

As fact.

Ilaha has played scores of matches, rarely losing, but she needs to acclimate for tournaments. Tournament play is why you hit all the balls, do all the work. Why you train. The point of all the practice.

To win through the field, in public, against anyone who shows up, to prove you are better.

Harmon knows Ilaha is better.

He wants to watch Ilaha prove it to the world.

Inflection Point

For her first tournament Harmon enters Ilaha into the open division of the Greater London Junior Championships. The field consists of the top juniors in Europe. Champions. Every girl in the field has won something, or multiple something.

The Greater London is a big, big deal. It attracts Europe's strongest junior field. Numerous Wimbledon champions played the Greater London as juniors. It has long history …

… And the winner in the open division is traditionally granted an invite into Wimbledon.

"You are playing open, eighteen-under, the toughest division," Harmon tells her.

Ilaha is pleased with the notion of being on court with top players. She has never played a tournament. Only arranged matches at Club Dagobah. Private friendlies. Harmon matches her exclusively against boys or men, older, usually, bigger and stronger.

Now she is just as big and just as strong as them.

With great discipline Ilaha isolates spot, speed, and spin. Over and over and over, to where she decides in an instant where to hit, and how to hit. High arcing topspin deep corner. Flat heavy pace cross court. Drop shot down the line. There is nothing she cannot hit.

Ilaha programs a faster than real-time shot graph process into her brain.

Where to hit and how to hit are always conjoined, and this is where Ilaha excels. What makes her special, really really special, is shot selection and execution.

She refines a set of rules. Ilaha sees the shot before she plays the shot, depicted against her mental shot graph. She knows how to send every shot to a spot with speed and spin that makes retaliating with a winner very difficult.

This is a cultivated gift, as if humankind has evolved over millions of years for exactly this purpose, for Ilaha Tudor to hit a tennis ball that is hard to send back.

Example. Ilaha hits a short ball. Her opponent steps in and hits back at her, hard, into Ilaha's ad corner. Ilaha anticipates where this ball will be hit, chases it down, and sets.

Before her opponent has hit, Ilaha indexes what her opponent will hit. If her opponent surprises Ilaha, her opponent has probably made a bad decision.

Ilaha simply needs to execute.

What shot works here? Ilaha is cornered, her angles are cut down, and her opponent is positioned well. But every position has holes, and Ilaha finds the hole.

Opponent in, at net, positioned laterally right where they belong. What is the play that turns the tables? Ilaha is not looking for a risky solution that may create an error. She wants to win this point. She plays to win every point.

Ilaha can try to power the ball through her opponent. Force her way through the reaction time window, perhaps simply blast a ball right at her opponent's belly button? Her instant scan of the shot graph shows her that this is not a high likelihood play, so she moves on.

She can lob, or hit for a precise spot that her opponent will need to move far to get to, resetting the point. Better, but not a shot that wins a point.

She continues to search. Player at net, what is the hard play for her opponent, the play that leads to Ilaha winning the point?

Ilaha now has the ball in her strike zone, and she hits down the line, a backhand with severe topspin, low over the net to her opponent's forehand side. The ball breaks down hard, below the net into the court. It is well within the sideline, and must be played.

This is a very hard shot to return, as her opponent is about to find out. Playing from the sideline and well below the net, all her opponent can do is lunge and work to get the ball deep, probably into the opposite deuce corner on Ilaha's side.

Ilaha knows this. She knows what they can do, how it must fly, where it must fly, and she is already there. The ball lifts softly across the low middle of the net and by the time it peaks Ilaha is there, ready, putting away a solid and easy overhead into a wide open court.

Like a boxer, like a chess player. She is a walking one-two punch sequence designed to knock 'em out. She is not idly sparring, or fighting to score points. Mindlessly playing one shot at a time to avoid error.

Every point is a prize fight, and every point must end with a KO. No standing counts, no decisions or draws. One player hits the mat every point.

Months and years of serious, intense training at Club Dagobah culminate into a maestro. She is elite, a rare genius, a mix of body and brain that comes along as frequently as never.

Harmon sees it.

Watches her every step of the way.

Ilaha works very hard to arrive. She can explain everything. Not to just anyone, because what she can explain demands a certain parity of knowledge and intelligence that very few have. Given a properly qualified listener, however, she can make it all as clear as it is to her.

Harmon is her compadre. She loves Harmon because Harmon always understands, deeply, and always treats her as a peer, not a child.

Harmon sees the thing that makes her who she is.

He walks with her down the most complicated intellectual paths that she is willing to follow. It is never, ever, "that is for a later time" with Harmon. You want to think about fluid dynamics? Let's go for it right now! What's the worst that can happen?

You find out you are ignorant and fix it.

Tennis players, at heart, are jocks. They go out on court with a racket and run and swing and grunt and sweat in real life in real time, making split second decisions while making even more rapid reactions and observations. They don't necessarily know what they are doing. They just do. Tennis is not an actual chess match, after all. You must go hit the balls. They move fast. No time to ruminate.

Ilaha's growth into a really great player is unusual.

With Harmon's help she is lucky to be able to develop her theoretically superior brain and then train her more than capable body to express it. She watches hours and hours of clips on YouTube, measuring and documenting and working backwards from the best results in tennis to reverse engineer their cause.

She sees that it is always caused, never random.

Ilaha grows into a killing machine. For her, the game moves so slow, and is so easy, that any opponent Harmon lines up is just a new form of fodder.

He is a brilliant manager, finding opponents with exactly the strengths to challenge Ilaha in exactly the right way for her at the time.

Example. When Ilaha is really gaining traction in her service game, after a growth spurt, he puts her across the net from men with very strong return games. Guys who are really hard to hit a serve past. Experienced players with great footwork who successfully read serves, because at Grand Slam speeds you must read, and deceive. There is no see ball chase ball hit ball. You guess. These matches push her farther, far enough to go from good service to great service.

Example. When she works at net play Harmon finds players with great ground games who can hit winners through any small hole.

"Just keep coming into the net," he tells her. "Don't stop. If they pass you, they pass you. Come up with a good approach, make them move, and come in. Close out points at the net. Do not give up and stay back."

She does. She is always a highly disciplined loser, willing to stick with a losing tactic in that moment until it is perfected.

This moment's outcome does not matter. Perfecting the tactic is the goal.

Harmon finds opponents with superior conditioning. With heavier pace. With outlandish junk action. With great court awareness. With serves that cannot be countered.

For every single axis of strength, there is always a player who has it. Harmon finds those players. He is a great talker, a great salesman, and he slips the opponent a few bucks or some merchandise or court time, whatever, and convinces them to treat the match as a friendly and really lay on the one strength.

They are sparring partners. Harmon has a genius for finding them, getting them on court with Ilaha, and letting her feed on them for her bigger purpose. A purpose she has yet to articulate. A purpose that she may well never articulate.

Harmon patiently waits for her to tell him her purpose.

He knows her purpose. He needs her to know it.

Ilaha can give up tennis at any point. For boys. For drugs. For friends. For school. God knows what or who.

She is free to quit.

She doesn't.

Harmon goes along one step at a time with a long vision but without any expectations.

It all rolls to an amazing place.

Everyone Has a Plan, 'Till They Get Punched in the Mouth

Ilaha takes the court at the Greater London against Europe's top female junior players.

Champions, all.

Future pros.

Future Grand Slam champions, in some cases.

She destroys everyone.

She doesn't drop a game.

Very few games get to deuce. The final match lasts under thirty minutes. It is so egregiously awful that her age is questioned.

There is no way that girl is under eighteen. Nobody that young can possibly be that good. Is she even a girl?

The matter is disposed of quickly. Ilaha has a birth certificate issued by the General Register Office during the adoption process.

The Crown says she is under eighteen and a girl.

A girl with a champion's trophy and an invite into Wimbledon.

Black Swan

"How old are you, Ilaha?" Harmon asks.

She is over six feet tall, and she can pass for old enough to buy beer in a pub. He thinks he recalls hearing her say something about Year 11, which makes her fifteen or sixteen, but he wants to be sure.

"I don't know," she tells him. "My family died in Greengrass. I was tossed from a window and lived. They never found out who I am, or how old. I hadn't been into school yet, when it happened, but I guess they think I was never sent."

Ilaha has never talked to Harmon about this stuff. She is quite indifferent in her tone. It is of very little interest to her.

"Mama Lily says I read right away, and I was tested, I think, to see where I was as far as school," Ilaha continues, "All I remember is going into Year 3 and it was boring so they put me into Year 4 and it was okay."

"I suppose I am sixteen? I am in Year 11, and my mates are all about sixteen," she asserts.

"In the early eighties the German tennis federation tested some of the country's top young tennis players," Harmon tells Ilaha.

"They tested basic athletic skills, tennis-specific skills, intelligence, and psychology. They followed up with those kids until they were eighteen. The idea was to find a way to identify the best tennis prospects to invest resources into," Harmon explains to Ilaha. "I am going to test you the same way, just to see where you stand."

Harmon runs Ilaha through a battery of tests. Physical skills, general and tennis-specific, psychological. Intelligence. All very tennis relevant. A comprehensive list of what the Germans did. When it is over, he takes the data into his office and goes to work analyzing and scoring it.

Okay, Harmon thinks, let's assume Ilaha is sixteen.

Harmon finishes his analysis assuming Ilaha is sixteen and immediately calls Mama Lily. He tells her to come to Club Dagobah, right now.

About half an hour later she sends a text that she is outside having a fag. He goes right outside to meet her.

"I did some tests on Ilaha, skills and such," Harmon tells Mama Lily. "I reproduced tests that the German Tennis Federation did on kids in the early eighties. Do you know who Steffi Graf is, Lily?"

Mama Lily tells him she does not.

"When the GTF tested all those kids, Steffi Graf was an overwhelming standout. On every score she was top. Her tests predicted she could be an Olympic fifteen hundred metre medalist. Incredible stamina. Strong. Rare drive. A perfect tennis talent, they say." Harmon continues, "Even very young, it could be seen that Graf would be great at tennis."

"So was she?" Mama Lily asks.

"Oh wow. Yeah. She was the best. No question," Harmon gushes. He always had a crush on Steffi Graf. Who wouldn't? A perfect female specimen, a virtual Wonder Woman.

"How did Ilaha do?" Mama Lily asks.

"Well, here's the thing. I had to check my work more than once, because she did too well, really.

"Ilaha scores way above Graf on every measure, in particular, the psychological scores. Ilaha is apparently some sort of savant in regard to the mind game of tennis.

"So I suspect something is off. Can you help me with her age? I know she has difficult circumstances, but being off by even a few months makes a big difference," Harmon explains, excited, a bit geeky about the whole thing really.

"I don't know how old Ilaha is," Mama Lily tells Harmon. "The child services did all they could to find out where she belongs, who she is, and they came up empty. The dentists helped, because of her teeth. Still had all her baby teeth. Precocious. Reading at too high a level to still have all her baby teeth. They sort of just decided she was eight years old when they issued her birth certificate."

Harmon, rarely taken fully aback by anything, because he simply thinks and imagines so much, is a bit stunned.

"Wow. Ok. That is remarkable. Let me explain something, show you something," Harmon ushers Mama Lily inside.

Harmon guides Mama Lily into a seat in front of his computer. She looks at the screen. There is a graph with two lines, rising steeply then gently, unevenly, from lower left to upper right. Above the lines there is a single dot toward the middle of the chart.

"I was never much for maths, Harmon, or science," Lily complains, "I dropped out of school early."

She is experiencing math phobia, and worse, for the first time in forever, a general sense of inferiority.

Feelings from school days, from adolescence, when a big jockey type like Harmon would be with the jerky crowd of lads and ladettes that make her so miserable.

He would think she is silly.

Harmon leans over Lily and points at the dot.

"That is Ilaha, assuming she is sixteen. She told me she is in Year 11, her mates are about sixteen, so I assumed she is sixteen," Harmon explains.

The dot is well above the two lines. Harmon grabs the mouse, maneuvers and clicks, plows through menus, types in settings, and hits some sort of "go" button. Another dot pops up on the chart.

"That," Harmon points, "Is Steffi Graf." The dot is a bit below Ilaha's dot, directly below. "At sixteen, after being tested again as part of follow up research."

It makes sense to Mama Lily to exactly the degree it should to anybody, even an arithmophobe distracted by miserable memories from difficult years of never fitting in.

"If Ilaha had all of her baby teeth, she was no older than six or seven when you took her in. That means she probably isn't sixteen, she is at least a year younger." Harmon clicks away again with the mouse and two more dots come up, to the left of the first two. "Ilaha and Graf. Look at that gap!!!!" Harmon runs his hand over his forehead and back through his hair. "Ilaha is so much more gifted than Graf. The gap narrows, of course, if we project out, but she is way ahead."

Lily has been pulled out of her bad memories and into the subject at hand. She is catching on. Ilaha is demonstrably special, ok.

Harmon goes back into hammering away at the mouse and the keyboard, and when he is done the graph changes again. The lines are there, and the single dots, but now there are "x" marks in stacks and two more dots.

"The 'x' marks are each individual kid they tested. See how far below Ilaha's and Graf's dots they are? That's regular people. None of them, not a single one, no matter how hard they try, is gonna be a great player. They just can't. They are just not working with sufficient raw material." Harmon says it with such a bizarre, diabolical joy.

Lily betrays a certain repulsion that Harmon catches onto.

"I know, it's diabolical, really. Germans. Only the Germans would think to even gather this data with this motive, so soon after running death camps and all," Harmon concedes. "I can't help it. God bless 'em, this kind of data is gold."

Lily rolls her eyes. Okay, I get it at some level, but honestly.

"Who is the other two dots?" Lily asks. She catches on quickly, Lily does. "You added another pair, so who is it?"

"Becker," he says. One word. Two syllables. He says it as if with regret. "Becker. Look at Ilaha compared to Becker!!! Can you believe it? She is right there, with Becker, slightly above, maybe. If we could just be sure of her age."

Lily has never heard of Becker, but she must have really been something, this Becker, testing even better than Steffi Graf.

"What happened with Becker? Did Becker fail or something?," Lily asks.

"No. No no no," Harmon laughs. "Becker was great. Best thing I ever saw, Becker winning Wimbledon. Seventeen, I think. Maybe eighteen. Incredible. The first time I watched. Never heard of tennis before that."

"So who was better, Becker or Graf?" Lily asks.

"Graf, but she was the best of all, by far. Maybe Serena Williams is better, but I suspect if you put them in a time machine at their best Graf would win." Harmon is biased toward Graf, crush and all.

"What if Graf and Becker played? Who would win?" Lily asks, naively.

"Becker would kill her!" Harmon laughs.

"Why? I thought Graf was the best?" Lily asks, once again, naively.

"Lily," Harmon pauses, realizing she is misunderstanding, "Becker is a *man*. Even Graf couldn't beat the men. Not then, anyway. And certainly not Becker. That little difference on the graph is actually a really big difference on the court."

Lily all of a sudden sees the light. Ilaha, apparently, is as gifted as a man, like this Becker, or perhaps even more.

"Can Ilaha really beat men?" Lily asks.

Wanting to believe.

Reluctant to believe.

"Maybe the top men, Lily," Harmon tells her. "You know how good you are at music? She is at least that good at tennis. Honest."

122

Lily pauses, eyes wide open, and attacks.

"How do you know how good I am at music, Harmon?" Lily demands.

Lily will not have her music treated lightly. At all. She is a lightning rod and a natural attention seeking trouble maker, but when it comes to her musical chops there will be no patronizing.

"Lily, I know your music. I listen to it all the time. I know every note, every lyric, every reference and sample," Harmon states. With reverence. He really does admire her, Lily Lacey, the pop star. "Your stuff is way too good for pop. Accessible, but brilliant. Saleable, sure, but no sellout. You are a genius. I know that."

Harmon says it as if it is the most obvious thing in the world.

It puts her off. He is so sure, always, but here, about this, how can anyone ever be so sure about art? Impossible. It's just not possible to know. Isn't it? She thinks about it.

He is so presumptuous!!!!

"What do you know?" Lily demands.

"Lily, listen," Harmon lectures her now, dismissing her suspicions and feelings, "I played Ravel for you, didn't I? On your Cincisprezece? Perfectly, by the way. You recognise the piece. You know how hard it is to play. I am not paying you lip service. I know music. I can see genius. You have it. You can't hide it from me."

He is in motion now, looking for which side is the good guys. He wants Lily on his side, for the war they will wage in coming months. Against the bad guys. As soon as you win, you are the good guys.

"Lily, do you know the saying about blood being thicker than water?" Harmon asks her.

She knows it, but like most she knows it wrong. He explains it, to be sure she understands.

"Warriors are thick from blood. The blood they risk, the blood they shed. Relatives are thick from milk, or water. Breast milk, womb water. We are off into a war, and we fight with and for each other," Harmon tells her.

"Are you daft?" Lily responds, laughing.

The whole thing has just taken a very weird turn.

"Birth is a random circumstance," Harmon goes on, brushing her off. "It happens. Everyone involved is passively involved. We do not choose our parents or children. They just happen. So the loyalty we have for them, deep as it may be is not the same as the loyalty warriors share. I will be hard with Ilaha, for a reason. She is special but young, and I need you as a willing ally to help her get where she is going. You cannot undermine her struggle."

Lily is utterly confused. She wants to interrupt, and he sees that, but he forces through one more assertion.

"Lily," Harmon literally holds up his hand, "If we don't push Ilaha, right now, nothing will ever be good enough. Not for her. Ultimately not for you. She will never, ever dream as big as we are going to shoot. Nobody does. It's not right and it's not fair but it's real … She is a woman, and she won't believe she can go where she can go until well after it happens, but it won't happen unless we push on her."

124

Lily is completely lost. She feels like she missed an essential part of the conversation or something. What in the world is Harmon rambling about?

"Harmon!," Lily shouts to interrupt him. "What in the world are you talking about? It appears pretty specific, but I do not understand at all."

Harmon snaps out of his fog. He has run away in his own mind just assuming that Lily was following. Duh. She isn't in there, inside his giant mind world. How can she understand?

"Ilaha is going to play Wimbledon, and she is going to win," Harmon tells Lily.

"Okay, Harmon, that's fine. I know she is playing Wimbledon. She won Greater London, so she is in. I suppose she could win, but let's not get everyone's hopes up …" Lily tries to anchor him back to earth.

Harmon fully understands now.

"No, no no no, you don't understand," Harmon explains, "She is not playing on that invite. We are going to pass. She is playing next year. For the next twelve months she is going to train."

Mama Lily is once again confused. Why in the world would she pass on a Wimbledon invite?

"That makes no sense, Harmon," Mama Lily counters. "Wimbledon is it, it is the end point. A tennis player shoots for Wimbledon, a musician shoots for Royal Albert Hall."

"Right, Ilaha is gonna play Wimbledon," Harmon agrees…

"Next year," he reiterates…

"Against the men," he clarifies.

Ennui

Lily becomes a celebrity because she is a genius, a brilliant, brilliant lyricist. A master pianist. Legendary guitar player. An encyclopedic melophile. She works so, so hard at her music, and it is brilliant beyond what work alone can ever make something.

Her catalogue is built on genius, buttressed by all the work.

If it was only that simple.

There is a problem.

Forget that she is from celebrity and the public knows who her father is, who her mum is. An "advantage" which diminishes any success she creates.

Lily also has the body of a supermodel. Very tall, and slim. Geometrically perfect. No bad angle.

She has intimidating beauty. Stark. Borderline androgynous. Severe cheeks. Slightly ethnic nose, but the ethnicity uncertain. Exotic. In no way basic.

Imagine the most beautiful woman you have ever seen and now make her fearless.

It is in her eyes.

Her fearless eyes magnify her beauty.

That's Lily Lacey.

She looks as if she thrives without food for months on end, then joins a spear hunt and kills a grizzly bear ...

without smudging her makeup or a single hair falling out of place.

She is not particularly feminine, but she is very Amazon sexy in a violent, horrifying way.

Fashion covets her. Women despise her. Men cower in fearful awe of her.

Lily is oh so commercial. Perfectly professionally pop. She makes her way out of her childhood celebrity Oz looking exactly like a female pop star three-d printed from a corporate algorithm.

The suits see her and ejaculate into an elevator pitch.

She is a much sexier Joan Jett who writes lyrics like Dylan and plays guitar better than Hendrix.

She hates it. Hates her own skin. Despises her easy access to fame, if she just sexualises herself and goes up for sale. Lily abhors the commerciality of her beauty.

It obscures her genius, occasionally even from her. It imposes upon her. It precludes freedom. It sours the deal.

They want her to be like the other girls, like that Tina girl. They want her to look like Taylor Tweedy.

It makes her feel so seedy.

They expect her to *comply.*

Lily Lacey Primrose Tudor, real person, is not compliant. And she won't comply as Lily Lacey, celebrity.

She hides. She insists on making it in music without monetizing her loins. She will do it her way.

Anon.

The record company.

Shylocks.

They pray the Lord sends them a bastard with talent. They do nothing and have a masterpiece multi platinum record foisted onto them by Lily's genius.

Yet they pressure her.

Doll up. Shorten your skirt. We will pay for a boob job. It never hurts to make so and so happy, if you follow.

They think it will be easy. She will be easy. She will eventually go along.

They all go along.

She will be compliant.

Not Lily Lacey.

Lily is from entertainers. Oz. The wizard tells her stuff, after vomiting on the sofa.

Don't get an advance. Get a job and take points. Never need the music for the money. Once you have the music, keep it. Tour for fun, not to pay off production. Never spend royalties from an unsold record. No complicated financial agreements. You own. The best way to finance something is to own it. Don't go onto the casting couch, it is for the ones who aren't any good. Oh! Oh oh oh!! Pay your bloody taxes!!! Never provoke Treasury.

They are all bastards with talent, the adults of Lily's youth. They are all big stars, at some point. Now they live hand to mouth. They ride on buses while the record company people drive Bentleys, or are driven about in a Rolls. The talented bastards pass on wisdom passed over in their own lives.

Lily pays attention.

Lily creates an "anon" web identity. She posts her tracks.

On social media her anonymous first single is downloaded hundreds of thousands of times within a few days.

Smart, savvy, belligerent, Lily cuts an aggressive deal for her first album.

No advance. Final say on the music. I make the music, you just manufacture it. Receipts. I get receipts for everything or it didn't happen. We go fifty-fifty on every record after you recover production costs. You tell me now how many records are breakeven. Outside auditors of my choosing count everything up. No touring. No publicity. I have final say on any spend of any kind. The record sells or sits based on the music.

They cave.

The pittance it actually costs to make music is nothing against such proven success. So many downloads, any conversion rate is a major score. There is no way we won't make it all back n-fold. Sure. Have it your way. We'd all make a lot more if you'd just take off your shirt, but so be it. We will make a lot instead of a lot and a lot more.

Lily's contract is one side of one page.

It is a blessing and a curse.

Blessing. Financially, it is game over for Lily. She makes so much money on that deal she will never be without. She has more than even a pop star can squander.

Curse. That kind of wealth is hard to deal with, creatively, and her work suffers. Spiral of doubt. Vortex of self-loathing. Bacchanalia prevails. Distraction rules one's days.

Ennui. Ennui is no good for an artist.

Lily pursues celebrity, the sex and drugs part of rock 'n roll, and neglects music.

Now I am a big celebrity
Millions of friends that I can't see
Got a Vermeer, just for me
Got it all, But I'm crippled by ennui

She flounders for years. Subsequent easy success from albums she knows are not quite as good as the first only exacerbates the problem. Now they buy it because they bought it. Pavlovian commercialism. Lily Lacey rings the album bell and "ding," the fans salivate all over iTunes.

She can't tell the good from the bad in her own work.

The meaning of life slowly disappears.

And then she finds Ilaha.

Project Apollo

Harmon walks out onto the court and Ilaha stops hitting. He holds out his hand and tells her to give him her racket.

"This axe is being set aside, Il. We are about to take the first steps toward putting you on court at Wimbledon, next year," Harmon beams.

Ilaha is confused.

"Harmon," she says, "I can play *this* year. I won the Greater London. I am in."

Harmon smiles and laughs softly.

"Nope, not this year," he asserts. Ilaha will skip the entry she won. It is for the Ladies' draw, not the Gentleman's.

Ilaha is going to play the men.

"Graf. Serena. Hingis. Seles. Sharapova. They all won Grand Slams young. Borg. Sampras. Becker. Wilander. All won as teens." Harmon points Ilaha's retired racket at her.

"Ilaha, next year you are going to go play Wimbledon in the men's."

She hears it, and understands it, and it sends a shockwave through her.

"The men's? Why?" she complains and protests. "It makes no sense. It will be so hard, and why not just play the women's this year? I can go for the men's next year."

She is not one to whine, and to whine about such a challenge is understandable, but Harmon will hear none of it.

"Ilaha, do you want to be the best woman, or the best player?" Harmon challenges her.

She burns. In her gut. The side of her that Harmon can see, that she can't even see yet, flares white hot.

I want to be the best. Not the best woman. The best.

"Say it out loud, Ilaha," Harmon confronts her, "Say, 'I want to settle for being the best woman, so I can be dismissed by history as lesser than the men.' Say that. Say it out loud."

Harmon is being harsh, but also brutally honest. Her age, her moment in life. It is right now, now or never, probably, that she decides how to go through life - as a woman, or as a person. There is no going back from this confrontation.

"I won't say that," Ilaha says a bit softly. "I want to be the best of all, not just the women. But I can play *this year* against the women. Why not? It seems so crazy and stupid."

Harmon is prepared for this. Ilaha is not.

"Ilaha, here is the deal," Harmon blandly threatens, "This all becomes very uninteresting for me if you decide to settle on playing the women. You can do that, and enjoy great success, but not with me involved. You don't need my help going for that."

She is overcome by a sense of terror. She simply cannot imagine not having Harmon in her life. Her life, her whole life, is tennis, and without Harmon's gravity field she will simply float away. He is inseparable from it, from her, from tennis.

She trembles. Tears up. Sobs.

Harmon stares at her, unblinking.

"Why in the world would we shoot for space when we can shoot for the moon? Ilaha was it fair, really, what you did to those girls at the Greater London?" he asks her.

She knows it wasn't.

In fact, during the Greater London, once she realises how much better she really is, Ilaha decides to play even harder, to hit even better, out of respect for her opponents as people. She pushes herself. She plays at one hundred per cent for no reason, against herself, when a fraction of that would dispose of them all.

"It is beneath you, and disrespectful, to enter the women's draw, Ilaha," Harmon tells her. "You belong with the men. You can beat any of them. But it will be a challenge. It will also be an achievement. Only you know what you want, but do you really want to prove the obvious, that it is awfully easy for you to beat women at tennis? Instead of going after the best players and showing everyone you can beat the men?"

Ilaha sees his point. There is an *enormous* temptation to just play the Ladies' draw and win, perhaps easily, and rush into glory, but she decides to forego it.

It will be the wrong glory. She knows he is right. Her place is to be among the best, of all, almost exclusively all of whom happen to be men.

The women cannot challenge her, so it will have to be the men.

"How do I win, Harmon?" she demands of him. "I will not play in the tournament like some freak and get killed. I want success. I want to win the tournament. Go deep. Not just take the court in round one."

"We make you stronger than the men," Harmon declares.

She is startled, really, stronger than the men? She has played against some of the men, and they are really, really strong. How is she going to become stronger than a Wimbledon Grand Slam player?

"How can we do that?" she protests, uncomprehending.

Harmon looks right at her. In the eyes. He smiles, mildly, unblinking. Ilaha wonders if she has ever actually seen Harmon blink.

"The only strength that matters, in tennis, is what sort of racket you can wield. Why do the all of the men hit it the same speed, and with the same action, more or less? Why doesn't anyone hit it altogether harder or livelier than all the rest?" Harmon asks, rhetorically, of Ilaha, who cannot answer.

"Everybody plays the same equipment, Ilaha, and they all hit it about the same. Some guys can make more or less from the same equipment, but within pretty narrow limits. It is the racket, Ilaha, and we can pull one over on 'em if we execute my plan," he tells her.

She believes.

When Harmon looks right at you and says it, you believe it.

135

Whatever it is.

Practice Gear

Harmon intends to purify and perfect Ilaha's ball striking. He has been watching her for a long time now, and she has a natural inclination to hit it right.

Sit into the shot. Bend the knees. Push on the earth. Uncoil from the ground up. Passive hands. Accelerate.

She is getting big enough and strong enough to get lazy, unfortunately, on occasion, and handsy, and Harmon blames the equipment.

He plans to fix this and compound the good things into utterly great. Harmon's goal is to follow through on what the greatest champions do.

Ilaha will take one small step with her equipment, to make one giant leap for mankind on the tennis court.

Harmon knows it is no accident that the rackets the two greatest champions in modern tennis play are different from what the rest of the field plays.

Pete Sampras plays soon after the turning point from wood rackets into modern equipment. His Wilson Pro Staff six point o eighty five, in fact, is something of a throwback by the time he retires. Much smaller and heavier than what is in vogue at the end.

Roger Federer plays with the same racket initially, and then switches into very slightly modified versions of it, for most of his career.

Those rackets lead Sampras and Federer into a decisive game. They *control* outcomes. They are like a heavyweight boxer who fights for a knockout. Not inclined to just dance and jab all night, they move forward, power through an opponent, control the result, win or lose.

Federer works with Wilson to design a new racket. The RF ninety seven is a grand achievement in modern racket design, as far as Harmon is concerned. But it can be improved. He can customise it, make it better, and make it a secret weapon.

Harmon orders frames. Identical. He calls his Wilson rep and tells her that he *must* have thirty three rackets from the same production run, in sequence. Pro Staff RF ninety seven frames, no modifications, no grip. No artwork etching or visuals, flat black. Don't even label the specs. Just send them out with naked handles, unstrung.

When the rackets arrived, Harmon goes to work on measuring. God bless Wilson! There is effectively no variance in the frames. Exactly the same weight. Exactly the same size. Exactly the same balance on both axes.

Perfect.

Harmon sets aside twenty one of the frames. Those will become Ilaha's match rackets.

With the remaining dozen, he goes to work on customizing rackets for training.

His plan is to incrementally move Ilaha into training with a very heavy, particularly head heavy racket. Her training will last thirty eight weeks, with her racket notching up from twelve ounces, unstrung, to sixteen ounces, unstrung, progressively head heavier.

A pound.

A heavy pound.

Nobody plays this heavy. Ilaha will train for this heavy. This heavy will feel like swinging Thor's hammer. There is no way Ilaha will be able to swing this axe with her hands. It will require her whole body, and mind, to hit right.

Harmon hands Ilaha her first training racket. She picks it up, extending her arm, and feels its weight.

"How does it feel?" he asks her.

She tells him it feels solid. Heavy, but evenly so. She is eager to go out onto the court and hit.

Before she does, Harmon gets the tape measure and tells Ilaha to extend her arm and raise the racket to shoulder height. He measures her wrist, elbow, and shoulder. He jots down his measurements.

"Ilaha, this is all about strict discipline. You absolutely must hit from the feet up," Harmon commands. "Every stroke, you must sit down into the shot, push against the ground, lift into the shot from your feet, and do not ever lead with your hands. The hand follows along and allows the strings to move through the ball, it does not mandate where the strings go."

Harmon is very stern and clear about this.

Ilaha goes off to hit. Harmon follows along soon after, to watch. Sure enough, she is working really hard, stressing her calves, her thighs, bending her knees deep into her stroke, hitting from the feet up, her hand and wrist passively allowing the whip action her body is creating to channel through the racket into the collision.

"Only two rounds, Ilaha," Harmon calls out to her, "We are not pounding thousands of balls. Intensity, not quantity."

By the end of the second load of balls, Ilaha is quite tired. Her muscles are strained and lacking pop. She is breathing heavy. Her joints ache a bit. Unusual feelings. Hitting never hurts. This hitting hurts.

Harmon summons Ilaha into his office and gets out the tape measure. Once again, he takes Ilaha's measurements at the wrist, elbow, and shoulder.

"Three per cent swelling," he lets her know. "Normal. Good. How does your arm feel? Your elbow, shoulder? Any sharp pain? Just sore?"

Ilaha tells Harmon that she is a bit sore, but there is no pain at all.

From his desk Harmon takes out a leather jump rope. Worn, but beautiful. Broken in and burnished like a fine antique. Clearly still in great shape for use. He hands the jump rope across his desk to her.

"Jump the rope," he commands, "It is hard to do. Honestly. You are going to miss and trip a lot, at first. Go force yourself to keep at it for ten minutes."

Ilaha takes the rope and heads off to jump.

Feeling a bit silly, she takes the rope onto the empty practice court and starts jumping. Tries to, anyway, as she misses more than she jumps. She takes to going very slowly just to get over the rope, working to build some sort of rhythm and picking up the pace. Then she trips, and then goes back to slow and then faster and then trip.

After what seems like forever she looks at the clock and realises, disheartened, that it has only been a couple of minutes. Her heart beats like a drum, and she is short of breath. She feels like she has sprinted a mile.

A natural battler, she keeps at it. By the five minute mark, her efforts are largely symbolic. Her form is awful, her pace is a snail's, her productivity lacks.

Harmon comes along and laughs at her.

"It's hard, right?" he provokes.

She battles through the final thirty seconds of her ten minutes and goes to her knees.

"Why do you think boxers jog? The rope is too hard. Jogging is a break from the hard work." Harmon leaves laughing.

Ilaha lays flat for a number of minutes, then gets up to give Harmon his rope.

"Keep it," he tells her. "I have used it plenty, you need it. You have a long way to go, Ilaha. Keep at it. Take it with you and every chance you get, go for five or ten minutes. If you can."

Exhausted, Ilaha puts the rope into her bag and goes home.

She sleeps. Straight away. When Mama Lily looks into her room, she is shocked to find her dead asleep, at six thirty. She feels compelled to make sure she is okay, so she shakes her and Ilaha grunts.

"I am fine. Let me sleep," she groans.

Mama Lily lets her be.

One Hand

Ilaha wakes sore, not in pain, but broadly and shallowly sore. Strained. Tired. She comes home after school rather than go to the club.

Not long after she usually arrives at the club, Harmon calls.

"Come to the club Ilaha. No day off today. You will regret skipping out tomorrow," he cajoles her.

She groans and then begs a ride to Club Dagobah.

At the club she is told by Harmon that they are going to hit together. Harmon never hits, so Ilaha is more than a bit excited. It makes her tingle. Hitting with Harmon has the effect of a painkiller; all of a sudden she is not sore.

Hitting with Harmon. Huh.

Harmon sends Ilaha out to one of the indoor hard courts. In a few minutes he comes out with two wooden rackets in his hand. Black. Donnay on them. Borg rackets made by Jose.

He hands one to Ilaha.

"Remember this?" Harmon holds up his racket, showing Ilaha and looking at it with great admiration. "We hit with these today."

They go out onto court and Harmon pulls a ball from his pocket. He holds it up.

"Ilaha hit it on the strings. That is the point of this. Think about nothing but hitting it on the strings," He implores her, "Strings. Hit the strings."

He drops the ball and sends it over the net.

She moves into position to play the ball, bends into her shot, pushes against the ground, takes her swing from the feet up, and promptly frames the ball sickly off the court short of the net.

Harmon gets out another ball and starts another rally.

Better, but bad. Awful, really.

"I only had two, go get 'em." Harmon stands calmly, waiting. Ilaha recovers the balls and tosses them to Harmon. "Let's go Ilaha. The sweet spot on that racket is in the same spot as your other gear. What's around it doesn't matter. Think sweet spot, and let's rally."

Harmon starts off another rally and this time Ilaha manages to get the ball over the net. Harmon hits it perfectly back to her, right into her strike zone. They rally back and forth, Harmon always hitting a perfect ball right into Ilaha's hitting zone. His ball flies so tight, so clean, with perfect spin, hitting the court and kicking just so for her to return.

Ilaha quickly gets the hang of the racket, noticing that it feels very different from her other rackets.

The geometry of it. Its narrowness, its small surface area. The mismatch lengthwise between handle length and lengthwise string bed. It feels so much in the hand, so much like a club. Wood is very head light, so it is heavy, but doesn't feel as heavy as it might.

Back and forth they rally, Ilaha hitting progressively more beautiful forehands, but having trouble with her two-handed backhand. Real trouble. She can hardly hit the ball on the strings. Harmon summons her to the net after a series of terribly mishit backhands.

"Ilaha, you are a big girl. Tall, strong. What the f&#% are you doing hitting two-handed?" Harsh. Ilaha has never heard Harmon curse.

In his more natural settings every sentence, practically, is profane. But never around the club, ever. With Ilaha he is opening up a bit, in subtle ways, and this unexpected dropping of an F-bomb is just one way.

"I have always hit two hands," she defends. "Just about everybody hits backhands with two hands. Serena. Nadal. Great players. What's wrong with it?"

Harmon laughs.

"Look, the greatest champions played one hand. Sampras. Federer. A straight line over time from that stick you have in your hand," Harmon points his wooden racket at her wooden racket, "Borg. I'll call him one-hand because he took his other hand off the racket during his backhand. So he used one hinge, really. A natural stroke. Feet up and out."

Harmon peers at Ilaha, seeing that she doesn't see it.

"Steffi Graf. The best woman. She was the best. Better than Serena," Harmon asserts. "Put Steffi in a time machine and move her forward, she beats Serena. Superior athlete. Not a great matchup for Serena."

Harmon feels himself falling into a vortex of misunderstood tennis history. So he stops, and gets back onto a point Ilaha can understand.

"Ilaha, you must watch Federer as much as possible. He is your model, by no accident," Harmon declares, "We are going to get you where he is. A one-hand backhand is essential. This will be your best stroke, your edge. You cannot play a vertical game with a two handed backhand. That is a baseline mindset. It is trench warfare, stalemate, defense driven. You cannot match men at the highest level ambling about on the baseline. You move forward, always forward."

Harmon holds up his racket, extended, where a backhand strikes the ball. He points at his eyes.

"Ilaha, you are right eye dominant," he informs her, "So when you hit a forehand, you must look across your nose at the ball. That is not the case on backhands. On the backhand side, you will not be blocked by your nose. You definitely see the ball better on your backhand side."

Ilaha is simply lost.

"This is an enormous opportunity that cannot be wasted. Do you know why Nadal hits such a forehand? He plays right eye left hand. Unusual. He sees his forehand better. Rare. Of course," Harmon smiles, "No forehand can be hit as well as the best one handed backhand, but his forehand is all right, still."

Ilaha, flummoxed and flustered, says nothing. Harmon understands why. She is a thinker and she is baffled. He reconnoiters. He will get through. It is just going to take some doing.

"You understand eye dominance?" he asks her. Let's nibble. Let's eat one bite at a time.

"No," she confesses.

Harmon boggles over how the eye's essential role in hitting things is overlooked. He has not invented this idea, by any means, but he sees it as essential and obvious once he reads it … in exactly the books that every hitter of anything should read over, and over.

"Make a circle with your thumb and pointer finger, like this," Harmon makes the "OK" sign with his fingers and Ilaha does as well. "Now extend your arm and look through the opening at something in the distance, something small, so it is inside your circle. Keep both eyes open."

Ilaha does it, placing a "W" Wilson logo in her finger scope.

"Okay, Ilaha, close only your left eye," Harmon tells her. She does. "Did whatever you put into the circle disappear?" She tells him, no, it is still there. "Now close only your right eye."

The "W" disappears. She can't believe it!!! She does it again, over and over, still disbelieving. Such a simple thing, and obvious, and she never knew.

"Right eye dominant. You see the ball better on the backhand side. You need to know that. It will pervade everything you do on the court. Never, ever give away your best sightline lightly," he preaches.

Ilaha doesn't fully understand, but intuition and the power of the display convince her. She has unlimited faith in Harmon, and decides to follow blindly until he shows her the light.

"Let's hit again, Ilaha, and you take that left hand off the racket," Harmon instructs her. "I am going to feed you backhands, and you slice them back. It's an easier place to start."

Harmon shows her how to slice a backhand, keeping the face of the racket with a relatively fixed orientation, and simply sweeping through the line of flight of the ball with a lever or two less action.

Ball after ball after ball, Harmon sends her every variation of action. He hits everything strike zone or down right into her hitting zone, easier shots to slice. He feeds her slices and heavy topspin, sends balls deep and shallow.

Throughout the course of this drilling he subtly pulls her into the net, and gently raises her hitting zone. Eventually she is at the net hitting volley after volley with her one hand backhand.

"Ilaha, where are you?" Harmon asks while they rally.

"I am at net," she responds.

"Yes, Ilaha, at net. You own the best property on court!" Harmon declares, with enthusiasm.

Ilaha wants the ball now, more, more. She is feasting upon all these balls, sitting there begging to be put away. So many places to put them away!!! She envisions her shot graph and the whole court, pretty much, is green. She sees the result of the chain of reasoning. Why a simple thing like the eye is essential.

With that little wooden racket she is hitting ball after ball right on the strings, directing it to spots. Putting it away clean with nothing close to strain.

This is impossible with two hands. Simply impossible. The footwork and turn with two hands is so unnatural. Her reach is cut off. The ideal hitting position for backhand volleys is a ball that a two hand backhand cannot reach.

They play out the last ball, which Harmon rifles into the tape to roll onto her side.

Ilaha rushes to the net.

"What is the catch? There must be a catch. One hand cannot be superior in every way," she protests, "Nobody would hit with two. Where is the hole?"

Harmon takes back his racket.

"You figure it out. Just keep looking at Federer, and keep hitting with one hand from both sides," he says as he walks off the court.

Ilaha chases after him, pleading.

"Come on!!! Just tell me," she begs.

Harmon waves the rackets back at her and keeps walking.

The God Doctor

Lily has not produced any new music, really, in years.

Not a word or a note.

Hasn't fingered a single string, even idly, just for the tactile pleasure.

Her vinyl is stored away somewhere, certainly safely, but she doesn't even have a turntable on which to play it.

Lily's Cincisprezece is out of storage and placed in the sun room at Elysium, but she has not played it since the fundraiser.

It is covered by unopened mail.

She wrote her first hit album, *Souliloquy,* lyrics and music, sitting at the Cincisprezece listening to her vinyl. It is her only piece of furniture at the time, in an efficiency dump with no loo. She goes potty down the hall in a shared. Sleeps on a mattress flopped down on the floor. Showers at the gym.

All she does at the gym, actually.

Lily hasn't played a chord on her guitar in years. Where is it, anyway? You better find that, she castigates herself.

It is a Strummer prototype, called Prometheus. The only one. A magnificently unsuccessful attempt to fuse acoustic with electric, made from parts of Stratocasters, Gibsons, Fenders, and other iconic axes that great players bust apart in fits of rage. Quirky. A failed attempt at sound engineering, but a Lily Lacey signature.

Her life, once so musical, so rock and roll, so full, starts to feel like a death.

There really isn't any excuse. Ilaha is a self-starter in every way. She is at school, at Club Dagobah, or out on her court. Three places. Never, ever a problem of any kind.

There are no demands on Lily. She is financially secure, has savings, actually invests well, and still has residual income, however much in decline, from her music.

She is free.

Free to wake up and just pass her days with no real obligations of any kind.

This is the problem.

Ennui.

One of her songs runs through her head. Over and over. She can't shake it. Not an earworm, because she wrote the song and knows all of the lyrics. It persists. It goads her. It is as if it is someone else's words. It haunts.

Starting in your womb
A different kind of tomb
A shudder and a freeze
Why can't you see?

Day turns into night
You've forever lost your sight
Before you had grand visions
Now your heart's a prison

Lily writes it in hospital after suffering a stillbirth. She loses her child. She loses her sight. She dulls and dies. Something is off after that.

Lily never forgets. Not for long. She can go back at any time, in an instant, anything's a trigger, smaller small big or bigger, and suffer it all again as if then is now and now is then …

… She is at home, and feels what must be labour coming on.

Early.

The baby will be premature, just like its father.

The thought goes through her mind with guilt and delight. A dastardly giggle.

What's so funny?

Her husband. He is there.

Lily becomes dizzy, nauseous, and fiery hot, and falls unconscious. The ambulance is called, and she goes to Chelsea Westminster.

As it turns out, the best place for her. Emergency quickly passes her onto maternity. She is mostly unconscious, but her husband is there, right there, for every second of it, and she knows and it makes her feel safer. Not safe. She cannot feel safe. She experiences varying degrees of terror. But it is all at least a bit better because he is there.

Lily regains clarity at a certain point, and she sees a very tall, lean, incredibly hygienic doctor looking at her. The doctor's face impresses upon her as if it is the face of God. She can hear one of her own lyrics, in her mind.

Of all the places God can be
He or She is next to me

151

God's right here, I feel so small
Because I can see God's very tall

She may have mumbled it. Not sure, to this day. Her husband tells her during the whole ordeal she occasionally laughs, as if from a dream. She probably laughs over that.

She misses phase one of her crisis. Her condition spirals down rapidly. The God doctor, God bless, is literally the best on the planet. One of those gifted types, the God doctor's gift is human birth.

The God doctor is fascinated by it from the earliest age and knows literally everything one can ever know about it.

The God doctor ruminates, deeply, over many years, about the Hippocratic Oath, upon morality, about a doctor's obligations. Decides, with no reservations, that the mother is the priority patient.

In cases where it comes down to saving mother or baby, it is mother.

Always mother.

The God doctor works very hard everyday to be able to save both, but if there is any making Sophie's choice it will not be to euthanise the mother. Ever. This is not ground ever to give.

The living have more of a right to life than the unborn. That is the bottom line, for the God doctor.

The God doctor moves fast, running a calculus that covers every remote rare and extreme possibility. The God doctor has developed a list, a universal checklist, a binary decision tree, to cover every possibility for when a pregnant woman comes into care. The most extremely explicitly confirmable or deniable possibilities are first on the list.

Spotting is not even considered. Too common, too widely seen across situations. The mother's symptoms, noticed but not primary. A distraction lesser doctors get stuck upon. Inside the mother, separate but enclosed, is another person. Direct testing.

The God doctor develops tools to be sure. Flash measurements. Heartbeat? None. Brain activity? None. Body temperature differential? None. The child is lost. This is exclusively a case of saving the mother. The child is gone.

When the God doctor determines the child is lost, there is no going back. Onto treating the mother.

The God doctor does not treat by committee. The team is well aware they are machine parts in a grand process. There will be no opinion. There will be fact. The God doctor goes to great length to train the team, to make their roles exact and clear and not vague. For the God doctor, and for them. Care is not collaboration; it is a conductor conducting players who are to play as conducted.

Instruments, really, with heartbeats and souls.

Lily is cognizant, briefly, long enough for the God doctor to communicate with her.

"Ms. Tudor, the child is dead," the God doctor decrees, as if reciting a commandment to Moses.

It has been thought through, exactly what to say and how to say it. State facts. Clearly. Leave no room to negotiate.

A pregnant woman's first thought, her only thought, will be "my child." She is no longer a woman, after all, a free entity, a singularity.

She is a mother.

The mental shift from person to mother is drawn out over pregnancy. At birth it is complete. The mother is never again a woman, a person, they are then and always a mother. With a dead child inside her, a now former mother to be will not think right. She will still think "my baby."

The God doctor knows it is best to castrate that notion. Right off. The condition of the child is known, and the entirety of the playbook for saving the child has been exhausted.

Great care and diligence went into a conclusion, fast, that the child is lost.

There is no going back.

The God doctor tells Lily she is to be sedated and given general anesthesia. Just breathe, and relax best can. Lily does not argue or reply or say anything. Between these communications and going black, she comprehends her situation.

Stillbirth never even occurs to her. It is happening. She cannot conceive of it. The whole thing sounds so bloody medieval. It is the twenty first century, after all, and WTF? Who ever hears of a stillbirth?

"My baby is dead," she states, to herself, aloud, with clarity.

She wells up, she heaves and cries, she feels her husband hold her hand, she feels her dead child inside her, and then she expires. Fine with being dead, if that is also her own fate.

The entirety of the weight of the world lifts, and a morbid lyric enters Lily's mind before going under.

She always hated this lyric.

Her lyric.

Non sequitur.

I lived all wrong
Went to hell
All the devil does is yell
Try and try
I just can't cool down
Hell is really loud
I never hear a sound

See It Through

Harmon's grandfather fights at Normandy, and at the Bulge, and beats the devil to get through alive to be in Berlin for the surrender. He never speaks of it, never makes a fuss.

Harmon sort of knows Gramps was in the War, but never concerns himself with it.

One day Gramps shows up at Harmon's house, alone, very rare, and tells his mom he is taking Harmon on a little trip.

Harmon gets into Gramps's car, an American sedan, modest but fully paid for in cash, of course, and they set off. Windows up, A/C blasting. He loves Gramps's car because of the A/C. Mum is paying off a Jap-lopy with no A/C. In summer her car is stifling.

They make off for Vermont, down the Mass Pike and then north into the Green Mountains. Harmon has no idea where they are going, but he is happy enough to sit in the A/C and watch the scenery pass. The Red Sox are on the radio, they are playing the Yankees, and Dave Righetti is working his way through a no-hitter.

Harmon is unaware that it is the Fourth of July, or what is in store.

Gramps pulls off the road onto a dirt path of sorts. He drives under a sign that says "Valhalla." The dirt road splits the forest and runs into an open field up in the hills. The field serves as a parking lot. Everything is surrounded by tall evergreens.

They park and get out. Gramps walks Harmon across the field and through another opening in the trees. A short walk through the tall trees leads to another open area, with an enormous lodge and a magnificent view of a valley and the surrounding mountains.

Harmon is very hungry. There is a tent. Under the tent there are tables piled high with food. Gramps motions to the feast and Harmon runs off.

Harmon eats. He devours everything in sight.

Gramps makes off for a small crowd of old men. They greet him zealously, and loudly. A handshake, hugs, laughs. He is immediately handed a glass of whiskey on ice, which he takes down in one gulp, ice and all. An immediate refill follows.

The day passes from midday to afternoon to night. The bugs come out. Giant fires are built. The men don windbreakers and Barracuda jackets and settle into circles on folding chairs around the fires. Harmon gravitates toward Gramps, always with food.

Harmon is not stuffed despite eating nonstop all day. The old men love it. They laugh and comment and just devour Harmon's delightful insatiable hunger.

It is pitch dark except the firelight. The old men are mostly quiet. They sip stiff drinks and guzzle beer. No wine. Only man's drink. Straight whiskey on ice or cans of beer some of which still have pull tabs.

Harmon sees a man pull his tab and drop it into his can.

"You better be careful. That tab can cut open your throat and kill you!" Harmon warns the man.

He looks at Harmon, with great seriousness, a bit drunk, and just laughs out loud. A deafening belly laugh. The rest of

157

the men around the fire join in. Gramps laughs loudest of all.

"The little devil is worried a beer tab will kill me!," the man howls through his laughs. "The f#%$ing Gerries try as they did couldn't, but some sliver of metal will get me!"

They all laugh even harder now.

Gramps stands and taps his wedding ring on the edge of his glass. Silence prevails. All of the men surrounding all of the fires turn to attention. He clears his throat.

"Boys boys boys," Gramps says, putting a verbal hook into the men. "It is July fourth. We celebrate America and we celebrate being alive. We all know we needn't be alive, perhaps shouldn't be alive, but we are. Here we are. Living."

An old man Harmon cannot see calls out "we live," and soon all of the old men join in. They chant it, at increasing volume, their cries carrying off into the valley and hills through darkness to dissipate and die.

"We are few. The ones not here, many more," Gramps carries on. "We saw and did the worst, and we bear that cross alone each day. So tonight, we unburden each other and offer an ear to any brother with a word to pass."

They all raise their right hands, all of them holding identical flasks with the word "Valkyrie" engraved on them, and cry out one time in unison, "brothers!"

They drink mead from the flasks, one big gulp, and then screw them shut.

Back to whiskey and beer.

Harmon sits next to Gramps, listening to him and a few other men talking. He understands that they talk around him. They are aware he is there, a boy, and they hold back.

Harmon gets up to leave, so they can talk freely, but Gramps stops him.

"Sit, Harmon," Gramps commands. He addresses the old men around him. "Boys, don't hold back over Harmon. He is smart as a whip and can handle 'R' rated or worse. I want him to hear. Let the pigeons loose!"

The men talk.

Harmon listens.

They are all soldiers. They fought WWII and survived varying degrees of pure horror. They won their war, but every single one of them was a casualty.

Every one of them died ...

A little bit inside ...

... Not a single shred of innocence left.

Harmon does not utter a word. He doesn't blink. He sits, and he compiles a story line. Specific individual stories and a general narrative. This goes on for hours and hours. The things he hears are diabolical, really.

Men testify about actual unprosecuted war crimes. Cold murders. Thefts. Vandalism and unnecessary destruction of property. Something else that they talk around ... Harmon intuits it involves abusing women, but cannot fathom much beyond that.

These apparently mild old men, harmless, more of a threat to soil your couch with urine than to harm a fly are actually cold, heartless, sociopathic bastards ...

... Who won a great war.

Harmon listens.

He should abhor what he hears. He cannot. It makes diabolical sense. It evokes sympathy, in some way. Empathy at least. Harmon uses logic to think through what he hears and it is so obvious, like it has been engineered according to a formula.

Such a complete waste.

At least a literary waste.

Human. Elegant.

Willful and historic.

No longer.

War is corporate and computerised and inhuman now. There isn't a guy from Kingston, Texas on a battlefield with a knack for operating cannon making the difference. There is a dweeb with a degree in computer science pecking away at a keyboard in Virginia writing Ada code to automate the cannon.

Everything is machine, nothing is man.

The old men drink and talk and the drinks empty and talk dies off. They recount various battles and events within the war. They console each other, insisting that whatever a man did was noble given the circumstances. The men admonish each other to keep their chin up and make it through one day at a time.

"See it through," one says, and the others join in and drink. After a few rounds of "see it through" one of the men interrupts the rest and speaks directly to Harmon, on their behalf.

"Son, 'see it through' is a philosophy of sorts. Your grandfather there came up with it," the old man tells Harmon. "Our commander was killed inside our Higgins off the beach on D-Day. His head was blown clean off. We all saw it.

"Everyone hit the floor, as if it would matter. Karys stood up tall, walked right over to where the commander's dead body was lying, and addressed us.

"'We are gonna see it through, boys,' he said. I can still hear it. Calm. Determined. He never ducked, stood as tall as he could, staring at the beach. Daring the snipers to kill him too.

"He told us to get off the boat fast. Get under water. Stay low. Helmet forward. Smallest target possible. Don't shoot. Just move forward. Inch by inch.

"The he says this. 'Most of us are gonna die. Use the dead as shields and get across the beach. Two to a carcass.' He was so calm about it. He was talking to the men who were about to die!

"We landed, and Karys picked up the commander's dead body as if it was a child's. The gate dropped and Karys led the way, using the commander as a shield. He got to the beach first, showed us all what to do.

"We inched across the beach. Hours later we took the first bunker, and Karys came up with a plan to take all of the bunkers along the beach. One at a time."

The only sound is the old man telling the story. Silence. Utter silence. Even nature goes silent in deference to the old man's testimony. Harmon hears his own heartbeat. The story scares him, makes him worry Gramps will die on the beach.

Of course, Gramps lives. He is right there, his hand on Harmon's shoulder.

Gramps stands up. He taps his wedding ring on his glass.

"Men, we had to do terrible things to be here today," Gramps asserts. "There is no guilt. There is no shame. Life, itself, is its own intrinsic good." Someone chants "we live" and a chorus interrupts Gramps. He pauses then continues. "Make it through another day. Another week. Another year."

Gramps raises his Valkyrie flask, and all of the old men do the same. They say "see it through" in unison and slug mead from their flasks.

Gramps sits down and Harmon stares at him. Harmon doesn't blink, he just stares.

"What, Harmon?," Gramps asks his staring grandson.

"How do you see it through, Gramps?," Harmon asks.

Gramps recognises the depth of Harmon's question. Harmon wants to really understand. Harmon is too smart, to incisive, cuts too deeply and too immediately to the point.

"You decide where you want to go," Gramps explains, "And then you look in that direction. Once you are sure you are looking the right way, you go. One step at a time. Just go …

"… And when you get there, don't wish you were somewhere else. Only go where you want to go. That is how you see it through. You decide where you want to go. The getting there is much easier than deciding where to go, believe me."

Harmon understands. He will see it through. He decides right then; always see it through.

Seeing it through is its own intrinsic good.

"Gramps," Harmon asks now, a question he has been dying to ask after hearing about all of the terrible things these old men did during the war, "What is the worst thing you did during the war?"

Gramps smiles, a small smile, a tired, comprehending, exhausted smile.

"The worst thing, Harmon?" Karys, not Gramps in that moment, Karys, the man who was ultimately alone on that beach when death provoked him, pauses, then answers.

"God forgive me, but I loved it so."

Journeyman

Harmon has someone in mind for Ilaha to play.

She must be tested against a solid, professional male player. Someone with experience. Someone accomplished. Not a Grand Slam champion, but a solid player with years of experience at professional tournament tennis.

A survivor.

Ilaha faces Gils Compagnon, a one-time top twenty five player who keeps playing for the money. He plays at every opportunity. It is a fine livelihood.

He travels the world all year, on a cycle, from tournament to tournament. He plays the singles, the doubles, and the mixed. He gets on court, and tries to stay on court, in one or another draw, long enough to pay for each trip.

Gils can grouse and be bitter about his lot, having never quite broken through, but he loves being a tennis pro. Even a middling tennis pro.

He isn't desperate. He is from a good family of professional people. He completes university and obtains Ordre des Experts-Comptable. At a moment's notice he can go home to France and be an accountant.

He just needs to give up on the game.

The tennis tour was once a real thrill. Roll into town, young, fit, tireless, check into a posh hotel where the entourage are staying, go right to a nightclub, connect with a party girl, and live out a two week vacation interrupted by matches.

Now it is mostly a rather lonely, stressful grind. Punctuated by pain and injury.

This stakes match he has accepted is a real boon for Gils. He agrees to play for the guarantee, fifty thousand US, and for the bonus, another fifty thousand US. He has no idea who he plays. He just knows where to go, when to be there, and what terms apply.

A five set singles match. At Club Dagobah, an hour or so outside London.

"Gils," Harmon greets him as he enters the lobby. "Long time no see, as they say."

Harmon speaks to Gils in fluent French.

Harmon learns French in four weeks. Week one, he blasts through a LinguaRapido program to learn vocabulary and grammar. Week two, he reads The Count of Monte Cristo. Weeks three and four, he travels in France, talking to anyone who will talk, watching French TV, and listening to French radio. Twenty eight days, fluent.

Gil is surprised to see Harmon.

"Harmon Elder. I don't play you today, do I?" he asks, hoping for "no."

Gils is relieved when Harmon tells him that no, he isn't playing.

That means Gils still has a chance at the second fifty thousand.

The Feet

Harmon looks as if he has not changed at all since years earlier, when Gils first met him.

In those days Gils is making an earnest run at a high ranking. He is fitter than ever, is more experienced, and his game is strong. He goes deep a few times that year and is optimistic about his chances at the US Open. He wants to play, to work, to toil, to be a consummate professional, but he needs a break.

Just a few days.

To party with a girl he knows, from Chicago.

Just a few days.

To refresh.

Just a few days.

She is one of a kind, Karly Marley. Beautiful. A goddess in flats standing well over six feet tall. Legendary party girl. World renowned, really.

From Glasto to Carnivàle, from Fuji Rock to Coachella, from Ibiza to Dubai, she is on every guest list. She never pays for drinks, or meals, or rooms. Gratis, everything, everywhere, always.

Top designers beg to give her clothes, because nobody wears them like she can.

Karly works on the trading floor at one of Chicago's futures exchanges, for some reason, but doesn't need to. Screaming and shouting all day, a breathtaking Amazon surrounded by lesser simians. It is funny, really, incongruous. It never looks right.

She is an heiress to an enormous fortune, and breathtakingly beautiful, but she chooses to stand down there eating pizza squares at nine AM among the halfwit brutes. She works there out of habit, or maybe nostalgia. It is home for her, in some sense, and she always comes back.

After about a week of debauchery, Gils tells Karly he wants to play a bit of tennis, that he needs to work on some things, and asks her to arrange it.

"I need a pro quality player who can test me and work me through some specific focused drills," he tells her. "I am working on service return, so I need a guy who can hit a professional serve."

Karly tells him she knows exactly the guy.

She arranges for Gils to go to Midtown Athletic Club, noon, on a Tuesday. He shows up, checks in at the desk, and is sent out to court seven.

When he gets there, he sees an enormous man. Magnificent, really. His gear draped upon his massive frame loosely, and perfectly. Obfuscating his enormity, actually. Gils sizes him up as a large framed six feet or so, from across the court.

When he reaches the man, he finds himself looking up at a practical giant, and feeling like a child. His proportions mask his magnitude.

"Gils, yes? I'm Harmon. Pleasure to meet you." He says it in perfect French, which surprises Gils. Karly never mentions that Gils would be playing a Frenchman.

"Are you from France?" Gils asks. Harmon tells him no, I am an American, from Boston. Gils can hardly believe how well he speaks. "Let's stick with English if it's okay," Gils asks, "I will be speaking it for the next couple of months."

Gils and Harmon warm up, and Gils observes that Harmon hits beautiful strokes. Effortless, but so powerful. Top players can tell, they can see through an opponent's second gear into how they move in fourth gear. Based on what Gils sees, he can tell Harmon knows how to hit a tennis ball.

"Okay, I want serves. Deuce court, wide," Gils instructs Harmon.

Harmon approaches the net.

"Listen," Harmon says, "I have never done this. Worked with a tournament player. So explain a bit more. Am I trying to win these points or do you want balls you can play?"

Gils chuckles, and tells Harmon to get his serves into the right areas, but go for it.

"Try to win the point, but serve into the area I indicate," Gils instructs.

Harmon takes position to serve into the deuce court to Gils. He tosses, goes into his service motion, and uncorks something that Gils understands immediately cannot be returned.

The ball comes over the net hot, high, breaks almost vertical into the sideline well short of the service line, and kicks even steeper into the screen between courts. Gils hardly moves an inch. Any inch he moves is wasted effort.

Harmon's next serve isn't as formidable. He backs off and hits into the same area of the service box, but with a lot less pace and action. Gils manages to get to the ball and defensively block back a return short into the middle of the court. Harmon is there, well ready to put away an easy forehand through the other side. He chips the ball into the court softly.

Harmon adjusts his serves until he reaches a stasis where Gils can make real plays on the ball. These serves are Grand Slam quality, but far from Harmon's best.

The point, of course, is for Gils to train, so Harmon is fine with it. He does a perfect job of being a sparring partner. Harmon serves, Gils plays a return, Harmon moves to play the return but the point ends there. Can Gils put pressure on Harmon with return? That is the point of the exercise.

Harmon gets to every return, well positioned in every case to play a great shot. Gils starts to notice this, and it aggravates him. He recognises that Harmon, an enormous man, is always already where the ball goes. He never lunges, is never out of position or off balance. He anticipates everything.

Such a man should be able to serve, sure, but move like a predator into perfect position for every return?

Gils raises his hand and goes to net. Harmon meets him there.

"How do you get to every ball?" Gils asks.

"It's the feet. I watch your feet," Harmon confesses. "You have no idea, but you are a strong ball striker, so you make use of your feet. The feet betray the ball every time."

Harmon will not divulge what he is looking for or exactly how to read an opponent's feet, because he has worked very hard for years to develop this insight, but in the spirit of fidelity he gives Gils the answer.

"Let's play a set," Gils proposes, "You can give me a great test ahead of Cincinnati. I would normally avoid playing anyone I don't know, but you will be a good sparring partner."

They play one super set, play to eight win by two. It goes terribly for Gils. Harmon is not broken or even taken to deuce on serve, and the other way Gils manages only one hold.

8-1.

This is a very bad outcome for a tournament professional playing some guy a party girl in Chicago knows. Gils is a bit devastated, honestly, because Harmon isn't even tested. Gils feels great, physically, feels ready to break through and go deep in a Grand Slam in a few weeks at the U.S. Open.

Now a club punter thrashes him.

It is so easy, really, for Harmon, and so hard for Gils. For starters, Harmon's serve is simply unplayable.

Gils has never seen anything like it.

Harmon's pace alone is too much. As Gils backs up to neutralise it, angles open that Harmon can drive a train through. Harmon hits ace after ace, or causes forced error after forced error. Gils rarely gets the ball back into play.

The whole thing is a brutal beating.

Gils serves fine, but Harmon is always exactly where the ball ends up. He never hits a defensive return. Harmon is always in control of the point from the moment he hits the ball.

They shake hands at the net.

"What is your story, Harmon?," Gils practically pleads, "I've played just about everybody and never seen anything like that."

"I hit a lot of balls, and I watch a lot of tape," Harmon tells him.

Litmus Test

Gils takes the court against Ilaha. They toss for serve and Ilaha chooses to receive. Gils assumes she must be weak on service. The professional's response is to open with a hold. You want wins, your serve is supposed to be your strength, you always serve first.

Gils takes position to serve. He tosses and hits the ball to the deep sideline corner of the deuce court, pulling Ilaha wide off court.

She is already in position, set and ready to return. Ilaha notices that Gils stays back, so she hits a hard return over the center of the net right at him. Deep, hard, lots of topspin. It catches Gils off guard, and he cannot handle the ball. Point Ilaha.

Gils serves next to the ad side and takes her wide, again. Ilaha sets and unloads a one-hand backhand sharp cross court, over the center of the net, but hard, at a severe angle that hits the sideline and follows into the wall. 0-30.

Gils double faults, and then hammers a hard serve down the T into the ad court from 0-40. Ilaha has time to chase it down, set, and block back a forehand with backspin deep into the center of the court. She resets the point like a pro, and when Gils hits her ball back she makes quick work of moving him into a bad spot and then hitting a winner through the opening she creates.

0-1.

Ilaha to serve. Having been broken, Gils finds himself in a bad spot. There is pressure to break back, because if Ilaha holds the set can end quickly.

That's the rub of serving first, lose and you are very much weakened. Gils takes solace in his assumption that Ilaha defers to cover up for a weak service game.

Ilaha hits her first serve right down the T for an ace. Gils barely moves. She surprises him, but he recognises big pace, and he knows that off guard doesn't matter. That serve does not go back over the net.

Her serve from 15-0 to the ad side is the same. A blast down the T for another ace. Ilaha serves hard, but not terribly flat. Gils observes that her ball moves a lot, so speed understates how hard that ball will be to handle, assuming he ever gets to one.

30-0 another ball hard down the T. Gils barely gets a racket on it. 40-0 now and Ilaha hits a perfectly placed serve hard with enormous kick off the sideline. It hits the sideline closer to the net than the service line, impossible to play even if Gils runs it down.

0-2.

Gils to serve.

The match goes fast. 6-0, 6-1, 6-4, Ilaha. Gils is gracious and offers Ilaha genuine encouragement at net when they shake hands.

After the match, Gils finds Harmon.

"Where did you find her?" he asks, in French.

"She can really hit it, right?" Harmon responds in fluent French. "She has only played one tournament. We set up friendlies. Hits a lot of balls, watches a lot of tape."

Gils grabs Harmon by both arms.

173

"That is what you told me you do!" Gils wails, "I've tried, but what am I supposed to be watching?"

"I told you. The other guy's feet," Harmon laughs.

Free Your Mind

Ilaha enters Harmon's office in great spirits. She beat a pro, a man, yesterday, and is more than a little bit puffed up. Harmon is proud of her, and very enthused about the prospect of moving forward toward the Wimbledon Men's next year.

"You have that rope I gave you in that bag?" Harmon asks her.

Ilaha opens her bag and takes out the jump rope.

"Go out to an empty court and jump for fifteen minutes. You are not hitting today," he explains. "You do not hit again until twenty four hours after jumping rope Mayweather style for a hundred minutes straight."

Ilaha is not enthused, because she lives to hit balls, but she acquiesces.

"Ilaha," Harmon follows, "Don't fret not hitting. You will be doing a lot of it soon enough, but to be ready you need to be stronger. And give me your shoes and socks. You jump barefoot."

Ilaha removes her shoes and socks. She puts them on Harmon's desk, and then takes the jump rope with her to an empty court.

She starts jumping, clunky, and ugly, hardly like Mayweather. She is at it until she can barely breathe, and then she keeps pushing, missing and starting over and so on, until she literally ceases to breathe. She collapses to the ground, fights to catch her breath, and looks at her timer.

Eleven minutes.

My god! A hundred minutes! Is he daft?

Ilaha stumbles back to Harmon's office, rope in hand, and falls onto his couch.

"Tough stuff, huh? Didja do fifteen?" Harmon mocks.

Ilaha waves him off. Harmon stands above her, and motions for the rope.

"I am no hypocrite, so I'll skip with you," Harmon tells her, "It may seem impossible, but you can get there within a week or two. An hour. We will do it together."

Ilaha dreads the next week or two. Harmon makes it worse, really, offering to suffer through it with her.

"Get me all of your gear. I have to get your rackets ready and I need to be sure you don't try to hit until you can do an hour on the rope," Harmon commands.

Ilaha gets her equipment bag and gives it to Harmon. She is spent, and tells him she is going home. He throws the rope at her and tells her to give it a go whenever she feels even slightly able, as long as possible, and to focus on rhythm and not missing.

"You don't need to be fast, just smooth. Smooth makes you fast. Think smooth," he tells her.

She leaves. That afternoon she makes a few efforts to get the hang of it, and eventually she starts to get the rhythm. She is dead tired, but is seeing a light.

That night she suffers awful cramps in her hamstrings, calves, even in her hands. It is just miserable. She screams and Mama Lily comes into her room. Mama Lily has never dealt with such cramps and has no idea what to do. She is ready to call an ambulance but instead calls Harmon.

"What should I do?" Mama Lily pleads.

"Give her dill pickle juice and quinine water, and as much drinking water as she can take," Harmon tells her.

Mama Lily complains that there are no pickles or quinine water in the house.

"Then go get some," Harmon says and hangs up on her.

Mama Lily rushes out, gets the pickles and quinine, and rushes home to Ilaha, who is still cramping. Ilaha gulps the pickle juice, wincing at the tartness of it, and starts chugging from a bottle of Schweppes. Immediately she feels her cramps loosen, a definite placebo effect, and slowly they go away. She sits on the sofa watching TV and drinking water, and then finally falls asleep.

For the next ten days Harmon and Ilaha skip rope on the clay courts, barefoot, as smoothly as possible. By the end of day five Ilaha is able to go for thirty minutes with less than a handful of misses.

Harmon never, ever misses and he shows no sign of ever wearing out. His form is perfect and he goes fast, his rope whistling from minimal movement, his technique driven by motion of the shoulders and not the hands. Ilaha watches, and copies, and becomes his doppelganger.

By day eight she makes her hundred minutes. Harmon skips along, his phone displaying a timer counting down from sixty minutes. The timer zeroes out, the alarm sounds, and Ilaha has done it.

"How do you feel?" Harmon asks.

She feels a bit heavy in the legs, but great, just fearsome. Cramping has become much better managed, and she feels very very strong under her cottony puff of tired.

Harmon is unaffected, apparently able to go on forever if necessary.

"Great work, Ilaha!" Harmon gushes. "There are probably a few dozen people on the planet that can do that, skip fast like that for that long. I doubt a single player on either pro tennis tour can. Maybe a few boxers. Some Navy SEALs or something. Nobody skips like that, Ilaha, it's a big deal."

Harmon is genuinely impressed. He tells Ilaha to skip rope for a hundred minutes. He sets her on an aggressive course to get there. He does it with her, to set an example.

If he tells her how hard what she is doing really is, she finds excuses and never succeeds. Not knowing any better, her best self can find its way out from within.

"Your ignorance allowed for that, Ilaha," he tells her. "You have no idea how hard what you just did really is. So you saw it through. Never, ever forget this. If you ever doubt, anything, at all, ever, remember this. You can see it through, unless you decide to refuse to believe it."

Grand Instrument

The next day Ilaha bounds into the club eager to hit balls. She wakes up before the crack of dawn, and would hit on her home court before daylight but she hasn't a racket.

Harmon has all of her gear.

She does a hundred minutes on the rope, so now, back to hitting.

Harmon sees Ilaha enter his office as soon as Club Dagobah opens and he brightens.

"Ilaha Tudor, Goddess of Greengrass, reigning Greater London girls eighteen under open champion, do I have a surprise for you," he beams.

She is going to be more surprised than she understands.

Harmon works on her rackets with Doctor Raglan's help during her jump rope training. What they create is truly a masterpiece, these rackets for Ilaha.

Harmon walks Ilaha over to three identical racket bags. Zipped shut. Beautiful leather, with her name etched into each. Ilaha is elated! She can hardly wait to open this cornucopia of riches and see what is inside.

Harmon opens one of the bags, unzipping it to a sound that is simply beautiful. Ilaha has never heard a zipper make music.

The slider is in the shape of a tennis racket, a bit large, but a work of art. It is a tiny replica of the rackets inside the bag, as it turns out, with strings and every detail of the wrap of the grip and even the labels on the frame. In the center of the string bed there is a horse with wings.

When the zipper is pulled, the musical scale is played back and forth … do-re-mi-fa-so-la-ti, ti-la-so-fa-mi-re-do.

Harmon folds back the flap of leather and Ilaha sees a large clef etched into the inside of the flap.

In the bag is an array of seven rackets, standing on their side, locked into place by an ingenious soft-grip bracket system that tightens upon inserting a racket into its slot and loosens upon removing it. It is amazing. Ilaha keeps putting in and taking out a racket, just to experience how the bracket system works.

All of the rackets are black, Wilson Pro Staff ninety seven model frames. The rackets are strung with black strings, no logo or artwork. The handles have black leather grips, all of them perfectly wrapped.

Ilaha takes out one of the rackets and handles it. It feels heavy, but perfectly balanced. It melts into her hand as if it belongs there and only there. The grip is a bit large, a bit larger than she has grown accustomed to, which creates some discomfort.

"Ilaha, the grip probably feels a bit puffy, but that is because you don't know how to hold a racket properly. Not your fault, but a problem we fix now," he tells her flatly.

Harmon talks her through the physiology of the hand, its relationship to the arm, and to the body, most important to the brain, all the way down to the feet.

He explains that the hands must be deadened, that the typical relationship between brain and hand must be shut down. The hand is passive in a proper tennis stroke, not active. Everything starts with the feet. The hands can too easily derail a proper stroke.

When he is done she literally feels her feet connecting to her racket as if a super nerve is running from the grip itself through to her toes.

"This is going to require you to do some thinking, Ilaha, so listen. Are you ready to pay attention?" Harmon makes it clear he does not intend to go through whatever is coming over and over.

She puts the racket back into the bag, into its soft-grip bracket. She knows that handling it will distract her. Ilaha nods that Harmon has her full attention, and he proceeds.

"Do, ray, me, fa, so, la, ti," Harmon ticks them off, discrete, and slow. Not musically. "Those are the notes. Seven of them. Those are the tools musicians have, seven notes. The whole musical scale is based on science, based on some very high math that was figured out a long time ago, and it holds today and it will hold forever. It held before anyone figured it out. It is a truth."

"A tennis ball is a truth, and a tennis racket is a truth," Harmon goes on, "The ball, and the racket, they don't care about you. Or the other player. Or the crowd, or anyone or anything."

"The ball goes where you hit it," Harmon states, emphatically, "The racket hits the ball the way it was designed to hit the ball. There is no random, no luck, no chance. Everything involved is a deterministic process that obeys the laws of nature. Those laws are inviolate and absolute. There are no feelings, no hopes, and no wants. The whole game is a simple laboratory for collision science."

Harmon looks close at Ilaha, making sure she is following.

181

"You have three sets of seven notes to play. The ball is your sound. You must play the ball with the right note for the situation. These rackets will cover any situation you are in. What we must do now is teach you how to figure out what situation you are in and make sure you always play the right note."

Harmon tells Ilaha to zip the bag shut and bring it with them out to the court. The bag is heavy, seven rackets and leather with the plastic soft-grip brackets.

She lugs at her bag. Harmon carries the other two bags, one each slung over a shoulder. He rests his arms on each bag and walks comfortably to the court behind Ilaha.

On court Harmon sets down his two bags and takes the third from Ilaha. He arranges them in a specific way, side by side, and unzips the bag in the middle.

"That is a cleft," Harmon points at the cleft on the inside of the flap that zipper closes. "You know music? It tells you what octave to play your notes in. This bag has the base octave."

Harmon pulls out the middle racket and hands it to Ilaha.

"D. It is labeled. ' D,' right here on the frame." Harmon shows Ilaha the mark. "All of them are marked as such, 'A' through 'G' in each bag. This bag is the base octave, so the letters have no notation. In the other bags the cleft is notated as a higher octave or lower octave, and the notes on the rackets are as well. We do not want rackets becoming disorganized, so keep the rackets together the way they are arranged now."

Harmon indicates that Ilaha should head out onto court, so she does, with her "D" racket from the base octave set.

Harmon takes the other side of the court with his own racket. He has a ball in his hand and a ball in his pocket.

"We rally to keep the ball in play, focus on hitting the strings," he instructs. Harmon hits a ball her way and they commence a rally.

They keep the ball in play for about an hour. Harmon taking her shots and sending them back just so, varying depth and action. Location is almost exclusively deep to center court, so they don't move much. When Ilaha finally hits a ball that Harmon apparently mishandles into the tape, which actually falls onto her side, they stop.

"Okay, Ilaha how did that feel? Your action was pretty good," Harmon observes.

She tells him the racket is heavy but it hits pure, and she feels herself adjusting into a much more balanced and controlled move in the course of hitting. Her action pace and quality of shot do not suffer at all, but her effort is greatly diminished.

"Right," Harmon agrees. "Get the same from less effort. That is leverage. There is a compound outcome there to be had. Go switch that racket for the 'D' racket in the bag to the right. This is tuned to be an octave higher. See the difference. We will hit again."

Ilaha dashes to the gear, switches rackets, and goes back onto court.

For another hour they rally back and forth, metronomic, pure, smooth, and powerful. Ilaha feels a difference in her racket, how it collides into the ball making a very different sound, and creating different action. She feels herself naturally move differently to play into the new racket, making subtle shifts in weight, and angles, and timing.

Harmon watches every move, eyes on her feet and hips and shoulders and then into the hitting zone. Always one eye on her wrist and hands, to confirm passive action there. He hits another ball into the tape that rolls over onto Ilaha's side. They stop.

"Okay Ilaha, switch again," he tells her. "Get the 'D' racket from the bag to the left."

Ilaha does so and goes back onto the court.

Another hour. At first, the new racket gives Ilaha trouble. Her shots fly long or whimper into net, and she just doesn't feel right unloading into the ball.

Harmon talks her through adjusting and she follows quickly, settling into a disorienting manner of playing what feels like a thick, soupy, stunted game. The new technique creates great results. Excellent action with great accuracy. Although there is no sacrifice of pace, she feels as if she is swinging in slow motion.

One last time, Harmon unleashes a vicious backhand that hits the tape and rolls onto Ilaha's side.

"Let's call it a day," he says, heading off the court toward the gear.

Ilaha puts away her racket and they gather up and leave for his office. When they get there, he fetches water from his fridge and hands a bottle to Ilaha.

"That was great, you hit well, you adjusted well, and you got a bit familiar with the gear." Harmon sits down and Ilaha takes a chair across from his desk.

184

"You leave everything here, and you only hit here," Harmon commands.

Ilaha is tired, more so than tennis usually makes her, and agrees without argument.

Torture Device

Ilaha's training goes quickly, and it must.

She has incrementally moved up into hitting with heavier and heavier rackets. This is a primary focus of her training. Moving forward toward hitting with a one pound racket. In matches she will play closer to fourteen and a half ounces, but Harmon wants her to get to where she can effectively hit with sixteen, and head heavy.

Ilaha's training shifts from hitting a lot of balls and working on swing mechanics to playing situations out with Harmon, conditioning, and watching even more tape that now includes opponent research.

Ilaha does not perform typical or common conditioning work. Not by any means. She never, ever does any form of road work. Jogging. Sprints. None of that. She never, ever runs. Not in any metronomic go forward sense.

She skips rope, a lot. So much that it becomes utterly automatic. Mindless. As natural and pervasive as breathing. She is so conditioned from skipping rope that she literally does not stop, can not stand at ease, if she is on her feet, she is micro skipping at all times.

She does a lot of pushups. She varies them to keep it interesting and to work the entirety of her shoulders and arms, not just one axis of muscle.

Harmon spends a lot of time teaching Ilaha about the physiology of tennis, of her body, of her skeleton and muscles. By adjusting the placement of her hands, and her feet, and shifting her center of gravity, Ilaha focuses her pushup work on all of her upper body muscle groups.

Ilaha canoes in a large, beautiful wooden flat bottomed canoe that Harmon built. Not a single screw or nail to be found. All joined with fitted mortise and tenon work that requires no glue or epoxy. The joins are made permanent by soaking the unfinished canoe and causing the wood fibers to expand. They will later contract, of course, but not quite all the way. It is crafted so perfectly that the surface finish of the canoe is enough to keep everything together.

Ilaha rows the canoe in kneeling position while Mama Lily lays in it twittering.

The conditioning program extends into some borderline bizarre exercises that Harmon instructs Ilaha to perform. He explains to her that tennis injuries are almost always injuries of the connective tissues, and that they happen in an apparent instant, from making one undisciplined move. They are completely avoidable, he says, and completely the fault of the player.

This will not happen to you, he asserts.

A part of her push up regime is to get halfway down into her push up and then vibrate. She is to perform micro push ups from that position as fast as possible, to a hundred count, then proceed through the down cycle very slowly. On the way up, Ilaha is to vibrate up, ratcheting until her arms are once again fully extended.

"Quality of rep, Ilaha, not quantity," Harmon preaches, "You are to do no more than three of these, in a day, but do at least one. It stresses and strengthens your joints. We would like for your joints to not be the weak link in your kinetic chain."

Ilaha dons a weighted vest when she is drilling with Harmon. It is outfitted to make it very difficult for her to get lazy and swing with her hands and arms. Feet up and out,

Harmon implores, on every stroke. Whenever he catches her cheating, and he never misses it when she cheats, he stops play and lectures her.

"I am going to find a way to punish you whenever you do that, Ilaha," he warns her, "You must never, ever get lazy and swing from your hands. It is a mortal sin."

This leads to the torture device. That is what Ilaha calls it. Whenever Harmon puts Ilaha onto the torture device, she wants to just cry. Run away. It is truly awful.

Harmon claims to have invented it, but Ilaha suspects that in fact he stole it from the Devil himself.

It looks innocent enough. Sort of a pull-up bar, but attached at each end to wheels. Picture an automobile axle that is attached at the outside edge of the wheel instead of at the center. It looks like that. It is attached to a motor that rotates the wheels, moving the bar up and over and then down. The motor is sophisticated and varies speed, at random, in addition to just rotating at a fixed rate.

The brutal thing, the thing that makes it torture, that makes the exercise Ilaha is assigned to do miserable, is that the bar that she is to hold onto that connects the two wheels is fixed. It does not spin. So as Ilaha dangles from it well above the ground, feet hanging free, even at the bottom of the cycle, she is forced to adjust her hands the whole time.

She tries not doing that, and by the time the bar goes far enough from where she grabs onto it her hands are put into such a painful state that every instinct in her body is to let go. Which she does. And falls to the ground. Hard. Harmon laughs.

"Ilaha, think about what happens if you actually hold on and don't adjust your hands," Harmon laughs, "You are going to get pulled over the top of that bar like a widget running through some sort of industrial stretcher. The point of the exercise is to keep letting go and grabbing back. It is all about adjusting your hands, fast, against gravity pulling at you."

Harmon invents the machine after studying injuries of the arm. He observes countless idiotic practices in weight rooms throughout his life, and never sees certain things that he believes should obviously be available.

As a young boy, six or seven, he reads a book by Tom Seaver, the baseball pitcher, which documents training techniques for pitchers. The science of it may or may not be sound, Harmon does not know at the time, and the approach of it is offbeat, but it all makes sense.

Seaver is evangelical about the need to strengthen the connective tissues of the shoulder and elbow. He advocates a variety of very light weight, leverage dependent exercises.

For example, Seaver says to get a one to three pound dumbbell, just heavy enough to feel it in your hand, and extend your arm down your side holding the weight. The exercise is to raise the arm, fully extended, to shoulder height, parallel to the ground, slowly, then rotate the arm as far as possible in both directions, first one, then all the way back the other, then back to start, then lower the arm slowly. Repeat.

Seaver says to do reps, ten or more, and create a burn up inside the shoulder. This type of exercise, he asserts, builds up the rotator cuff and prevents a common injury suffered by hard throwing pitchers. Harmon sets to work on the regime and is doing dozens of reps at a relatively high weight soon enough.

Harmon saves the torture device for exactly that.

Torture.

From Ilaha's point of view, he only does it to punish her, and the process is basically random. He always seems to find an excuse to put her on the torture device. She hits with her hands. She is too upright and doesn't bend enough. Always one form or another of failing to make a good swing, feet, knees, hips, core, shoulder, release the strings into the collision. Feet up and out.

In fact, Harmon has a very specific plan for Ilaha. He puts her on the torture device at exactly the times he wants her to be on it. There is a plan. It is all driven by safety, actually. Harmon never really vocalises it, but he is first and foremost safety driven.

He is always measuring Ilaha. The circumference of her wrist elbow shoulder, and now her knees and ankles. He jots down the measurements and keeps them in a pocket calendar. Ilaha thinks it is just strange, but Harmon knows that any damage her training may cause betrays itself in swelling, very early on, and from there he can back Ilaha off and prevent real injury.

Harmon is a believer that the human body is best at curing itself, and that not damaging it is a huge move forward toward healing. The body wants to be healthy, he has been told over and over by Assad. Plants want to grow. Nature finds a way.

There is a simple lesson in life that people obfuscate at every opportunity; nature, including the human body, can function just fine without man's meddling.

Ilaha is directed onto the torture device. Harmon turns it on, and as soon as Ilaha is off the stool she uses to grab onto the bar he removes it and sets a timer.

"Three minutes, Ilaha. Then rest thirty seconds. Three on, thirty off, three rounds." He has measured her joints before putting her on the machine.

After about fifteen minutes she is done, has rested some, and Harmon comes back. He tosses her an ice pack, measures her joints, and sits with her.

"You are swelling within normal. You feel sore? No pain?" he asks.

She confirms that yes she is sore, but not exactly in pain. The burn is spread out away from her joints down her limbs. The joints are a peak burn and from there it is less.

"Ice up," Harmon instructs. "Twenty ice ten off twenty ice. No hitting. Take tomorrow off to just stretch and recover. You did great work. We will do the bodybuilding part once a week, and then recover and hit. We start playing points, games, and matches. I will arrange them."

"You will play me, right?" Ilaha is quick to plead.

Harmon confirms that yes, they will play plenty. But mostly she will play matches against opponents he will arrange.

"We train Monday. Full power building of your body. Severe rope, lots of the rotator. Push Ups, plyometrics for your legs. We batter you on Mondays," he explains. "Tuesday you just rest. Stretch. Recover. Eat protein. Drink a lot of water, always, every day, drink a lot of water, but especially Tuesday. Wednesday I hit with you, structured practice to perfect points. You always play to control points. You find an entry as soon as you can and use it to take over the point. We do that together. Thursday you play a match. I'll find opponents to test you in specific ways. Friday we

191

watch tape and do science. Your brain grows Friday. Fridays are when you win Wimbledon."

It is all laid out.

"What about the weekend?" Ilaha asks.

"If you have anything left, Ilaha," Harmon chides, "You can do anything you want on the weekend."

Fancy a Pint?

The training cycle starts with a match against a former junior boys Grand Slam winner. Harmon solicits him from a bank in London where he works. He is from a privileged background, and gives up tennis to attend a prestigious uni and then go into banking.

His parents indulge his tennis, but despite being boys Grand Slam champion at the French Open, he knows and they know he is much better equipped to win at banking. And he does. By his mid-twenties he has already made much, much more money than he ever would at tennis.

He still plays. Locally, including some professional doubles. As a hobby now. Harmon brings him out to the club and tells him to push on Ilaha. Intimidate her if you can. Play a strong man's game. Do not take it easy on her at all. Try to batter her.

He takes this to heart. He is a fine player better suited to a fast surface like grass. His win on clay as a junior at the French Open is very much unexpected. Not a favorable surface, not a favorable opponent.

He wins on pure fire and on being very good but even more so tough. Harmon chooses Essex to challenge Ilaha because he is a cold and vicious bastard on court. Ruthless and violently purposeful.

Ilaha needs an emotional test.

The two take the grass court and Ilaha elects to receive. She always chooses to receive. She concludes that tennis is about breaking and holding, and every chance to break is an extra chance to win. Service takes care of itself. You are supposed to win service. Making a break is what matters.

Harmon watches loosely, not sitting courtside or studying the points live. He will study tape and data later. For now, he just comes and goes.

Ilaha is having very real trouble with receiving service. Essex is able to really boom and is hitting corners quite often. When his best serves hit intended spots Ilaha has terrible trouble. When his good serves get near her, she still has only limited choices for what to do with them. Too often she feels no chance to control his service points, and it becomes frustrating.

She can't break him through 6-6, so they play a tiebreaker. Her service game is very effective, rarely going to deuce and more or less coasting into her next chance to break.

In the tiebreaker Ilaha receives first and loses the point, aced. She sets to serve and wins her two points expeditiously.

Now, 2-1, standing to receive, she pauses a moment, raising her racket. She is pulled into thought, not sure why, but all of a sudden her brain explodes with insight.

She understands why she has yet to break serve. Look at his feet! Harmon is always talking about feet. Feet feet feet. You'd think they are at football and not tennis. She just now understands why you start with feet.

Essex sets to serve and Ilaha shifts her focus to his feet. He serves pinpoint, which is an enormous disadvantage because the extra move gives him a chance to betray his intentions. Ilaha watches his feet move, watches him orient just so for the T, and starts moving a bit before the ball is hit. She doesn't guess. She watches and responds.

He hits a booming serve, and she steps right into it and rips back a ball that whistles through the deep corner and into the tarp around the court.

Down the gangway Harmon hears the two shots, Essex's serve, Ilaha's return, and then a thump as the ball hits the tarp. That sound!! She finds it. Finds what she is looking for. On her own. Brilliant.

Harmon returns to courtside and watches the tiebreaker play out with Ilaha cruising into a 7-3 win. Essex walks off court muttering curses and heads to the locker room for a break. Ilaha stays with Harmon.

"I couldn't figure him, he serves so hard, and then I figured to watch his feet," she gushes. Harmon smiles and bumps knuckles with her. "After that it's like a light was turned on. I hit a serve that he blasted down the T back at him so hard I doubt he could've played it back if I'd hit it right at his racket."

She has seen the trick, now to ingrain the trick.

"Ilaha," Harmon instructs her, "In the next set you focus on moving into his serve. Don't worry about hitting it out. Just put it back into a safe spot. Let the point develop, but neutralize his serve and convert the point into deep points, layer four points."

Layer One. Serve decides point. Powerful service players pursue this. Ace, unplayable ball. Faults are fine if batting averages are high enough. I toss I serve point over.

Layer Two. Return decides point. The best return players can pursue this. A weak serve, a spun in second or someone who just has no serve, you exploit this. You plan to put the ball away and end the point. Once again, errors here are fine if the batting average is high enough.

Layer Three. Serve plus one, as it is known. Serve is strong enough to take control of the point but not strong enough to finish the point. Serve plus one creates a return that the service player can put away. Volley works, but so does a short ball that can be hit for a winner by stepping into the court and putting the ball away.

Layer Four. By now the serve has been neutralized and the point is just a point, where neither player has any obvious or structural advantage driven by service. For a traditional baseliner, Layer Four is what needs to be reached because the longer a point lasts the more certain the more stable player will win the point.

Harmon does not believe in Layer Four tennis, but for today's purposes he wants Ilaha to experience it.

On grass, against the top service players, it begins to feel impossible to get anywhere. Ilaha needs to feel comfort from knowing that for those guys, Layer Four is simple death. They cannot function at Layer Four. So if you just take away the first three layers, that's it. They push harder and harder on Layer One and Layer Three and punch themselves out.

The second set goes quickly. Ilaha wins 6-1 and the game she loses has no aces. Essex manages to win in Layer Three on shots that are not likely to line up in sequence again, and Ilaha is fine with it. She reads his feet, steps right into his service, and slices back returns into great spots, focusing on spot the whole set.

Essex is ready to shake hands when Harmon calls out to the players.

"Play best of five, guys. Conditioning," he instructs them.

Essex brightens and catches a second wind. He is a gamer, and feels resurrected by his chance to fight back.

In the third set Ilaha begins very slightly to tire and Essex takes full advantage. He starts by moving inside the baseline to receive serve, doing to Ilaha what she does to him, playing to simply block the ball back onto her court with a focus on spot.

All of a sudden Ilaha is getting many less free or easy service points. And Essex is coming into net, a tactic Ilaha has not faced. This throws her off, and she loses the third set 4-6. Essex pushes to break and manages it twice. On service he becomes bold and follows in lesser serves to frustrate Ilaha with net play that produces angles she can not counter.

After the set, Ilaha summons Harmon over.

"What should I do? I am a bit stuck," she laments.

Harmon, unsympathetic, just tells her to figure it out her best. That's the challenge. Rise to it.

In the fourth set they go to tiebreaker. Ilaha a bit more tired misses on a couple of serves, producing a double-fault and an effective double-fault on a lazy spin-in second serve that Essex pounds away easily. Essex wins the tiebreaker 7-3.

For the fifth set, Ilaha takes a water break and sits on her side, thinking back. I have him, I win, 2-0, but Harmon says to play three of five and now I am in deep. I wasn't ready for five, she whines to herself.

What now? She sparks and decides she will see it through. I can figure this out. There is an answer. See the answer.

She serves. She decides to go for bigger action on first serve, delivering a kick that clears net by a wide distance and breaks hard into the court. High bounce, this puts Essex in a difficult spot standing just inside the baseline. He quickly backs up to play the ball deeper after it drops.

Ilaha feels great about gaining back control and feels much more at ease. In an aggressive and clever ploy, she starts using her first serve to set up her second, going for perfection with her first serve kick and then taking advantage of his expectations for even more spin on second to power through him with flatter balls.

This is usually done in opposite sequence, but Ilaha is as accurate flat and hard as she is with more spin and she understands that on a relative basis the flat first serve on second serve can be that much more effective.

It is very effective. She goes back to cruising through service games. But now what to do about return? Essex starts hitting hard kicks at her and coming to net behind them. She is having trouble getting those serves into her strike zone so she sort of blocks balls back less than strongly. He is eating her up at net.

She decides to go for Layer Two, so she adopts a tactic of stealth stepping into his serve. She takes it on the rise and cuts his time by not letting his kick buy him time and force her into a defensive strike.

This works well enough that Essex stops coming in. He is also getting tired, in fact faster than Ilaha, who has caught a second wind having solved serve and now feeling great about the low burn in her legs.

Game by game Essex falls into not only failing to come to net, but hardly trying to do much with her return. Ilaha finds a way to either control the point from Layer Two or simply seize it from Layer Four or beyond. Essex deflates, losing the fifth set 6-2.

They meet at net and shake hands. Ilaha is tired, and getting sore. Essex is completely worn out.

"I haven't played that hard in ages," he confesses. Ilaha feels great about the whole match and is dying to do her tape and data work.

"Fancy a pint?" Essex asks her.

He is more than a bit captivated by Ilaha, he makes clear, and brashly asks her up.

"Um," Ilaha sort of starts, a bit unsure as she has never really been involved with boys and is actually well underage.

Before she stammers much longer, Harmon cuts in.

"Essex, buddy, she is only sixteen so no pub," he pats Essex on the back, "But I tell you what, her mum is single. Want me to set you up with her?"

Essex feels a bit daft about the whole thing and gracefully declines.

Ilaha jogs off to put her gear away. Elated, at some level, for the ask out to the pub, but silly nervous and brain frozen over it also. For the moment tennis is not on her mind, but that will not last.

One track Ilaha will obsess over her match point by point soon enough.

"She's a hell of a player, Harmon," Essex says as they make their way to his office. "She hits it better than any girl

I've ever hit with. Strong. Man strong, really. Is she going for Wimbledon? She can make a run, probably?"

Harmon pulls two near freezing cold oil cans of Foster's from his fridge and tosses one to Essex.

"Yep," he says before draining the whole can, "She is going for Wimbledon. And she can't just make a run, she will win."

"I won't tell you that's impossible, mate," Essex agrees, "But a bit aggressive. What's her record? Has she played much?"

"She won the Greater London, Open," Harmon informs Essex. "Didn't drop a game. And she beat Gils Compagnon out there."

"She beat Gils? And won Greater London? That's something. So she's in? Ilaha, eh? What's her full name? I'm gonna want to get some action on her at Wimbledon," Essex pleads.

"Ilaha Tudor," Harmon tells him. "She was adopted by Lily Lacey, the singer. Survived being tossed from Greengrass when it burned down."

Essex is surprised.

"Maybe I should take you up on setting me up?" he quips.

He has heard of Lily, even has some of her music on his phone.

Essex gathers up his gear and is off. Before he leaves the office, Harmon calls to him.

"Essex," he says, "Ilaha is not playing Wimbledon. We are not accepting the invite."

"Why not?" Essex asks, a bit shocked.

"It is beneath her. She belongs with the men," Harmon states.

Essex stops. He turns and laughs out loud.

"She belongs with the men!" Essex exclaims. "Harmon, how is she going to beat the men?"

Harmon raises his eyebrow.

"She just beat you, wanker," Harmon reminds him.

"Sure, sure, but I am a broker and haven't played seriously in years," Essex defends, "Those guys? Harmon, those guys are so good."

Harmon sits back and finishes off another Foster's, his third.

"She beat Gils, and he is one of the men," Harmon reminds him, "And I hit with her. She will be a lot better by next year. Just watch for her name in the men's. Expect really long odds. It will be free money."

Teenage Dropout

Ilaha's training continues into the school year, same schedule, never varying.

She builds her body Monday, sessions that she dreads, as they get progressively harder and harder. Tuesday she recovers and talks with Harmon all day about tennis. Wednesday is on court training with Harmon. Thursday she plays a match, and Friday is for science.

The schedule is clearly too much for Ilaha, so very early in the school year Harmon sits Mama Lily down.

"Pull her out of school, Lily," he demands.

"No way, Harmon. She is too smart and must finish school," Mama Lily insists.

Harmon immediately flashes frustration. He stands at full height, inflates, and lectures Lily.

"Oh baloney! Honestly. *You* dropped out," he taunts, "She is too smart to waste her time with school."

Mama Lily digs in, defensive, but Harmon's points are too overwhelmingly true and she is quickly forced to ease off her position.

"Lily," Harmon hammers away, "She is learning more here than she is in school. The math and science alone is better than anything she will ever get from some teacher in a posh private, let alone a state school. And the work she is doing is brain work. This isn't zumba we are at."

Harmon is impatient. It makes no sense to him, at all, to waste an opportunity for the sake of convention and conformity. This is what he sees Mama Lily doing.

"Harmon she needs friends and a life and a kid's existence. All this tennis becomes too much, I think." Mama Lily wants so badly for Ilaha, of all little girls in the world, to have the normal life she does not have herself.

Mama Lily shields Ilaha from the things Lily's parents expose her to. The celebrity life, the extended vacations and all-nights at posh clubs. Ilaha is never dragged anywhere for the benefit of Lily.

And *Lily* misses that life! God, she gave it up way too soon. What she would give for an indefinite stay in Ibiza filled with booze and drugs and raving and crashing and carousing with every sort!!!

"Lily, this is childish and stupid. Let's just ask her what she wants to do," Harmon challenges her.

Harmon is inclined to grow very impatient when those with whom he allies appear to lose their mind and not follow his plan. When he senses fear or ignorance or just being a little dim is leading to resistance and verging on defiance or disloyalty, he flares.

He will not put up with extrapolated momentary panic.

Harmon calls Ilaha into the office. He abruptly addresses her, cutting Mama Lily off before she starts.

"Ilaha, do you want to quit school and go full time at tennis to win Wimbledon, or stay in school and sit there bored all day waiting for the dimwits in your classes to catch up?" he snarks.

Harmon states it so evenly. Mama Lily rolls her eyes and looks at Ilaha.

"Well, then, Ilaha? Do you want to drop school?" she asks.

She does. She needs to. She is committed to tennis and feels herself ramping into places she never imagined going. When she watches tennis on TV now she has these powerful thoughts. *I can definitely handle him. That was not the right play. I would have done this, and it would have worked.* She watches with a critical eye that makes her sure she will win, out there, if she is the one on telly, not watching the telly.

Every champion has exactly those thoughts, very young, premature really. Precocious notions of grandeur. They see someone great do something great and think …

I CAN DO THAT.

It is that simple.

From there, a journey.

Ilaha is on that journey. She knows it, and she wants it. And yes, school is slowing her down. It is a series of distractions from her path and becoming a nuisance.

"Mama Lily, I want to drop," she tells her. "It is all too much, and I want tennis. I want Wimbledon, and I want to beat the men. I can do it, but this training and school both is killing me."

Lily, still bitter about being bullied by Harmon, is well pleased enough to go along. It's not like the girl is just sitting around on Snapchat all day. All this tennis is clearly a real thing and she is probably lightning strike lucky to have fallen in with Harmon.

"Ok, it's a go, I will tell the school," Mama Lily states.

Harmon reminds her to just tell them she will be homeschooled, and reiterates that in fact she will receive a better education than at the school. She ignores him and leaves to work on pulling Ilaha from school.

Ilaha is left with Harmon in the office. Harmon comes around the desk and sits next to her.

"When do you sleep best?" he asks, "Sleep is your number one priority. You must get as much sleep as you can. So you tell me when you sleep best. We will schedule everything around you getting a lot of sleep."

Ilaha never thought about it. She tends to stay up pretty late, but has been crashing hard early since school starts because training is exhausting her.

"Take a week to adjust to not having school and training. Figure the best time to get a lot of sleep. Like, twelve hours would be great if you can do it," Harmon instructs her, "Then next Monday we will set a hard full time schedule. Twelve tennis, twelve asleep. Monday through Friday."

That sounds like a tall order, and almost as exhausting as staying with school. All of a sudden Ilaha feels overwhelmed.

Harmon catches on.

"Ilaha, yes, we do more tennis, but wouldn't you rather spend all day at tennis? We are not gonna be on the rotator all day!" Harmon puts her at ease. "The extra time we have is going into your brain, not your body. You have much to study. Academic, historical, scientific brain work. Serious stuff. Books and all. So it won't be all skipping rope and

Mondays. Your brain can go farther than your body at the moment. We have to push on it."

Operation Overlord

Ilaha takes a week off. She has dropped school. She is good about sticking with a routine centered on sleep.

Every night Harmon demands a text from Ilaha telling him when she goes to bed. She is to hand Mama Lily her phone and then sleep. No light. The room is to be completely dark. Every morning Harmon sends a text to Mama Lily demanding Ilaha's wake time.

By Sunday Ilaha has settled into a go to bed between nine and ten and wake between nine and ten cycle. Sunday night Harmon knocks at the door at Elysium and hands over printed schedules. A booklet of sorts. Two copies. One for Ilaha, one for Mama Lily.

The schedule starts with Monday, ten in the morning, for intensity training. Skipping rope, the rotator, plyometrics, and bodyweight resistance. Power increasing work. For one hour.

Then a break for lunch. A big, heavy, hearty lunch. It is understood Ilaha will eat a very light breakfast, if any at all, and will aggressively hydrate at all times. Lunch is a feast. Ilaha eats all she wants, almost exclusively meat, seafood, cheese, and the harshest most truly nutritious greens. Watercress, lots of it. Spinach, lightly blanched close to raw. Mushrooms. Eggplant. Peppers of every sort.

The food bill is astronomical.

After lunch, technique work. Severe mechanics. Service. Kinetic chain. Drilling feet up knees hips core shoulders release. Power maximizing perfection. Technique is done without hitting balls, with excessively heavy rackets, weighted whole ounces beyond her playing weight. Also excessively head heavy. For Ilaha, technique on Monday feels like swinging a sledgehammer, not a tennis racket.

Tuesday is a very light day, cool down type stretching. Some push ups. Some footwork drills. Light hitting for precision.

After a modest lunch, which is later in the day than Monday, lots of technique analysis. Play-Sight day. Watch film, watch data of the film, and learn how the data is created. Feeding off Ilaha's problem solving brain. Ball strike engineering. Form equals data. How does form create the data?

Wednesday Ilaha plays out scenarios with Harmon. Ilaha's favorite day. Hitting with Harmon, hands down, the best thing Ilaha ever does. She simply cannot imagine a better striker of the ball. His shots are magical, always just challenging but not impossible. The better she plays, the better she hits it, the better he sends it back.

He has this thing he does, every time, uncanny, to end a rally. He hits a lightning strike right into the tape, and it always rolls over onto her side. He never mentions it, never makes anything of it. And he never, ever has a ball he hits go into the tape and come back onto his side.

Ilaha notices this, and then she always always watches closely to keep track. Just once she wants to see him hit the tape and have the ball come back onto his side.

She never does.

She never will.

Thursday Harmon always has a match for Ilaha. Always a great match.

Quickly she comes to see his process.

He lines up an opponent with outlier strength.

They are all really really great at positioning, or service, or return, or hitting high kicking balls, or coming to net. Something specific.

Ilaha's job is to figure out how to beat that strength. And not by avoiding it, by beating it directly. Harmon tells her there is no hiding. You knock 'em out, you don't win on a scorecard.

Friday is for analysis. Ilaha watches the tape of her match, and the data along with it, and comes to understand the opponent, the shots, and the playbook.

A guy who hits really heavy topspin but plays deep behind the baseline? Step in and hit it on the rise. Create hard angles. Come to net. A guy with a severe heavy flat powerful serve? Read the right side, block it deep, and get to Layer Four. Every strength has a direct and neutralizing counter. Ilaha is to learn the counters.

On Saturday and Sunday Ilaha rests from tennis. No Club Dagobah, no tape, nothing but life. She still has mates, perhaps more so now, with total weekends free.

Her social life actually catches fire after dropping school. Before she is a bit awkward. Distracted by tennis, not really there for school. Now she is able to immerse during the week and looks very much forward to weekend hangouts and pizzas and films and walkabouts in town. She shops, coffees, and sleeps over.

Her friends are always eager to see her because they never wear out from constancy.

Harmon lines everything up.

Wimbledon starts in two hundred eighty days.

The Art of the Deal

Harmon has an attorney, a powerful and effective killer shark of a barrister. Counsel he can rely upon.

For amusement he drums up outrage and lathers himself up for a fight.

Harmon stalks off to the All England Lawn Tennis Club, storms the tournament committee offices, and throws down a gauntlet ...

... Ilaha Tudor will be playing the Gentlemen's next year. What must she do to be invited?

They waffle and laugh and try to blow him off.

Who is she, exactly? A girl? Huh. What has she won? She did? Why isn't she playing the Ladies'? Why would she skip an invitation?

Harmon plays along, sparring, and then communicates his intentions.

"I am very serious about this," Harmon declares. "I am trying to prevent a big problem for you. You are not going to pull any shenanigans on the fly later on. Tell me right now what Ilaha must do to get an invite into the Gentlemen's singles and she will do it."

Sensing a shift in tone, the people Harmon is provoking call in the Tournament Director.

"The Tournament is by invitation. Players participate at the pleasure of the Club," Harmon is lectured. "There is no entitlement involved. Traditionally," the lecture goes on, "We invite according to a consistent structure, with limited discretion involved in certain cases."

Harmon raises his hand to end the lecture.

"You invited her into the Ladies' based on winning Greater London. You also invite the boy who won the boy's open division, right?" he states, not really asking.

"Traditionally we invite the boy's and girl's Greater London open division champions, yes," the Tournament Director confirms. "Traditionally. As I have stated …"

Yeah yeah, Harmon shuts the Director down. Everything is discretionary.

"Ilaha will play the Greater London Boys Open, and she will win," he declares.

"Well, if she does, that is traditionally an invite into the Gentleman's," Harmon is told.

"Into the Gentleman's?" he demands, for clarity.

"Yes, the winner of the Greater London boys is invited into the Gentleman's," the Director confirms.

Harmon writes it down, exactly how it is stated, on a piece of paper.

The winner of the Greater London boys is invited into the Gentleman's.

Harmon foists the sheet onto the Tournament Director's desk.

"Sign," he demands.

The Tournament Director signs, grateful that a blood smear is not also demanded.

Harmon leaves it at that. He does not push to clarify, or offer any chance to back off. The AELTC has been very clear. If they renege, it will be as clear as that.

Off he goes, to see his barrister.

The people at the AELTC are very much relieved when Harmon leaves their offices, especially the Tournament Director.

"I am old," the Tournament Director says, aloud, to nobody, "And I remember Blitzkrieg. Dealing with that man is a lot more stressful than the bombings were!"

Infuriate, Negotiate, Have a Really Deep Pocket & Threaten to Litigate

Clara Brett Martin, Esquire, stands and smiles wide at Harmon, her favorite client.

He enters her office and sits in the large, burnished, beautiful antique leather club chair she has opposite her desk. Harmon loves her office, loves her desk, which has occupied its place since well before London was bombed by the Nazis, and he really, really loves the chair.

"Twenty grand, pounds, whaddya say?" Harmon offers for the chair.

He tries to buy it since the first time he visits with her, and every time she lamentably rebuffs him.

"Harmon, I'd give you the chair but it is property of the firm and they simply won't let it go. Churchill sat in that chair. He got drunk." Clara can only imagine how many times they have been through this.

It is a ritual of sorts for them.

"Clara," Harmon leads in, "I am teaching a young girl some tennis and want her to enter the Greater London tournament in the boys division. Do you think that is going to be a problem?"

She is not involved with tennis and is not familiar with the event.

"Is this privately run, or part of a public institution? Like a City facility or some sort of state school? Public uni?" she asks.

"Not sure," Harmon confesses his ignorance. "Can you find out and deal with it either way? She played in the girls division last year, and won, but we want her to play the boys. The winner gets an invitation to Wimbledon. She is really, really good. Good enough to beat the men, I suspect, so we want to win that invite."

Clara thinks she may not have heard right. Did Harmon just say she already won the girls division?

"Do the girls get an invite?" she asks him.

"Yes," he confirms. "She is not going to accept. We are shooting for next year, the men's."

"You are skipping Wimbledon this year and holding out for next year, for the men's?" Clara is incredulous.

Why would a young girl invited to Wimbledon skip it?

"I know, it sounds crazy, but we have a plan," Harmon explains. "Playing the women would be counterproductive, believe it or not. And beneath her, frankly."

Clara takes down some notes and opens a case file. She does not imagine that entry into a junior tennis tournament will be hard to secure, but she will look into it.

"Okay, Harmon, I'll get on it. I don't see any issue with getting her into the Greater London, but there may be an issue with that invite." Clara suspects that the invite is a courtesy.

Wimbledon is a prestigious, sacred event and the AELTC is a very powerful entity. Legally obliging the Club to honor a courtesy is a much different matter.

Harmon stands and gets the sheet of paper with the quote he wrote down, signed by the Tournament Director, from his pocket. He hands it to Clara.

"You got the tournament director to sign this?" she asks, giggling. Harmon confirms that he did. "You know this is not legally binding, Harmon?" Clara tells him.

She is on the verge of laughing now, because she knows Harmon, and she has seen him deal. She pictures the Tournament Director at the stodgy AELTC signing *anything* Harmon hands over just to be free of the terror he inspires.

"It may not be legally binding, but it is morally binding," Harmon asserts. Clara can no longer hold in her laughter. "Morally binding is enough. You can make them cave if need be, with that signature," Harmon asserts.

Harmon. So intellectually strict and comprehensively aware, but in matters of law so sickeningly pragmatic. What a barrister he would be!!!

"Bill me at full rate," Harmon instructs, "I want for Ilaha to get what she deserves. I won't be happy with a capricious fight over public perception. I want the power of law to protect the girl. No politics. Law."

When Harmon reaches the door to her office, he turns back to Clara.

"Fifty thousand?"

She smiles and waves him off.

Compounding

Ilaha is accelerating, rapidly, surging really. The brain training is spilling over into the physical aspects of her game. She is smarter, better prepared, and thus faster. Stronger. Her shots are better. Her game is easier while producing superior results. It is a compounding process that mushrooms.

The better she gets, the better she gets, more rapidly.

Einstein is smart. Awful, awful smart. He sees into nature. Disputed, at the time, but obvious to him. Einstein understands the most basic forces in nature, and the most powerful, according to him, is compound interest.

Ilaha has become a creditor. Her game is on loan, probably from God, and is improving at a compound rate.

Harmon pushes her physically, to a necessary point for power. Her power levels match those of the most powerful men. Her peak ball is as good as any peak ball. Then he nudges her just a little bit further with an equipment insight that is risky, but can be executed with some specialised training of the joints in the arm.

The rotator. The rotator allows Ilaha to wield a racket of a mass not seen since wood. Very nearly a pound. This is her primary practice racket.

Harmon nudges her into heavier and heavier, always measuring and anticipating, preventing injury. Like a frog in a pot of water, Harmon very slowly boils Ilaha into wielding an axe that makes where she is going not possible, but rather not getting there impossible.

Feet knees hips core shoulders release into collision. Ilaha proactively and positively does this on every stroke. The heavy racket reinforces the foot. It pushes on her, forcing her to set and then push back, from her feet. With her knees. With her butt. Up from the earth. A lighter racket, a different training regiment, a slip into quantity rather than laser beam focus on quality, and Ilaha is not who she is becoming.

The physical would not develop nearly as well without tape and data. We are well past the space age and by the day fewer and fewer recall that journey. "One small step for a man" gets the headlines.

The thousands and thousands of failed launches that precede the moon landing unknown. Not ignored, unknown. That is the shame of ignorance, right? It isn't forgetting, it is simply not bothering to know.

Harmon has slowly become less involved. For Ilaha's best interest, it is now up to her to direct her own development. All part of Harmon's process. He plans a progression including her independence. He hands her a blueprint. The schedule. The techniques. The philosophy. It is hers to use. Hers to waste, hers to cultivate.

He honestly doesn't care. He is not living through Ilaha. He is sharing, with a brother of blood, a warrior's path that he maps. Part of the gift is the detachment.

Harmon has his own path and will not be diverted from it forever.

Ilaha, his club, a life in Britain. It is a diversion for him. He has a plan, a big plan, but along the way he enjoys amusements. This is a grand amusement. There will be another. There is always another.

It becomes a schedule of mentorship. Harmon teaches the philosophy: counter strength directly. Once you undermine an opponent's strength, they are defeated. In the sense of the word that matters. They give up. They compliantly surrender. They don't expose their own ineptitude; they simply succumb to a greater force.

You are the greater force.

You win by countering strength.

Harmon offers a philosophy. From there, things can go rapidly. You can immediately skip ahead from "what?" as in, "what am I trying to do?" to "how?" as in, "how do I do that?"

"How" is easy. How can be as easy as trial and error. There are Bayesians all over the Matrix employing trial and error to happen on soft adequate acceptable outcomes who will never really know how anything they are involved in works, and not even caring.

Ilaha will never be that girl. She uses trial and error to find answers, not as a lifestyle choice.

There are great players who learn early on to vary, to try different things, to apply single layer tactics. Those tactics work or don't. When they don't work, they try something else. When nothing works, they lose. Then they mostly just hope they don't see that opponent again. Or they misunderstand a random outcome as driven by a given tactic. They are unaware, lacking insight, and honestly don't care.

Harmon recognises in Ilaha a sympathetic brother who needs to know.

Truth.

"God does not play dice," Einstein says.

He is uncomfortable with quantum mechanics. With its demonstrable paradoxes that are observed, it can be supposed, but clearly in violation of some truth aesthetic. The same entity cannot be in more than one location in one instant. Quantum mechanics proves, in some observational way, it can.

It cannot.

Ipso facto.

Einstein. Science. It must be truth. Things like the same particle in two places at once cannot be truths.

Ilaha carries on with the schedule. Monday build body. Tuesday rest body. Wednesday specific tactics. Perfection day. Thursday a match. Friday tape and data. The cycle lasts a week, but it can compress into a day, for tournaments.

It is a generic format that is scale independent. Ultimately, Ilaha discovers that it can be compressed into minutes, during matches, and she is unbeatable.

Tennis taps into a beauty. Two opponents. On a fixed field. One ball. Each equipped with one weapon. Simple trials.

Game, four points to be won by two. Sets, six games to be won by two. Matches, three of five sets to be won. By the end of a match, it is very hard to argue that the player who wins didn't win.

Arguments over "whether" happen.

A top seed loses to a qualifier and it is sort of concluded that something is amiss. The top seed has a bad day. The qualifier plays beyond their ability.

The better player should win a five set match.

By definition, in fact, the better player does win that match. The better player wins every match. The human nonsense element of the whole thing is a false notion. In the face of actual outcomes another theoretical outcome was supposed to occur.

Oh, the humanity.

Ilaha learns from Harmon not to fall into this trap. He tells her about the ball, more than once. To the point where a slight reference unleashes the whole sermon.

"The ball doesn't care, Ilaha," he tells her. Preaching a form of his religion. "The ball goes exactly where you hit it. The ball is a perfect thing. It is a single point in physical space, where it is can be forecast very precisely by a formula with limited variables.

"You are one of the variables. The air. The location. Time of day. It all factors in. Creates miniscule changes. Fractions of millimeters. The ball is all that matters. It is what moves, what is being moved.

"You move the ball, it never ever moves where it is not being sent. The ball does not defy. It does not decide. It is passive. It sits there, and gets hit until it wears out, and then it is tossed aside. For another ball.

"Always focus on the ball. Understand the ball, and you can figure out anything you need to know."

Ilaha has Harmon instructing her early on. He polices the sideline, watching for things that at the time Ilaha simply does not understand.

"Ilaha, all of your toes should press on the ground," he complains. Huh? She resolves to bend her knees deeper, push off more consciously, and be sure to start from her feet. How does he know anything about her toes? Inside a shoe?

"Ilaha, you are not seeing his ball warp," he claims. Ball warp? Huh? She finds some workaround to solve the same problem after a series of trials. I am missing into net. Decelerating. Must move forward, do not reach for the ball. Let it get into my strike zone.

Harmon sees it all differently. Things that sound completely off the wall, for him they are essential and obvious. The whole ball of wax can be melted into one simple notion.

He can explain it, and he does if properly prompted.

The toes thing. Ilaha asks him what he is talking about. How he can even know what her toes are doing inside a trainer.

He tells her to take off her shoes and socks. She is standing there, barefoot.

"Set to hit a backhand," Harmon commands. She does. He lifts her pinky toe off the floor.

"Now go into your strike, feet up and out," he challenges. Ilaha does, and feels terribly clumsy. Her move is derailed right off and an ugly series of Bayesian compensations feed through into a handsy and awful stroke.

"I see how it ends, and know where it started, because I know how it works," Harmon declares.

Ilaha is rapidly getting to where she sees when it isn't working, and then quickly makes changes to get it right. Good enough. More than one way to skin a cat, as they say.

Harmon simply will not sell his philosophy as if a carnival barker offering bizarre delights on a boardwalk.

He is deeply content in his own understandings, and wants not for confirmation. Willing to share with a brother of blood, but not rushing to share with the uninterested. He makes his own journey. At the end of the road he meets up with others who have done the same. Or not. He is going there in any case.

Things settle into where Ilaha is basically a PhD student, fully equipped to do her own work, expected to do so, and Harmon is her advisor. It is not possible for Ilaha to match his experience, his years, or his bigger view. That demands time. But she is about as far as she can go without more time.

Harmon begins offering more life advice and less specific mechanical insight. She has all of the theories. Now to just play with them.

"There is history," Harmon tells Ilaha, "If you have an idea, check with history to see if others did also, and if it got kicked into a dustbin. The idea may actually be stupid."

It is his way. The active expression of his philosophy. You do the work. You look backwards, question a false truth, and then move forward, to prove a true truth.

Ilaha keeps at her thesis work. She takes to telling Harmon what she needs to drill. She does tape and data alone. She becomes a wizard at the computer, working her way through the analytical tools Harmon builds and even does her own programming.

She is able to follow his proofs of Einstein, while he is doing them, but can't quite do them on her own.

Yet. Someday.

Harmon is scattered in his teaching. He will as soon explain esoteric considerations for reinsurance policy pricing as give a dissertation on the economic implications of Dorian Grey. He discusses pop music and eastern medicine. All at once on any occasion.

Connecting the unconnectable.

Ilaha follows word by word soaking in more an oeuvre than the reality of the ideas.

She believes.

She may not know what, exactly, she believes, but Harmon makes her a believer.

Operation Desert Storm

The Greater London. Ilaha is entered for the boy's, slated to play every round. No byes. In fact, playing against number one, perhaps as retribution for agitating, insisting, threatening, and then litigating her way in.

They are forced to take her. An effort is made to refuse her entry, and a judge orders that she must be allowed to play. Public facility, gender equality, etc and so on.

Clara Brett Martin, Esquire, does her job.

Ilaha destroys the poor boy. It goes 0/0 and she barely works. The whole affair takes well under an hour. Ilaha never goes beyond hitting a hard, flat, kicking serve at his backhand side. She never goes to deuce on service.

Receiving she is able to overwhelm by hitting deep and hard right back at the boy, then moving in to cut his time and volleying winners at a very high rate. She misses more than a few volleys and makes a note mid-match to focus her work on that for next round.

Ilaha is to play next day, so she does a mental tape and data session, with outcome data Harmon has compiled. There is no BallMap data to consult. A quick practice at volleys next morning to prep and then onto round two. Another drubbing. Nothing to be learned there, really. An overwhelming overmatch.

Round three, a pummeling. Loses a game, broken at service, but just a pointless lapse. It happens because Ilaha pushes herself to overplay. She insists on a game where she hits the line on every serve and just cannot. Gets back quickly to proper play and done.

0/1.

Semis. Drubbing. English may not offer enough synonyms for "destroy" to describe how many flavors of severe beating Ilaha hands to her opponents.

0/0.

Again.

Final.

By now a bit of buzz is in place. The crowd for the final is large, actually, much larger than anyone ever recalls for the Greater London. Her opponent, a standing junior Grand Slam champion, U.S. Open, expects to at least put up a fight.

The First Class sends a tennis reporter, a gossip reporter, and a photographer.

Ilaha is unaware of the press, but excited about the crowd. She is blossoming into as much a showman as a champion. A goldmine, her, once she hits the big stage.

She dismantles her opponent. It is remarkably uninteresting. There are maybe a handful of people capable of appreciating how good she really is given the ease with which she disposes of the boy. He is not even close to her class.

After the final point she goes to net and shakes hands. The shutterbug and scribe carry onto court to take photos and attempt an interview.

"You are playing the men's at Wimbledon, then?" the reporter asks, holding a voice recorder.

"Yes, I understand that winning here entitles me to an invite, and I plan to accept," Ilaha states proudly.

The reporter follows in with questions about tennis, her background, her coach, and etcetera.

Harmon immediately takes over the interview.

"Here is what you write," he dictates, "'Ilaha Tudor, Goddess of Greengrass, adopted daughter of the pop star Lily Lacey, and first female to play in the men's at Wimbledon, is the REAL deal' - use all caps for 'REAL,'" he insists, "'Call Ladbrokes, dear reader, because she will go off way too high.'"

Harmon ushers Ilaha away and leaves the tennis reporter to figure a story without enough information from her.

The gossip reporter knows Lily, and anchors to her at the beginning of the match. They interview during the whole match, and during that time Lily is more or less non stop chatter about Harmon.

She doesn't know much, really, but she gushes about everything she does know.

"He has this amazing credit card, it's a piece of jewelry, really, and he can use it for anything he wants," Lily gushes. "Everywhere he goes important people either know him or gravitate to him. It's a rush. Honestly!"

The gossip girl records all of it. She is good. She never actually burns Lily Lacey, pop star, but she plays Lily to the hilt, so well that even Lily Tudor loves reading about herself, as if Lily Lacey is a fictional always wonderful person.

"This Harmon sounds like the story, Lily," the gossip reporter observes. "I ought to hit him up, no?"

Lily misses this assertion completely and just keeps rambling on. As the match progresses, she comments with great insight lost on the reporter. She senses Lily is actually knowledgeable and pushes on that.

"You know tennis? How did you learn it? Do you play?" the gossip girl asks.

"No no no," Lily rebuffs her. "Harmon explained some ideas and I caught a bit. I can watch, not hopelessly, but I never hit a single ball. I used to toss to Ilaha in the park, so she could hit. That's all."

When the match ends the gossip reporter leaves, quickly, to write her story.

The story she submits focuses more than a bit on Harmon, mentioning him by name.

It is killed.

Orders from the top. It won't be printed.

Mama Lily makes her way to find Harmon and Ilaha, in an office, where Harmon sits behind a desk as if it is his. They talk over the match. Mama Lily enters and they wrap up. Mama Lily hugs and squeezes and fist bumps Ilaha.

"You bugger you were never in doubt!" she practically squeals.

Lily is feeling a rush. She has been on stages, has felt that rush herself, and is a bit envious

Harmon stands. Points his fingers at both ladies.

"What's the best thing you ever ate?" he asks, one at a time.

"Moro. In the City. The chicken. Mama Lily took me. Hands down," Ilaha declares. Mama Lily laughs.

"Chicken! Who'd think it? Me too. French Laundry. Thomas Keller recognised me. Insisted I get his chicken. He made it himself, just for me!" she brags.

"Tonight you eat the best meal you will ever eat, and the best meal anyone in the British Empire will have today," he declares, emphatically.

Feast

Harmon tells Ilaha and Mama Lily he will meet them in front of the building.

He drives up in a highest end Range Rover, a magical black matte finish with an all-glass dome over the entire cabin. Harmon takes Ilaha's gear, her three custom leather racket bags, and puts them into the rear of the Rover.

Lily sits into the front cabin chair and feels herself melt. The leather is not just soft, or just luxurious, or just any other descriptor she can manage.

It is perfect in ways she cannot articulate.

It is like being body to body against someone you are in love with. It feels like perfect, unblemished, human skin. It is dark in color, not a flesh tone, but makes one think of unclothed intimacy.

"They skin Irish babies to make the leather," Harmon says, aloud. "Before preparing them to be eaten. Irish babies are the most succulent, tastiest babies you can eat. But nobody likes the skin. Doesn't prepare well, doesn't really crisp, but it makes great upholstery."

Mama Lily looks at Ilaha in the rearview, aghast that she may hear this, but she is immersed in her music and staring up at the sky through the dome glass. The roof glass is no longer full black. The Rover has a setting that changes it to clear when the car is occupied.

The dome also works as a lense that enhances one's view of the stars.

"Irish babies? You are sick, that's not funny," Lily laments.

"Jonathan Swift Tanneries," Harmon continues, "They make the leather, from the Irish babies. Been doing it forever. Since the seventeen hundreds. When they started out, they made fine gloves, and provided material to furniture makers. There are rumors that De Sade bought an enormous quantity for making bondage gear, and that he actually cornered the market for years. You know what 'Victoria's Secret' really was? Irish baby leather intimates. Insisted on nothing else covering her there."

Harmon continues, Lily half listening, hardly sure whether to believe.

"Harmon, none of this is true," she complains, "These seats are not covered with the skins of Irish babies! Nobody is eating Irish babies."

"They taste incredible," Harmon goads her, "'A young healthy child well nursed, is, at a year old, a most delicious nourishing and wholesome food, whether stewed, roasted, baked or boiled; and I make no doubt that it will equally serve in a fricassee, or a ragout,'" Harmon taunts Lily, her unaware, but sort of aware. Something is off, but she knows not exactly what. "That's what we are having, for dinner. Irish baby. By far the best baby one can eat. Name three races of baby that taste better than the Irish baby."

Lily knows, now, this is some sort of joke. It plays because Harmon is so odd, really, and it is believable that he could arrange dining on a baby.

This car, for one!

"Harmon, where did you get this car?" Lily demands.

She pines for a highest end Range Rover from a child, and one of her first big buys when she hits it in music is a really

231

expensive, enormous, luxurious one. She pays way over a hundred grand for it.

She refuses to even test drive the one she is buying. Insists it be sent from the factory and never driven, with 000,000 miles on the odometer. They send her a Rover with 000,000 miles on the odometer, but unbeknownst the car has been driven.

Like every Rover.

To insure highest quality.

They just roll the odometer back for her.

"It's great, right? You've had a Rover, right? Going straight to heaven in one, I think, right?" Harmon samples.

Lily hits his arm.

"That's Lily *Allen* ya twat," she objects.

He knows.

"It's a version of a production model. A lot of it is custom," Harmon explains the details of the Rover. "The glass dome is not Rover. I had that done and it was a lot of work. Took forever. It's a glass that Apple owns. Better stuff than they use to make your iPhone screen. Much more than bullet proof. Not worried about bullets, want it safe in a roll-over. It is. Safer than the factory roof."

Harmon points out all of the amazing details in the car. There is a sound system that allows for personal listening at any volume, that no other passenger in the car hears. He admits to Lily that right then he is listening to her music at really high volume. She can't hear, so he tells her to lean over. She leans into a cone of powerful sound and hears herself singing "2BR02B," wailing about Wonder Woman pondering suicide over her shredding guitar.

They keep driving and Harmon explains more about the car. Every next fact is even more interesting than the prior. Solid tyres, impossible to deflate. The seats, that feel so good, are made from a special pig skin material, not the skins of Irish babies, and heated to exactly the occupant's body temperature, to start, based on a reading that the car takes when the occupant gets in. The seat temperature can be set at will to cool or warm.

Lily is shown where the control is and she plays with it like a child for the rest of the ride. She is so excited she turns to the back seat and shakes Ilaha.

"You have to try this!" she squeals at her. Ilaha has already set her seat to warm, but lets Mama Lily believe she discovered the whole thing anyway.

They arrive. No signage, no line, no evidence of a proper restaurant. Harmon parks and they get out. He leads them through a door into a very comfortable entry area. Through an inside door they see a large dining table and some staff moving about. There is no host or hostess, but they are quickly greeted by a breathtakingly beautiful woman in chef's gear.

The woman smiles wide and embraces Harmon. She holds him at arm's length by the shoulders and simply marvels at him. This goes on just long enough to not make Ilaha or Lily uncomfortable. At exactly the moment when any longer becomes weird, Harmon presents the woman.

Lily knows exactly who she is.

"Ladies this is my great and dear friend Ozgu. She is going to cook us the most fabulous meal we will ever eat,"

Harmon reaches out and hugs her, again, lifting her well off the ground and causing her to laugh out loud like a little girl being squeezed by her daddy.

The woman is beautiful. Stunningly, blindingly, breathtakingly beautiful. Petite, but occupying greater space than her flesh with her spirit. She fills the area she occupies with warmth, soothing.

Lily knows her as an actress. Foreign. Lily must read subtitles and does not recognise the settings, but after happening upon one of her films one night idling around on Netflix she makes it her mission to see everything in which she has ever appeared. She binges it all, down to a soapy telly series that is not very good where she plays only a small and infrequent role.

Ozgu instructs someone on her staff, in perfect French, to seat them. Quickly a staffer appears. She will handle their evening. She isn't really a server. More of a host, or concierge.

Harmon excuses himself from table. The woman charged with catering to them stays table side and chats with Ilaha and Lily. She appears to well know who Lily is, and mentions having seen her play at various venues. They find common acquaintances to discuss and bond lightly. She also knows that Ilaha just won Greater London and intends to play the men's at Wimbledon.

Quickly she creates a more than casually familiar rapport and extracts information about food preferences. She picks up that Lily prefers certain ingredients and that Ilaha has a tree nut allergy that has dissipated into mild if not past.

Everything the woman culls is reported to the kitchen, where Harmon and Ozgu are catching up. Ozgu is preparing mise en place, rummaging for ingredients, chatting at full speed, in Arabic, and spontaneously embracing Harmon as if she has not seen him for too long and may never again. He keeps up the conversation, in Arabic, and hugs back with great zeal in every embrace.

Nobody in the kitchen understands Arabic, so they speak freely. They have not seen each other in a long time.

"No more films? No more acting? Now you cook for friends and what, do yoga and pray and love?" Harmon practically confronts Ozgu.

"Harmon I did what I wanted to do. My path is the path I want to be on," Ozgu defends.

Harmon scoffs, nibbling at her mise en place and having his hand gently pushed away.

"You are a great, great actress. When I first saw you, on screen, it was infinity. Hollywood deserves a chance at you. The world is not a better place with you cooking for me. I am better, everyone else loses." He means this.

"You of all people, bastard, lament my selfishness toward the world?" she mocks. "Are you where you belong, or want to be?"

Harmon pleads his hypocrisy.

He knows that in fact for years, too many years, he has skated along gratifying himself and not giving what he has to anyone. It is so easy to isolate, to connect only via transaction, to withhold the basic generosity his abilities offer. Ozgu hits a chord not played in years, and Harmon breaks down.

"I miss her, Oz, I miss her so, so much," Harmon bubbles over. Tears stream, and he heaves, "I feel so, so empty. I sit, stare, and see only a Godless darkness, a vacuum, so empty. The worst is that I understand it. It is awful, Oz, just unbearable. All I can do is distract and amuse, to momentarily forget."

Ozgu wipes off her hands and holds Harmon, a giant of a man, his head on her chest. Her arms barely able to reach around his enormous shoulders, a makeshift pieta in an almost comical inverse proportion.

He sobs and cries. She strokes his hair back

"Harmon," Ozgu whispers, "She is with us in some way. I miss her so. I sob like you. And I miss you. But the missing passes and we have lives to celebrate. Hers, for one. Buck up." She guides Harmon upright, places her hands on his cheeks, kisses him upon his mouth, and stands.

"Go to table. Be with your wonderful guests, I must cook," she commands.

Harmon stands to leave the kitchen. He wipes his face and composes himself. Ozgu tells him she will dine, but she must get things underway.

Harmon sits down into Ilaha and Lily talking like schoolgirls. Lily is youthful at heart, despite her aged state, able to fall into Ilaha's entire milieu as if it is her own. She knows all of the current cultural earmarks, and remains a virtuoso social media user. Ilaha has her phone out and is sharing Snaps and Tweets and the two of them are friending and following for the first time.

Lily notes Harmon's face and bluntly laughs, inappropriate but genuine.

"Harmon, have you been having a cry!" she impulsively teases.

He understands the good nature of her ribbing and does not react.

"Yeah, I have. Ozgu does it to me. We share someone and when I see Oz I cannot help but relive the loss," he explains.

Ilaha has never seen such a human side. Harmon offers no evidence at all of any form of human connection. He never mentions friends or family or anyone outside the context of transactions.

So and so can get this done. Whosey whatsit can do this. Howya knows Whoya, let me ask about thingamajig.

This crystallises for Ilaha right there. *Harmon is a transactional being.* She assumes a bond with him, unclear exactly what kind, but realises what they really do is exchange … ideas, techniques, plans.

Lily loses her laughter and feels for him. She has lost, certainly not the same specifics but deep, deathly loss. She recognises the hollow. The empty that occupies the bereaved. They are there, they are them, but the empty is now inside, glimmering through, through the eyes.

Aside animate, separate but surrounded. Where once a body was is now a form of shell. She doesn't feel bad, exactly, about the laugh, but feels energy disconnect. She pierces a deep nerve and doesn't really want to. Harmon, great enough, is not an intimate. What transpires is too intimate.

The queer incident passes, and they fall into casual ease. A first ever gathering away from tennis. Harmon explains what will transpire.

"Oz has all sorts of contacts in food," he explains, "If it is eaten, in London, she can get some of it. And she gets the best. The sellers love her. So they tip her off. 'We have perfect cremini mushrooms. We have the best Iowa chop. We have rare Amish butter.' She gathers the day's best and makes magic." Ilaha and Lily show their delight. "I have no idea what she is making, but whatever it is, it can't be better. Just eat everything she puts in front of you until it is gone. And talk about it. We all agree. We will talk about it?"

They agree.

Ozgu comes out of the kitchen, now dressed in very fashionable party couture, and joins her guests at table.

Amuse-bouche. Cucumber sandwiches. Harmon scoffs at the notion of no meat or cheese - "Why don't I just eat the tablecloth!" - But even he takes his small bite, and it is magic. Startling. More flavor than one would ever expect of a cucumber. The bread is a miniature bun, still warm, just, flaky and offering some pull all at once. Slightly salty. The cucumber is cold to cool, lightly pickled with a hint of cinnamon, and plump. Fresh.

So fresh, in fact, that the stem in the kitchen remains moist.

Petite collation. A single egg, "that egg," as it is announced by the staff. In the shell, soft boiled, certainly perfectly. The egg is placed, and then tapped on top, very gently cracking the shell, which is lifted away with a tiny spoon, exposing the yolk. A dab of butter is dropped into the yolk, and salt is sprinkled on top. The butter and salt are left at table with the tiny spoon. They each devour it as if urchins living on the dole in nineteen thirties Limerick.

No trace of egg remains when they are done.

238

Plat principal. Rendang. Harmon sees it placed and stands at full height. His long, powerful arms spread wide, wider than the table, he stands over the large platter and adores. Ozgu locks his eyes, smiles wide, and they both laugh physical joy.

Ozgu introduces the meal for her guests, taking over for her staff.

"Codfish rendang. It is a spicy meat dish served at celebrations. It honours a guest, and is associated with ceremony," Ozgu explains. "Today we celebrate Ilaha, who has achieved the first of many great things."

Lily's eyes drip tears, unaccompanied by sob or sniffle or cry. A silent spring. Ozgu stares unblinking at Harmon. Her gaze has not wavered since the rendang was set. He is soaking in Ilaha, who is giggling in a bit of discomfort having all of a sudden been christened as the focus of the event. The mood is deep, but not heavy or morose.

Very real.

Rice and a vegetable dish accompany the rendang. Harmon leads the way, dumping some rice and the veg onto his plate then depositing a disproportionately large scoop of the rendang on top.

"In twenty eleven a CNN online poll had this as the most delicious dish on earth," Harmon begins what will be a short course on rendang. Ozgu rolls her eyes at Lily and smiles, settling in to listen.

"It is not curry," Harmon goes on. "Foodie types call it curry but it isn't. Too dry. With purpose. The spices preserve the meat, for up to a month. Perfect for the jungle. Sort of like jerky, really.

"Rendang makes me think about the Minang people of Indonesia. I have a soft spot for them. Largest matrilineal society on earth. Property, family name, it all passes through the mother. Men do the politics and religion. The Minang are famous for their commitment to education. The Minang diaspora is one of radiating influence and success.

"The dish is four ingredients, each representing a part of their society. The meat is for the clan leaders. The coconut milk intellectuals. Teachers, poets, writers. The chili is for clerics. The heat of the chili for Sharia. The spices are a mix that stands for everyone else in Minang society."

Harmon eats while he lectures, and Lily, Ozgu, and Ilaha only half listen, focused much more on the dish and on a nonverbal conversation of their own.

"Ilaha," Harmon summons her attention, raising a very old bottle of Veuve Clicquot Ponsardin. It sank with the Titanic and now sits exhumed from undersea in Harmon's huge powerful hands, perfectly chilled. "Fortuna led you into my life, and for that I experience grace. To you and to watching you fly."

Harmon pops the cork and hands off the bottle to staff, which fills flutes. Harmon sits, raises his glass, and tips for toast.

Ilaha appears unsure whether to toast. Harmon cuts in.

"Drink, Ilaha," he instructs her, "Franklin says beer is proof that God wants us to be happy. Champagne proves we can have good taste doing it."

They all toast.

The champagne tastes more or less like modern champagne, but it is a lot sweeter. Storage below the ocean for a century turns out to be an ideal process. It tastes perfect.

Ozgu and Lily scrutinize the near empty bottle. It looks awful, really, as if it was buried in a hole and not completely cleaned off after being dug out.

"What is this, Harmon?" Ozgu asks. She is a real gastronome, but generally not a wine enthusiast.

"Eighteen sixty three Veuve Clicquot Ponsardin," Harmon tells her, "It was on the Titanic. Now it is in your glass. Remarkable, no?"

Lily cannot contain a bellowing cackle.

"Irish babies and now bubbly from the Titanic!" she screams laughing. "You are really something, Harmon. What next? Everlasting gobstoppers?"

Even Harmon is laughing now.

Ilaha, a bit put off by the notion of drinking something so old, finishes her flute. Ozgu pours what she has left into Lily's flute, and Lily tops off with what remains in the bottle. Harmon has long since emptied his glass.

Upon Lily finishing her last sip, there is silence. Completion. Arrival. These four, for an instant, are one, and still, and all right, and at peace. Each and all, at peace.

The table is cleared, and desserts are presented.

Baklava, Ozgu's family recipe, perfect and warm, and an apple pie, hot from the oven, steam rising from openings in the crust. Harmon always insists on apple pie, frosted lightly with some form of cinnamon powdered miracle.

The apple pie crust is a complicated, interlacing pattern. Three interlocking triangles. Valknut. Ozgu always makes Harmon his apple pie with a Valknut crust.

Harmon sees the apple pie, sheds a tear, and breathes deep. Only Ozgu notices.

It takes some time but soon enough all is gone. A feast like one might imagine depicted in a film, then if they see the film, they are disappointed by what is depicted on screen, because food never looks quite right on screen, then the film ends and Ozgu's feast is presented, in real life, and Pavlov is again confirmed.

The adults coffee. Ilaha teas. Everything is eaten. Harmon sees to that. He confirms everyone else is full and then lets no crumb go to waste. Ozgu falls into deep talk with Lily. They have much to share, having experience with fame and being artists.

After some number of hours, with the food eaten and the table cleared, and the talk dying on its own very comfortably, Ilaha falls asleep curled up into an impossibly small ball for her greatness of size. Lily yawns. Ozgu reaches for Harmon's hand. He takes hers into both of his. Then he stands up.

"You don't need to drive, Lily. Ozgu can have a minion do that, but you and Ilaha should go home. All of her gear is stowed, so let's get her into the Rover and you two can go get some proper sleep." Harmon walks over to Ilaha, reaches under her, lifts her with too great an ease, never waking her, and turns to table.

Mama Lily sees them as a magnificent statue, a scene that belongs in marble, a vision one cannot fully appreciate after being blind washed by all of the pixel tomfoolery that passes for visual life.

Harmon holds Ilaha, a very large girl, as if a small child. She is unshakably asleep, deep sleep, dreaming of something, and he holds her in exactly a perfect way. Her hands exquisite, exactly where they belong. His arms bulging just so, offering engineering support for Ilaha's solid frame.

Everything looks so permanent, so idealised, so necessarily then and also eternal. Mama Lily works hard to snap the image, to never forget the image. Knowing her eye, trained enough, but not a genius of an eye, cannot do justice to the visual.

Harmon turns with Ilaha and heads out to the waiting car. He places her in the back, fetches a cashmere blanket from a hatch in the rear, and covers her. Mama Lily follows outside and approaches Harmon, who is closing the rear door of the car.

Shocking and surprising, completely unexpected, Harmon hugs Lily and lifts her off the ground. She feels as if freed from gravity, without the disorientation or pit in the stomach. He handles her in a way that makes her wish he would literally never, ever let go.

It could be so very awkward, but in a deft swoop he cradles her into his arms as he just held Ilaha. Lily settles into the chance to feel once again like a little girl, being held by a loving daddy. Harmon dances her one or two steps into position to place her into the passenger seat.

She never, ever, at any single instant ever feels like she will fall or get scratched or bumped or come to any form of harm. Ever. That moment, as short as it is, reminds Lily of a feeling from deep youth that a child cannot fully appreciate. Safety. The truest safest safety.

Harmon fetches another cashmere blanket from the rear of the car and tucks it around Lily. He closes the passenger door. She rolls down the window.

"So you stay on with Ozgu, then, Harmon?" Lily teases. She senses they are more than just casual acquaintances. "Gonna stay ovah, send us off in ya Range Rovah?"

Harmon smiles back. Pats her on the head.

"Lils Lils Lils," he lilts, "Oz is a blood brother like you and Ilaha, and it's been too long since we were together. For all I know this is the last time I will ever see her. Gotta make it worth it."

Harmon slaps the hood of the car and indicates the minion ought to take off. The window rolls up, and the car drives away, Mama Lily and Ilaha both asleep.

Inside Harmon and Ozgu sit at the empty table. They hold hands and talk. Ozgu tells Harmon they should go spend the night together. They agree to walk the Thames to the Goring and sleep the non-sleep sleep of little deaths, and then spend all day in London properly catching up.

Anne Rainsford French

Lily wanders into Harmon's office and sees Ilaha doing her tape and data work on his computer.

"Where's Harmon?" she asks.

Ilaha tells her Harmon is out on the courts, supervising renovations.

Lily walks out to the courts and sees Harmon instructing some men. He speaks very quietly and closely to one man, who jots some notes on a pad and then goes off to complete some mission.

"Final prep for Wimbledon," Harmon explains, "I am getting every court and net at the club to exact precise perfect specs, as a dry run, and then we are reproducing a Centre Court for Ilaha to use. She is going onto that grass as if it is her own."

Harmon is always invigorated by a deeper layer of complexity in a plan.

Lily waves Harmon's car keys at him.

"I've got your keys. The Rover is outside. How about a lift home?" Lily has had the Rover for at least a couple weeks, actually, and has taken full advantage of it.

It is just wonderful, Harmon's Range Rover! She looks for excuses to drive ever since being dropped off. Has even emptied the tank from near full and refilled it more than once. Harmon raises his hand, Lily tosses the keys, he catches them, and they are off. They pass the office, and Ilaha tells Mama Lily she is staying to do more tape and data.

Harmon heads for the passenger seat. Lily, cut off, has the keys dangled in front of her.

"You drive," he says, and gets into the car, closing the door. Lily lightly races around to the driver's side and fires up the car.

She drives the long way, really, not the shortest fastest way. Stops for drive thru coffee, plays a CD she has been listening to while using the car. She becomes very comfortable about it. Honestly, she is already missing it.

They reach Elysium and Lily stops the car but leaves it running. Harmon does not get out. He looks at Lily.

"What was your first car?" he asks.

She laughs and tells him it is a crummy little Alfa Romeo convertible with a roof that does not close. It is ruined, the interior, but the engine works fine. Filthy, really, but on summer days when everything dries out and she drives with the wind in her hair it is dreamy.

"What happened to it?" Harmon asks.

She tells him she leaves it parked with the keys in it in the City and it is not where she left it when she goes looking.

"You a big fan of cars?" Harmon asks.

Sure, she tells him, I've got a really nice car. I have means, you know, she defends. Harmon pleads miscommunication.

"Does Ilaha have a car?" he asks Lily.

Ilaha shows no inclination to drive, Mama Lily thinks aloud. It occurs to her that, yea, Ilaha basically shows little to

246

no interest in driving. Never talks about getting a license or anything. She is at that age, too.

Harmon gets out of the car, and Lily does as well. He comes around to the driver's side and puts his right hand out.

"One thousand seven hundred and seventy six pounds," he states.

Lily is unsure what he means. She has already taken his hand, an instinct, and is shaking on an unexplained deal.

"Go fetch me one thousand seven hundred and seventy six pounds and the Rover is yours. Give Ilaha whatever you drive and make her get a license," he explains.

Lily is shocked and elated. But reluctant to take such a gift. Harmon's Rover is the finest car she has ever come across. Honestly. It is so, so nice. And powerful and custom and all. She feels bad enough about wanting to pilfer the cashmere blankets, but to basically steal the whole car?

"Harmon, this is too much. I simply can't," Lily protests. "At a minimum I'll insist on paying some fair price for the car. But I don't really need such a buy right now and I am sure fair is pretty high, so thanks, but I just cannot."

He walks away, turns, and stares at Lily.

"Bring the money by the club. There is contact info inside the glove box for service. Anything you need, it's all paid already, excepting petrol. Perpetuity. Just contact the guys on the card in the glove box and they will come fetch the car, get it fixed, and get it back same day," he gruffly asserts.

Lily hesitates. God, she wants the car. It is soooo soooo wonderful. But far too large a gift, even in the face of the formal "sale" at his bizarre price.

Harmon shifts from amused by her hesitation to a bit insulted by it.

"Lily, listen, stop being such a wanker about the whole thing. You love the car, yes? You emptied the tank, yes? You imagine excuses to drive it, yes?" he practically accuses.

She just nods.

Yesyesyes. Of course. I love the bloody beautiful perfect thing, all right still.

"Just say thanks and love having it. Go straight to heaven in it. I had my fill of it, honest, it's great but it just wasn't ever me. Better it be you, and now give Ilaha her own car and get her a driver's license. Honestly. A woman should drive," he scoffs.

What kid Ilaha's age doesn't pine to drive!

Harmon turns and takes off at a run, looking like a machine in perfect gearing trampling after prey.

The poor, poor, prey, Lily thinks.

She can only imagine what he is chasing, but when he catches it, well, there will be a magnificent ending.

Reappear

Harmon disappears.

Before he does, he arranges matches for Ilaha.

He hands her a detailed schedule to train by. He arranges a hitting partner for Wednesday, not anywhere near his equal, but adequate.

Then he just goes somewhere ... else.

Ilaha drills. She is a bit bored and certainly not feeling any thrills, but goes about her work like a professional person. She focuses on form, and quality, and does not press for quantity or idle justification.

Almost two weeks Harmon is gone and Ilaha starts to worry a bit.

No word.

Of any kind.

He has no cell number of which anyone is aware, and his station at the club appears unclear. The rest of the staff just carries on as if he was never there.

Ilaha's grass court is complete. Harmon instructs her to use it for all matches and drilling with another player. She does.

She loves it. Playing the grass has been a revelation. The skid of the ball, sliding into strokes, the softness of the earth. She takes to it naturally and feels and senses a balance advantage. Her opponents struggle, ever so slightly, despite all of them being grass court champions, one of whom plays into the quarters at the men's at Wimbledon itself.

By week three, Ilaha is in near panic. Just about a month to go until the actual event and nothing. She is alone, training, not sure at all how to proceed. Mama Lily has little to offer, as she has not been managing Ilaha and has no idea where to begin. Ilaha still has a schedule to follow and she does, with great discipline.

She is studying tape and data when Harmon walks into the office, as if he never left. She stands bolt upright and calls out his name.

"Harmon!" she exclaims.

He holds his arms apart and she is drawn into them. He squeezes her then puts her at arm's length, holding her by the shoulders.

"Are you feeling okay, Ilaha?" Harmon asks.

She is a bit off, answering him - yes? - As if not sure whether she is, or what he is asking.

"I mean, are you at full speed? Can you play, tonight? Are you rested, feeling a hundred per cent?" he clarifies.

Ah, she understands.

"Yes," she tells him. "I feel great. Strong. Hitting the ball really well. Great balance. I am ready to play, yeah."

"Great. Come back here at midnight. I have a match for you, a final tune up for the real thing in a few weeks. Gotta run. I'll see you later." Harmon opens a drawer, removes a bundle of papers, and leaves.

Ilaha finishes her tape and data work and leaves just prior to the club closing. It is about nine o'clock. She goes home and preps for her midnight match. No idea who she plays, or why it is so late.

In the Higgins Boat

Ilaha is excited to get at it and heads to Club Dagobah at about eleven, early, dying to get on court. She gets there and the door is unlocked, a note taped to it instructing her to lock it after coming in.

She makes her way into the lobby area where she first hears it.

Deafening noise.

Very, very loud music. Hard core rock and roll music. The loudest thing she has ever heard. She fetches her gear from Harmon's office and moves toward the sound, lugging her three leather racket bags. With every step it grows louder and louder.

But not noisy. Pure, she hears it perfectly as if playing at modest volume on a super high quality sound system. She walks down the gangway to the grass court, the source of the music, and enters the court area.

She sees Harmon and a man she recognises but cannot identify on court, playing points. Playing hard. Almost playing in a slam dance with the music. It is like watching a music video. She cannot identify the music, but it sounds very familiar to her.

The music is exploding from a single small round tower resting on a bench next to the court. It is matte black, and appears that the entire outer surface of the short tube tower is a speaker. Light moves behind the speaker surface in harmony with the music, colors changing and ripple adjusting. She literally sees the music as it is being heard and felt. She can almost taste it.

Is that possible? To taste music?

Harmon and the man play service points, in a game of back and forth where winner serves next. They alternate between deuce and ad side, serving out until broken.

The man on the other end of the court from Harmon is tall, thick, with very short but very rich colored hair. They are playing with wooden rackets. Both. Tiny. The string beds look hardly any bigger than the ball.

Ilaha sits and watches them play. They appear unaware she is there, but she is not hiding. She just stares.

What she sees is amazing. She can't believe her eyes. BallMap is installed on the court, and Ilaha goes to the screen and watches the data come in. Harmon is hitting serves that are well in excess of any pace she has ever seen. One hundred fifty five miles per hour. He touches one hundred sixty miles per hour at least once.

The ground strokes being hit are rockets. Backhands well over a hundred miles per hour. Harmon winning point after point on service. His opponent rarely captures serve. They have some system of switching after four points that allows the other man to get serve back, but Harmon is able to break so often it is as if service is only a rarity for his opponent.

The music stops, and the men meet at net. They shake hands, and walk off court with the man's arm on Harmon's shoulder. The man is tall. Perhaps as tall as Harmon, but not nearly as well built.

Ilaha meets them at the post of the net.

"Ilaha," Harmon calls to her, "This is a great friend and a greater champion. Do you know who it is?"

Ilaha looks at his face, a much older face than she realises from off court. His hair, very short, throws her off, but then she indexes the moves she sees him make on court and it hits her!

"Pete Sampras?" she offers.

"Indeed," Harmon bumps her fist. "The one, and only. Name three greater champions than Sampras. You can't." Harmon passes Ilaha to put his wooden racket into his gear bag. While he does, Sampras holds his hand out to Ilaha.

"I understand you are supposed to play the men's?" he observes. She confirms that yes, she expects to enter. "And you have beaten men, preparing?" Yes, she asserts.

"Gil Compagnon," she declares.

Sampras smiles. He knows. He follows her progress.

"I know. I have seen you play. You are quite a strong player. Very well suited to grass. Good luck, nice meeting you." He pats Ilaha on her shoulder and goes to get his gear.

Harmon seated on the bench at the side of the court, shutting off the music player, stands and tells Ilaha he will be right back.

"She is really good enough to win?" Sampras asks.

He sees her film, and looks over a lot of data with Harmon prior to their sparring session. It is objectively true that she hits as well as the best men and moves as well as above average men. But can she actually win, on that grass, in just about a month, in front of the world?

"Can she win?" Harmon restates, rhetorically, "Pete, you did. Becker did. Graf did. Nadal did. Can she win?" Harmon echoes, laughing.

"We are about to see," Harmon concedes.

With that Harmon says goodbye to Sampras and heads back to the grass court.

It is silent. Ilaha is there, sitting, numb, and nervous. Her mind floods with all sorts of ideas. She can't believe Pete Sampras was just playing with Harmon, and getting whooped from what she saw. She cannot believe Harmon is so good. I mean my god!! Hitting those serves with a wooden racket? How hard can he hit with proper modern gear?

Harmon walks onto the court. Ilaha notices he is barefoot. She swears he was wearing shoes when she came in, but his feet are green and she realises he never wears shoes.

Ever.

Some theory about the feet really being hands, and wiring the ground into the brain.

"Okay, Ilaha, it's midnight, let's play," Harmon beams.

He goes into his bag and removes an RF ninety seven Wilson racket just like hers. He opens a can of balls, walks cleanly out to his side of the court, and offers to hit with her.

"I am warm," she states, deciding to get right into it.

He tells her she can decide on serve, and she takes.

Harmon hits the balls to her and sets himself to receive. Ilaha sets herself at the baseline to serve and tosses.

Her first serve is hit very well, down the T, with great pace and moderate action. It kicks hard, high, toward the ad court slightly. Harmon steps into the court and deftly blocks the ball deep into her ad court with mild topspin. Ilaha moves for the ball, to her backhand, and plays a shot with heavy spin down the line, trying to get it deep and well over the net. Harmon anticipates this and is there to volley the shot severely away from Ilaha cross court for the point.

0-15.

From the ad court Ilaha serves hard and flat hitting the sideline short, forcing Harmon into a full run at an angle to play a shot that few players could or would play. He is forced into an awful position, so he counters directly and hits a drop shot at a very severe angle across the middle of the net, the lowest part of the net, short into Ilaha's ad court. Knowing that he has in fact forced her into a much compromised spot, he makes his only move and charges hard into the middle of the court along the net.

Ilaha gets to the ball and realises she is stuck. The ball stays below the net line, forcing her to hit almost vertical. She cannot hit it back where it came from, because she has not quite gotten all the way into position, so she does the best thing she can. She fabricates a lob hitting as hard as she can manage more or less straight up. The ball does not get deep enough and having carried to a high apex Harmon has plenty of time to move and hit an easy overhead into a wide open court.

0-30.

From deuce side Ilaha pushes, trying to do just a little more with service, and it works. Harmon doesn't quite get all the way into his backhand and it flies just long through her ad court corner.

15-30.

From the ad side Ilaha changes up, hitting a heavy topspin kick down the T that is too much topspin. Harmon steps into it, takes it on the rise, and whistles it back through her deuce court side. She barely moves after it, but is not going to get to it in any case.

15-40.

From the deuce side Ilaha does the right thing and hits hard, into the court, right at Harmon's body. He is forced to sidestep and play a defensive shot back at her, deep into the middle of the court. She steps into the court and hits a great forehand back at him, deep into the middle of his court.

Harmon is a bit too far in and is stuck with playing a short hop on the rise, which he deftly bends over the net into her deep deuce corner. She runs after the ball but is forced just a bit to go backwards toward her baseline. Harmon sees this and moves into net like a jaguar closing in on prey. Ilaha does not see him move in, hits for the sideline, and right into Harmon's string bed. He puts away the volley into a wide open court. Game.

Changing sides Harmon stops to say a few things to Ilaha.

"Ilaha, that was a really good game," he concludes. "I made some shots that were much better outcomes than should be expected. You put me into tough spots on every point, really. Now, on my serve I am going to give you the balls you will actually face. So you are going to get good hard A serves in tough spots. How do we read serve?" Ilaha does a duet with Harmon, *we watch his feet*. "Right. The feet betray the shot. Breathe. Hit on exhale. It's a puzzle. Just see the pieces and put them together."

Harmon takes position to serve. He hits his serves in the fashion that a typical top seeded player would. Live action, good to great pace, reasonably often into tough spots. He is watching Ilaha for the binary quality of her response. If he hits a hard serve down the T at her, he wants to see her leaning that way and giving herself a chance to do something with it. He is looking for her to not get wrong-footed or frozen.

She does an admirable job of reading and responding. As she grows accustomed to a complete game, an unrelenting A level game from every aspect on every shot, she improves rapidly. She adapts to simply blocking back a great, hard, dominant type serve into a good spot to reset the terms of the point. She pushes harder to step in as far as possible to make the most of openings. She stops desperately reaching for the possible winner and begins calmly playing a shot or more ahead into sequences that lead to probable winners.

On her service games Ilaha is disciplined about not pressing too hard. She simply does not have the service to hit many or any aces against Harmon. She also can't really produce service winners. Harmon is just too good, always there; always ready to hit more than a defensive block back at her.

Spot. Spin. Speed. Ilaha produces any one of these on just about every serve Harmon hits at her. She thinks it through and decides to focus on spot, on where she hits the ball back, as the attribute most important in tennis. It is her only choice, and she commits to it, and after a bleeding one way rout she turns things around and ends up actually breaking serve once.

What is headed for a 0-6 type manhandling turns into a 3-6 loss, to be true, but from there winning a set and then even a match, and then multiple matches and maybe the whole tournament, is possible.

Science, possible.

As the set ends Ilaha heads to the benches next to the court. She notices Sampras standing a bit down the gangway. He has watched, apparently, out of sight. Ilaha follows through into the gangway.

"You watched, yeah?" she asks him. He confirms that yes, he watched. "What do you think? Is this hopeless? Am I gonna be a laughingstock?"

Sampras laughs gently.

"Ilaha, you won against Gils, right?" She nods that yes, she did. "Gils is a solid professional player. Everyone on tour respects him and his game. He never, ever, beats himself. He only loses to better players." Sampras pauses, touches Ilaha, who is looking at her feet, and has her look up at him.

"We all have a Gils, a guy who we beat and realise that we belong. Everybody can hit the ball and run the ball down and stay at it for five hours. The difference," Sampras stands fully tall, becoming as large as possible, "Isn't in the body. It's in here," he points at his temple, "and in here," he points at his heart, "and only you really know what's there."

Ilaha breathes, deep, soaks in what Sampras tells her, and says "thanks." Before turning to go back to the court, she asks, "Am I supposed to be winning tonight? What is this whole thing all about?"

Sampras laughs, and Harmon approaches.

"Ilaha," Sampras tells her, "There is no way you are gonna beat him. Hell, I wouldn't have been able to beat him on my best day. That is why I snuck back to watch. I never, ever miss a chance to watch him play. Ask for his A game. You will never want to set foot on a court again."

Harmon and Sampras make their way down the gangway, through the doors, and then out of the club. They say a goodbye, and Harmon goes back inside to the grass court.

"Questions, Ilaha, you must have questions for me. Tonight is the night we get everything clear," he invites her.

She sits down on the bench next to the court.

"Okay, first, can I really do this?" she pleads.

Harmon loses any trace of a smile and responds a bit harshly.

"Ilaha, I can't tell you that. *You* tell you that. You decide that. You see that through. Really. Inside your brain there is a switch. Turn it on, or leave it off. Simple. I cannot help you there. Don't ever ask that again, either. It is ugly and weak and between you and you," he scolds.

"You choose to believe, Ilaha," Harmon castigates, "Or you choose not to believe. You cannot know, for a fact, but you can believe. Be brave enough to believe."

Ilaha is shaken into the seriousness of the moment. This is not a kid blindly walking through a learning process any more. This is the battle she prepares for. For real. Soon enough she storms the beach and bullets fly and she will exist only in that moment to deal with them.

"I don't see any way that I could have won the set," she states. Not whiny, just factually.

"Okay, let's use the right words," Harmon begins, "'Could' is really a terrible word. It flips time in ways time won't flip. The set already happened, and you did not win. So there is no 'could,' there is 'didn't.'

"As far as if you had a time machine and went backwards to replay the set, of course you could win the set. All sorts of things could change. You could be a better player, I could be worse; we could be the same and hit different shots. What is the thing worth focusing on? Why do we do tape and data, Ilaha?" he laments aloud.

Harmon literally snaps his huge fingers right at her.

"Wake up, small little woman!" he booms. "Honestly. What have we been doing all this time? Is it just one step at a time, you think? Now is where you wake up or stay asleep."

Ilaha feels a bit of shame. Moments ago realizing how serious it all is, she feels a surge of readiness to meet her challenge. Now she lapses into a stupor and feels so stupid about losing that mindset.

"I wasted at least two of your service games figuring out to just block back into good spots," Ilaha blurts.

Harmon releases a deep breath and agrees.

"Yes!" he pulls her forward with his tone and manner and energy. "It's a game of breaks. Why did you take serve?"

She admits she is afraid to face his serve. She sees him playing with Sampras and hitting impossible bombs with a wooden racket! She does not want to be across from that.

"Okay, is that a good analytical decision?" Harmon asks. Ilaha immediately says it is not. "You always always always receive. You need every chance you get to figure out where there is a crack, for one," Harmon explains, "For another, every serve a guy hits comes out of a limited reserve. His last

261

serve will not be as lively and energetic and, well, good, as his first serves, as his completely warmed up serves. So catch the other player off guard, maybe steal an early break before the guy is really grooved, and then push him into an empty tank as soon as possible. Play to deny easy one swing points. Frustrate. Reset. Turn tables."

Ilaha soaks it in, in a different way. She etches it hard into a playbook. A playbook she is already writing, rapidly, from memory. Things she learns beforehand and just did not handle well. Things that only make sense now, in this moment, that kick around for some time waiting to be archived properly.

"Ilaha, the ball doesn't care. Always anchor on that. The guy hits the ball, you hit the ball, the ball goes where it is sent," Harmon preaches, "And you only need to deal with the ball. Deal with it via science and reason. It will never fail you. There is always an answer. Chances are you can go with the answer. Chances are the other guy will be the one who falls into playing like a halfwit unthinking rube. Tennis players are athletes, after all, rarely educated people, and unlikely to be terribly clever."

Ilaha expects to play another set, but she is to be disappointed.

"Nope," Harmon tells her, "We are done. I gave you an A player's Grand Slam best, you handled it fine. With preparation you won't burn games early taking serve and being slow to find the right pieces of the puzzle. No point in playing any more."

Ilaha practically begs him for more.

"Please Harmon. Come on! Let me at least see your A game. Just a few games? Points even? Please," she pleads.

"Didn't Sampras tell you it would just make you want to quit, seeing me play my best?" Harmon toys with her.

Amused.

Drifting toward being a hostile opponent now, not an ally.

"I don't care. I want to see for myself. I am not afraid. It's only a tennis ball. I can take it on, let's go." Ilaha stalks onto the court and motions Harmon to get to his side. "You serve, and give me the A stuff. Your best stuff."

Harmon goes into his racket bag, switches rackets, grabs fresh balls and takes position to serve. He holds a ball up, tells Ilaha these serves are live, and goes into his service motion.

He does it perfectly, and she is frozen watching it. She looks to his feet, out of habit now, and her brain registers that he is barefoot. Odd, she thinks, odd at all and odd she has forgotten.

His knees bend, his feet spread slightly, he rotates his torso, his toss arm lifts one way, and his racket arm goes back and down the other. He presses his toes into the grass and begins to push off, from the ground, the earth, up. Ilaha literally sees a bit of the mass of the planet channel up through his enormous muscular calves into even bigger and more powerful thighs. He lifts off the ground and his torso unwinds up into his shoulders, down through his arm.

His racket now at an impossible angle to where the ball will be hit. It cannot get there. It cannot get there. It will never make it.

The earth pulse he harvests converges into a more limited channel through his arm into his racket, and he unleashes it all into a nuclear explosion that mushrooms through the ball, through the air, down onto the grass court, and then up into the air coming right at Ilaha.

Hot.

The sound of steam coming off a red hot griddle in a greasy spoon. His ball can cook an egg, she thinks.

The ball whistles past her ear, scary close. She never moves. Never budges, never even blinks. Her heart races, faster than she can ever realise. As the ball passes, thankfully not splitting her head wide open, she feels a drowning rush of relief. As if she was just hanged and the rope broke, instead of her neck.

Harmon waltzes to net, Ilaha still standing frozen, coming down from a de facto chemical high. She hates this high. It is the high reckless seekers of death pursue. She loves being alive so this particular cocktail is not her poison.

"Is that quite enough, Ilaha?" Harmon insists of her.

She makes a final descent into being at ease.

"Um, yeh. Um, sure that's enough," she mumbles.

Veni, vidi, vici. She is hardly Caesar in this. Caesar salad, maybe. Not a victorious general by any means. She came. She saw. She hardly conquered.

Veni, vidi.

"So how did that go, Ilaha?" Harmon mocks.

She does not get defensive, or resurrect any sense of conflict with him.

"You know what, Harmon," she responds, with a confidence he admires, "I can be pretty sure I won't see anything as difficult as that at Wimbledon, so it should all seem easy I suppose."

She is ready. The switch is turned to 'on' and now she will see it through because she wants to see it through.

Harmon agrees.

"You won't see anything like that, anywhere else, Ilaha. I am the only one who can do that," he mutters, a bit sadly.

A Higher Power

The AELTC does not invite Ilaha to play the Gentlemen's.

For the first time in over a century, the boys Greater London champion is not invited into the Wimbledon field. Inviting the runner up, whom Ilaha drubbed in the finals, is considered. It is decided not to extend an invite at all.

They fill the spot with another player.

Harmon will have none of it, so he sets Clara to work on getting a court order. She has a difficult time of it, because Wimbledon is run by a private organization and the invite is a tradition, not an obligation. Judges are reluctant at best to demand anything of Wimbledon. Strictly speaking, the law is not on Ilaha's side.

Lucky for Ilaha, Clara knows a judge who will be on her side.

She arranges a hearing, produces the signed declaration Harmon extracts, and successfully obtains a court order. She explains to Harmon that it will not hold up, that Wimbledon will succeed in having it quashed, but for the moment, the law speaks.

As a favor to Clara.

To make a point.

Harmon immediately storms the offices at the AELTC waving the court order and the signed declaration. He demands to speak with whoever issues invitations. They surprisingly agree to let him plead his case.

"She won the Greater London, the boys, and a judge has issued a court order. Not to mention you stated clearly and signed attesting that the winner of the Greater London boys gets an invite into the Gentleman's," Harmon trumpets, "I know the court order won't hold up, but the public may not be terribly receptive to refusing a deserved entry into the field for the Goddess of Greengrass."

The members of the tournament committee look at each other a bit bewildered.

"Who is she?" one of them asks.

An assistant informs them that Ilaha is the little girl who survived being thrown from Greengrass Tower the night it burned down. They only vaguely recall any such thing. She was adopted by Lily Lacey, the pop star. Who? *Oh, that awful Labour agitator!* Really?

"Look," Harmon presses them, "She is a girl. Fine. She won. She beat the boys. Like a drum, to be fair. She was far and away the best player in the field and she deserves the invite. Do the right thing and extend the same invite you have extended for over a century to a really great player that won and deserves a chance to play."

They are unwilling. Resistant. *We will offer her a place in the ladies.* No, Harmon insists. She beat the boys so she could play the men. She won the girls last year. She could have played the Ladies' last year. *It wastes a spot, she will get killed.* She won't, and what will happen to one of the boys she obliterated?

The meeting is interrupted. The chairperson of the tournament committee has a call that must be taken.

Upon returning, the chairperson immediately addresses Harmon.

"She's in. First round, she will play on Centre Court. Probably Murray. We will inquire how he feels about it." The committee abruptly leaves the room.

The assistant hands Harmon a player pack and tells him to make sure Ilaha has it with her at all times on premises.

Harmon's phone signals he has a text from Clara.

"The Crown has spoken, yes?"

Chops

Ilaha wakes early, spilling over energy. Not nervous, not fearful, just at full power. Today is day one. She has access to the facilities at the All England Lawn Tennis Club.

Her goal has been achieved.

Ilaha leaves her room to go into the kitchen for coffee. She has taken to coffee, in massive quantities. She has abandoned tea for weeks now. Her googling and researching and full-fledged efforts to get ready and get better lead her to a health guru who swears by the benefits of caffeine.

Drink as much coffee as you can stomach, to the point where you have trouble sleeping, then cut back one cup at a time until you sleep well. THAT is how much caffeine you need!

She does it, and feels great. She even commits to this whole caffeine thing to the point of buying caffeinated soap and caffeinated shampoo. She drinks it; she bathes and washes in it. She nibbles at espresso beans covered in dark chocolate, too. Another Rorschach remedy. Dark chocolate.

She craves it all, deeply, like it is the only thing that can fill a hole in her. It makes her want to bound, to move, to be a live wire of energy in the world.

Mama Lily hears Ilaha about in the kitchen and wakes, not in nearly same go get 'em state.

Lily twitters and drinks wine until late and wakes a bit fuzzy and under slept. She grabs at the French press and fills an awfully big cup with coffee. It is just the right temperature, having cooled a bit from when it was pressed, so she chugs.

Ilaha is humming and murmuring some words to a song that Lily recognises. She has all of her gear out on the island, three beautiful leather racket bags side by side filled with twenty one very carefully customised rackets, literally musically tuned to cover three tennis octaves. Ilaha n-tuple checks how they are arranged, inside the bag, in the soft-lock slots, and then zips shut all three bags through the musical scale.

Ilaha has not let the player pack she is told she needs out of her sight since she got it from Harmon. Her other gear, clothes and what not, are in a matching sling bag Harmon gives her, just beautiful, with her name etched into the leather and "Wimbledon 2018 - Gentlemen's Singles - Ilaha Tudor" right below it.

Ilaha nearly cries when she slings the bag over her shoulder, at how it fits, how it feels, how it looks. This item, above all else, no matter what may come, is an artifact she will keep and cherish. It is likely she will have it on her person every day of her life.

Ilaha keeps on murmuring along to the song she is singing for much longer than the song should last. Lily half hears it, sure she recognises it. Ilaha is caught in an earworm loop, unaware and not caring at all, because she doesn't know the words. Lily begins listening, closer and closer, to unlock the secret of the murmur worm

"Ilaha," she demands, "Sing it louder. What is that?"

Ilaha blushes and resists.

"No!" Ilaha squeals. "I didn't even realise. It's way too embarrassing. No way."

Lily insists, and Ilaha caves in. Doing her best impression of an unknown song she hears that sticks in her brain and now will not let her alone, she does her best.

"Born and then bye you … Born and then bye you … Born and then bye you," Ilaha drones.

Lily slaps her hands. She knew it! Ilaha must have heard it at random, because Lily's vinyl is shut away somewhere.

Coming to life now, Lily climbs up onto the island and performs a cappella.

Lily belts out a passionate rendition of *Born on the Bayou* for herself and Ilaha, lifting her volume and antics word by word. She loves it, losing herself altogether into this moment, this shared musical ever warm.

Lily really gets into it, to Ilaha's delight. All at once Lily comes to full life, her biggest form, filling the kitchen and the house and Ilaha as well, with energy and verve. There is no more fuzz. There is no unslept sleep. There is life.

Pure life.

Lily runs through the whole song, and there is never a moment where it is creepy or uncomfortable. She finishes and Ilaha gives her a raucous standing ovation.

Her earworm extinguished.

"That was great!! So great!!! You can really really sing, Mama Lily!!! You could win Magic Dust!!!! Wow!!!!!" Ilaha is frankly caught off guard by it, and Lily is a little bit insulted.

"Win Magic Dust?" Lily exclaims, "Are you kidding, little girl? I've already gone multi-platinum!"

Lily defends her professional self realizing that those days have maybe passed, and that poor Ilaha is a bit young to be a Lily Lacey fan. To even know who Lily Lacey is, perhaps. She is Mama Lily. Real person. Not celebrity.

"Mama Lily, I'd like to head out. I want to be at the site as soon as I can to get everything in order." Lily gulps the last of her coffee and heads off to shower and dress.

Ilaha asks her if she'd like tea for the road.

"Sure," Lily tells her. "That would be great."

Ilaha opens the cabinet and grabs at tea bags. Lily, feeling a bit saucy and confrontational in the face of being written off by her youthful daughter, pulls her own version of a "Brooks was here" before leaving the kitchen.

"F#%$ your tea bags, Ilaha. Use the tea caddy!" Lily declares cheekily.

Ilaha starts, completely missing any reference.

Taking Mama Lily literally, and a bit surprised by the cursing, she puts back the tea bags and finds the tea caddy to make loose tea, for the road.

Oblivious in her youth.

Akiyama

Murray agrees to play Ilaha.

He is very much deferential to the wishes of The Crown.

The committee approaches him to get a sense of how he feels about it. It could be a circus, it could be too easy and an undermining farcical warm up, it could be disrespectful. Murray is revered at the AELTC, after all, and the committee will not insult him by trying to manufacture artificial excitement.

He gracefully consents.

It is assumed Ilaha will lose to Murray, round one, and that from there the interest level in the event will follow from a bit higher starting level than it otherwise may. Good publicity and a freebie bump in ratings.

Murray and Ilaha are scheduled to play at prime time, early evening, late afternoon, depending on when the earlier matches complete. Ilaha makes use of the ladies locker room facilities. She has never met Murray, but knows all about him, of course. She is told that they are starting in ten minutes and to gather her gear. She zips up her three racket bags, wears one as a backpack, and picks up the other two one in each hand.

Ilaha is waved into the hallway leading to Centre Court. She walks to an area from which she and Murray will go onto court. He is there. Tall, but not surprisingly so. A much smaller man than Harmon. He turns to greet Ilaha. Smiles wide and extends his hand, introduces himself.

"I'm Andy Murray, nice to meet you." They shake hands, and Ilaha responds in kind.

"Ilaha Tudor thanks. Nice to meet you." Harmon tells her to keep exchanges to a minimum. Just be polite and move onto your work. She does.

Ilaha places the two racket bags that she is holding in her hands onto the floor. When the handlers tell the players it is time to go onto court Murray turns and reaches for one of the bags.

"Let me help you with one of those," he offers.

It is a genuine act of politesse. It is definitely not intended as an insult in any way. Just a natural instinctive kindness and obligation for a man like Murray, from a certain station in Britain and in a public place where there are expectations upon him.

Ilaha goes red hot.

"No," she barks.

Murray pauses not exactly sure what is happening.

"Would ya offer to carry a man's bag? Don't touch my f#%$ing gear. I will carry it," she growls.

Silence. This is exactly what Wimbledon does not want. Any sort of ugly socially sensitive skirmish. This is to be a friendly barrier-breaking formality. Not some sort of steel cage death match. Murray, truly sorry, immediately stands upright and apologises.

"I am very, very sorry. Honest. It was just an instinct. I did not mean at all to insult," Murray apologises.

Ilaha does not feel sympathy, none. She feels aggrieved in a very real way that she will never forget or let go of.

Yes, my brain understands. You have instincts. Instincts that tell you the woman with the womb is supposed to be helped by you, the man, because she cannot carry on by herself.

Ilaha stays red hot.

"You worry about you; I can take care of me and my gear." Ilaha picks up both racket bags, stalks past Murray and the officials from the tournament, and marches across the court to her assigned bench. She puts her equipment down and opens water.

"ILAHA," Harmon shouts. Centre Court goes silent from a state of quiet befuddled murmur. He is standing, at full height, in her box. Mama Lily next to him, small in every way by comparison. He summons Ilaha to the box.

"What happened?" Harmon demands.

Ilaha tells him about the incident. Murray tried to help her with one of her rackets bags.

Only for her ears, Harmon instructs her.

Ilaha appears comatose, and Harmon will not settle on her not having heard him.

"ILAHA," he deeply growls.

Everybody hears that. She snaps to.

Once again, only for her, very specific instructions. Ilaha looks Harmon in the eyes to confirm she understands.

Ilaha goes back to her bench and sits, furious, hot, and pulsating. She drinks water and clenches her hands. Murray is standing on court waiting for her to warm up.

Everybody in the crowd is watching, uncomfortable, unsure, waiting for they know not what. The whole thing is very odd, because the crowd did not actually witness the incident in the tunnel. Only slowly is what happened filtering through the crowd, thanks to the Matrix in every hand.

The chair umpire finally addresses Ilaha, over the microphone.

"Ms. Tudor you are to warm up." Ilaha says she is ready to play. The chair persists. "You are to warm. It is courtesy."

"No."

Murray passes from guilt to near ire. He moves toward Ilaha, onto her court, and yells at her.

"Enough. Let's hit," he demands.

She stands and stares right at him. Glares right into him. Right through him.

"Warm yourself, wanker."

The crowd falls into uncontrolled laughter.

She sits and Murray stands there frozen. If she is a man, he charges. As it is, he is stuck. *I can't punch her in the throat, but I am gonna destroy her.* He summons his hitting partner onto court and quickly warms up.

Ilaha is summoned to the net with Murray. They stand for uncomfortable pictures, toss for serve, and go through the pre-match motions in cold rage. Ilaha wins the toss and elects to receive. They go to their benches, swig water, Ilaha selects her racket, and then onto court.

276

In Ilaha's box, Mama Lily is completely unsure of what is going on and very much emotional.

"Harmon are you daft?" she accosts him. "What are you at? Telling her not to warm up? Telling her to pick a fight with Murray? Are you all there?" She punches him.

Harmon laughs and pulls her ear to his mouth. He whispers an explanation that brings a huge smile to her face. He explains his plan, she laughs out loud, and they bump fists. A photographer catches that moment, perfectly.

Murray serves to start the match. His first is a rocket down the T that from his racket he knows is not coming back. It hits the line, explodes off the grass and …

… Lands right in Ilaha's string bed. She is there, ready, inside the baseline, fully set, and unloading into a backhand that goes back over the net right at Murray even harder than he hits the serve. Her ball darts right down into the baseline, and he is unable to even get a racket on it.

A hundred in, one twenty out, Murray, she mumbles to herself.

0-15 …

… Ilaha walks right at the chair. Murray on his ad side preparing to serve almost doesn't notice her addressing the chair.

"I challenge his serve," she declares.

Murray, and the chair, and the entire crowd are uncomprehending. She won the point. Why in the world would she challenge?

The chair announces "player challenge" over the PA. PerfOculus plays the tape and sure enough, the serve is out. By a millimeter. So, so close, but out.

The crowd gasps.

Instead of 0-15, Murray is back at deuce court on second serve. Murray has never seen such a thing, or even heard of such a thing, and he shifts back to deuce side in a bit of a fog. Ilaha is already in position, ready to play his second. The crowd is silent.

Murray just keeps bouncing his ball, looking up at Ilaha, ruminating, bouncing his ball, setting but not serving.

Finally he stops bouncing the ball and stands upright. Takes a deep breath. Tries to settle down. He looks across at Ilaha now, and she steps into the court, inside her baseline, stands fully upright, and motions toward herself from outstretched arms like Muhammad Ali on a hot night in Manila.

"Come on then, let's play," she provokes.

The crowd simply erupts.

Coming in, Ilaha is an oddity and an amusement and a soft spectacle. Ladbrokes and the like have her at ten thousand to one to win the match. They are loath to make odds for the tournament. In that instant, Ilaha takes control of the stadium, and now, at home, Murray finds himself on the way to becoming an opponent of Ilaha and the whole Centre Court crowd.

Murray hits his second, another very strong serve, to Ilaha's forehand, wide, and she slams it back through his ad side down the line into the wall. It goes right past the line judge before said line judge can even move. Lucky not to be hit.

The crowd surges into the stratosphere of decibels. She plays one point, hits two shots that nobody on the planet, save Harmon, could ever hit, and the road ahead becomes clear.

TV is not broadcasting. Another match, on another court, has TV. Murray against the young lady is a storyline that is assumed away as 0/0/0 and they will just deliver a broadcast highlight later.

Very quickly the television broadcast producer rushes to send the A broadcast team into the Centre Court booth and picks up coverage. The team is brought up to speed, fast. *Her first backhand was hit at one hundred fourteen mph. Mph, not kmh. The forehand she hits back on second is one hundred twenty two mph. Mph. Nobody has hit a winner that hard all year. Men's or ladies'. She is serving now, up a break.*

Ilaha sets to serve, going through her routine like a machine. She sets her feet, steals a glance at Murray's feet, bends her knees presses her feet into the grass loads her torso begins her toss motion presses up off the ground pushes up into the air unwinds her core gets her racket arm into cocked position and then unleashes her strings into the ball.

Her serve hits the very middle of the service line and kicks high and hard right at Murray, who scurries aside and misplays a dead duck into the net.

The match is quick, and painful for Murray, until he becomes comfortably numb about halfway through the second set and resolves to just play out with dignity.

Ilaha is not broken or taken to deuce on serve. She hits a lot of aces and oodles of service winners. She never really plays into layer four and disposes of points on serve or at serve plus one in every game.

It is a drubbing. 6-1, 6-1, 6-0. Murray is gracious, and at net after the match, once again, he apologises for the ugliness prior to the match.

"You were a great gentleman and I am terribly proud to have played you," Ilaha tells him with complete sincerity. "You are a hero for me and it was an honor. Honest. I admire that you gave me your real fight and played me as an equal. You didn't have to do that. Really. I hope to go at it with you many times."

They speak too quietly for anyone to hear. A private conversation at Centre Court. Murray goes to his bench to gather up his gear, trying to be quick about it so he will not make Ilaha wait to leave court. Tradition dictates that the players walk off court together.

Murray stuffs his gear into his bag and stands. He is in pain. Plagued by injuries, but so tough, and so committed to Wimbledon, he plays without complaint. Suffering in silence. No excuses.

He is surprised to see that Ilaha is waiting for him, patiently, smiling and waving to the crowd.

She does not and will not shake any hands or sign anything on court. She simply curtseys for the Royal box. She has seen this walk off after battle ceremony and resolves to be quick about it for Murray.

She knows Murray hurts, but says nothing, out of respect. Harmon tips her off, before the match, his private insight.

Feel your own balance. Soak it in. He can't. He's hurt. Derive strength from that. The poor guy is gonna wilt. Tough bastard. He won't show it, but it will happen. Never say anything about this. Ever. He deserves his secret. Don't warm up with him. It just uses him up. Get him angry, he will feel better. It will be a fairer fight.

Murray approaches her, she reaches out for his hand, raises it above both their heads, and they walk off court to enormous clapping and cheers.

For the press, Murray is utterly eloquent.

She is an amazing player and I just didn't have answers for her shots. My best serves kept coming back hard, and all day I found myself in corners where there was only one really narrow escape. I am utterly impressed.

What did she say to you after the match?

She was gracious. I have unlimited respect for her and will not be surprised at all when she wins this tournament. It may not be this run, but one day, for sure.

Murray answers a few more questions and then exits. The press let him go easily enough as he is a former champion who is jettisoned in round one, a tough situation anyway, but also by the first female player in the men's. They let him off easy out of respect, but also out of a bit of greed.

They want Ilaha. So letting Murray go just means getting her.

Ilaha comes into the press room with Mama Lily. Many in the press corps knows who Lily is. A few oddballs have no idea but quickly catch on. She was a pop star in country. As soon as they sit, a scrum of questioning journos starts shouting to be called.

Ilaha handles the mic and gives it a go.

"I guess, hello, world," she starts, "I am Ilaha Tudor and this is my mum, Mama Lily. Some of you may know who she is." A chorus of laughs at her naïveté.

What happened before the match?

"I was nervous of course and excited to be going on court with Murray, a hero of mine since a little girl," Ilaha explains, "But I came here to win and something in me snapped when he reached for my bag. It made me feel like a girl, and when I play tennis I don't feel like a girl, I feel like the best player on the court. So I cursed at him over it."

You came out really strong, did the incident help you?

"I guess it did," Ilaha confirms, "I came out raring to go unlike my usual game. So yeah I suppose I shifted right into a higher gear."

A man in your box called you over before the match. What did you discuss?

"That is my coach, Harmon," Ilaha tells them, "He told me not to warm with Murray, so I didn't. It worked so well maybe I won't warm with anyone I play?"

Who is Harmon? Are you the only player he coaches?

"I met Harmon at the club in town where I live," Ilaha says, "Honest I don't know much about him beyond he knows everything about tennis. He has helped me a lot, and hopefully we can get through to a trophy here."

It all goes on for quite a while. A brand new phenomenon that beats the favored son of British tennis on Centre Court is a big, big story. To boot, Lily Lacey is her mum and sitting right there. They are onto her next.

I do not recall you having kids. Am I correct you had stillbirth? How are you now Ilaha's mum?

"Right well I found her outside Greengrass the night it burned down and I have had her ever since," Mama Lily tells them, hugging Ilaha. "She is my adopted daughter and I could not be more proud. She really put on a show today!"

Do you play?

"No!" she laughs, "Not at all. Not in a million years. I am awful. I used to toss balls to Ilaha as a little girl, for her to hit, but no, I never play."

Do you know anything about her coach?

"I know he knows everything about tennis, and everything else in the world from what I can tell," Lily snarks at Harmon, who is not visible. "Not sure where he is, my advice is to find him and ask him yourself."

The reporters go back and forth a bit from Mama Lily to Ilaha and finally, eventually, start to circle back over covered ground. At that point, Harmon walks out from behind the curtain around the dais and dismisses everyone.

"That will do scribes. This won't be her last rodeo. You will get another shot at her soon enough," he tells everybody in the room.

They clamor to shout questions at Harmon, which he has little interest in answering.

As Mama Lily and Ilaha rise to leave, however, Harmon spots one woman, dark skinned, in fashionable modest garb, head cover, being dignified but communicating clearly a desire to ask a question. He addresses her, in perfect Arabic.

"You speak Arabic, yes?" he asks.

She smiles wide and confirms that yes, she does, in Arabic.

"Ask away, please," Harmon tells her, still in Arabic. "I will tell you whatever you'd like to know."

"Is she an Arab?" the woman asks.

Harmon looks at her and smiles as if he is Buddha. His smile and manner is affecting the room, the way they say the Dalai Lama moves people.

They all stare at him as he answers the woman, in perfect Arabic.

"Tell your readers that yes, she is an orphan of Arabic milk and water, brave like the Prophet," Harmon instructs the woman. "She plays with the spirit of a warrior and she is loyal like a blood brother."

The woman records it all, so does not need notes. The whole thing in Arabic, none of the press understands a word.

The biggest scoop of the day, they miss it.

Harmon follows up with an invitation.

"Please come find me in the player lot in a few minutes. You should cover this story," he tells the woman.

A few minutes later the woman is waiting for him when Ilaha, Mama Lily and Harmon exit for the car. She approaches them and introduces herself as Tasmin, shaking hands and mentioning to Lily that she is a fan. Harmon puts all of Ilaha's gear into the rear of the Rover and then turns to Tasmin.

"You must be anywhere?" he asks her, in English now. She says no, she is free.

"Great, Lily, you have a passable guest room?" Harmon confirms.

Mama Lily is in a great mood but has no idea a guest is staying. Mortified, she blanches, but not at having a guest. She likes Tasmin right off and wants her to stay, but, well.

"The room is a bit of a mess, so, I suppose, maybe, but please forgive me if it's a bit rough," Mama Lily pre-apologises.

Harmon assures Mama Lily and Tasmin that the room is fine, they will clean it up, and tells them all to get in the Rover and let's go.

Al-sīra al-Nabawiyya

Tasmin sits next to Ilaha in the back for the drive. Tasmin is tall and fit. She was a serious tennis player prior to uni.

Injury puts her off from playing past youth, and she goes onto high brow classical education in Britain then onto the press corps.

She does not normally cover tennis, but she is tipped off that the story of a lifetime is to be had on Centre Court at Wimbledon today. She loves going to the AELTC, for the tournament, and the tip makes for a great excuse to see something she never imagines she will ever see.

It isn't the "she is a girl" part; it is the "I can't believe I just saw that" part that amazes her.

Tasmin has a trained eye and appreciates what she sees Ilaha doing. The girl is powerful. More powerful than Murray. And Murray is hardly a soft hitting player.

The data bears it out.

Ilaha's average first serves one hundred twenty three miles per hour. Seconds at one hundred eight miles per hour. Ground strokes averaging over eighty miles per hour from both sides. She hits a lot of winners, forces a lot of errors, and spends most of the match inside the baseline.

Imagine a boxer.

They step into the ring, and they spend all night getting in close to their opponent and landing hard punches to the head. Clean shots into the ribs. Not jabbing away glove into glove, moving around doing a lot of watching and waiting. Intently moving forward into their opponent and forcing

286

wide openings through which damaging strikes can pass into an exposed body.

Ilaha does this to Murray.

If this is a boxing match, there is an early knockout. In tennis that doesn't happen, the knockout victim suffers through at least three sets of micro KO's point by point. Every winner, forced error, ace and put away its own small scale KO.

Tasmin is very interested in Ilaha, and does her best right away to engage her.

"Ilaha I am in love with your racket bags. Honest. The coolest I have ever seen. Where did you get them?" she asks.

Ilaha tells her that Harmon gave them to her. She explains all about the soft-lock slots inside the bags and how they were arranged to mimic a musical scale, across three octaves.

At this point Harmon looks into the rear view and visually commands that Tasmin take no notes.

"This is all off the record, right? The technical stuff about her gear. No trade secrets, yet," he demands.

Tasmin understands and keeps on with Ilaha.

This Harmon knows things.

His language, clean and easy, for her reporter sense, speaks volumes. They barely leave London and Tasmin understands what this is all about. She has been selected, by Harmon, to ride a tidal wave of his creation, with her help, into a place that one way or another is bound to be very exciting.

The car pulls into the drive at Elysium and stops. The ride passes quickly, and Tasmin engages Ilaha into becoming a new friend.

She sees more than a bit of a forgotten self in Ilaha, a brown skinned Brit who loves tennis and grows up with privilege. Ilaha is so much better at the game than Tasmin ever was, of course. But as de facto outsiders inside the Kingdom, Tasmin feels a compulsion to mentor and befriend and be an ally.

She is sure Harmon bet on this.

Ilaha bounds inside and goes to work on coffee. Harmon hands her a thumb drive and she takes her coffee and her tape and data and goes off to the computer.

It is a ritual, her schedule, which she is ready to compress into shorter time now, in the midst of a tournament. You follow a match with tape and data. Then you work at the holes until they are plugged. Then you prep for next if you can.

Harm∞n E

There is another player following the same ritualistic process, in the village in Wimbledon, in a flat that he has occupied every year during his journey to become the greatest player of all time.

Roger Federer wins Wimbledon seven times. The flat he rents every year has previously been rented annually by Pete Sampras, who wins the event seven times. Between them, these two men dominate the event for decades, one GOAT passing the torch to the next GOAT, and always while staying in the very same flat.

Inside that flat Federer is studying tape. Not his own tape, and not tape on his next opponent. He knows the book cold on everyone in the field …

… Except this one.

Federer watches Ilaha, focuses on her feet.

He takes to watching the other player's feet in two thousand two. He is a rising professional, twenty two, who has not broken through in the Grand Slams. Makes a couple quarter final rounds the prior year, appears poised to break into the high ranks, but in oh two he is fumbling.

Mid-year after a fast exit at the French Open he takes time off and leaves the tennis circuit for Wisconsin, USA, of all places.

A Chicago area finance magnate with whom Federer's family is acquainted invites Federer's dad and mum to a huge scale annual shindig he hosts at his historic Lake Geneva mansion. Roger, having nothing to do, really, is asked along by his dad, and decides why not?

The property is simply beautiful and he needs to be away from tennis, if even for a few days. It is a great reprieve, really, from self imposed pressure he is creating by being stuck inside the tennis machine.

In Lake Geneva he is basically anonymous. Certainly not the headliner of the event. He makes his way around the grounds, around the lake, and among the guests, and enjoys being treated like a real person with no expectations baggage.

The property has a tennis court, grass, a real rarity for Midwest USA. After a few days of having not so much as touched a racket Roger makes his way over to the court where something of a crowd is being delighted by quite an exhibition.

A very large man wielding a Wilson Pro Staff six point o St. Vincent racket is hitting serves at coins that are placed inside the service box by a group of children on the other side of the net. It is a game, of sorts.

Federer goes to courtside and watches, amazed. The man tosses to serve, a boy calls out "Eleven!" and the man hits a hard kicking serve that hits a coin. The boy runs to retrieve the coin and holds it up.

The number "11" is written on it with a Sharpie.

The other kids laugh and razz the boy, who takes the coin and deposits it into a large clear glass jar with a number of other such coins. The boy's mother calls to him and instructs him to fetch a matching coin from her, which he takes back to the jar and drops in with the others.

A man next to Federer explains what is going on.

"They started doing this last year," he tells him, "It's a fundraiser. You gamble a coin by writing a number on it and placing it inside the service box, number up. When your turn comes up, you call the number during toss, and if Harmon hits the coin you donate it. If he misses, he donates two."

Federer looks into the jar.

"Those are krugerrands," he observes with surprise.

"Yeah," the man says, "They raise a lot of money doing this. Harmon will stay out here until every last coin is wiped off the court."

Federer watches, for hours, staying on until that very last coin is swept off the court by one of this man Harmon's serves. By the time he is done there are multiple jars filled with krugerrands sitting courtside on a table.

Harmon walks off court to the table and Federer approaches him.

"That was really something," he observes. "Are you a player? I am not familiar with you, and I play a bit."

Harmon laughs a "HA!" at Federer.

"Play a bit. Sandbagger," he goads, "I know who you are, I just watched you wipe out of the French Open. You are a better player than that."

Harmon dumps out the krugerrands into a large cloth bag. He lifts and moves the bag, apparently assessing its weight.

"Half a million bucks," Harmon says aloud.

Federer does not quite understand what he just heard.

"There is that much money in the bag?" he asks.

Harmon repeats it.

"Gold is three hundred twenty two dollars per ounce, there are sixteen hundred seven krugs in the bag, five hundred seventeen thousand four hundred fifty four dollars," he states.

Harmon sits on a bench next to the court. Federer sits next to him.

"How do you do that?" he asks Harmon, astonished.

"I know how much the bag weighs and what gold costs, and I multiply," Harmon says flatly.

Federer doesn't understand. He means something else.

"No, hit the coins with serve. How do you do that?" he asks again.

It would be one thing if Harmon had just hit any given coin from the coins scattered in the service box.

But he didn't just have to do that.

He must hit a particular coin after hearing its number named during his toss. So he has to hear that number, see which coin has that number on it, then hit his serve at that coin and not miss. They say every miss costs him two coins.

"I listen for the number, find the right coin, and hit it," Harmon replies blandly.

The whole thing is surreal, as if happening in a dream. Federer aspires to be as good as Sampras and he will, but at that moment he feels as if he will never ever under any circumstance match this Harmon.

He won't.

Harmon observes Federer is sinking fast into a low point. He doesn't want that. He is not one to crush a spirit. So he stands, hands his racket over, and indicates Federer should go out onto the court. Harmon fetches another identical racket from his gear bag and takes a place on the other side of the net.

"Let's hit, I'll tell you a secret. Not how to hit the coins. But good." Harmon drops a ball and sends it over to Federer.

They hit the ball back and forth for quite some time. Federer is not used to Harmon's gear, very very heavy, so he is more than a bit conscious about how he hits and is not his clear minded best self.

Harmon watches Federer's eyes, to assess where Federer is looking during the course of a rally. He catches on right away that Federer is very quick to focus onto the ball. He has certainly been taught this, and does it with deliberate discipline. It is not the way to go. It is a marginal, reactive way.

Not a way in the sense that one should have a way for getting through life. There is at least one better way.

Harmon uncorks a vicious forehand into the tape at the top of the net that falls over the net into Federer's court. He approaches the net and summons Federer.

"You do a great job of seeing the ball," Harmon observes, "The problem is you are missing a great game by doing that.

293

It is killing you. You have no idea how badly it is killing you."

Federer is immediately defensive. He has been taught to see the ball, to play the ball, and he does. It takes great effort to immediately see the ball and immediately move to play it.

Harmon anticipates a defensive response and laughs it off.

"You are giving up the ghost before ever chasing after it. Come on, I'll show you first. Let's play out some points. You serve." Harmon hands the balls to Federer and takes position to return.

Federer builds his game around a powerful service in the manner of Sampras. He takes understandable pride in his service game, and like the young Sampras, has foregone greater success at the youth levels to cultivate a bigger game for a longer run. He has yet to encounter many if any players he cannot overwhelm with his service game.

Federer sets to serve from the deuce side. He goes into his motion and tosses, winds the racket into the ball, and sends a really great serve into a terribly tough spot down the T.

Harmon is well ready when the ball gets to him, a few feet inside the baseline, and he hits back a very solid topspin one-hand backhand right into Federer's forehand strike zone. Federer sets himself and unloads into the ball, hitting a missile deep and hard into Harmon's deuce corner.

Harmon is there, as if waiting and he unloads a severe and heavy topspin forehand right into Federer's backhand strike zone.

Federer lines up his shot and simply explodes into a perfect backhand at a very sharp angle to Harmon's advantage sideline.

Harmon is already there, and he fine tunes into position and actually runs around the shot to hit an even more severe topspin forehand through Federer's ad court into the fence beside the court.

This process repeats a few times. Federer is toyed with by Harmon until Harmon decides to terminate the point in his favor.

Harmon approaches the net, and Federer meets him.

"You hit me with your best shots, right? How did that go?" he asks. Federer, apoplectic, has no response. "You play the best players in the world. They play full time and have every advantage for being in top form. So how does a guy who stands around yelling on a trading floor all week beat you like that?"

Federer is stumped. He feels weak, hopeless, and pointless. This is not Harmon's intent, but he understands it.

"You have settled on an inferior priority," Harmon instructs, "Tracking the ball the length of its run is pointless. Never, ever watch the ball for where it is; focus on where it is going to be."

Federer takes this in as some sort of wisecrack truism, and is inclined to get upset.

But then he pauses, just a moment, and reconsiders.

This man has just played him like a fiddle, honest, and in the face of some of the best shots he can hit he is drummed out of points mercilessly. Harmon has him on every shot, from the serve on, and mocks him by hitting right back into his strike zone. He invites Federer to give him his best and he just brushes it off.

"You need to see the ball for only a moment. And you don't even need to see it to know where it is going," Harmon leads him, "Think about it, think about your own shots. When do you determine where the ball is going? When you are hitting it? Right before? When? When the racket starts forward? When you push off the ground? When?"

Federer instantly sees light. Not fully comprehending, but he sees brightness. His spirit lifts, as it turns out, for good.

"I get it!! I get it!! The feet!" he practically shouts.

Harmon articulates a feeling Federer has rarely had, but has had on occasion. In sports it is often known as being "in the zone" but in fact, as Harmon explains, it is actually about having the right moment focus.

Athletes must anticipate and confirm, not watch and react.

"There is a big, giant, enormous difference," Harmon preaches. "One is a proactive attack oriented act. The other is reactive and defense oriented."

Harmon does not believe in holding ground, he is a practitioner of gaining ground.

Federer insists on playing more points, and Harmon agrees. They go back and forth, playing out points and alternating service on breaks. Harmon is nearly impossible to break so they adjust the game to changing serve after four consecutive points, rather than handicap by allowing only one serve or some such scheme.

After about an hour, in a great rally, Harmon unleashes into a backhand that hits the tape and lands on Federer's side. He waves off the start of the next point and approaches net. Federer meets him there. Harmon extends his hand.

"Nice run. I think you will get the shift quickly. Look ahead, the other player gives away their plan well before they hit," he reiterates.

Federer is bursting with energy now, very very eager to get back to work and focus himself on a new way of playing. He has a way. He will read, and he will eventually deceive.

Walking away from the courts, Federer addresses a bit of a peeve that comes up during their play.

"You know, you hit a number of balls into the tape that carried to my side," Federer observes. "Players usually offer some indication or apology for that, to appease karma and own up to luck."

Harmon stops, turns, and stares.

"If it was luck, I would do that," he asserts.

Federer, once again, is uncomprehending.

"What do you mean?" he asks.

"Did any of my balls fall back onto my side?" Harmon asks him.

A simple question. Federer reaches into his mind and realises that no, not a single ball falls back onto Harmon's side.

"Well," Harmon follows through, "Maybe it wasn't luck?"

No Eyed Man

Round two is greeted with a much bigger buzz than the match against Murray.

Tasmin's ongoing bio of Ilaha is well on its way to becoming an historically important biography, and getting front page coverage. The Goddess of Greengrass and her wild ride across the gender line are driving the news cycle.

Ilaha is going viral.

In a mosque in Birmingham a group of angry men, very upset, are bickering in Arabic and passing that day's paper back and forth. On the cover, full page, is a picture of Ilaha following through on a serve, in perfect form, strong, powerful, and beautiful.

Her skirt has hiked up in the photo, and the entirety of her beautiful, toned, muscular thighs and derriere can be seen. She is not displaying any skin above her knees, but her form is clearly visible.

By the racier "sex sells" standards of the western media this photo is incredibly tame, but to these men, in this mosque, it is blasphemy.

The girl is named 'goddess' this is an outrage!! With that name out in public like that, showing off her ass! Allah himself should smite her but he leaves us to do his earthly work.

The words and the sentiment come from a blind sheikh. He has not actually seen the picture, of course, but it is described to him by trusted minions. Over and over, over and over, the sheer beauty of Ilaha's ass is described to the man.

298

Tell me about her thighs, again, and the curve of her glute, how her quads gently and subtly connect into her uncovered knees.

Tell me again about her skin, he demands.

His minions tell him it is perfectly smooth and the color of freshly poured café au lait, light.

And her face. Tell me about her cheekbones, and her brows. Her nose. Is it narrow?

They assure the sheikh that yes, she has prominent high cheeks, and perfectly arranged brows. Her nose is ideal, exquisite, blessed, they promise.

The sheikh is powerful and devout. Righteous. Openly at war with the west. He does not want to assimilate. He desires caliphate. To conquer Britain, and then mainland Europe, to succeed his ancestor the Prophet Muhammad.

The great blind caliph.

Everywhere one goes in the west, images of women in various appalling states of undress are displayed in public. Not to mention the women themselves.

There are actually retail stores that openly sell intimates to them! Western women shamelessly walk the streets or ride the tube carrying bags from such stores, probably containing every example of erotic and provocative garb.

Out in the open!

The blind sheikh demands that a minion describe it all to him, right there, in public.

Tell me about that blonde woman, in the yoga pants. About her bust. Is it prominent? Does it heave when she walks?

She is jogging, sheikh.

Do her buttocks flex with each step? Her breasts, do they heave when she exhales?

She is very fit, sheikh, you can see her muscles flexing, yes.

And her labia. Can you actually make them out through her yoga pants?

Yes, sheikh, they confirm they can make out the woman's labia, nervous to be discussing the most intimate parts of a woman, even a heathen slut out for a jog, audibly in public.

The sheikh responds to Ilaha with great ire. Her back story cannot be confirmed, but given her name and her look and what the Muslim community knows of Greengrass, it is certain she has lost her way from Allah.

Very quickly a jihadist atmosphere builds up inside the mosque with Ilaha as the target. It is brought to the sheik's attention that Ilaha is to play today, at Wimbledon, late in the afternoon.

"We will not allow that," the sheikh announces.

Intifada

Ilaha arrives at the AELTC to more than a bit of pomp. The Rover pulls up, and attendants are quick to insist on fetching her gear from the back. Harmon steps in, with cash to tip, and insists that no, they cannot carry her gear. Show her to her locker, thanks. He gets her gear.

Harmon tells Lily and Tasmin to don their player passes and head into the lounge area. He takes Ilaha's gear to the locker room and then heads to security.

Harmon finds the person in charge. They have established a relationship. Prior to the event, prior to her completely unexpected win over Murray and today's highly anticipated match, Harmon finds the person, in a pub, and sits down with them over pints.

Harmon explains how they are really, really, a key person in what is coming. How nobody can possibly be prepared for what a run through the men's draw by Ilaha, the Goddess of Greengrass, can cause. He puts the person at ease but also at attention.

"This is not about probable," Harmon implores, "It is about possible. Wimbledon is sleepy, insulated, not perhaps fully prepared for the, well, larger social impact this may have."

Harmon speaks to the person on their terms, with respect and understanding of their role. He discusses the matter in terms of risks. Unknown knowns, and known unknowns. The person sees the light.

Harmon gives the person a very much unexpected heads up. More important, Harmon gives them specific tells to watch for that will precede any real concern. Now, today,

Harmon is in the person's office expressing some of those concerns. Harmon hands the person his phone.

"Look, look at all the Heil cars in the village today. I have been tracking Heil in the village for weeks. And sure, the event should create a bump in activity," Harmon acknowledges, "But look at who is doing the driving."

The person taps onto car icons, and notices a lot of brown faces, young men. All with beards. Harmon concedes that yes, that is perhaps an outlier, but look closer. The person scans the profiles … None of these men has given many rides. Some of them have given no rides. Some of them, too many, are driving on their first day with Heil.

"Here's the real concern," Harmon goes on, "Not a single one of the dozen or so Heil drivers out there circling around not picking anyone up is also registered with Rickshaw, best I can tell." Harmon pauses as the person registers this, but not quite at the deeper level of meaning.

"Nobody in a Heil car doesn't also drive for Rickshaw," Harmon explains, "Driving is a yield game. You take whoever is there to drive right now. Two sources of rides make twice as much sense, and every Heil driver doubles up. Assuming they are serious about making money," he points out. "Also, on the way in I saw a bunch of Heil stickers on cars that were parked and unattended. Cars Heil would never approve. More Heil cars than I see on the app."

Security at the stately and serene AELTC is not MI6.

They deal mostly with people who fall sick, the rare drunk, the even more uncommon rabble rouser, and maybe, just maybe, specific concerns about a stalker. Even a stalker is generally a situation where the player in question already has a top security team that is simply informing the event what they are dealing with, as a courtesy.

The security person feels their pulse kick into the next gear and goes to work on securing the event. They start by calling in reserve staff, and then call a select few personnel into a meeting to reassign them.

The security person contacts the local police, passes on their intel, and specifically mentions the scheduled match that Ilaha is to play and when it is to occur. The police contact takes the info, perhaps not terribly seriously, at first, but as things are explained urgency prevails.

One Man Builds a Bomb, One Woman Plays a Game

Harmon catches up with Lily and Tasmin in the player lounge. They are surrounded by a crowd, all of whom are excited about the match, about Lily, about Tasmin.

Ilaha is a cause celeb.

Harmon stands at the back of the gathering, above the gathering, so big, watching the gaggle giggle.

Lily is recognised by many of the people there, as a pop star and as a child of her petite prominent parents. They hold no grudge that she is militant Labour. In such settings the Pimm's and the caviar, the couture and the Chanel No. 5 cleanse away the grime of democracy. Tasmin is frequently in these circles and appears to know everyone socially. Let alone everyone who she is aware of as a reporter.

Lily and Tasmin see Harmon, at the same time, towering over the gathering, and they go silent. They look up, smiling, in a modest state of joy, not completely cognizant of what is going on at so many commingling levels. Those gathered hush and turn to follow their gaze.

The crowd turns away from Lily and Tasmin to stare at Harmon. He looks them over, and then reaches above and through them for Lily's hand, then Tasmin's hand. The crowd parts and Harmon, Lily, and Tasmin cross through. Harmon leads them over to the bar leaving the gathering behind to gossip among themselves.

"Three Pimm's," Harmon instructs the bartender, handing over a hundred as he does. The tender acknowledges the generosity, makes three perfect Pimm's, and serves them.

"To Ilaha," Harmon toasts.

"To Ilaha," Tasmin repeats, raising her glass.

"To Ilaha," Mama Lily three peats, "And to this club!!! This place is posh. I feel so silly about never coming out before."

Harmon finishes off his Pimm's in one gulp, ice and garnish and all, but Lily and Tasmin only sip. The drink is wonderful, and the day is shaping up to be among the best days they will enjoy.

The three of them make their way into Centre Court to the player's box. Ilaha plays, once again, in front of a full crowd and at prime time.

Her match starts on time, and it is easy going for her. Her opponent is not in the same category as Murray, simply cannot answer any of the questions she is posing to him. He is a bit flamboyant and acts out repeatedly, but it is very clear this is simply an expression of frustration over his own play, and not directed at Ilaha. To her credit, she simply goes about her business and accommodates her opponent's fits with great patience.

She wins the first set 6-1 in about half an hour.

During crossovers her opponent makes it a practice to apologise for his mini tantrums. He understands his own shortcomings and cannot go off game just because it is Wimbledon and he is playing a viral phenomenon. Ilaha is a great, great player, but she is also rapidly becoming a real celebrity. Genuinely famous. Certainly bigger than tennis.

Her opponent is a lowly journeyman player trying to muddle his way into a living, relying largely on doubles and development circuit events to get by. He is hardly ready to even play at Wimbledon, having gotten in through a convoluted spot filling process, and he is actually losing badly in the first round when his opponent comes up lame and must retire. So through to the second round by default.

After the end of the second set, 6-1, Ilaha is sitting on her bench drinking water and thinking through her list of checks. Feel? Great. What's working? Serve, moving forward, a pretty long list today. What can keep working? Serve and pushing in. What is not working? Don't rush through, don't try to shorten points.

Her list of checks is being assessed diligently when a loud BOOM! is heard outside the stadium. The boom is quickly followed by sirens, and distant shouting, and then gunshots.

The crowd begins to buzz. Almost immediately the twitter sphere goes wild with tweets, including video. Outside the AELTC, in the village, not very far away, a car is driven into a crowded square and a bomb inside it is set off. It is a disaster, with many presumed dead.

Unsure what is supposed to happen, the crowds inside the AELTC and the players grow anxious. Security takes over the PA and all visual displays.

It is announced that the matches will go on.

An attack in the village has been perpetrated. All inside this event are safe and are being asked to stay calm and on the grounds. No exit will be permitted until further notice. Matches will continue, and until exit is allowed concessions, excluding souvenirs, will be complimentary.

Ilaha looks over to her box and Harmon summons her.

"Just think about the ball, Ilaha. Just play the ball. One more set and then you can think about anything else." Ilaha understands the practical wisdom in this and does exactly that.

She finishes off her opponent expeditiously, at 6-1. Her service games go very quickly and his go with ease of score but not without self-imposed drama. He presses, he really, really presses hard, to hold, but in the end the mismatch is just too great and Ilaha handles everything he has with complete ease.

As the matches progress patrons spend more time on their phones than watching the tennis. Social networks literally explode. The events outside the AELTC become clear, but official reports reject the earliest internet rumors.

There is an attempt to attack Wimbledon that is foiled before it is carried out, thanks to a brilliant insight by Wimbledon security and London's terror specialty police.

Heil cars are to be used to plow into crowds and set off bombs. They attempt to plow through onto the Wimbledon grounds.

The signal is a Heil request to be driven to Mecca 24231, Saudi Arabia.

London's terror squad is closely monitoring Heil the whole day, and recognises the ride request as certainly bogus.

As soon as Heil cars in the area that have been idling and not picking up riders mobilise, teams of officers swoop in and surround them.

The explosion occurs when one of the Heil cars tries to escape police and the driver decides to carry out an ad hoc suicide mission to kill as many people as possible in a desperate effort to salvage his failed intifada.

He manages to set off his faulty bomb, badly burns himself, and then dies suffering great pain within hours. There are no other fatalities.

On the dark web the usual suspects immediately take credit for the attack, boasting over a phantom death count and pledging to continue the fight in the name of Allah, and their blind sheikh.

In real time, Ilaha is not linked in any way to the attack. The motive for the attack and the specifics regarding the real target are not disclosed, not yet. Harmon has an idea, a suspicion, but keeps it to himself.

Harmon protects Ilaha, Mama Lily, and Tasmin, keeping them safe and together with him in a strictly members only private club room deep inside the AELTC. No non-member has ever been in the room in the absence of a member. Staff does not even enter the room unless a member is present.

Harmon secures access by obtaining membership to the AELTC for Lily.

Harmon suggests locking down the grounds to Club security should a worst case occur. He insists on footing the bill for gratis concessions. He pays Lily's membership for life.

He offers the AELTC a deal they cannot refuse.

Nobody is ever to find out. At Harmon's insistence. Tell Lily an anonymous patron gifted her membership. Make up a story. Officially deny Harmon is involved if it ever comes up.

Lily and Tasmin are smart phone wizards, and between them they paint the entire picture, in detail.

A radical Islamic jihadist group associated with a notorious Birmingham mosque organises the attack. An infamous blind sheikh takes offense at Ilaha's attire in her match against Murray. As retribution for the sexual degradation of a Muslim girl in public, the blind sheikh means to destroy the infidel and Wimbledon, a decadent symbol of western godlessness.

Ilaha does not understand. She is aware of what she wore; she is wearing the same outfit now, and feels very strongly that it is exclusively utilitarian.

Ilaha always wears the same thing.

Like Einstein's suits, Ilaha has seven identical tennis outfits, all white, modest really, hardly revealing at all by western standards.

Her top is a crew neck T, very modest, not in any way fashionable or revealing. Her skirt is not short. If anything, it is perhaps a bit longer than ideal for the purpose of moving on a tennis court. Her spandex undershorts run down her thighs to a few inches above the knee.

She takes this whole thing hard, at first, feeling responsible for deaths, however absurd that really is, since one jihadist is the only casualty.

She wails, she heaves, and she despairs.

Why can't it just be about tennis? Why not just the ball and the points and the games?

Then she drifts into rage, very much aggrieved by the notion that anyone should co-opt her freedom to be as she chooses. Is she to don a burqa and play under a veil? Why can't she wear what she wears without facing a violent backlash?

Suddenly the whole notion of Islam occurs to her.

Am I a Muslim?

An odd thought, but she cannot shake the idea. Ilaha was found outside Greengrass clutching a white horse and talking about flying. Her name is Arabic; she has googled it, and based on what was known about who lived in Greengrass it is likely she is of Muslim descent. She has never practiced or followed, but she is probably of those people.

Harmon has nothing to say. A rarity, but right for the moment. Ilaha is confused and terrified and angry and needs his input.

"What the bloody hell is going on?" she pleads.

Harmon looks at her, extends his hand, which she takes, and just holds onto it. She keeps saying things, aloud, and Harmon, Mama Lily, and Tasmin watch her, silent.

"It's not my fault. It's tennis why would anyone attack a tournament? Am I supposed to withdraw now? What the f#%$?" she laments.

Harmon smiles gently at the cursing. Mama Lily smiles half giggling. Not funny, right, but Ilaha just said 'f#%$' so honestly WTF?

Tasmin is the one who breaks in.

"Ilaha, you are a symbol now and for some you are too big to ignore," she explains, "They have spoken, but you need not be silent. You have a voice. You can speak."

Harmon nods. Mama Lily is made a bit nervous by this, based on her own experiences with the media machine and political machine, but she supports Ilaha.

"Is there press today?" Ilaha asks.

"You bet, Ilaha, want to go in front of them?" Tasmin confirms.

Ilaha says emphatically that yes, she does.

Ilaha starts to gather up her gear, opening her attire bag to look for a hoodie or sweatshirt. She has cooled down from her match now and is getting cold. There is nothing in her bag to put on.

Harmon sees her rooting around and asks what she needs. She tells him a hoodie would be perfect. He leaves the room briefly, and then comes back with a tournament hoodie from the gift shop. Across the chest is a Union Jack. Harmon tosses her the hoodie, and she puts it on, not appearing to notice anything about the hoodie other than that it is very comfortable.

Tasmin balks.

"Harmon, was there something less, well, political she could put on?" she suggests.

Ilaha cuts everybody off.

"This is exactly what I want to wear," she insists.

Tasmin reiterates her concerns.

"Ilaha, it has a Union Jack on it. Today's attack was against that symbol as much as against you. Do you want to provoke?" she warns.

"Yes," Ilaha responds, "I want to provoke. Me and this Union Jack are gonna hit back right now, against them. I may be from a Muslim family, but I am British no matter what and this is my f#%$ing country."

British Jig and Reel

Ilaha sits at the front of the press room, packed with everyone on site from every media outlet. Nobody is allowed to leave the grounds yet.

She has on her hoodie, hood up, Union Jack impossible to miss.

As soon as Ilaha looks up, the reporters clamor shouting questions. Ilaha points at a reporter.

Did you have any idea an attack like today could happen?

"Of course not," she says, "I am only thinking about tennis, about winning my matches and getting through to play again."

Are you a Muslim?

Ilaha looks to Mama Lily, in the seat next to her. She speaks for Ilaha.

"Ilaha is a Greengrass survivor and we don't know who her family was. It would appear none of them survived," she explains, "An extensive search was done and nobody has ever come forward to offer any information so we just don't know. She has not been raised in religion."

Ilaha adds her own take.

"Mama Lily is my mum," she declares, "She is my only mum. She adopted me and I love her as a mum like any other kid."

She pauses.

"And Britain is my country. I have lived here my whole life and it is my only country," she declares.

Her assertion creates cheers from the media. There is a chance this will go hostile. Now they turn, all of them, and see Ilaha as a girl bearing a cross for her country. She is just far too genuine and sincere to be viewed or portrayed as anything but pure.

Was it hard to stay focused after the lock down? Should play have been suspended?

"It was not very hard," Ilaha says, "On court I have routines that are designed to make me focus on what matters. It is all very analytical, honest, so all I did was anchor onto my routine and focus on the ball."

Mama Lily and Ilaha remain to answer questions for a long time. Eventually the lockdown ends and the reporters rush away to file stories and go on air live. This is a big, big news cycle for the event, and the primary headline is more or less as follows:

GODDESS OF GREENGRASS FLIES THROUGH, IN A UNION JACK

Every tabloid and every TV report uses the same image of Ilaha, standing tall, in her Union Jack hoodie, hood up, eyes wide open, looking as if by some miracle right into every camera that takes the shot.

Layer Four

In round three Ilaha faces a real challenge, but it is more a challenge of execution than understanding. Ilaha watches hours upon hours of tape on her opponent, a player with a giant serve that is very difficult to break, especially on grass.

For years, Isner plays without breaking through despite winning roughly ninety per cent of service games. Standing close to seven feet tall, Isner has the luxury of more or less hitting an overhead put away on his serve.

It is very easy to grossly underestimate just how strong giants are. A man like Isner, a competent athlete who declines to play college basketball, standing nearly seven feet, weighing nearly eighteen stone, is certain to be strong. Perhaps not on scale metrics, but in absolute terms, it is damn well impossible for someone that big not to be strong.

Isner routinely hits serves up near one hundred fifty mph in matches.

He is very, very hard to break, increasingly so over time as his plus one game improves a lot from his younger developing days. His return game is perhaps a bit sub par, but not hopeless, and up to a certain level of opposing player he holds his own on return.

The key to beating Isner is to just block his serve back into play and hope to get past serve plus one. If Ilaha gets into layer four of the point, her chances increase dramatically.

To prepare, she has the luxury of having Harmon blast serves at her. He obliges, with great zeal. For Harmon, having an excuse to really unload serves at someone equipped to deal with them is a form of a dream.

Harmon always, always plays down. There isn't really anyone he can play up to.

This is why he doesn't play much.

It is dangerous, honestly, because how hard Harmon hits, things can go very bad. He is always holding back. In Ilaha he has a foe and a reason, and he is excited.

They take the grass court at the club and Harmon explains his plan.

"Ilaha, we are gonna start off at peak velocity," he tells her, "I am gonna hit at the beginning as hard as possible. I won't be focused on spot or action, just on pace and hitting the service box. I assure you, hard hitters who can overwhelm with pace do exactly that. Hit for the box, hard, not even sure where in the box the ball will go." Harmon pauses on this. "Very important, Ilaha, you must read this kind of serve. I am hitting it, and I won't even know where it is going, but you must. These are the serves you can pick off."

Harmon takes position to hit serves at Ilaha. It is understood he will just serve out points, alternating from deuce to ad side, in a never ending service game.

His first serve is mishit a bit, coming over the net really, really hard but not so hard that Ilaha cannot move and flail at the ball. She barely scrapes it with the racket, failing to get it back. Harmon does not follow the serve into a point. He does not intend to play out points, yet. Just condition her for heat.

Ilaha and Harmon go back and forth, him hitting really really hard but incrementally softer. He has forbidden her from asking about pace measures or looking at the BallMap display.

"Condition yourself to the ball, with your eyes and ears and sense of touch. Forget data," he directs her.

They keep at it, Ilaha experiments with different starting spots and different attack angles. She tries to step in, but it doesn't really work and Harmon suggests that she does not need to compound pace, rather just focus on a solid directed block.

Ilaha finally figures out a tactic that works, where she starts a bit behind the baseline and simply focuses on reading the correct side. If she at least recognises what side to move to, forehand or backhand, she can go there and cut off the ball. She finds an optimum depth to cover the whole triangle of the service box and soon starts blocking balls back into the court with great consistency. She even gets to where she direct the blocks, at least going for one or the other deep corners of the court.

"Okay that is great work," Harmon compliments. "Now we have a run at playing out points."

Harmon resumes service, but now he is following up into a serve plus one approach. He moves very well, and is very often able to get into net and put away Ilaha's blocked back return.

"Isner won't really be able to do that, or willing to try, so I am going to stay back now," Harmon tells Ilaha, "But understand where the power a dominating serve comes from. It is from forcing the other guy to hopelessly block balls back that you can step up and put away. I am showing you what you should do, not what he will do. His return game is weak enough that you can do to him what I am doing to you now."

They carry on, all the while Harmon is calibrating down from impossible pace and action, and placement, into the more Normalstan of where the most ferocious service players like Isner play. When they reach stalemate and Ilaha can break service and consistently get serves back into play, they quit.

Ilaha is chomping at the bit to see the BallMap data. Harmon insists on keeping it from her during practice. Before she jumps on the machine to get a data run, Harmon takes over and bangs away at the keyboard. He insists that Ilaha stay away while he prepares a report for her.

"Okay Ilaha, come on over here," he summons her.

On screen is a report that Harmon prepares from which he has removed the labels. It contains tables of service accuracy, return accuracy, and data on the nature of Ilaha's returns. Speed spot spin on her blocks back into play.

Ilaha sees a pattern in the graph of the data that progresses from being incapable of getting serves back at all then converges toward getting back nearly one hundred per cent of serves. Toward the end of the session Ilaha sends back good shots that reset control of the point. Ilaha cracks it.

"So," Harmon says to her, "You can see the qualitative trend, right? We've identified your limits. Obviously at some pace you are just frozen out. For you," Harmon produces another report, targeting serves by speed, "two hundred mph is end game. At that pace you are just not relevant to the point"

He shows her on the report where she is able to block serves consistently into play, but not really seize control of the point with those returns.

"Guess the pace for these outcomes," he instructs.

She offers up a lowball number. 135mph. Attachment, he figures. She thinks in terms of commonly seen rates of speed.

"Higher," he tells her, "These serves are 165mph-185mph. You won't see that."

Now Harmon pulls up a final report. This one is a sentence and a sequence of "?" marks.

"At this pace Ilaha is expected to break serve: ???," is what the sentence says.

"Make a guess," Harmon tells her.

This time she guesses much better.

"A hundred forty mph?" she offers.

Harmon explains that she is still a bit low, but it is a good guess.

"That pace is 145mph-155mph," Harmon discloses. "Isner can hit it that hard, but his accuracy drops. Meaning second serves, meaning you can control his service games."

Ilaha attempts to comprehend.

"I must get to layer four," she asserts, correctly, "And I can do that."

"Yes," Harmon tells her, "Forget layer two, even on his second serve. Just keep pushing him past serve plus one."

Ilaha smiles big, understanding.

"As soon as you get past serve plus one," Harmon tells her, "The probabilities flip. You win."

God Save the Queen

Ilaha and Isner stand in the entrance area courtside waiting to be announced. Ilaha reminds Isner that she does not warm up her opponent and that he should arrange a hitting partner. He chuckles and assures her that he knows. They are the only words they will exchange until the match ends.

Isner warms up while Ilaha sits on her bench, hydrating and going through her mental checklist. Block returns of serve. Get to layer four. Do not try for more on second serve, just block to a spot and get to layer four.

Isner is completing warm up so Ilaha goes into her racket bag to select her starting racket. She gets comfortable preparing with Harmon by using one of her most tightly strung rackets, a high note within her higher octave of gear. Ilaha opens her bag, reaches for her racket, and pulls it out from its perfectly functioning flex grip slot.

She removes the racket from the bag and holds it up, a bit surprised, recognizing what she sees but not fully understanding …

… Then Ilaha drowns in a surging explosion of sound from the crowd.

Isner looks up from his gear bag and sees the crowd rising to its feet, screaming and cheering. Ilaha is standing, holding her racket aloft above her head. Prompting the crowd to go on, to continue, to reach a crescendo of national pride.

Ilaha's racket strings have a Union Jack painted upon them.

Ilaha walks across court, faces the royal box, and bows, deep.

"God Save the Queen," she says, aloud.

The crowd consumes itself with vocalised nationalist ecstasy.

Britain hosts the most prestigious tennis championship, but Brits do not enjoy great success in that tournament. In the modern era, they harvest just a handful of championships. Murray wins twice, the only man. Ann Jones and Virginia Wade win the ladies, years and years ago. Four wins. In about fifty years, over a hundred singles champions.

Now Britain has a modern daughter playing in the men's draw and wielding a Union Jack on Centre Court. And bloody winning! It is a flashpoint. It is a recipe that cannot be remade. It is a moment none will forget.

It turns into a very difficult day for Isner.

Ilaha wins the coin toss and selects to receive. Isner is broken in game one, and again in game five. Ilaha's service games are like a pleasant breeze. Isner has no answer for her ability to place her serve with sufficient speed and spin to frustrate.

Ilaha's service games are being won without ever getting near deuce. She breaks him twice. Quickly, with the crowd having barely settled down from its nationalistic frenzy, Ilaha takes the first set 6-3.

The second set is a bit tighter, with Ilaha only breaking once, but once again, she prevails mechanically. 6-4.

Isner plays admirably, sticking to tremendous discipline on serve. He does not succumb to desperation and over hit; he stays within himself and avoids giving away points. He serves very well, and actually doesn't double fault all day, but despite playing a great match he falls in the third 6-4.

Match, Ilaha.

The crowd cheers Ilaha, and does not jeer Isner.

At net after the match, Ilaha grabs Isner's hand and leads him over to her bench, where she climbs up onto the seat, stands, now a bit taller than Isner, and raises his hands above hers while waving to the crowd. It is a wonderfully sportsmanlike celebration and a great moment for Britain. Ilaha lets Isner's hand go, gestures toward him, and urges the crowd to give him his due.

They do with a deafening roar.

Isner is a great sport and he waits patiently, enjoying the enthusiasm, as Ilaha makes a lap high fiving the crowd. She stops at the royal box, does a deep curtsy, and then runs to gather her gear. Ilaha and Isner make their way off the court with the crowd singing "God Save the Queen" along with the instrumental version playing over the sound system.

Isner does his duty with the press.

How do you feel about the Union Jack incident before the match? Was it in bad taste?

Isner asserts that he thinks it was great, and he has to give credit to Ilaha if it was engineered gamesmanship. It throws him off, yeah. He knows he is playing the crowd as much as Ilaha and it will be tough.

Do you believe she can get all the way through?

Isner is analytical, and he is very clear with his answer. He knows that he did not double fault, that he hit few unforced errors, and that he played very well against Ilaha.

His A game is on display, he explains, and it just isn't enough.

"I've played everybody left in this field," Isner asserts, "I've beaten all of them at times. I thought I could get all the way through, so yeah, I think she can get through. She beat me. I didn't beat myself."

Reincarnation

There is no play during middle Sunday at Wimbledon. Harmon is correct in being a bit concerned that Ilaha is wearing down, ever so slightly. He sees it in her match against Isner. Very subtle, but there. Signs.

Harmon goes to Elysium early Sunday, planning to cut Ilaha off from any attempt to do anything. Lily is awake, but a bit put off because at that hour on Sunday she is never, ever, awake.

Ilaha is not up yet.

Harmon sits with Lily at the island counter. She is perusing the paper, taking tea, nibbling jammy cakes. A wonderful Sunday. Windows wide open, breezes filtering past drapes across the kitchen.

"Why are you here?" she demands.

"Where's Tasmin?" Harmon asks.

Lily mocks him.

"She's off with her bae, why? Are you jealous?" She taunts. "Do you want me to ask her if she 'likes you' likes you?"

Harmon golf claps, impressed by Lily's snark. Lily explains that Tasmin is taking the day to go home and gather up a proper suitcase of necessaries.

Harmon shifts to a bit serious.

"I want to take Ilaha to meet someone. She needs a day off and she needs to do myself and herself a favor. You can come with, if you want," he demands and invites.

Lily dreads going anywhere, the day is shaping up so wonderfully empty, but she knows that soon enough she will be restless and Twitter will not gratify and Tasmin won't be around and she will feel she is missing out … on … something. She agrees to go along.

"I'll rouse Ilaha and get dressed and be going. Where are we going, exactly?" Lily asks.

Harmon tells her Cambridge.

Once ready they leave the house. Lily assumes they will take her car, the Rover, but parked in the drive is the most beautiful vehicle she has ever seen. It is real, it is right there, but it cannot be believed. She does not recognise the car, but she does recognise the logo upon the hood.

It is a Jaguar, a magical green with the most luxurious, dark coffee colored leather interior. She wants to sit into it, to never not be absorbed into it. It is convertible and the roof is down. Four seats, obviously luxurious. Four bucket seats, each looking like the finest piece of ergonomic perfection. The wood details are perfect and of a visible grain she has never seen. It is just enthralling, the whole thing.

"Jump in and let's be off," Harmon commands.

Ilaha jumps over the door into the back driver's side seat. Lily opens the passenger door and gets in. There are rear doors, facing mirror images of the front. If Ilaha opens the rear door she sees the front seat tilt forward slightly enabling her to get into the back seat with great ease.

Harmon starts the engine. Lily feels it in her loins as much as hears it in her ears. It is magical, the whole thing. She fantasises about being nude for the ride, perfect buttery leather caressing her skin.

"It is a prototype," Harmon tells Lily. "I asked Jaguar to make me a totally impractical car, said they should let their engineers run wild with features and designs that are not economical. I said I'd foot the bill and they could keep the ideas, but give me the car," he explains. "It's a beast, honest. I won't air it out. Governed down to one hundred eighty mph but before that I had it at two hundred eighty mph on a test track. It's like sitting inside pure power."

Lily listens and feels and just luxuriates in it. God oh god oh god will he sell me this magnificent machine for a few thousand? She feels a bit guilty as soon as she thinks the thought.

Harmon makes the drive from Lily's farmhouse to Cambridge at well above the posted speed limits, apparently unconcerned about getting ticketed. Lily comments on his speed and he brushes her off.

"The car has radar detect that works perfectly," Harmon says. "We share that patent. If the filth can clock me, they don't know where I am. I call it 'quantum paradox' but in production it will probably get another name."

Harmon maintains a gaze at Lily after his answer.

"Do you notice something?," he asks her.

She is stumped. She notices so many things, the longer she rides the more detail catches her eye, but exactly what Harmon is talking about she does not follow.

"Not sure, what?" she begs back.

"Look at your hair," he instructs. Lily flips down the sun visor and looks into her mirror. Her hair is still, dead still, despite their motoring down the road at well over one hundred mph. With the top down, no less. It is amazing. Convertible without the hair-ruining wind.

Then she notices the silence. It is so quiet inside the car. She never has to raise her voice to be heard. The radio comes through crystal clear with no distortion and at a low volume. Harmon speaks mildly, and she hears it as if he is speaking calmly right into her ear.

"How …?" she just stammers. She would curse, but chooses to refrain … Out of some bizarre respect for the car. "How can it be so quiet?"

"It's all done with aerodynamic tricks," Harmon explains, "The shape and surface material of the hood and windshield glass funnel the air just so."

Harmon points out the ridge atop the wind glass.

"See those little fibers?" he gestures, "They are actually tiny air blowers. They adjust into place to insure that the air coming across the top of the car flows away from the cabin. It's brilliant, really, because the faster you go, the better it works. The whole thing is dynamic, it is impossible to see but the wind management system is adjusting constantly to maintain stillness in the cabin."

"Wow, just, wow," Lily says aloud.

She settles herself deep deep into her seat, realizing that it is just a bit warm. She does not turn on any seat heat or any other comfort feature. She does nothing at all.

"Does the seat automatically warm?" she asks.

"Actually, it knows your settings from the Rover," Harmon answers excitedly, "It all goes to the cloud and adjusts as soon as you sit down."

Lily thinks he must be mistaken. How does the car know they are her settings?

"The seats can tell it is you, from how much you weigh … eight stone? Mmm? Huh?" Harmon points at Lily.

Lily freezes in shame, from the harsh immediacy of hearing her own weight. Not from weighing that much, but from hearing it spoken aloud and addressed at her directly.

"It's not just how much you weigh, though. Both seats have sensors that measure how you spread your weight, your body temperature at various spots. It is more accurate than a fingerprint, really. So when you get in, it uses your own settings to perfect your seat for you." Harmon explains.

They arrive on the Cambridge campus. Harmon parks and closes the roof of the car. Once closed it becomes impossible to tell it is convertible. The roof of the car is mostly clear, not possibly glass, as it must fold and warp to tuck away, but clear. Once completely closed the non-glass glass goes dark.

Harmon leads Lily and Ilaha into a magnificent building. Certainly old. Hundreds of years old.

"The main library," Harmon explains, "It's really something."

They walk to the entrance and Lily sees a mark on the building, a date from nineteen thirty four, marking the completion of construction. So much for hundreds of years old.

The library is a vast, voluminous collection of items, dating back for hundreds of years to the fifteenth century and earlier. The loss of the Great Library at Alexandria pales in comparison to what the loss of this collection would mean.

Some of the greatest of great minds access and produce this collection. It is possible to touch the very same books and read the same pages that some of the greatest minds read or hold. Elizabeth Blackburn, Dorothy Hodgkin, Dian Fossey, Jane Goodall, Anita Brookner, Dame Iris Murdoch. Many many more.

Harmon navigates the stacks and rooms as if he is in his own home, appearing to know exactly where he should go. After a bit of maneuvering he gets to an aisle where an old man is scanning a shelf. Harmon walks right over to the man, looks where he is looking, and then reaches up and grabs a book from the shelf. He hands it to the man, and says "Babbage."

The man smiles at Harmon, zealously hugging him while grasping the dusty old book in his hand. They separate and Harmon continues.

"Page four o six; there is a scribble that is hard to make out. It's a drawing of a ghost," he tells the man.

The man opens to the page and looks. Harmon motions for Lily and Ilaha to circle around the man. The four of them look at the book, page four o six, and see the drawing, clearly of a ghost.

"'C.D.', that's Dickens. Babbage is 'CB,'" Harmon explains, "They would mark the books that the ghosts occupied. They were of a pair, Dickens and Babbage. I always imagine them as ancient Ghostbusters tramping the library looking for spooks and spectres. Probably drunk."

A pause. They just sort of stand, together, unintroduced, but comfortable. Harmon times the break just right and makes introductions.

"Assad, this is Lily Tudor, perhaps better known to some as Lily Lacey, the musician." Assad extends his hand and Lily takes it.

They do not shake. Assad places his other hand over hers and with both his hands simply holds hers looking in her eyes with a great smile on his face.

"I love your music," he says, to Lily's great surprise and delight, "And meeting you after hearing it seems so complete. You really come through in your music."

She takes it as a great compliment.

Harmon puts his hands on Ilaha's shoulders and moves her toward the man.

"This is Ilaha," Harmon presents her. "Can you believe it? It's as if she is once again alive, right?"

The man does not extend his hand, or motion in any way. Ilaha stands, still, with Harmon's hands on her shoulders. The man's eyes start to water, slightly. He chokes up very slightly, and mumbles.

"Harmon," Assad is barely able to mumble the name, "I feel like I am holding her again, as a tiny child, the first time we were home in the States."

The man quickly shakes off his deep nostalgia and extends a fist toward Ilaha, indicating a desire to bump, like all the kids are doing. Ilaha bumps his fist and the heavy mood lightens.

"Oz fed us, Assad," Harmon tells the man, catching him up. "It was impossible to believe. The meals she makes! Better off acting, but wow, she can cook."

Assad tells Harmon that he has also met up with Ozgu, and has enjoyed a meal. He already misses her.

The four start out of the stacks and make their way outside to Harmon's car. They get in and drive a short distance to Assad's flat. Inside he makes them tea, and they sit around in a comfortable living room.

Assad addresses Lily first.

"You have retired? It's been a long time since I heard a new record. I loved the commercial on telly, that was great," Assad compliments her.

Lily denies retiring. She defends herself by pointing out that she is planning a new record, a departure from her younger days. She is very excited about it.

"I really look forward to that," Assad assures her.

He turns to Ilaha.

"So this is the Goddess of Greengrass?" he asks.

Ilaha is more than a little uncomfortable with that moniker, but graciously confirms that yes, she is indeed the same.

"Harmon has been teaching you some tennis?" he confirms.

Ilaha is very eager to talk about that.

"Yes!" she practically yells. "So, so much. Everything about it. I think I've learned more math and science with him than I ever did in school. We have a great process. A cycle. I wake up every day so excited to do my work."

Assad reaches over the coffee table and squeezes her hands.

"He is so clean minded, right?" he observes.

"Yes!! Exactly. It all seems so easy the way he lays it out," Ilaha agrees.

Lily rolls her eyes at Harmon, who is sitting there watching Assad, closely, tenderly. Assad is alight, looking at Ilaha, engaging her with deep feeling, asking her things, listening to her every word. Harmon does not talk; he just absorbs Assad absorbing his dead daughter, Harmon's deceased wife, via Ilaha as medium.

They visit for a few hours and then Harmon stands and announces that they must go, Ilaha needs to rest up, tomorrow the tournament resumes and she has a tough opponent.

Assad, looking a bit worn, older than he looks at any point in the day, allows his eyelids to droop a bit and concedes their exit. Harmon hands Lily his keys and leads her and Ilaha to the door.

"I will be down in just a bit," he tells them.

Lily feels a greedy rush to own the Jag, and frantically suppresses it. She feels so awful about wanting to take all of Harmon's stuff, but damn if everything he has isn't just so perfect. It is as if he possesses the one ring to unite us all, but he is completely immune to its darker pull.

Hospice

Inside the flat Harmon takes Assad's hand. He squeezes, prompting Assad to squeeze back. Assad generates no force. It is as if a butterfly is squeezing at the paw of a grizzly bear. Assad is always powerful, dexterous, and strong. His handshake cripples many a powerful man, physical and otherwise. Today he barely creates any pressure.

"How long has the slide been going, Assad?" Harmon asks.

He misses a few visits with him, at Assad's urging, and is now dealing with a gap in his assessment arc. Assad is very old, and nobody lives forever. Harmon is going cold seeing too great a contrast between robust and running out.

Assad is running out.

"Harmon," Assad speaks quietly, "You always cut right to the salient point. Grip strength goes and life itself follows fast. It's been about a month. It's accelerating. Not much longer now, my son."

Harmon chokes up, his eyes watering. He understands. Assad teaches him so much, and he teaches so much to Assad. Medicine, healing, and most important, a shared philosophy of hospice.

Assad saves countless lives, directly and via his influence on his peers in medicine. He is a solver, and much more a definer of the real problem. When death is certain, as it often is, Assad is quick to concede this. Best to simply apply the most effective spiritual treatments to make the big death as pleasant as it can be.

Assad is a talker, a comrade, and he heals the dying with palliative connection. He pulls the story of their lives from them, befriends them, and provides a storehouse for the meaning of their life. Not everyone maintains an ongoing mission statement. The dying is almost perfectly incoherent. Assad helps them make sense of who they are, ultimately, astronomically, in the big sense of the big picture.

He guides them past superficial "father" or "mother" or any other relational identities.

Yes, you are all those things, but you are you without them. So who are you?

Most do not understand, so he explains in personal terms.

As a boy I was raised a strict Muslim, but something about that just didn't sit. It was because of an eclipse. As a small child I stood outside, watching the sky darken. An old man in my village warned me, 'Do not stare at it, Shaytan will steal your soul.' 'Shaytan' is our devil.

I was overtaken by a desire to argue. This made no sense, a devil stealing souls. I sensed the merit of not staring at an eclipse, and I did not. But I could not let his reasoning go. It stayed with me.

A few years later I read some science and learned why you do not stare at an eclipse. The pupils dilate when it gets dark, and then in an instant your eyes are flooded with sunlight. You should never stare at the sun, but when your pupils dilate it is especially bad. There was a real answer.

When I found it, I realised I existed to find out the truth and forgive my people their superstitions.

"So why are you here?" Assad asks the dying.

He gets so many wonderful, varied, wide ranging answers over the years of practicing his hospice hobby.

336

"I am here for cheese," one man from Wisconsin says, and they both laugh aloud for many minutes. The man smiles a lot after that, dying within a few days but perhaps more gently.

A woman tells him she is here to read the best words ever written. Assad points out that may be a fool's errand. Why don't you guarantee that, by *writing* them? She does. She leaves a beautiful love letter to her husband, who is with her every second that he can be, to the very end. She dies smiling, holding his hand.

Assad walks himself through his own hospice process for about a month. Here, now, he has Harmon. Harmon, still holding his hands, looking at him with tender love.

"Assad, would you stay with me, for the last days?" he pleads. Assad tells Harmon, no, I prefer it here. "I will visit then, daily now, until it comes."

Harmon makes sure Assad has all he needs, and makes sure his phone is charged and getting a signal. He stands and makes his way to the door.

Before he opens it, Assad calls to him.

"Harmon," he says, "Do you remember discussing the theory of hospice with me?" Yes, Harmon confirms, like it was today. "And how you offered the notion that it was really about framing your own story to feel like life was worth it?"

Yes, Harmon confirms, you need to be able to say "yes" if asked, "If you had it to do all over, would you?"

"And you remember how we argued, how I could not accept your assertion that a life has no past, that it has now, and that if you agree on your own meaning right now, you can carry your own final draft of your life into your death?" Harmon says yes, he remembers it all. "And the Africans, the ones who believe you live until nobody has any memory of you?" Yes, Assad, yes.

"She missed it, Harmon," Assad cries out, tears streaming down his face. "She went too fast, she missed this. She never wrote her own final draft, Harmon."

His crying becomes uncontrolled. Memories of his girl, his Kay, Harmon's wife, he feels sick for her loss, for her incomplete story.

Harmon comes back to Assad, also crying now, and holds him.

"Assad, my father, she had her final draft. We have lived her final draft. She is not forgotten, and will not be. I promise you this," Harmon assures.

Assad grips back now, around Harmon's wrist. Harmon can tell that even in just a few minutes the grip has weakened a bit more.

"I cannot explain my life, Harmon," Assad bawls, "I told those people in hospice I existed to find the truth and forgive my people their superstitions. I didn't. That is not why I am here. It can't be."

Harmon now talks Assad through his own hospice process.

That is fine, Assad. Perhaps you were too literal, but you helped them. Why was it so important to you to help? Why did you give with such generosity, Assad? Why do you mourn now, so deeply, our Kay? Why do you feel so deeply, Assad? I think you know your own answer, Assad.

Say it out loud.

Assad, eyes closed, trembling with tears, wails and clutches at Harmon, and then inhales and says his piece, quietly, but with a clear voice.

"I existed to love."

Harmon laughs and cries and squeezes the old man in his arms.

"Yes, Assad, you existed to love," Harmon celebrates him. "And you did. You loved as the giant you are, and if you had it to do all over again …"

Assad cuts him off now, and finishes his idea shouting …

"I would, I would over and over, changing nothing."

Mythos

Ilaha plays her next match on Centre Court.

She has yet to play on any of the other courts, or even hit a single ball on any of them. Ilaha never, ever hits at the tournament site. Her work is done at Club Dagobah, and only at Club Dagobah. Her training becomes a matter of deep secrecy, slowly, without her being very aware. Nobody is able to see her hit, ever, except in matches.

Tasmin posts stories about Ilaha that are not strictly, well, documented fact. So many stories. She hits on a notion that the better story, for covering Ilaha, is the story of the story. So she adopts a style that makes her the one to chronicle a legend.

Ilaha's past is unclear, so why clarify into the mundane if one can play up the ambiguity into wonderful maybes?

Tasmin has committed to creating a mythology.

An example is Tasmin's story about how Lily comes to find Ilaha, on top of that abandoned car, no tyres, surrounded by tall grass, soaking wet in her white sweats and white hoodie, clutching Buraq.

The car is remarkably far away from the Greengrass tower. At the time nobody is in a position to locate Ilaha's people, and it is probably the case that Mama Lily's assertions about where she finds Ilaha are simply disbelieved.

Tasmin and Mama Lily go to the site one day, and Mama Lily shows Tasmin exactly where she finds Ilaha. Tasmin stands there, in what is now an empty lot, and looks at the tower that replaces Greengrass quite far away. She is no engineer, but she has a very difficult time seeing how a child tossed out a window could have landed on a car this far away.

Tasmin interviews Ilaha about it, and the best she can recall is being told she can fly. She appears to think little of the whole thing, to hardly remember any of it. Nobody is sure how old she is. Nobody can ever be sure how trauma will be remembered, so Tasmin doesn't do much more than take what Ilaha has to say on its face.

Tasmin knows witnesses make for terrible witnesses.

She consults a scientist about the proximity of the car to the building and he flatly rejects the idea Ilaha landed there after being thrown from the building.

It is way too far. Just not possible. She'd have to be able to fly. Tasmin, brilliant, demands that she quote him on that. That she'd have to be able to fly? Sure. Quote me. No way she lands on that car unless she can fly.

Tasmin's story appears in the middle Sunday paper, and it is a huge seller. A second printed run, unheard of in many, many years for a printed newspaper, must be produced, because papers are flying off the stand. It is a great, great read. Perhaps not the strictest example of journalistic truth, but received with limitless enthusiasm by a country falling in love with an adopted daughter …

Night Flight

Tasmin Murasil reporting for the Empire Prophet

The Night Flight of the Goddess of Greengrass

On the night of the Greengrass Tower fire, too quickly forgotten, for some, the pop singer Lily Lacey, formally Lily Lacey Primrose Tudor, was drawn from her posh Babel home toward a fire in the sky. Moved by instinct, twittering away every step, she donned a pair of sheepskin boots and made her way toward the fire.

At the site she witnessed a terrible and horrifying tragedy in the making, and did her best to help. A bit overwhelmed, and a bit unprepared, she took a moment to step away for some air.

Some distance away from Greengrass, in a shuttered parking lot on the estate property, she discovered an apparently abandoned car with a collapsed roof and no tyres. She heard a voice and approached the car to see what was atop.

She found a miracle.

Clutching a stuffed animal, a white horse with wings, was a small girl muttering a cryptic sentence. Ms. Tudor, very tall and even greater of spirit, took the girl down from the roof of the car and carried her the two miles to the nearest emergency to get care.

"It was exhausting," Ms. Tudor recalls now, "I am not very strong and she was not so little at all. I had to stop, more than once, for a rest. I confess I had more than one fag during those rests," she laughs today, a tear running down her cheek remembering that night.

In the chaos that followed, Ms. Tudor informally and then legally adopted the girl. On the emergency admission forms, Ms. Tudor wrote her name down as 'Ilaha,' because she had been saying it over and over when she was found.

"When I found her she said, 'Ilaha can fly.' Clear as day. I recall that I believed her. Never any doubt. 'Ilaha can fly.' She kept saying it all the way to the emergency. I figured her name must be 'Ilaha' so I put that on the forms."

Ms. Tudor showed me where she found Ilaha, today an empty lot quite far away from the former Greengrass Tower. Standing there now, many years later, she agrees that it seems impossible that Ilaha could have landed on that abandoned car after being tossed from the building.

Dr. Archimedes Siracusa, a physicist at Oxford, investigated the matter and concluded that it was in fact impossible.

"There is no way Ilaha Tudor landed on a car in that location after being tossed from Greengrass Tower. It is simply too far a distance to cover."

When pressed on his conclusion, Dr. Siracusa reiterated his certainty.

"Impossible! To get to that car, she would have had to fly. There is no way she was tossed onto that car."

Ms. Tudor insists that she found Ilaha atop an abandoned car in that exact spot. Records confirm that the location was in fact a Greengrass parking facility. No record of the specific car could be found, but Ms. Tudor is insistent.

"This is where I found her," she states from the spot. "I don't know how she got here, but this is where she was. I believe she flew."

Ilaha cannot explain it either, but she does offer one insight.

"I don't remember much, from that night, but I do remember being told I could fly, and then feeling like I was flying."

It would appear that in fact, Ilaha can fly …

… And that she is destined to fly right through the Gentlemen's field at Wimbledon.

Match Point

The story is hokey and editorial and embellished to the nines, but it is so well received it is reprinted again, that Monday, ahead of Ilaha's match.

The Prophet has never sold as many papers.

Prior to this, Ilaha enjoys favoring crowds. From the first match against Murray, once she proves her worth as an adversary, the Wimbledon crowds betray an inclination to get behind her. With her match against Isner, she establishes herself as this year's runaway fan favorite.

Britain is for Ilaha, and only for Ilaha.

Now, moments before heading on court for her Monday match, a literal frenzy is building.

Her opponent warms up and Ilaha prepares. She selects a racket and heads out to the net for the coin toss. Harmon has her rackets strung back to flat black, no artwork. His Union Jacks have their moment. Now is time to refocus on tennis.

Ilaha loses the toss and her opponent elects to receive. She chooses the favorable end of the court, given the bit of wind blowing and the path of the sun.

Ilaha makes short work of her service game, winning at 15. 1-0. The players switch sides, and Ilaha manages a break right off. Now serving 2-0, the pattern continues through the first set ending at 6-2.

The second set breezes along and once again, Ilaha wins at 6-2.

She is cruising, and her opponent is struggling to find answers to the problems she presents. Her opponent leaves the court after the second set for treatment of some sort. After about ten minutes, play resumes.

In the third set both players hold serve into 6-6, so a tie break is to be played. The tie break shifts in favor of Ilaha's opponent early, with a mini break on a very rare double fault. Her opponent holds onto that advantage and wins the third 7-6 (7-5).

Ilaha drops her first set of the tournament. She is not shaken, but she understands that she is perhaps hitting a bit of fatigue. Harmon prepares her for all of this, for every possibility, so she just consults her mental index and finds the answer.

You are fatigued. You are just a bit sluggish. Account for it. Hit with more clearance, hit with more spin, go to a bit lighter racket.

She swaps rackets to start the fourth set.

Once again, the set is tight and both players hold serve into 6-6. Off to another tie break. Ilaha sits on her bench, doing an inventory of where she is. She is sensitive to the notion that fatigue is affecting her, so she once again consults her index of problems and solutions.

You are even more tired now. You hit at least a few balls into net, but that is not because you need a lighter racket. You are getting tight. If you get tight, get heavier and longer.

Ilaha switches rackets again, this time to a heavier one in the middle of her low octave. She comes out for the tie break and holds serve through to 12-11 in the tie break.

Her next serve is well struck but called out. It is close, but she does not challenge. On second she hits too easy a serve and for the first time all match, all tournament, really, she is read perfectly and her opponent blasts a return through her deuce court. Mini break, 12-12.

Her opponent holds and takes the fourth set 7-6 (14-12).

Now into the fifth set. Her opponent, feeling a burst of adrenaline, breaks Ilaha early in the set. They hold to 6-5, where her opponent is serving for set and match.

His first is blasted through the court down the T. 15-0. His second is blasted down the T and Ilaha can only lamely flail at it, not getting it back. 30-0.

It is happening so fast, her demise. The next serve is one that Ilaha can play, and she does, but a great forehand is called out.

Ilaha challenges and the PerfOculus shows that it was literally right on the line, and as such the original call has to stand. PerfOculus has a tiny miniscule sliver of a margin for error. This shot lands right inside it.

0-40. Triple set point. Triple match point.

Ilaha stops.

She just stops, standing well back of the baseline. She scrutinises her racket. One of the strings is visibly worn. She summons her towel from the ball girl behind her. She very, very slowly wipes her hands, arms, face, and grip. She sets to receive, then backs off, turning her back to the court. She scrutinises her strings, again. She already knows her string is worn.

She is buying time, freezing her opponent. She turns back to the court, but rather than set to receive she walks to the chair.

"My string is worn, and could break on any ball. I am switching rackets." The chair confirms the wear and grants her two minutes to switch her gear.

Ilaha uses the full two minutes. She very slowly summons a ball girl to fetch her racket. She gives instructions for having it restrung. She may need it later. She goes into her gear bag and selects a new racket, a bit lighter but in the same octave. Then she very slowly and deliberately makes her way back to the baseline to receive.

Her opponent sets to serve, tosses, and blasts a ball hard at the sideline. Ilaha reads it, perfectly, having now all at once cracked the DNA strand of his mannerisms on serve, and hammers a beautiful backhand down the line and into the wall. 15-40.

The next serve is long. Ilaha sees her opponent very subtly turning a corner. He is in a hurry, wanting to serve second right away. She steps away and rubs at her eyes. She calls for her towel. She scrutinises her grip. She approaches the chair.

"My grip has torn, I must rewrap." The chair confirms the damage and grants her two minutes to rewrap. Ilaha does so, deliberately, and then goes back on court to receive.

Her opponent over reaches on second, but manages to hit a bomb right at her. She reads it perfectly, and takes advantage of his instinct to assume the point by hitting a perfect drop return into the shortest area of his ad court. He never even moves for it. 30-40.

Now frustrated, and tiring rapidly, her opponent hits two faults to even the game. 40-40. Deuce.

This leads to a tantrum of sorts. A fit. Cursing in his native tongue, directing curses at the chair, waving and pointing at

Ilaha, he seethes. The chair warns of a time violation and instructs that serve must be hit. This simply sets him off.

She is f#%$ing around with her strings and grips and I am getting warned on time?

He faults on the first, spins the second into the court. Ilaha kills it, hammering it right back at him. He is unprepared to play it, and bunts it weakly into the net.

Break point. First serve in, down the T, Ilaha blocks it back, deep, to his forehand corner. Ilaha sneaks toward net just as he is playing the ball, and he does what she expects. He gets a bit lazy, falls into swinging from the hands, and misses right in front of her into the net.

Ilaha has him. She knows it. It has been a struggle in the third and fourth sets but now she sees the whites of his eyes, and she is ready to shoot. Right into his heart, right through his brain.

Harmon sees her see it. He gets up from his seat, and is leaving Ilaha's box. Lily grabs at his arm.

"Where are you going? These are huge points!" she bleats.

Harmon smiles down at her.

"No. It's over."

Ilaha serves out at love, hitting everything at her opponent's fraying forehand. He simply cannot keep the ball in play. The more he misplays, the worse he hits and the more he misplays. It is a self-fulfilling prophecy of doom.

7-6 now. Her opponent serves. Ilaha sets to receive. Ilaha's opponent tightens, goes over to bunting in his serves, just to avoid fault. Ilaha can hit lasers back through his court, but refuses.

On every serve, she blocks the ball back into his deuce corner, follows it in, and soaks in the pleasure of knowing all he can do is flail away and hope to pass. She knows what he can hit in such a state, what he cannot, and where he will try to pass. He has no response she will not put away.

She wins four straight points. To his credit, three of his balls get over the net into what would be tough spots for a less insightful player than Ilaha. But for her, they are easy put away volleys into open courts as vast as the sea.

Game. Set. Match. Ilaha goes through, again, now into the quarters.

Mary Kay

Harmon opens Assad's door and finds him watching the matches. He is dozing, and the telly is on a match following Ilaha's win. Assad hears Harmon, wakes, and announces the result.

"She won! I was worried but she pulled it out," he exclaims.

Harmon pats Assad on the leg.

"I know, she hasn't gone five. She was worn, but she adjusted. She absorbs everything, she uses everything. Brilliant, really," Harmon marvels.

Ilaha is truly, genuinely gifted. Not just the physicality, she is significantly more brain than brawn, a must, really, a definite essential, for tennis.

Harmon sees that Assad is weak, that he can barely stay awake. So he launches into a narrative for him. And for himself. To ease Assad into dreams…

I knew Ilaha was special the first time I heard her ball. I couldn't see who was hitting, but I could hear the ball. It popped, just so. A perfect note. I felt joy at the sound. Like a man lucky enough to have a special ear, dining, who hears a server present the day's specials, and recognises that it is Callas, earning her rent money.

The special ones are special, and they cannot be mundane. Ilaha is special.

Even the special ones need to train, and once I engaged her it was clear that her greatest talent is a talent for work and learning. Sometimes I wonder if we would all be better off with her at curing a disease rather than banging on a yellow ball, but it's her heart, not mine. She loves it. She loves it more the more she learns about it.

I have not told her everything, because I would never tell anyone everything, but I have told her enough to figure the rest. She will want to figure it, rather than just be told.

She will definitely win. The whole thing. And you must hold out to see it, Assad.

They are the same, in spirit. It is so hard for me, to see her, close, intimate, see the subtle mannerisms, the tells and the ticks. It is as if she is alive, again, or at least reincarnate. I get chills.

I have kept a distance, Assad; I have shielded her and myself from my deepest heart. I have been in a moment I do not want to ever end, but it will end. Everything ends, Assad, nothing can persist in purity. Even if it does, even if it can be shielded and sheltered and protected, it soils itself from want of vital air. The filth and dreck, it is essential. There must be risk.

Stay with us, Assad, a few more days. Stay long enough to see. And see our Kay in Ilaha, and see what you dreamed, and know the dream is the truth and that you are not alone in seeing it.

Assad is now dead asleep. Not dead, but completely out. Harmon covers him, places him prostrate onto his big comfortable sofa, and shuts down the lights. He turns down the TV volume and leaves.

Tomorrow. I'll be back tomorrow.

Sandwich of Brotherly Love

Ilaha is sore. She is not injured, she is just sore. Her muscles are under a great strain, for which it is not really possible to prepare. Her conditioning is as good as possible, but a five set Grand Slam match that goes into two tie breaks and then beyond 6-6 in the fifth wears.

Harmon goes directly from Assad's flat to Elysium. He knocks at the door while walking in and finds Ilaha on the sofa, next to Mama Lily, watching TV, looking worn.

"Get up," he tells her.

She dreads it, fears the worst, but does as she is told. Lily sort of half motions to follow, but Harmon cuts her off with an extended hand.

"Exactly how would you help?" he mocks and she settles back in, relieved.

Harmon leads Ilaha out to her court. It is dark but the outdoor house lights throw off enough for them to do what Harmon has in mind. He hands Ilaha a rope and they both skip, lightly, in a metronomic fashion.

After about fifteen minutes they stop and Harmon asks Ilaha how she feels.

"Blood flowing. A bit less sore. Better." Ilaha is not all better, but feels improvement.

"Okay," Harmon tells her, "Now we go inside. Have you eaten?" She tells him she had noodles with vegetables. "That will not do," he says, dismissively. "You need meat. Cheese. Grease."

Ilaha is very surprised to hear that, given everything she has ever been told about nutrition.

"Trust me, worst case, you actually enjoy a meal," Harmon assures her.

Harmon tells Ilaha to go inside, drink a glass of dill pickle juice, a glass of quinine water, and take a very hot shower. Borderline scalding, he tells her. As hot as you can stand. Then he leaves, letting her know he will be back shortly to make her a dinner she will absolutely love.

"As good as Oz?" she jokes.

"Of course not," Harmon admits, "But really good."

After about an hour Harmon returns with bags from the supermarket. He puts the bags on the island counter and does a play by play as he empties their contents in front of Mama Lily and Ilaha.

"First, a couple beautiful prime rib eyes. Fresh. Best they had. The butcher assures me this cow was alive yesterday." Harmon lights up at the notion, the diabolical type that he is. "Food tastes better if you catch some of its soul."

He continues to display his ingredients. A container of Cheez Whiz. White American cheese sliced thin. Crushed red pepper relish. Fresh, beautiful, warm baguettes. Three of them. An arm's length each. Fresh butter, still soft. He hands a baguette over to Mama Lily and Ilaha, pushing butter at them with a knife.

"Get to work on that. Anyone who does not devour a fresh baguette smothered in butter is not worthy of their next breath," he insists.

Lily takes exception to this.

"What about people with celiac?" she defends.

"Poor hopeless culinary rubes," Harmon mocks, "They should at least wish they could devour the baguette. A little upset stomach is probably worth it."

Harmon rifles through Lily's kitchen searching for tools.

"You don't have a deli slicer?" he condemns. She tells him no, I don't, I am not a supermarket. He finds a cutting board and a decent knife. "Wood? Why don't you just cut stuff in the toilet?"

He places a rib eye on the cutting board and slices it into impossibly thin sheets at a diagonal across the fibers of the muscles. Then he does the same with the second rib eye.

"Lawry's?" He demands.

Lily, mouth filled with warm baguette dripping butter, opens her eyes wide to indicate 'what are you talking about?' She knows not of Lawry's.

"Spices, then. Salt, paprika, whatever you have," Harmon pleads.

She points to the cabinet where it all is.

Lily's kitchen, very high end, has a beautiful flat top grill. Harmon turns it on, high, and lets it get hot. While he is waiting he puts together his own version of a seasoned salt, a bit closer, probably, to Tony Chachere's than Lawry's. The grill, now sizzling, is ready.

Harmon takes a large scoop of the fresh butter and slaps it onto the grill. It melts and bubbles into a foam that he spreads evenly across the surface. Then he dumps the sliced rib eye onto the buttered grill. He lets it sit, and opens the Cheez Whiz. The can itself goes into a pan with boiling water.

After a minute or so it is back to the grill to work on the rib eye slices, spreading and flipping them to get every square inch of surface directly onto the grill. He shakes on some of his seasoned salt, keeps working at the rib eye, and then turns to cut the baguettes.

He cuts each baguette in half, and then splits them leaving a hinge. He slathers Cheez Whiz onto all four halves. Spreads crushed red pepper relish on them. Then he turns back to the grill and places a thick layer of American cheese onto the rib eye.

Quickly the American cheese melts and Harmon brings over the baguette halves. He heaps piles of the rib eye with melted American onto them. He uses a knife to hold in the meaty cheesy melty miracle and folds each one shut.

Harmon places the steaks onto a platter and puts it on the island counter. Lily and Ilaha, a bit full from gorging on baguette and butter, are loath to eat, but drawn to the hoagies strongly enough to reach. Harmon pulls away the platter.

"Not yet," he admonishes.

Within a minute the door is knocked. Harmon answers it, and then comes back with a brown bag that smells of heaven. Chips! Lily immediately thinks, and then says aloud. Harmon empties the bag onto a large plate and spreads a generous helping of salt all over them. Lily jumps up from her stool, runs over to the cabinet, comes back with vinegar, and splashes it all over them.

"Mayo," she says, "These need Mayo." She opens the fridge and to her disappointment, there is none.

"I'll make it, just eat," Harmon tells her. He finds an egg and olive oil, drips in some vinegar, and squeezes in some lemon. Whisk whisk whisk and add a bit of salt and pepper and bam, fresh mayo.

Ilaha picks up her enormous Philly cheese steak hoagie and bites into it. Heaven. It is as if she is an empty vessel and with every bite she is being filled with waters from the fountain of youth. Literally by the bite her soreness is melting away.

It is magical. The Cheez Whiz, an eyebrow raiser, is a perfect tangy counter to the salty spice of the seasoned salt mix Harmon makes. The fat from the rib eye permeates the layers of rib eye flesh and marries to the melted American cheese, and it all pairs with the Whiz and dry salt into bites one at once does not want to release and demands to swallow. The baguette is simply perfect, holding the whole thing together and offering a wonderfully flavor neutral delivery system for the headline act inside.

Ilaha finishes the whole thing. Mindlessly. She just keeps biting and chewing and eating until there is nothing left. She feels full, but she also feels strong. Her muscles feel like they are actually healing, micro tears in her fibers fusing back into something stronger than what precedes. After a pause she digs into the frites, sent from the area's highest end French bistro. Harmon arranges an exact drop off and coordinates the whole feast around the frites.

Lily is in an uncomfortable heaven. Her social circles consist of fashionables who stick with lighter, much more gourmet faire. Models, musicians, leftists of every sort. The cool kids are too cool for school, as they say.

357

Now Lily finds her inner carnivore unleashed. She placates her soul devouring side openly enough, frequenting greasy spoon type diners, because they proffer grease and salt and have coolness for her crowd. Costume designers will tolerate a big plate of bangers and mash or a midnight run at steak and eggs sloppy in the right setting.

This, this is so very Tory. So jockey, so not her. So masculine. So violent, really. It is all, so, well, embarrassing. If only her mates from years gone by could see her now, devouring an ugly American concoction like a Philly steak, in her farmhouse sitting at an island. A stone or two overweight, certainly not a size six, frumping around in Cholesterol Town.

Harmon asks Ilaha how she feels.

"No soreness. At all. I feel great," she says, surprised.

"Good," Harmon tells her. "That will not be the case tomorrow. You will get sore, and tonight you may get leg cramps."

"Drink at least another glass of dill pickle juice, and at least another glass of quinine water. That will help the cramping," Harmon tells her. "Then, tomorrow when you get up, stretch and take another really hot shower. You will be sore, but it's fine. We can hit easy and focus on tape and data."

Harmon also reminds her to drink as much water as she can stomach. Just keep forcing it in.

The next day Ilaha is sore, and wakes starving. Ilaha and Harmon go over tape and data, go over the scout report Harmon prepares, and then when it is time to hit she stands and realises she is very sore. Too sore to hit. She tells Harmon.

"Don't worry," he assures her, "It will be fine. We can skip hitting."

Ilaha is worried. She has never been in such a state. She is normally tireless.

"Harmon, what if I am still this sore tomorrow?" She is a bit scared.

"You won't be," he assures her, again.

"How can you be so sure?" she challenges.

"Today we will get you a massage, and then we will give you powerful narcotic anti-inflammatory drugs, muscle relaxers, and painkillers," he states, flatly. "Drugs work."

The next day, the day of her match after her massage and drug treatments, Ilaha sits, entirely pain free, fully recovered. She wonders, aloud, what athletes did before they had drugs to deal with soreness and pain.

"They got drunk," Harmon tells her. "Alcohol is as good as all of that, really, but you are just a kid. Can't well get you pissed."

Weapons of Massive Consumption

Quarters. Interest growing. The world watching. Not quite a panic, not quite as big as possible. If Ilaha gets through, to the semis, you get an enormous audience. Probably the biggest audience to ever watch a tennis match. Wimbledon. The semis. A female playing the men. No brainer.

At this point a commerce monster previously held at bay by Harmon breaks free of its shackles and explodes into Ilaha's world.

Big shoe, big gear, big fashion.

Cosmetic companies want her.

Retailers want her.

Every magazine, from the sports to the fashions to Motor Trend. They all want her. Motor Trend sees Mama Lily driving Ilaha to the AELTC in her Rover and for the first time they send a reporter to cover Wimbledon.

Ilaha, oblivious, is amused by it all. It never occurs to her, submerged completely into a sea of promotion, that much of what was going on is really about selling stuff.

The matches? One big commercial. A side-show, really. The bread and circus multinational merchants offer to the weapons of massive consumption, not their fault, just how they are programmed to function, to keep them consuming stuff.

Harmon protects Ilaha from the reps and agents and rainmakers. He has a real way of it. A leading French racket maker sends a rep to pitch Ilaha on a racket swap. Harmon sits idly by listening and when the rep pauses, he accosts her.

"She plays Wilson. And we buy the rackets. We use your strings. We pay for them. No endorsements. That's it," he barks at the young lady, who practically trembles while offering free strings. "Are you simple? I said we buy our gear."

No sale.

Ilaha is given complete wardrobes of free outfits. The one more feminine and sexualizing than the next.

She always wears the same thing. Modest, really. Whites, always, no matter the setting. She can bleach whites. She can keep whites white. And she feels better in whites. Colors and designs? Garish. Distracting.

Harmon sees to it that all the swag is collected and deposited into Mama Lily's Rover, to be gone over later. They can keep what they want and then he will donate the rest. It is all garbage, really, but for some other kid it maybe creates a form of escape velocity.

Centre Court, again.

Primest prime time, again.

Ilaha wins, in straight sets, again.

6-3, 6-3, 6-1. Her opponent, the number eight ranked man, winner of the Australian Open earlier in the year, fodder. The hole was second serve. He is shaky, and Ilaha's read allows her to hit winner after winner through his court. The more it happens, the more he misses on first, under too much pressure, and the more he resorts to just getting second into the court. Those balls Ilaha simply puts away, with greater and greater ease, at higher and higher success rates.

By now the men's field and the media and the pundits accept that Ilaha is a force, and that she is not a circus act.

The gambling firms have conceded as well. She is now six to one, down from ten thousand to one.

Harmon has made many, many millions from this, but his money stays on the table. He will not cash out now. He will make that next six from his one because he knows, for a fact, Ilaha is going win.

Achilles

For the semis Ilaha faces a great warrior.

Ten-time French Open winner, fifteen time Grand Slam winner, and a lefty. It will be Nadal in the semis. Not on his best surface, but still formidable.

Harmon warns Ilaha that Nadal's severe ball action will require an adjustment. She has never seen such severe action on ground strokes.

"Service, eh, he is so-so," Harmon tells her. "He will serve to get to layer four, mostly. He hits a good serve, don't get me wrong, but on its face hardly an A serve. A- to B+ type serves. His serve is to set up the rest of the point, not win the point."

Harmon tells Ilaha that to prepare they will simply hit balls.

A lot of balls.

Ilaha assumes Harmon will do the hitting, but she has it wrong. He has been hacking the ball machine. She takes a place on court, on the grass at Club Dagobah, and he turns on the machine.

He rests it upon a rolling platform. This allows the balls to launch from closer to the height that a groundstroke will be hit. It also allows the machine to be moved around the court.

He programs the machine to send shots over the net that are an exact match to Nadal's ball, in terms of speed and spin. He goes over reams of PerfOculus data and derives the average speed and spin characteristics for every shot Nadal has ever hit, from every spot on court.

Harmon attaches a sensor to the machine that insures the balls land in the court wherever aimed. He programs an algorithm into the machine to select from a variety of shots based on buttons he pushes.

"So here is how this works," he explains to Ilaha, "I will push the machine around the court. I will press a button to send off a shot. An exact match for what Nadal would hit. You hit back and go for winners. I will mix up his shots and move around the court."

Harmon starts off at center of court near the baseline. He turns on the machine and a ball is sent over the net at Ilaha. It flies hard, with severe spin, clearing the net high and breaking very hard into the back third of the court. The ball kicks, hard, appearing to accelerate as it lifts almost vertical up into a terrible spot for Ilaha. She lamely punches at it.

Harmon stays put and keeps sending the same ball at Ilaha. She keeps having a hell of a time doing anything with it. After about a dozen balls, she motions for him to stop.

"I am just not seeing it, not understanding how to hit that ball," she declares. She has grown into a scientific thinker who does not get upset. She simply looks for answers. Harmon appreciates this about her, her analytical bent. He approaches the net.

"What is the biggest problem for you?" he asks.

"The ball is at an awful height," she observes, "I cannot get over it, and I cannot hit an overhead. I am stuck making a swing at a terrible angle that feels completely disconnected from my feet."

Harmon nods.

"Exactly," he confirms, "You are being forced into swinging with your arm and hands. Very, very bad. In fact, it's good we stopped before you make it a habit."

Ilaha feels better having sized up the problem, but still has no answer.

"So what do I do?" she asks.

Harmon comes around the net and sends her to the machine.

"Just hit the 'A' button. Send me balls, I will show you a few things," he tells her.

Ilaha takes the controls, turns on the machine, and then sends a ball at Harmon, who is standing where she was.

His strikes look like hers, but better quality. He is taller, and stronger, so he overpowers the ball's action more easily. But it is obvious this will not do. Too much shot variance. So now he adjusts by backing up, well behind the baseline.

From so far back the balls have time to sink back down into his strike zone, and he is able to hit very high quality strokes back over the net. But from her side of the net Ilaha sees that what he sends back is much easier to handle because of how far the ball travels. Balls slow down, so from far enough back even Harmon's ground strokes become easier to handle.

Harmon amps up his pace shot by shot, and as he maxes out hitting blinding balls off the strings Ilaha sees it is pace in vain. His normally unreachable balls are easy enough to chase down when hit from ten feet behind the baseline. He also cannot produce severe angles.

She keeps sending over shots, and now he moves in toward net. About three feet inside the baseline he stops, and she watches as he takes the balls on a short hop. He is forced to assume a lot, and what he is doing looks impossible, but ball after ball he manages to catch the ball on the way up just after it bounces and smothers it into a return that whistles through the court. His error rate is high, but these balls are much harder to chase down. He can create severe angles.

She continues to send him balls, and now he does something she would never figure to do. He moves in even farther, to the service line, and positions himself dead into no man's land. He is not at net, and he is not back, he is in the middle ground. A bad spot, usually. From there, hitting a high quality shot is usually quite difficult.

She sends over the balls and watches. It becomes clear now. He is exactly where he should be!!!

Nadal's ball loops. It clears the net very high, carries deep, and breaks sharply to get into the back of the court. Harmon moves to where he can hit the ball in the air before it lands. These balls are right in his strike zone, and he forcefully puts them away. There is no chance, from where he is, that a good punching volley will come back. He has too much green area to hit into from here.

Ilaha shuts off the machine and goes to net.

"That is the answer!" she exclaims, "Go where nobody ever wants to go, and you have his number. The exact things that make his shot hard to play from the good spots make it easier to play from the bad spot."

There is always an answer. She has the answer. Harmon sends her back to the other side and resumes manning the machine.

Given the notion, Ilaha starts controlling the balls being sent over and turning them around into shots that take over points. He moves the machine around the court, and adjusts the speed and spin of the ball accordingly, and after a couple of hours Ilaha has the whole fingerprint in her grasp. She sees the action, sees the weak spots, and sees how to build the points.

"It will be all about getting him into a spot where I can get to my spot and take it on the fly," she asserts.

Harmon confirms that idea.

"Yes," he says, "You can open him up by getting him to spots he will be comfortable going to. He has exploited an inefficiency that his opponents refuse to pursue. Understandable. But he is very much at a disadvantage against a great volley player. Be the great volley player. You'd be the only one. His ball flies too high through the volley zone. Get into it and put balls away."

One Small Step, One Giant Leap

Wimbledon semifinal.

Nadal versus Tudor.

Centre Court.

They schedule it for first match to insure a prompt start. The broadcast will go out to more potential viewers than any broadcast in history.

ESPN has offered it up to every station worldwide that has asked, even in countries where ESPN is available. They want everyone on earth to be able to see it for free. They are even unlocking the ESPN.com live broadcast online.

All of it free.

This event will be available to anyone and everyone, gratis.

Confirmable audience counts of the broadcast stun.

The cable companies know actual viewers and observe over fifty per cent of all cable subscribers tune in. Overseas cable companies confirm similar rates. Satellite operators also know, and confirm the fifty per cent or higher rates.

The internet in one form or another sees hundreds of millions of streams being opened. Airwave broadcasts, still common in many places, cannot be counted directly, but estimates of viewership rates based on the countable and sampling make it very clear …

… This is the most watched event in history, bona fide and verified.

Fact.

In nineteen sixty nine, when man lands on the moon, an estimated five hundred thirty million people watch on telly. That is fourteen per cent of the world's population at the time.

One in seven humans.

For this match, effectively everybody on earth can and does watch telly, via cable or satellite or airwaves or the web. Given the measurable rates of viewing and the availability of the broadcast, the best guess for the number of people watching the match is well over two billion. That covers twenty five per cent of world population at the time, more or less.

One in four humans.

The real question, for Harmon, is why so low? Who is not watching this, he marvels? At a minimum every single female on the planet should tune in. Just to start.

A bit more than half of all humans should be watching, at least.

The match is an instant classic. Five sets, four tie breaks, and a 15-13 final set.

Ilaha prevails, and she does it by force of will. By the fifth set they both figure each other out, largely, and Nadal makes adjustments to neutralise his unwitting weakness from balls carrying the net in the sweet spot for a volley player. He starts hitting flatter, to pass, which leads to a series of very exciting points with wild swings of momentum within them.

Ilaha is smart enough to keep playing in, despite point variance and getting blitzed more than once in hopeless situations. They both win point after point, neither giving ground, neither playing just to let the other falter. It is all proactive and offensive, and marvelous to watch.

After the match, Ilaha makes her way into the entryway where the other two semi-finalists wait to be called on court.

Federer plays Del Potro.

Del Potro is as impressed by Ilaha as anyone, and he openly roots for her as a spectator during her matches when he is not playing his own. He is approached by TV in his seat next to Centre Court. The TV people as him why he is so enthusiastic about a potential opponent.

"I have a mother, and a sister, and aunts," he beams, "Someday I'd like to have daughters. I want to live in a world where women can be as good as men at tennis. Ilaha is as good as men at tennis!"

Del Potro, a bit shyly, approaches Ilaha.

"Great match, again," he gushes, as if just a fan boy. "I hope you don't get a chance to do what I did."

His joke is not lost on her. Ilaha is a walking encyclopedia of tennis, and she knows he is the only one to beat Nadal and Federer at the same Grand Slam. She watches replays of those matches over and over as inspiration.

"Me too, I'd love to play you next," she beams.

He reaches out to hug her, and surprised, she accepts and hugs him back.

"How did you do it?" she asks.

She wonders how a guy like him, only twenty one, storms through the two greatest players of their generation, perhaps of all time, back to back to win the US Open.

"One point at a time," he smiles back at her.

There is a bond, driven by Del Potro, a man beloved on the professional tour. He is a giant of a man, and so lovable. Now a bit older and having missed perhaps his greatest days to injury, but once a prodigy of sorts, humble, but powerful, he is inclined to appreciate Ilaha, and root for her, and just gushes at wanting to share with her.

"The ball doesn't care about any of it, Ilaha," he assures her. "Take solace in the ball. It is the same ball you've hit a million times."

They part when Del Potro and Federer are called onto the court.

G∞d Is Infinite

It is not Del Potro.

He gets another chance to root for Ilaha from the Royal Box. He fights hard, taking Federer to five sets, but the fifth goes very badly at 1-6.

The anticipation is just incomprehensibly overwhelmingly enormously gigantic.

The GOAT versus the Goddess.

There is talk of moving the final to Wembley Stadium, which accommodates a hundred thousand, but it is decided to simply televise on giant screens at Wembley and play as always at the sacred site. Centre Court may only seat fifteen thousand, but it has a monopoly on the tournament's history.

To prepare for Federer, Ilaha is taken on a long walk by Harmon, through the fields and hills beyond Elysium.

"Ilaha," Harmon explains to her, "We can walk as we please across private property because we have 'everyman's right.' Freedom to roam. There is a law. It says that the public can access certain forms of private property for recreation and exercise. Land like this. Hills and fields, not being used for farming or commerce. Natural property left alone that happens to be owned by someone. A God given right. Not bestowed by man."

The idea is pleasing to her. Freedom to roam. Like when she dreams. Freedom to fly.

They walk and talk for quite a while. Small talk. No tennis. Primarily they walk. Quiet. Occasional observations. Mostly they are just in each other's company.

Eventually they approach a National Trust site.

"Do you know where we are?" Harmon asks.

Ilaha does not.

"We are at Runnymede. No idea what it is?" Ilaha tells Harmon she has no idea. "The Magna Carta was signed here. Hundreds of years ago. Right here. In twelve fifteen. Democracy was born right here."

Harmon leads Ilaha to a monument, a gazebo of sorts made from stone. A man is standing there, watching them approach. He is holding a green shopping bag from Harrods. Tall, dressed in a gray suit jacket over a light khaki linen dress shirt that hangs down past his knees. He also has on a headpiece, made from the same material as the shirt.

Traditional Muslim garb. Quite dapper.

Harmon and the man shake hands and embrace, addressing each other in a language Ilaha does not understand but recognises as Arabic. Harmon turns and introduces the man to Ilaha.

"This is Grand Mufti Ainfasal," Harmon tells her. "A friend. He would like to speak with you, and has something for you."

The Grand Mufti, a man of giant presence, is perhaps the most highly esteemed religious figure in modern Islam.

Ibrahim Ainfasal is the youngest Muslim to become a Grand Mufti. He descends from Islamic religious royalty.

His great grandfather is a Grand Mufti of Istanbul, among the most prestigious positions in Islam. He has uncles and cousins ensconced all over the Islamic world serving at the highest levels of religious scholarship and law. He completes a doctorate at Al Azhar in Cairo at age fifteen. His knowledge of the Quran is held in sheer awe by his peers.

Having an affinity for the west, he aspires to lead a reform movement to celebrate the finest elements of Islam without requiring the faithful to be fundamentally at odds with western culture.

Grand Mufti Ainfasal works his whole life to derive interpretations from the Quran and Hadith. He wants a more modern set of practices to make assimilation into the West easier.

The devout need not wear a veil, he preaches. They can believe as deeply with an uncovered face. Of course, they are free to choose to cover their faces if they wish. Western freedom cuts both ways. Religious tolerance is a foundation of that.

The Mufti hands Ilaha the bag from Harrods. She takes it and looks inside. There are clothes in the bag, white, made from some sort of athletic gear material.

"Ilaha, some fans of yours made those garments for you," Mufti Ainfasal explains, "They will be humbled and honored if you consider wearing them for the final match. It all conforms to Hadith. Seeing you in it would make many hundreds of millions of Muslims incredibly proud."

Ilaha protests.

"I am not a Muslim," she asserts, "They attacked me, set off bombs over my gear."

She becomes upset. Understandably.

Harmon intervenes.

"Ilaha, you are certainly from Muslim folk," he insists, "An Arab. It's a fact."

"I am not religious," she shoots back, "I eat bacon, and pork chops. I celebrate Christmas with Mama Lily, for f#%$'s sake."

"And you curse … Okay, sure, you aren't religious," Harmon concedes, "You may not believe, but you are still a Muslim. They are your people."

Nobody speaks, briefly, and then the Grand Mufti offers an insight.

"Ilaha, are you familiar with the phrase 'Allāhu 'akbar!'?" he asks.

Ilaha tells him she has heard it on the news. A man who drives a van into a crowd on London Bridge shouts it before hitting the gas and killing a dozen people.

"This is an unfortunate truth, yes," the Grand Mufti acknowledges, "There are disturbed people who abuse Islam for violent purposes. They too often invoke that phrase while committing horrible acts."

The Mufti pauses, and then goes on.

"Can I explain a little about that phrase, Ilaha?" he asks. She nods yes, he can. "It is Arabic. Arabic does not translate into western language perfectly. Many languages are like that. There are often disputes regarding translations. I have spent a great deal of time studying that phrase, Ilaha, and I would like to tell you what I think it means."

Ilaha is interested now, and wants to hear.

"People in the west tend to translate it as 'God is great,'" he tells her, "Which has a certain linguistic justification, but fails to capture the nuance. 'Allāhu 'akbar' refers to a 'great' that is much bigger, much more profound, than large in size or great like 'great time' or other western uses of the idea of greatness."

Ilaha is following now, rapt, wanting to hear more.

"God is great in the greatest sense," the Grand Mufti continues, "In the sense of greatness without limit. Boundless …"

"INFINITE," Harmon declares.

"Yes, infinite," the Mufti resumes, "God is infinite. The human mind cannot comprehend infinity. It should not comprehend infinity. Infinity is for God, not man."

Ilaha's brain teems. She is fully engaged now. She is thinking the biggest thoughts. It excites her.

"The core of belief, Ilaha, is faith in God," the Mufti asserts, "Faith. You cannot know God, you cannot comprehend God, you must simply believe. There is no proof, only the heart. You accept infinity and submit to God, freely, consciously, faithfully."

Ilaha comprehends. She has always understood. She finds great comfort in the face of infinity. She likes this idea, of a boundless yet distinct being we have a relationship to.

She believes.

She has always believed.

Harmon intervenes now, again.

"Ilaha," he addresses her, "You are bigger than tennis. You mean more than you can understand to so many people. Muslims, your people. It may not seem like it, but wearing that gear can change the world."

"I don't want to take sides," Ilaha declares. "I just want to play tennis."

Harmon reaches out with open arms and hugs her to him.

"Ilaha, you can be on *both* sides, you know. Just try on the outfit when we get back and if you are okay with it and want to wear it, do it. If not, just stick with your gear."

Comparative Advantage

As soon as they leave Runnymede, Ilaha has a question for Harmon.

"What am I to do tomorrow?" she asks him, "I have watched Federer more than anyone and I just can't see his hole. He is just so good at everything. I cannot see where I would be able to corner him."

Harmon smiles, because unwittingly she finds her own answer. He will not just tell her, though. She must see it first, on her own.

"What did you just say?" he demands.

"He is so good at everything ..." she repeats.

Harmon cuts her off.

"Listen, and do not lose that idea," Harmon instructs. "David Ricardo. A thinker. Great mind. His greatest idea is 'comparative advantage'," he asserts, "It was radical, really. Ricardo had an insight about trade. You know, buying and selling stuff. It can be proven with a little math. If one country does everything better than the other, they should still trade."

Ilaha does not understand.

"Why would they bother?" she asks.

"Imagine we both grow apples and bananas," Harmon explains, "I grow more of both. But you grow just a very little fewer bananas. If I focus on apples and you focus on bananas, neither of us is wasting time. For every banana I don't grow, I grow a whole bunch more apples. For every apple you don't grow, you grow a whole bunch more bananas. In the end there are so many apples and bananas to go around when we trade we are both better off."

"But I am not trading with Federer, I am playing against him," Ilaha argues.

"Right," Harmon affirms, "But what really matters is the relative advantage. Federer is supposed to do what he does best, to win, right? What if you can lure him into doing what he does worst?"

Ilaha understands.

"Even if he does everything better than me, whatever he does relatively worst is what I want him doing. That at least gives me a chance!" she exclaims.

"Right," Harmon tells her. "Just make him play his weakest game. And if you can, match his weakest game to your strongest."

Ilaha feels better. Briefly.

Then she deflates.

"What is his weakest game?" she asks aloud.

Harmon studies it. He gets his hands on all of Federer's match data from IBM and runs a complete analysis. Even the GOAT, the guy who does everything better than Ilaha, has a hole.

"Guess," Harmon tortures Ilaha. "Think it through, imagine it. Be on the court. Where is Federer least threatening?"

He is hard to push back, she thinks. He does not drift way behind the baseline. He fights for ground on or inside it. He can hit winners from either side, especially if he can step into his shot inside the baseline. His service game is not exploitable, really. He is so good and hard to read. And on return he is really tough, because he reads so well and has such great hands. He can block back almost anything and get into layer four almost at will.

Ilaha is stumped, so Harmon lets her off.

"It is a lost art, but Federer is from a prior era so you may be able to pull a fast one," Harmon observes. "If you can pull him to net and make him hit high pressure volleys, you turn him into a much more average player."

Ilaha sees it, and actually understands what Harmon really means.

"He would be the best volley player," she states, "But even the best volley player isn't terribly effective today. Nobody plays to be at net. They suffer through being at net. Net isn't where anyone wins anymore."

She figures it out. Federer is more willing to come in than most. So use that. Draw him in, where he is more exposed, and guide him into playing the worst of his many excellent games.

Fólkvangr

They reach Mama Lily's farmhouse, Elysium. Ilaha carries the Harrods bag. She is tired, from a very long walk, and wants to go inside and just rest.

"Ilaha," Harmon says, reaching for her hand, "I am not going to be there for the final."

Ilaha's heart stops. She feels so alone, so abandoned, and it hasn't even happened yet.

"WHY!?" she screams.

She just cannot understand.

Her scream draws Mama Lily outside.

"Do you remember the man you met, Assad, at Cambridge? We spent a day with him." Ilaha confirms that yes, she remembers. "He has passed, and I must bury him, in his family plot, in his home country. It will be dangerous, really. It must be done now. There will not be another chance."

Ilaha is very unhappy with this.

"This is the final at Wimbledon, Harmon. For f#%$'s sake! How can it not wait? How can you miss this?" she laments.

Mama Lily wanders over, just in time to hear Ilaha curse.

"What's wrong?" she asks.

Ilaha tells Mama Lily that Harmon is skipping the final.

"Assad was a father to me," Harmon declares, "He wanted to lie for eternity next to his daughter, my wife, and his wife and his family from generations past. I swore I would see to it, so I must. The grave site is in a very dangerous place and I will not get another chance to do this. Great, great trouble has been taken for it."

"So it is more important than me in the final of the men's at Wimbledon?" Ilaha confronts him.

"Yeah. It is. It is the final act one warrior blood brother can perform for another," Harmon explains. "Someday you may do such a thing for me. But a choice must be made and I am choosing to bury Assad."

Lily feels for Ilaha, but her sympathy in this case is with Harmon.

"Ilaha," she says, squeezing her on the arm, "Losing someone is really hard. And proper burial is really important, so give Harmon a break."

Lily Tudor, real person, reaches out and hugs Harmon, imploring him to be safe, but knowing in her heart that whoever may try to harm him has more to fear from him than he has from them.

Ilaha wails. Heaving, uncontrolled sobs. She reaches out and hugs Harmon. Realizing his enormity, his massiveness, that he is in fact a giant. Never wanting to let go, she finally does, understanding that she will feel that hug forever, similar to how an amputee feels a lost limb.

"I will watch, Ilaha," Harmon tells her, "I won't miss a shot. I may not be in a seat, but I am there with you. I know how it ends, Ilaha. I have already seen how it all ends."

Something is not right about this, Ilaha thinks. This feels wrong. She grows nauseous, her stomach becoming a pit. Dizzy. Synaesthesia. Loss of breath.

She feels like the moment one is hit by a literal ton of bricks.

"Harmon," she says, choking up, "I am never going to see you again, am I?"

"Of course you will," he assures her, "Warriors who share blood and become brothers always meet again. We will meet again at Fólkvangr, if nowhere else."

Jehanne la Pucelle

Ilaha, alone inside the Ladies' locker room, soaks in the last moments of solitude before her planned burst onto the grandest stage.

Official photos of past champions adorn the walls. Maud Watson. First Ladies' Singles champion, eighteen eighty four. Lottie Dod. Youngest winner, fifteen years and two hundred eighty five days. Althea Gibson. First champion of color, nineteen fifty seven.

Billie Jean King. First Open Era champion. Gender warrior. Succeeded in forcing purse parity at the U.S. Open, nineteen seventy three.

Ilaha strolls and looks at the photos of the women who preceded her, here, at this place. Soaked in history. These women occupied this space before Ilaha. She feels a presence. A collective soul.

Doubles champions. Ilaha waltzes along the wall, through time.

She stops. Nineteen eighty eight. She stares.

Steffi Graf and Gabriela Sabatini.

Ilaha has heard Harmon talk about Steffi Graf as if a schoolboy with a crush. Ilaha has studied Graf, her forehand. Timeless. Service. An inspiration. But not on par with the great men. Ilaha did not dwell on Graf's technique. Driven for more, for bigger, for the biggest dream.

Ilaha shifts her focus to Sabatini. Something about her face ... Familiar.

She is overcome.

Mama.

Ilaha collapses to her knees.

She faces east, and feels, in her soul, the entirety of all meaning. It chills her. She ceases to breathe, ceases to see or hear or smell or feel or taste.

Momentary death.

She thinks about Jadd, about her dreams, about infinity and tennis and Mama Lily. She strains to imagine what came before her, the mum she cannot remember and the dad she does not know. She envisions Greengrass aflame, all who died. The lives to go unlived and the dead forgotten in tandem by all who knew them.

Then she stands, tall, to full height, and resumes her journey. This is not over, I will see it through.

Ilaha opens her sling bag, the one she absolutely always has on her person, and fetches scissors. She walks very deliberately to the sinks and raises the scissors.

"Allāhu 'akbar!"

She says it aloud, a great impassioned cry that nobody hears …

… And then commences to cut her hair.

It has never been cut. Her parents never cut it from her birth. When Mama Lily suggests it, Ilaha insists no, I want it left alone. Not once in her life has she ever had her hair cut.

She cuts it now. Short. Roughly. No regard for styling. She crops it at her neck and lets the mass of beautiful, dark, prefect silky hair fall to the floor in a pile.

Finished, she puts down the scissors and stares into her own eyes, in the mirror, and sees it all.

Everything.

Past present future.

On the mirror she draws the mathematical symbol for infinity with a bar of soap.

She understands what she is about to do. For the first time fully aware that she will perform, and that the show matters well beyond the tennis.

While she dresses she thinks about all those women, all over the world, at every hour of the day, who will watch and listen, not understanding, not knowing what any of the tennis means, converging together into her, a single conductor, making a much larger point than who can hit a better tennis ball on a given day.

Ragnarök

Ilaha dons her racket bag as a backpack, picks up the other two one in each hand, and strides down the hallway toward Centre Court.

Not a single seat is empty, anywhere at the All England Club. In the other stadium courts the match is displayed on large screens. On the grounds, the large open courtyard with a giant screen is at standing room. There are nearly a quarter of a million patrons on site and many many tens of thousands more watching on big screens in Wimbledon Village.

A hundred thousand British Muslims gather early that morning at Buckingham Palace. At sunrise they pray in unison for Fajr, surprising and waking the Queen.

Her Majesty comes out onto a balcony, beholds the massive crowd, immediately understands what she is seeing, and sheds a tear and waves.

The hundred thousand cheer a great cheer and then serenade her with "God Save the Queen."

Then march the eight miles or so to Wimbledon to watch Ilaha play the final. They all bear small gift bags of Turkish delight candy. Some of it home made, some store bought.

The hundred thousand pass out the candy during their march and at their destination. Every bag is handed out while looking the recipient right in the eyes.

"As-salāmu ʿalaykum."

Peace be with you.

At no point in the day is there a single incident involving violence or confrontation or fighting or cruelty of any kind.

Anywhere in the world.

For this day, this one day, there is global peace.

Opponents accustom themselves to Ilaha not warming up, so Federer has a hitting partner ready. He is warming up, innocently hitting overheads, when he hears a deafening surging roar from the crowd.

All of them, every one of them, shout with great zeal when Ilaha comes out onto Centre Court.

She is wearing whites in the form of pants and a long sleeve shirt. Head covered, in a matching headpiece. All white and only white. Excepting a black logo over her heart.

The mathematical symbol for infinity.

It is magical. Her outfit. It flows and rests and looks so, so comfortable. Ilaha looks every bit the goddess she has become.

Bare feet. She is wearing no trainers.

Ilaha opens her racket bag, base octave, 'D' note, and takes out her racket. All black, black strings. On her strings, she has a silhouette of a white horse with wings.

Buraq.

Ilaha strides out to net, summons Federer, and when he reaches her, she leans over the net and hugs him. He hugs back, and the crowd simply goes berserk. The shouts and cheers are heard for miles. A tsunami of sound originating inside their hug ripples across Britain, Europe, perhaps the whole world.

"I thought you do not warm up your opponents," Federer says to Ilaha.

"You aren't my opponent. We are here, together, to put on a show. Let's put on a show, Roger," she suggests.

He understands she is not suggesting they simply play a gentle exhibition. It runs deeper. They will fight it out, but in the spirit of respect that only tennis really lends itself toward.

They complete warm up and go to center court, to toss for serve. Federer wins and elects to receive. The smart move. Game on.

Ilaha does not uncover for the match. Her apparent warm up outfit, covering all but her feet, hands, and face, is her attire. Her whites are perfectly opaque, even when they become soaked.

Modest and in utter conformity with Islam.

The bare feet, on the other hand, are an act of defiance. Muslim women do not go about barefoot.

The Goddess of Greengrass is barefoot for the whole world to see.

The match starts. Ilaha opens with service, and she is really on. Her serves are being hit right on the strings, with explosive action and variety in location. She is pitching a masterpiece, throwing Federer off with changes of pace, location, and action that appear to make full use of the infinity of serves that a great player can create.

In the first set they go to tiebreaker. Ilaha manages to win the only break of the set, placing a completely unexpected drop return on a Federer second serve into a perfect spot to win the set 7-6 (9-7). Federer slips slightly in attempting to go after the ball, preventing him from getting to it.

As they change sides Ilaha once again hugs him, takes his hand in hers, and turns to the crowd with both of their hands raised to the sky, an enormous smile upon her face and his. The moment, bigger than tennis, in exactly the right gracious hands.

The second set goes into another tie break. Score 10-11, Ilaha to serve. She hits a perfectly placed high kicking ball down the T that actually bounces over to the ad side, from such severe action. Federer gambles on a serve down the T and is aggressively moving in to his backhand. That prevents the ace that probably should have come of the serve. He is barely able to handle the odd and severe kick, blocking the ball back to the middle of the court, deep.

Ilaha is very much ready for it, and hits a blistering forehand into Federer's deuce corner deep. He chases it down, lobbing the ball back high to buy time and reset the point. This gives Ilaha an overhead she should step forward to put away, but instead chooses to let it drop into a forehand that she hits sharply at his ad sideline with hard topspin.

An impossible ball, but somehow Federer anticipates this once he sees her forego the overhead. He rushes at full speed toward the spot before the ball is hit. He chases it down and slices back even more severely across the net into Ilaha's deuce court. She dives and volleys from below the net toward his deep ad corner. The volley is not high enough, and Federer manages to punch a half overhead through her deuce court.

Set.

It is a remarkable and spectacular point, and everybody including Ilaha, most of all, savors it. She comes up off the grass clapping Federer's shot with great zeal and chases him down for another big hug. A set a piece, and by now there is nobody who really cares as much about who will win as they desperately want this kind of play to never, ever end.

The third and fourth sets are once again into tie break, with only one mini break deep into tie break the difference.

Fifth set, Centre Court, men's final, Wimbledon, playing Roger Federer, GOAT. The match is as even as a match can be, literally down to the point. Neither player is broken on serve, save the two points each in the tie breaks.

Ilaha serves her first game, getting through with ease, 1-0. Federer follows, winning after deuce. Back and forth they go, holding, with varying degrees of ease.

They play to 6-6 and the fifth goes on. 7-7. 8-8. Wimbledon offers no tie break in the fifth. You play out to win by two. 9-9. 10-10. The games have their moments, but for the most part, it is very mechanical. Neither player faltering, neither player moving to any advantage.

Daylight is not an issue. The match starts early enough that there is plenty of time to finish, unless, of course, it turns into a 60-58 type Isner marathon.

By 15-15 Ilaha is showing signs of wanting to push harder. She starts taking bigger chances on Federer's serves, especially his seconds, and she is making overtures to play for a steal of break. In his service game, after a double fault at 15-15 that puts her at 15-30, she succeeds with a return on first serve that Federer cannot play. 15-40 now and double break point.

Ilaha buckles down, determined to use both breakpoints for maximum payoff. There will be no blocking back a serve here, she will swing, full, and bet on her side of the coin coming up just once. She knows the probabilities cold. It is one in three that she loses both points. She plays for the two in three to make one of them a win.

Federer tosses and Ilaha reads his feet. They betray his intention to hit to the sideline, to pull her wide. This puts her well out of position if she defensively plays back into the court to try for layer four of the point. She has no intention of doing that. She starts sideways, then forward, and is well ahead of his serve when it in fact breaks down onto the sideline and kicks wide off the court.

Ilaha, ready, in position, is well ahead of the ball and able to cut it off, using the extreme angle Federer creates to hammer back a forehand with severe topspin that breaks low over the center of the net and darts down into the shallow front of the court, well inside Federer's deuce sideline, and away into the wall aside the court. Break.

Game, Ilaha.

An enormous cheer and Federer appreciates her gamble with a clap. Not such a gamble, she knows, because she reads him like a book and simply responds to what he is telling her.

16-15, and Ilaha serving for the match.

Throughout the day she makes opportunistic use of drawing Federer in and forcing him to volley. It works, and is done in such a way as to avoid detection as a tactic. It is disguised by her, apparently a situation of lucky mishit, at some level, not an intended draw. In this game, Ilaha commits to that tactic to completion.

I am gonna see it through. I have my comparative advantage, and I will live or die by it.

Her first serve is a bullet, hit very, very hard, at one hundred thirty four miles per hour, right into his body. He cannot manage a return, and the ball lands weakly, short of the net.

15-0.

Her next, from the ad side, is a wide kicking serve off the sideline that pulls Federer off the court. He hits a soft, high ball down the line and immediately races back onto the court. By the time Ilaha plays the ball, he is back in position and the point ends up going many strokes into a stalemate situation. Ilaha eventually misplays, just, and Federer wins the point on her error.

15-15.

Deuce side and once again, a bullet, this time more down the T, for an ace. One hundred thirty seven miles per hour. This is the two hardest serves any woman has ever hit in a match.

30-15 Ilaha.

Back to the ad side. Once again, Ilaha serves wide, hitting the sideline in exactly the same spot. This time she does not squander the serve, coming in hard behind it. When Federer hits the same shot, arcing deep, to buy time, he ends up hitting right into her strike zone for an easy forehand swinging volley put away into a wide open court.

40-15.

Double match point.

Now Ilaha pauses. From the deuce side she has hit two straight winning serves. She gets four serves to go for match point. It is only one of three that she double fault out and get to deuce. She should go for it, end it with a service winner.

But she knows better. He is the one under duress. He is the one under pressure. And a service winner is not her plan. See it through. She reminds herself of her plan, to use the tactic, to draw him in, to exploit comparative advantage.

Her first serve is soft, with a gentle kick, into a great spot down the T that Federer plays easily. He really steps into a backhand. He gets a full move at the ball, but from the center he has no great angle to play. The same serve into the ad sideline results in him hitting a winner down the line. From here, he cannot really expect to win the point with one swing.

He hits hard, deep, into her ad corner. She commits to her plan, slicing a ball back short enough and to his ad sideline that Federer is drawn forward to play. He could try for down the line, but her ball stays low and that is not a good shot to hit down the line. He elects to go cross court over the low part of the net, but directs a bit deep back into her ad corner.

Ilaha is there, and runs around his ball to hit a forehand. Federer moves into the middle of the court, at net, and is ready to volley.

Ilaha unleashes into a forehand and hits it perfectly, low over the net, right at him. The ball breaks hard toward his feet. His marvelous reflexes take over, and he manages a return middle deep that is something of a miracle.

Ilaha unloads, once again, right at him, grazing the top of the net and then darting, low, at his feet. Once again, a miraculous volley on an impossible ball, this time toward her deuce sideline, not deep.

Ilaha moves, almost feeling like motion has slowed, time has ceased, and geometry has prevailed. As if now living in Flatland and not on earth, she sees it. She sees the whole thing. She sees hours upon hours hitting, hitting, training, tape and data, thinking, bleeding, inhaling it all, an obsession, a vocation, a passion.

Her religion.

She sees Harmon hitting with her. She sees his bare feet. She sees his strength, his grace, his ability to channel the power of the earth through his feet into the ball. She feels the weight of her racket, can literally feel the tension in the strings. Her hand her toes her core her shoulders the surface of her eyes. She takes it all in.

She smiles.

Excessus.

The picture that graces all of the papers, worldwide, shows Federer's back, and the ball, in frame, and Ilaha smiling behind the ball just before hitting it.

She sees the ball, sees it more or less stop moving, sees it sit there, sees the line it has followed and the line it will trace going back. She sets; she can feel every blade of grass under her feet. Ilaha pushes off from the earth, and harnesses the power of the earth through her into the ball.

It hits perfectly on her strings, where it is intended to, and flies, hard, rising, whistling, exactly where it is sent. She can see it press into Buraq; can hear it leave her strings.

It flies hard, and fast, picking up spin as it flies, as if the spin is latent in the collision, taking time to unwind from within the burst of energy that her impact creates.

The ball flies fast, right into the tape …

… And it does not stop.

The ball pulls itself up the tape, to the top of the tape, trading off motion for climb, trading off spin for vertical inches.

Just like it is supposed to.

Just like she hits it.

Just like she plans.

The ball makes a final roll and falls onto Federer's side, dead, to the ground. It dies there, and he never makes a real play. It is an impossible ball to play back.

Game. Set. Match.

Ilaha falls to the ground, lying there, flat on her back, arms clutching at her tennis racket. Buraq in silhouette painted on the strings.

From directly above, she appears not unlike a version of the crucifixion.

Brown skin, white pants, white top, white headpiece. Clutching Buraq.

There are clear blue skies all day, but now a cloud races across the sky, as clouds will do, and a dark shadow washes over everything and everyone.

It rains, it pours, and warm water falls from heaven in a collective baptism.

The shadow passes, the rain stops, and the sun shines brightly on Ilaha's face, kissing it.

Jadd.

THE DREAM ENDS

Call Me Ishmael

Jadd Ishmael sits in his black cab at Heathrow leafing through *Motor Trend*, waiting in the taxi queue. His workplace is a sanctuary. He drives six days a week, every week, ten hours daily.

It is not labourious work. It is quite pleasant, really. Jadd, personable, enjoys the stream of riders who come through his cab. He is easygoing and willing to make conversation, but not intrusive; also willing to let silence prevail.

Jadd is always listening to something, but his fare never hears. The cab has a very special stereo speaker installed directly above the driver's seat. It creates a physically contained shower of sound that only the driver can hear, perfectly, and nobody else in the car can hear, at all.

Jadd uses his many hours driving to listen to audio books, pop music, and news. Sports talk radio. Sporting events. Podcasts on every subject. The Great Courses. He processes so many words everyday, day after day, over so many years, that he can easily pass himself off as a genuine intellectual.

He wishes that he could watch films while driving. He has tried. Ruins the film, and too dangerous. Films are for off hours. But oh, the films Jadd would watch if he could watch while he drove!

His turn comes and he pulls ahead to pick up the next fare. Jadd stops the cab, gets out, and helps the very tall and very fashionable woman with her very high end trunk. Into the boot with the trunk, into the cab with the woman, and off.

"Carlisle, please, the Marina, 5459 Allen Street," the fare instructs him. She has a pleasant voice and manner, but very quickly dives into her phone as soon as her destination is provided.

Jadd recognises her. Normally he would leave a fare alone, to her phone, but he feels compelled to speak.

"Excuse me, miss? You are Lily Lacey, the singer?" he inquires.

The fare confirms that yes; she is Lily Lacey, the singer.

Lily Lacey, the singer, smiles, pulls away from her phone, and looks forward into the front seat of the cab through the glass barrier that separates the driver from the fare. The glass has many signatures upon it. Lily Lacey, the singer, scans them and recognises Mick Jagger.

"Is that Mick Jagger's signature?" she inquires, now more interested in talking with the driver than tinkering on her phone.

"Yes, I've actually driven him more than once," Jadd tells her. "He was kind enough to sign for me one night, late, sun nearly up. I picked him up in Camden Town. Dropped him at The Goring."

"George Best is there. Right in front of you," Jadd tells her.

His signature is a cartoon. His initials "GB" are on the hood of a convertible sports car. A liquor bottle is driving and a bird is in the passenger seat. Hundred pound notes fly from the tailpipe.

"Banksy is up there," Jadd tells Lily Lacey, the singer.

He gives her Banksy's real name, directs her to the signature, and laughs. Just a name, no flourish, no cartoon. Nothing artistic about it. Not even written in cursive.

"How do you know it was Banksy for real?" she challenges him.

"I watched Banksy finish 'Falling Shopper' from my car," Jadd explains, "When Banksy finished, I pulled over and asked if Banksy would like a ride, free of charge. Banksy said, 'Penguins must get bored of fish … Take me to the zoo.' Banksy signed my glass as Banksy's fare."

Lily Lacey, cab fare, squeals with delight! She scans the glass, unable to recognise anyone else among the dozens of signatures. She asks who else? who else? as if a child.

Jadd lists names and tells her where to look.

"You have a favorite?" she asks.

"Yes, to your left, near the window, large, above the seat," Jadd tells Lily Lacey, cab fare, enthusiastically.

Lily Lacey, cab fare, finds what must be the signature. It stands out, signed with a flourish, in gold paint pen. A tennis racket with a musical clef symbol in the string bed below the name, 'Harmon E.' The 'o' in 'Harmon' is the mathematical symbol for infinity.

"Harmon Elder, the tennis player. Wasn't famous when he signed," Jadd explains. "Great coincidence. I ended up driving him to see a dear old childhood friend, in Cambridge. Hadn't seen him in years, my friend Assad. Didn't even know he lived in Britain. Then a random fare drops me right into his lap! Now I see him every Thursday!"

Lily Lacey is nosey, and she looks into Jadd's portion of the carriage. She sees a picture of a little girl taped to the rear view.

"Who is that, then? The girl? I don't want to be rude, but your daughter?" Lily Lacey is uncertain, as the man's age is hard to determine.

He appears to be quite old, in some way, but comes across as very fit, youthful, almost, so the girl, young, smiling, could be his daughter, she supposes. If it is his daughter, and she assumes grandchild, wouldn't that be rude, really?

"No, Miss," Jadd laughs, "That is my beloved granddaughter, Ilaha."

Lily Lacey has daughters, she tells him. In state school, at Agatha Christie Academy.

"My Ilaha was to go there," Jadd laments, "But she is precocious, and they insisted that she start in Reception. I was able to get them to approve skipping to Year 1, but decided instead on Independent school."

"How old is she?" Lily, real person, asks, falling prey as any parent might to nagging notions of offspring competition.

"She just turned five," Jadd admits, almost apologising.

"So where is she going?" Lily follows, calmed by Jadd's subtle insistence there is no competition in this conversation.

"Abbey School," he tells her. "Daft of me, I applied to Farrow, and she appeared on her way to being accepted!

401

Then they realised 'Ilaha' is a girl, and they rather rudely terminated her application. Actually refunded my fee and sent a stern letter stating the boys only admission policy. I kept the letter and cheque."

Lily flares at this. Bollocks Independent schools and their posh tosh!

"I am very happy with Abbey School," Jadd continues, "Ilaha will be the first girl admitted to Under School there. They assure me that will not last very long. They plan on admitting other girls right away, perhaps even by year end. She may have mates!"

Lily is more than a bit impressed. How much do cabbies make? She can't help succumbing to the fear. She is a real person, after all.

"So is she on scholarship there? At Abbey School?" Lily asks, regretting her hopeful rudeness as soon as she asks.

Jadd understands the nature of her faux pas. He is not insulted. Not defensive.

Jadd informs Lily that he owns his cab, and half dozen others, and passes his card to her. *Jadd Ishmael, Proprietor, Greater London Hackney Carriages - An Equal Opportunity Employer.*

"If you ever want a more personal touch, call or text. If I am driving I'll be there quickly, or one of my ladies or gentleman will show," Jadd assures Lily.

Lily puts his card into her very expensive Hermes handbag. She is impressed and surprised.

Lily has rarely gotten a female driver. Male dominated business. And this man appears obviously not western. Probably Arab? Ishmael ... *Shall I call him Ishmael?* she laughs to herself.

Not exactly the type one would assume a feminist, Lily marvels.

"You have women driving?" she asks.

Jadd confirms that he does.

"I much prefer hiring women, mothers, they are much better drivers," Jadd explains.

Mothers simply love the job, especially his liberal policy regarding scheduling.

His drivers are free to handle family matters during their shifts. Pickups, drop offs, sick days, doctor visits, haircuts, etc. Jadd has production standards, but is not a micro bossy type as far as reaching them. Very flexible about scheduling. His drivers stay on for years and years, and they never cause any sort of problem. It is designed to be a mutually beneficial situation.

Equal pay. The meter does not know man from woman. It simply clicks off time and assigns a rate.

"Your girl's name is 'Ilaha'? Is that it, I have it right? 'Ilaha.'" Jadd compliments her on her pronunciation. Exactly, he tells her. "That is a wonderfully interesting name," Lily observes.

"It means 'goddess'," Jadd explains. "We all have big dreams for our children. For Ilaha I have the biggest of all dreams."

Lily is warmed by this man, by his manner and grace. Not boastfully in love with his Ilaha, but unreserved about it.

"We are neighbors, then? Ilaha was to attend Agatha Christie?" Lily asks.

Jadd confirms that yes; he lives in Carlisle, in Greengrass Tower with his children and grandchildren.

"It must get a bit cramped," Lily suggests.

Jadd tells her, no, it is wonderful, the generations together. They can move elsewhere, but choose to stay in Greengrass.

"My wife and I settled there," he tells Lily. "She has passed, and I own our flat. I could lease it out and move, but we all like it, my children and grandchildren."

The ride continues. Jadd and Lily converse gently, as neighbors now, not just fare and driver. Jadd gets comfortable enough to admit to Lily that he is a fan.

"I often listen to your music," he confesses. "I was listening to 'Lily Lacey radio' on AlgoRhythm earlier today."

Lily is quite surprised. She has met many fans, but not any who are Arab grandfather cab drivers.

"Ilaha is also a big fan," Jadd tells her. "She especially loves your 'Lilybies.' She has fallen asleep to them thousands of times." Jadd pauses, and then goes on, a bit reluctant. "We filter her listening, of course, because, well, some of your other lyrics are maybe not the best thing for a Year 2."

Lily laughs out loud, agreeing.

"Of course not! Imagine my dread when my girls google me!" she giggles.

Jadd laughs with her. He is worldly enough to understand. He knows who she is, and knows of her youthful high jinks and debauchery. It is wonderfully western, he has always thought. He understands her milieu, and does not condemn it. He is a true fan boy, incongruous as that is.

Lily reaches into her handbag and takes out a CD in a case. She signs the case with a Sharpie.

"This is for your Ilaha. It is one of a few remaining mix tapes from when I was starting out. I'd like her to have it," Lily says, handing the case forward through the opening in the glass. "But perhaps not until she is a bit older?"

Jadd is very grateful and tells her thank you.

"I may listen to it, if that's okay," he confesses. "Never got a chance to hear your famous mix tapes."

The ride goes on, with Lily and Jadd discussing restaurants. This prompts Jadd to tell Lily about the best meal he has ever eaten, prepared by a Turkish actress with whom his friend Assad is acquainted.

They pass Old Dagobah Park and Jadd enthusiastically tells Lily about how Ilaha loves tennis. She is always begging to be taken there to play. He indulges her, but at his age it takes a toll and the next day driving can be a bit uncomfortable.

"I played when I was younger, then gave it up until Ilaha dragged me back in. I get sore, but she is so happy out there," he laments, smiling.

Lily asks if Jadd has taken his Ilaha out to the matches at Wimbledon.

"No, we have never gone, but we watch on telly. Ilaha watches every match. We may go this year, though," Jadd

404

asserts, "To see Harmon Elder. I am rooting for him to finish his Grand Slam."

Lily is oblivious to tennis, but is always being invited out to the matches. Never went. Too uppity for her, tennis. Tory game. Lily is Labour.

"Jadd," Lily says, "I am always being invited to the matches. If you'd like, I would love to pass on tickets for you and Ilaha."

Jadd, truly grateful, is humbled. He does not demur, too mature and graceful for that, he simply expresses deep gratitude in accepting the offer.

"You have my card, Ms. Tudor. I would very much love that." Lily asks how he knows her proper name. "I told you, I am a huge fan," he reminds her.

They reach her address. Jadd exits the carriage and opens Lily's door.

"Ms. Tudor," he has a favor to ask, "Would you sign my glass?"

She happily agrees. Jadd hands her the same gold paint pen Harmon Elder used to sign.

"Sign right next to Harmon Elder, if you would," he requests.

Lily scoots across the seat to the other side of the carriage. Inspired by Harmon Elder's signature, she signs with her own flourish, writing out 'Lily Lacey' with the 'l's' as lily flowers, and a lace pattern accent below. Jadd is delighted.

He carries her trunk to the door. She pays and tries to include a generous but appropriate tip. Jadd insists that her signing the glass was more than enough and tells her to keep her money.

Months later, mid-June, very hot outside, rummaging through her very expensive Hermes handbag, in her air-conditioned home, looking for a lighter, Lily comes across Jadd's business card.

She remembers him, that he lives in Greengrass, his precocious granddaughter who loves tennis off to break the gender barrier at Abbey School. She set aside the bag and totally forgot she offered him tickets to Wimbledon.

Until now.

She decides to contact him. She will see through her promise of tickets.

Text. No reply. Multiple texts. No response. She calls, straight to voicemail. Multiple tries. No luck. She sets the card aside with some other dreck that will finally be removed from the very, very expensive Hermes handbag, and goes about wasting her night smoking fags and twittering.

Until she hears great noise outside, and gets up to see what it is all about.

Nosey. A buttinsky. She must go see what is happening.

73974771R00243

Made in the USA
Middletown, DE
20 May 2018